Harbour Plaza

Built on Dreams

Kayla Danoli

Copyright

First published in 2016

Copyright © Kayla Danoli 2016

All rights reserved.

No part of this book may be reproduced or transmitted in any form or by any means, electronic or mechanical, including photocopying, recording or by any information storage and retrieval system, without the prior approval in writing of the publisher.

National Library of Australia

Cataloguing-in-publication data

Danoli, Kayla, 1946-

Australian fiction
ISBN: 9780975028742 (paperback)

ISBN: 9780975028759 (eBook)

Dewey Number: A823.4

Contents

On Reflection

Let me introduce myself. I am Ezra Green. You do not know me. In fact, you might never have heard of me, for I have been dead for a long time. My association with Oyster Point stretches back over many decades. I came to this place as a young boy with my father at the start of the town in the 1860s.

Disgruntled with his position, Father swapped the Civil Service for private enterprise and opened a ships chandlery. Oyster Point became a busy port handling goods for the hinterland. The gamble paid off. At an appropriate age, I joined him in his chandlery, and learned about running a business. I discovered being a ships chandler was not for me. There were other opportunities at Oyster Point. At the ripe old age of 25 years, I disappointed my father by striking out on my own to open Green's General Store.

The settlement grew fast. Settlers needed supplies. My business boomed. I expanded the store. My son, Thomas, eventually joined me in the store, but never seemed to grasp what running a business was all about. As my end approached, I held grave misgivings. With only the one son, there was no one else to pass the business on to, although I severely doubted Thomas's ability to take up the reins. There was nothing for it. I had to stick around, at least for a while, to ensure the place continued to operate. Oh, the number of times I had to intervene to prevent disasters. Thomas's ownership was a busy time for me. Then his son, William, came to work in the store. William showed a little more promise, and I held high hope I might be able to move on when he took over the business.

It wasn't to be. Although William ran the store better than his father, he too had a poor head for business. His wife had more understanding. It was thanks to her – with my help -- the business didn't go under. Again, I had to help when things were getting out of hand. I realised I needed to stay around a bit longer. William named his son Ezra, after me, and young Ezra took over the store when William died in 1970.

This young Ezra hadn't inherited any business acumen. Well, from whom would he get it? Neither of his parents possessed much to pass on to him. Still, in spite of this, he managed to keep the business afloat and my need to intervene lessened to some degree. On young Ezra's death in 2001, his son and only child, Edward (Ted), inherited the store. Ted proved to be a 'back room' man rather than store manager, so he worked out the back with the stock while his wife ran the place and dealt with the customers. She was a dynamo. The future of the store looked safe.

Together, they expanded the store, installed large plate glass windows, built a residence on top and installed a large cold room. My only concern then was this couple's lack of offspring. Who would take over the store when Ted and his wife were gone? This troubled me. I felt compelled to stick around to find a solution to this problem. Since my death, I have done many things to save the store, but doing something to ensure there are offspring is beyond even my ability. Then a potential problem became a reality. Young Ted passed away while still in the prime of life. His wife's quick thinking was all that saved her. The cyclone of December 2014 ended the Green family's line and wiped out my legacy. Greens General Store was no more, as was much of Oyster Point. Such a devastating event; I couldn't leave. Other things I had invested in during my time in this place also disappeared. The construction of a shopping precinct, lately so run down, was something I invested in just prior to my death. It too became a flattened heap of rubble. Ah, the cyclone was a sad and disturbing time, but I sensed something new -- something exciting -- flickering in the future. I wanted to see what it was and how it might develop. I had to stay.

A new, young investor would change the face of Oyster Point. The devastation from the December cyclone provided all the impetus he needed to marshal whatever resources he required. Like Phoenix rising from the ashes, he helped re-establish what the cyclone took away. A new supermarket complex and the Harbour Plaza shopping precinct arrived. It was fascinating to watch. I could hardly believe the speed at which this young fellow Robinson made things happen. It was exciting. I couldn't leave. Everything was so enthralling. ...And that Harbour Plaza! What a world of dreams that turned out to be.

Now, 12 months after the cyclone, I sit here reflecting on the past year, and remember those dreams on which Harbour Plaza is built... so many dreams, so many stories and, for some, so much heartbreak and despair. Dreams can become nightmares.

Ooh, the stories I could tell you about those dreams that were part of Harbour Plaza. If you have the time, I will share those I remember more clearly – some happy, some poignant. Now then, where shall I start...? The beginning seems a good place...

Resurrection

I shall begin with that cyclone at the end of 2014, its devastation, and the resurrection of the town and its community that followed.

A small seaside town in North Queensland, Oyster Point, just off the main north-south highway, has good beaches, some rocky hilly areas, and rich soil supporting mainly horticultural agribusiness. Its once thriving fishing industry has almost disappeared, with only a few hardy souls continuing to fish.

The place slowly went downhill for years, offering few employment opportunities. Adverse weather conditions affected the productivity and viability of vegetable growers. The population declined and the town became run down with increasing numbers of derelict buildings evident throughout the urban area. Many shops closed. Those that remained cut back on stock and the range of services provided. The global financial crisis (GFC) all but sounded the death knell for this town.

Oyster Point's demographic includes a high proportion of older people, especially retirees. The onset of cold weather in southern states triggers a northern migration to warmer coastal areas in this part of Queensland, causing a population explosion during the tourist season between May and November each year. For much of the tourist season, a large caravan park is host to an influx of grey nomads. There are few other accommodation options: backpackers' hostel and two pubs. The local council is concerned that, if the decline continues, tourists will no longer be interested in this part of the world, resulting in the district's considerable loss of revenue.

Noticeable variances occur between residential areas. Substantial upmarket homes predominate in some of the elevated areas, including a gated community. The main urban residential area now looks shabby with a high proportion of older homes interspersed only occasionally by more modern residences.

However, for some time now a glimmer of hope for salvation existed, and maybe an upturn in the fortunes of those who managed to hang on. After two years of planning, an proposed new mine some distance inland now finds itself bogged down in the bureaucracy and environmental processes attached to opening a new mine. A further complication is that its coal requires transport to the coast for shipment to domestic and overseas markets. This necessitates the construction of a new rail corridor or haul road from the mine site to the coast, with the most likely site for the port identified as the Oyster Point area.

Locals, initially excited that their harbour might see redevelopment as a coal port, were gutted by the news the harbour proved too shallow and had insufficient area to create a suitable port facility. A more suitable site is about eight kilometres further north along the highway. If the mine, transport and port infrastructures proceed, most of the construction workers along with relevant management personnel and their families will live at Oyster Point.

"So this is Oyster Point. Not exactly the land of milk and honey… but plenty of potential," Geoff Robinson announced aloud to no one but himself and a couple of seagulls strutting along The Esplanade.

Robinson, a property developer, arrived in Oyster Point around the beginning of September. Keen for a new investment opportunity outside the metropolitan area, insider information lured him to Oyster Point. After leaving The Esplanade, he drove around the town assessing it, before calling in at the larger of the town's two hotels for a pub lunch. As he sat sipping his cold beer, he thought back on what prompted this trip.

Matthew Pritchard married Geoff Robinson's favourite cousin, Margot. More importantly, Matthew was Chief of Staff in the Office of the Minster for Resources and Energy – as well as being an exceptionally fine example of a pompous high-ranking public servant. On a number of occasions, Geoff commented to his wife, Gillian, "Matthew is an absolute pain in the arse until he becomes almost human after a couple of wines." So, Geoff's uncharacteristic enthusiasm over Margot's dinner invitation to see the Pritchards' new house intrigued Gillian.

Geoff kept an eye on the progress of an application for a new mine near Oyster Point and was keen to know progress on its approval. He planned his strategy carefully and arrived well armed. With something of an overly dramatic flourish Matthew, sporting the latest in trendy casual wear, ushered them through the front door and into the tiny foyer. Geoff thrust the fancy carrier bag into Matthew's hand.

"To help us christen the place," he suggested with a conspiratorial wink.

Matthew peered at the contents of the bag and gave an appreciative nod. It contained two bottles of wine: one white, one red, and both very expensive. After saying hello to Margot who was busy in the kitchen, they set off on a tour of the house with Matthew as tour guide. Afterwards, they joined Margot for a celebratory drink before enjoying an excellent meal. By sheer good luck, Geoff's wines proved a perfect complement to dinner.

The wine did its trick and Geoff congratulated himself as Matthew led him through to Matthew's new den -- his 'man cave'. Matthew was positively yappy from the wine, but his ego remained intact. Just the situation Geoff wanted, as it rendered Matthew easily manipulated… and Geoff knew how to be persuasive. Conversation began on a lighter note, but quickly headed elsewhere as Geoff nudged it in the desired direction. Soon the situation was primed and Geoff launched his attack -- stealthily.

"I don't envy you blokes in the State's big house at the moment, particularly the Ministers," he led in. "The State budget took a beating with the drop in overseas demand for mining resources coupled with low prices."

"It certainly made a huge hole in royalties coming into State coffers," Matthew agreed.

"You know, no one should be surprised at the mess some of the mines are in; so many closing down and so many workers already laid off." Geoff knew just the right mix of concern and sympathy required. "Some of those mines around for decades started in the glory days at the beginning of the mining boom. Their methods are outmoded. There was no consideration of long-term sustainability -- or viability – and poor management saw them haemorrhaging money from day one."

Matthew couldn't resist the temptation and launched into a long dissertation on the present ills of the mining industry. This was going exactly as Geoff wanted.

"The way I see it, we still need those mining royalties, but we need a new mine to open up, one that employs 21st century technology and practices, and is well-managed. I don't suppose there's much chance of that happening though given the current financial situation," Geoff suggested thoughtfully.

"That's where you're wrong," Matthew announced with glee. "There's a proposal for a new mine up north that will do just that."

"Oh yeah, I know the one you mean. That proposal has been around for a couple of years now. It's never going to get the nod."

"Granted, there were a few problems with the transportation of ore to the port that took a bit of working out, but the infrastructure details have been agreed now." Matthew loved demonstrating a superior knowledge.

"Argh, they'll find something else wrong with the proposal and it will end up going nowhere. It's probably costing all sides a lot of money trying to get it through the approval process. Maybe the kindest thing would be to knock it on the head."

"Yes, it has been a protracted exercise, but everything is in place for its approval. Now that the transportation infrastructure issues have approval, the developers are modifying the proposal documentation accordingly. There is 'in principle' approval for the mine. It just needs due process to occur now. The developers have until October to resubmit the documents. The mine and its associated infrastructure will have approval before the House rises at the end of the year. It just needs to be seen to go through due process before its approval is rubberstamped."

"I dunno. I'm still not convinced it's going to happen. I bet you a mega Lotto entry it won't."

"You are on... start saving up now to buy me that ticket."

That was what he had been fishing for and, with the wager in place, Geoff knew Matthew would brag to him about the mine's approval as soon as it happened. With the information safely tucked away, he abruptly took the conversation off in the direction of Matthew's golf handicap. That filled in the evening until it was time to leave.

So, here he was lunching at a pub in Oyster Point and weighing up his options. The bartender said the local real estate agent usually lunched here if he was in town, and offered to send him over to Geoff if he came in. Geoff had almost finished his lunch when a scruffy, overweight bloke sidled up to his table.

"Rick Winston, real estate agent," he announced, extending his hand. "Leon, the barman, said you wanted to talk to me."

"Yeah Rick, thanks for coming over. I was wondering what properties might be for sale -- business properties preferably, not residential."

"Hmm, well there are a few, but it depends on what you want. I have an appointment in a few minutes, but I'll give you my card. Give me a call if you see something you're interested in."

"I noticed a couple of fairly old properties down at the marina end of The Esplanade. They look a bit unloved. Are they on the market?"

"They could be. Let me know if you want me to follow up." With that, Winston collected his steak sandwich from the bar and left.

Geoff left the pub and drove to the end of the next block. He parked and walked around the two buildings he mentioned to Rick Winston. Together with a third parcel of land, they occupied about half of a town block. They both looked abandoned. A small shopping mall of sorts occupied the other part of the block. It was old, and contained six shops in need of a lot of attention. Two were empty and one advertised a closing down sale. The remaining three looked poorly stocked. Geoff rang Rick Winston and arranged to meet him at the hotel that evening. He had booked a room at the hotel for the night and returned there to plan for the meeting.

Robinson capitalised on the mining boom, owning residential properties in several of the mining towns, all of which brought in extraordinary rents. An astute player in the property development market, he realised early that the boom was ending and sold off his properties. Snapped up, they provided Robinson with a handsome profit and a nice bucket of cash to invest in his next project. If he was to use those funds to invest in Oyster Point, he needed to have a plan for the future development of the land and, more importantly, have a strong idea of what the overall project might look like … and what it might cost.

Winston waited in the lounge area for their meeting. If it was at all possible, the agent looked more dishevelled than he did earlier. The word 'sleaze' came to mind as Robinson made his way over to join Winston. The agent's jet black locks held so firmly in place had nothing to do with nature, and his shirt, now gaping from the strain of trying to cover an enormous gut, was sorely in need of a wash and press. Winston wore his trousers low on his hips to allow his gut hang over them, providing observers with the expectation they might soon descend to the agent's ankles. Nevertheless, Geoff consoled himself this was the only show in town so to speak. There was no other local agent.

Geoff got straight down to business, not wanting to spend any more time with Winston than necessary. "Right, I've had a good look around and the two parcels of land I'm interested in are the two at the far end of Main Street. The end one has an old warehouse style building on it and the one next to it has a derelict looking shed or hall of some sort. Can you determine the owners and whether they're interested in selling and, of course, what their asking price might be."

"Yeah, that shouldn't be a problem. I should have something for you by the end of tomorrow, if that's not too late. I haven't heard they are for sale but, by the look of them, the owners aren't particularly interested in them and might jump at the opportunity to sell. As I said, I should have something for you by the end of tomorrow. Is there anything else I could help you with while I'm about it?"

"Er, now that you mention it and, if you're going to be chasing up owners, you might see what you can dig up on that next property – the third one from the end. The one with the old Queenslander and the ramshackle shed on it. I've no real interest in it, but you never know. Oh, and what do you know about Green's General Store? It seems to be the only thing that passes for a supermarket in town these days."

"The store has been here for ever, owned and run by a few generations of the same family. It's not for sale, and I doubt you could tempt them."

"I wasn't interested in buying it. It looked as though it had a long history with the place. I was interested in its story."

Geoff looked closely at that third block when he checked out the area, but his cautious instinct suggested a wait-and-see approach might serve him better. Still, there was no harm in giving Winston something to do. Whatever he dug up on the old Queenslander block might prove useful if the new mine actually got the green light. The meeting was brief. They shook hands and Winston left the hotel. Geoff felt in need of a drink to wash away the bad taste that lingered after the agent's departure. As he sat with his drink, he decided to ring a man who knew a man that could play an important part in his embryonic ideas for the development of the two blocks -- if he managed to secure them.

"Hello Manny, this is Geoff Robinson. I thought I might give you a ring to call in that favour you owe me. I know you've done a bit of work with a couple of other supermarket developments in the past. I'm thinking about a similar development in a place up north and wondered who I might talk to."

"Geoff, hi, long time since we've spoken. Yeah, I know a bloke who would be interested in whatever your plans are. I'll give him a ring and suggest he calls you for a chat. Remember, if you need a few extra bucks to make it happen, I might be interested."

The conversation ended with some good-natured banter and the sharing of information and Geoff promising to keep Manny in mind as a potential investor if an injection of cash were required.

Reduced to filling in time during the next day, Geoff went down to breakfast late and enjoyed the luxury of the dining room to himself, as all other guests had already departed for the day. He was skimming the local newspaper and sipping his coffee when his phone rang.

"Good morning, Geoff. I'm Bernard Cartwright. Manny called me last night saying you might have a project in mind that could interest me."

Bernard was keen, and Geoff was happy to have his supermarket chain involved with his project. The conversation lasted about forty-five minutes, and ended with Geoff agreeing to meet with Bernard and others when he returned south in a couple of days. He left the hotel and drove to the end of Main Street again. Only a quick look around, before he parked beside Green's General Store. The small customers' carpark provided an excellent view of the store's profile.

Like Topsy, it grew and grew over its decades to evolve into its present configuration of a supermarket with a street frontage, a warehouse structure tacked on the back, and owner's residence and office above. As was the case with so many old stores, originally the residence attached to its rear. Geoff entered and bought bottled water, a pocket pack of tissues and a chocolate bar. Searching for these items gave him an excuse to wander up and down every aisle and inspect every corner of the store. He counted three people working in the place: a woman on the checkout who he assumed was Mrs Green, and a sullen looking teenage girl with straggly bleached blonde hair and many piercings engaged in rotating stock in one of the aisles. Through the thick plastic curtained doorway into the stock room, Geoff spied a man, probably in his 50s, loading cartons onto a trolley. He assumed this was the owner, Mr Green.

Satisfied he had all the information he needed about the store, Geoff drove a further two blocks along the street to his next port of call, the local newspaper office. His phone rang as he parked: Bernard Cartwright.

"Hey, Geoff, sorry to bother you again so soon, but my boss is keen to start discussions straightaway. Are you available for a call at eleven o'clock today? It could take up to an hour so, if you're busy with other stuff, suggest another time that might be better."

"This is a surprise, Bernard. No, eleven o'clock is fine. I'll make a point of being in my room a few minutes beforehand to make sure I'm ready. I've got something to do right now, so I won't keep you, but I will be fine for a call at eleven o'clock." He closed his phone and, still slightly stunned by the phone call, entered the newspaper office.

He asked if he could look at their archives to get some background history on a couple of buildings in the area. The helpful receptionist explained how the local historical group were slowly indexing all the back editions of the paper. That index might have what he wanted. A quick search gave him details of which editions contained articles on the warehouse and the old Queenslander. It didn't mention the current owners. There was nothing in the index about the large shed like building. The receptionist suggested it was a more modern building and the indexers hadn't reached the papers from its construction era. However, she could tell him a bit about its more recent history if it would help.

"I don't know anything about its early history but, back in the 1970s, the local gymnastics club sourced funding from somewhere to do up the hall for their activities. Then the club folded, leaving the building idle for the best part of ten years until a dance teacher, new to the area, took it over for a studio for her classes. Classes ended when she left the district about six years ago. The hall's remained unused ever since. I don't know anything about its early history or who the owner might be."

After spending some time going through images of early issues of the newspaper and printing off relevant bits and pieces, Geoff paid for his printouts and hurried back to the hotel. Reception was good and the Skype call happened as planned. As Bernard suggested, it went for almost an hour. Geoff almost felt elated as he made his way down for lunch, and ordered himself a very nice wine to have with it. The supermarket chain bosses were keen to get involved and outlined deals they previously struck with other developers for similar projects. He would still meet with them when he returned south to negotiate, and hopefully sign, a heads of agreement with the supermarket chain.

He booked a flight home for the next day and, with nothing else to do, would read some papers and have a snooze to fill in the afternoon. He had just reached the snooze stage when his phone rang: Rick Winston.

"Geoff, I have the information you wanted on those couple of parcels of land. You want to meet up to discuss it? I'm available from about 5.00pm if that suits you."

"Okay, let's meet at the hotel again and discuss it over a drink." Things were falling into place much better – and faster -- than expected. He would go home tomorrow with the project further advanced than anticipated.

Winston reported the Local Council owned both parcels of land. "They foreclosed on the properties some time ago after rates remained unpaid for a number of years. The person I spoke to believed Council would be happy to dispose of the properties and that they probably would be available at a reasonable price."

"I'm returning south tomorrow. Can you follow up to see if you can get a firm price? No doubt, the person you are speaking to will need to run it through all the right people before that can occur. Once you get a price, let me know and we'll see what happens then."

"The bloke I was talking to suggested the asking price might be something like the amount of the rate arrears plus any other expenses Council incurred along the way. I'll follow up and get a firm price in writing for you. Oh, the other thing you asked about was that block with the old Queenslander on it. The current owner supposedly lives in Melbourne. The last owner anyone here remembers was an elderly bloke who died many years ago and left the place to his son. It was empty for quite a while before the old fellow bought it, and it remained empty after he died. His wife ran off many years before with some other bloke, taking their infant son with her. The boy grew up in Melbourne and, from all accounts, turned out to be overly indulged, likes the bright lights and plays hard."

"…Sounds like he has no interest in the property. Anyway, I don't want to do anything about it at the moment, but it's worth knowing something of its background in case that situation changes."

"Apparently, immediately on inheriting the building, the son tried to sell it but the asking price was unreasonable for anywhere in this region let alone Oyster Point. It didn't sell, and he left it sit and decay."

"Well, he won't have much to sell very shortly. The white ants have made it their own."

Geoff instructed the real estate agent to do nothing more about the Queenslander block – caution remained the keyword at this time – but reaffirmed his instruction to seek firm price from the Council for the other two blocks. With nothing more to discuss, Geoff gave the agent a business card with his contact details and ended the meeting.

Things continued to move fast. Discussions continued with the supermarket chain and resulted in a signed agreement. About two weeks later, Winston contacted him with the Council's price for the two blocks of land. Geoff couldn't believe his ears; they were almost giving them away. The agent reiterated that council based the price on recovery of the rates arrears, plus any expenses incurred in maintaining the properties during the period of the Council's ownership. Geoff secretly believed it might be difficult for Council to itemise those expenses, as he believed it probably included a nice little profit margin. He read recently of that Council's financial woes and reckoned they could not dispose of the property without making a profit on the deal.

Nevertheless, the asking price was cheap. He instructed the agent to have a contract drawn up ready for signature. Before the end of October, the deal was finalised and Geoff Robinson was the new owner of the two blocks at the end of Main Street. The sale came with a Council proviso: the purchaser must render the blocks cyclone proof immediately on purchase. This necessitated another visit, and Robinson soon returned to Oyster Point to arrange for compliance with the sale provisions.

Inspections by various people confirmed Geoff's opinion that the old warehouse was solid and needed no work to make it cyclone proof. However, the adjoining block was a different story. The large derelict shed-like hall required demolition. Heavy rain delayed work until the ground dried out again.

Margot Pritchard's birthday was in early November and Gillian Robinson invited the Pritchards over for a barbecue. While the women busied themselves with salads and the like in the kitchen, Geoff heated the barbecue. Matthew sidled up to him and shot a cautious glance over his shoulder in the direction of the house before speaking.

"You might like to buy me that Lotto entry about now. An entry in the big New Year jackpot would be good."

"Why would I do that? I haven't seen where anything has been approved."

"Ah, well, keep an eye open for what comes out of the last week of sittings for this year. The new mine, and its associated infrastructure, are on the calendar for approval at that sitting. The developers, already advised accordingly, start moving resources into the area around the end of January. You just have to accept it, Geoff, it's going to happen."

"I don't really believe it, but I suppose I'm going to have to. I guess you would know."

At that point, the wives, laden with bowls and platters, came out, effectively ending the men's conversation. Geoff floated through the rest of the night. The party flew past in a blur. All he thought about was what else he could do to capitalise on this information. By the time he dropped into bed, he knew the first thing he would do was look into buying that extra block now occupied by the old Queenslander. He still had cash to play with … enough, if he could get it at the right price.

First thing the next morning, he put a call through to Rick Winston. The agent seemed a little ambivalent about pursuing the purchase of the extra block. After some pointed questioning, Winston admitted he thought the chances of buying it were slim, and chances of buying it at a realistic price were non-existent. However, as their discussion continued, Winston seemed to warm to the idea. Finally, he came round.

"There might be a way; no guarantees of course. There are a few negative aspects to consider. The owner might not want to sell; he might want to sell but you might not want to pay the price he asks. There might be a way around the first problem … but it might cost."

"I'll leave it in your capable hands to work out what might be possible."

Geoff was no stranger to the property game. He knew better than to question how they could get around the possibility of the owner not wanting to sell. Winston's mention that it 'might cost' needed no interpretation. Some sort of deal would be involved. Geoff did not want to know about it. That way there would be deniability later if questions ever arose.

Winston didn't waste time on a phone call, opting instead for a face-to-face discussion with his contact in the Council office.

"Good morning, Bert; remember that Oyster Point block with the derelict Queenslander we spoke about a few weeks ago? My client decided he is keen to buy."

"As you know, unless your client has very deep pockets – and no savvy about property prices, he is going to be disappointed."

"Look, it's almost coffee time and I'm dying for a cup. How about we wander up the street for a latte?"

Bert wasn't exactly a babe in the woods. He knew how to play the game. He couldn't see how he could help Winston, but he would put up with his company for half an hour or so for a free latte. Once the coffees arrived, the agent made his pitch.

"I noticed the Council is reminding all residents that the cyclone season is about to descend upon us again. What happens in the case of absentee property owners? The locals receive reminders via the media and letterbox flyers. What about out-of-towners? Perhaps the Melbourne owner of this block needs reminding of his liabilities in the event of a cyclone and should his property cause damage to other surrounding properties."

Bert saw where this was going, and liked the sound of it. "You are right. Out-of-towners don't get the reminders. That's a shortcoming in my department's processes. I should look into rectifying that situation. Of course, it would incur additional expense and, with the current financial crisis plaguing the Council, I need to consider whether the cost is warranted or not."

"As you say, with Council currently under investigation for financial mismanagement by its previous elected members, you need to think about how to handle that extra cost. Shall we say $1000 might cover the cost and inconvenience?"

"Hmm, yes, I think that should just about do it." They shook hands and went their separate ways. As the matter fell within his jurisdiction, Bert drafted a letter to go out under his signature.

In effect, the local Council, as part of its cyclone preparedness campaign, advised the owner of their concern regarding the old house, pointing out that, in the event of a cyclone, should the house suffer damage, the owner could be liable for any damage it caused to other properties in the vicinity. The letter added that, in the event of the owner not taking immediate positive action, the Council would need to undertake the work to ensure the safety of other buildings in the area, and would seek to recover costs from the owner. It also suggested that the owner check with his insurance firm whether his policy covered the liability for damage caused to other properties in such circumstances.

This brought the owner scurrying to Oyster Point to reignite sale discussions with the real estate agent. Winston prepared his slick sales pitch in anticipation. He assured the owner that quotes obtained to make safe the building showed there would be very little cash left from a realistic sale price … if an interested buyer could be located. The agent handed the owner a lifeline.

"However, for a much reduced sale price and no responsibility for making the building safe or paying the outstanding rate arrears – I see the property is listed in the Council's annual list of rate arrears – there might be opportunity to find a gullible buyer."

With the owner hooked, the agent reeled him in. They discussed what might constitute a reasonable though much reduced sale price, given the extra costs to the buyer of the rate arrears and immediate demolition the Council required. By the end of the meeting, Rick Winston was pleased with himself, and the relieved owner was on the next flight back to Melbourne.

The deal was done. Geoff Robinson insisted on a shortened two-week settlement period. He did not want to give the owner time to reconsider. The quick settlement also allowed Robinson's currently engaged demolition contractor to complete work on both blocks at the same time. Geoff briefly wondered how much of the purchase price went to 'grease palms' to secure the sale, and how much greased Winston's palm over and above his commission. By the end of November, Robinson owned all three blocks at the far end of Main Street. The hall and the Queenslander and its shed, now razed to the ground, left only concrete slabs and foundations as evidence of their previous existence.

In the second week in December, in its final sitting before it rose for the year, Parliament approved the new mine and associated infrastructure. Matthew received his entry in the major New Year Lotto draw. The wet season was about to set in. Stifling hot humid weather greeted politicians as they left their air-conditioned offices to head home following the last session of Parliament. The Bureau of Meteorology predicted at least four cyclones would develop off the Queensland coast during the forthcoming wet season, and one or possibly two would cross somewhere along the coast.

Just over a week out from Christmas, a small low-pressure system developed in the Coral Sea. It was a long way off and not particularly significant. The situation soon changed. By the next day, it had deepened and moved towards the coast. Cyclone watch notices broadcast that night had it as a category two and probably a category three by the following morning. They were right. By the following day, it was a category three and threatening to become category four. Cyclone watches now became cyclone warnings. It picked up speed as it raced towards the coast. Residents along a long strip of the coastline hurriedly taped windows and generally battened down for a nervous night.

After a sleepless night for many, the cyclone crossed the coast late the following afternoon. Although predicted to cross close to Oyster Point it crossed the coast in a largely unpopulated area some distance to the north of the town. However, that was close enough to create severe damage in the town itself and in the surrounding farming areas. The town lost power and water supplies. As so often happens with cyclones, there wasn't blanket damage across the district, merely swathes of destruction through town and farmland areas.

Amongst the worst hit areas was the commercial centre of town. The shopping centre was completely demolished. Green's General Store, located across Main Street from the shopping centre also sustained severe damage. At the height of the cyclone, Ted Green went downstairs and ventured outside to investigate a worrying noised coming from behind the store. Tragically, the main power service connection to the building, brought down by the wind was unseen in the dark. Ted's contact with the fallen live wire was fatal. If power had been lost earlier, or he had gone out a little later, he might have survived.

Rain fell all night and next morning, but the wind abated. People ventured out to inspect the damage and learn of the Greens' tragedy. Every shop in the small shopping arcade sustained severe damage and loss of stock. Flying debris breached the plate glass front of Green's Store. The upstairs residence was unroofed and walls and furniture blown away. Mrs Green took refuge in a new cold room installed only the week before in the warehouse area of the place but not yet made operational. The shop, warehouse and all stock were lost.

Only a few days to Christmas and no power, no water – fortunately it kept raining – no food supplies, and, for many families, previously purchased presents lost. Surprisingly, in many instances, old houses survived better than some of their modern counterparts did.

Geoff Robinson weathered the cyclone in his rented villa about a hundred kilometres south of Oyster Point, where the night proved windy and wet but no real concern for residents. He needed to stay in the area while work progressed on his Oyster Point properties, but one overnight stay at the local pub was enough. As soon as the highway was open to vehicular traffic after the cyclone, Geoff Robinson returned to Oyster Point to check on his properties. He congratulated himself on having demolished both the old Queenslander and the old hall when he did.

The cement slabs and foundations remaining on those sites presented no cause for concern during the cyclone. The warehouse escaped unscathed. The devastation at Green's General Store and their tragedy had Robinson on the phone to Bernard Cartwright, his supermarket chain contact, to offer the use of the warehouse as a temporary supermarket. The firm jumped at the opportunity and organised a fleet of trucks. At least the townsfolk would have food for Christmas -- if the trucks could get through.

Next day, the first semitrailers arrived, bringing three large cold rooms and a number of fridge and freezer display units. Various shelving arrangements and flat-pack checkouts arrived on another truck along with cash registers and other sundry electrical items. The various utility supply providers, supported by many local tradespeople, worked feverishly throughout the previous day and into the night to ensure adequate power supply to the warehouse for the cold rooms and other equipment in readiness for the food when it arrived. … And the food did arrive the next day on a long convoy of trucks, including a refrigerated ones loaded with hams and various frozen poultry.

Insurance company representatives swarmed across the area. Never one to miss an opportunity, Robinson quickly sought out his slick real estate friend to enquire after the future of the obliterated shopping arcade. Winston advised that the elderly owner bought up big as the town started to die. In much the same way as Geoff Robinson had done, he based his buying spree on the premise that the place would come to life again when/if the new mine opened. Undercapitalised to begin with, the elderly buyer wasn't concerned. His terminally ill independently wealthy wife of many years had no more than a few months to live. With no other family, he believed he would inherit on her death, and was confident he could sit things out until that anticipated windfall arrived. His wife, however, had other ideas. She left the house (which was in her name) and a small sum of cash – a very small amount of cash -- to her husband, and distributed the rest of her estate across a number of organisations with which she had long been involved.

Loss of the anticipated windfall, forced her husband to cut corners. Those corners included ignoring maintenance of the arcade buildings, and reducing insurance cover on the property to the minimum. In the wake of the cyclone, the insurance agent's advice was that the payout would barely cover the cost of clearing the site. In danger of retribution from his tenants and townsfolk alike, the owner retreated to a holiday apartment he owned on the Gold Coast.

Robinson recognised an opportunity when he saw it, but purchase of the three blocks at the end of Main Street depleted his cash reserves. Nevertheless, he put through another call to his sleazy acquaintance, Rick Winston. The real estate agent sprang into action, located the owner and began negotiating the sale of the shopping arcade site. While Winston haggled with the owner, Robinson took measures to remedy his liquidity situation.

His dilemma was that he could afford to buy the property, but then wouldn't have the cash to develop it. Robinson urgently needed to source a fair lump of investment capital for reconstruction. He had married well. Gillian came from an affluent family, and she was wealthy in her own right. She and her sister inherited from grandparents. As his first targets, Robinson canvassed his wife and her other more affluent family members for investment money. Matthew Pritchard he bypassed as Matthew's involvement could raise awkward questions at high levels. However, his favourite cousin and solicitor, Margot Pritchard, was another matter, as were a couple of other business colleagues. Gillian and Margot grilled him about his vision for Oyster Point and its potential investment potential.

He explained, "I have enough cash reserves to buy the former arcade land and to build at least stage one of the planned new supermarket. However, I won't have enough to build a new shopping complex on the site of the old arcade, and might struggle to find enough for stage two of the supermarket. From the outset, I was prepared to go to the bank if I needed extra cash for stage two. However, with the town's shopping facilities now wiped out, the development opportunities have increased exponentially while the timeline for everything has shortened considerably."

"How can you be sure it's worth the investment? I though you said the place was dying. Why invest in a place that, if not dead already, now probably soon will be?" Gillian asked. Geoff knew her caution was justified.

"The new mine in the hinterland and its attendant infrastructure received approval by Parliament a couple of weeks ago. Work is to begin around the end of January. Oyster Point will be the mine's town. It's where workers will live and the mine's administration function will be located. The population will explode … and probably more rapidly than the place can cope with, I imagine. We would be getting in on the ground floor – no pun intended – and, if we start building now, we should be ready by the time there is a reasonable build-up of population."

That swayed the women. They promised to invest what they could. Business colleagues took less convincing and immediately gave investment guarantees. Not wanting to bring in too many outsiders, Geoff then went to the bank with his detailed proposal. Before doing so, however, he spoke to the Mayor of the local Council responsible for Oyster Point. The Council was keen to see the town re-established and expressed appropriate concern for the welfare of its constituents.

Concern existed about how the place would accommodate the predicted forthcoming expansion. The Council was unable to assist with funding – 'our current embarrassing financial situation, you understand' – but immediately provided Robinson with a strong letter of support. That letter, plus the more than abundant available collateral and confirmed financial support from investors, resulted in a guaranteed bank loan. Geoff structured his consortium so that their investment was in building the new shopping complex, leaving the supermarket development in his name alone. The gods smiled on him. During the week after he secured the bank loan, the Council contacted him. They advised there was a strong likelihood some natural disaster assistance funding would be available to help with reconstruction.

The makeshift supermarket in the old warehouse building opened its doors for business three days before Christmas. Many of the locals who owned and/ or worked in various businesses throughout the town, and who now found themselves unemployed, became shelf-packers and checkout operators. Intensive discussions occurred between the Council and Robinson regarding future development of this town block. Preliminary plans (hardly more than ideas) received Council's 'in principle' approval.

A public meeting on Christmas Eve afternoon shared with the community Robinson's vision for the new supermarket and shopping precinct. Not surprisingly perhaps, all those who attended lauded him as something of a saviour. As explained to the crowd, the finer details of the shopping complex weren't available yet, as its final make-up depended on interest from potential businesses. However, Robinson knew that his development projects had to provide the mine developers with something they could use to entice workers to relocate to Oyster Point, a place that at this time looked exceptionally unappealing.

Prior to the public meeting, Geoff met with Mrs Green. He was sufficiently astute, to realise the community might take a dim view of his capitalising on another's misfortune and tragedy. In recognising Mrs Green's long-time capable management of Green's General Store, he offered her a management role in the new supermarket's operation. It proved a wise move. She wasn't interested then as she was still recovering from recent events and was going to spend some time with her daughter and grandchildren down south, but she thought that, perhaps some time in the future, she might be interested in some involvement. Word of his offer to Mrs Green rapidly spread through town. It resulted in many of the locals commending him on his approach. The move worked a treat. He genuinely liked Mrs Green and thought she would be a valuable asset to the business, but the big win was avoiding getting the townspeople offside – while scoring a few Brownie points as well.

Nothing much happened in the week between Christmas and New Year except that the supermarket kept trading and an array of front-end loaders and other heavy equipment arrived and parked around the shopping centre site. Immediately following New Year, work began on clearing the site. The insurance payout for clearing the arcade site that would have gone to the previous owner, but now paid to Robinson, more than covered the cost. However, when work began, Robinson wasn't around. After arranging all the on-site work, he flew south to work with his architect on plans for the supermarket. He anticipated this would not be a lengthy process. The architect had been involved in similar projects in the past, and plans from another precinct only required minor tweaking to align with Robinson's vision.

After discussions with all concerned, firm plans were on the table. As Robinson envisaged, building the supermarket would be in two stages, the first stage on the block previously occupied by the old hall. When this stage was complete, the temporary supermarket housed in the old warehouse building would relocate to stage one, and the warehouse building demolished. Stage two of the supermarket development would follow. The original open spaces on the warehouse and hall blocks would become car parks, as would the old Queenslander's block -- eventually.

The new shopping complex required a bit more thought. From the outset, it was obvious it needed to be large and simple but, more importantly, its design needed to incorporate a high degree of flexibility. As the architect pointed out, over time, the size of the individual shops might vary depending on the nature of the businesses occupying them. Robinson had his own ideas about the types of businesses he wanted to attract. Businesses that he imagined would meet the needs of a burgeoning cosmopolitan population, but he realised it would take a sound marketing plan to make reality match his vision.

Geoff also realised that, once the precinct neared completion, he would need someone local to manage rentals and allocation of spaces, and to ensure the spaces were set up ready for the proprietors to fit out according to their needs. This wasn't something he wanted to take on himself. As much as he hated the thought, Geoff had to accept that Rick Winston might be a logical – part-time – manager, at least for the initial establishment phase. However, that was something for later. Right now, getting the place designed and built as quickly as possible was paramount.

Preliminary drawings to hand, Robinson called a meeting of his fellow shopping complex investors. One of the non-family investors, Manny, liked what had been done so far but posed a question that caused pause for thought. Manny was Robinson's lead into discussions with the supermarket chain but, more than that, he was someone Robinson knew was involved in the design of several other shopping malls. As he observed some time earlier, Geoff's vision amounted to the resurrection of a place already in its death throes, and Manny wanted a part of it, saying it was 'as close to a resurrection as he'd ever get'.

"Has there been any consideration of a second storey for the building?" he asked. "I can see from the architect's plans, the building is structurally sound enough to take another level. Remember, my background is in construction."

They all looked at Geoff, who simply shook his head and said, "No."

"I think it's worth a thought," Manny pushed on. "If the town goes ahead as we think, there will be a need for more than what this single story building can provide."

"What sort of things might occupy the second storey?" Gillian queried.

"If you are going to have more shops up there, you would need to build in multiple means of accessing the upper floor to ensure everyone has access to whatever is up there," Margot added thoughtfully.

"I hadn't thought that far ahead," Manny confessed, "But you are right about the universal access aspect. Speaking off the top of my head now, things to consider for upstairs might be the centre's management office … and some sort of functions room. And it just occurred to me how we might build in those access facilities so they not only serve their primary function, but also serve a secondary purpose along that bit of blank back wall."

"What sort of functions room? I envisage there will be a restaurant on the ground floor. Do we really need something else?" Geoff asked a little aggressively. This was his development and someone questioning his thinking and design didn't sit too comfortably.

"Restaurants are for dining out and maybe the odd small party – like maybe a family birthday party. What I'm talking about is somewhere for seminars, workshops, conferences, meetings, weddings and the like, and possibly other events like book launches and parties to celebrate other events. The restaurant could be the caterers for any function involving eating and/or drinking," Manny explained in the hope of placating Geoff

Geoff looked around his fellow investors as Manny spoke. They looked thoughtful and nodded in agreement. Reluctantly Geoff joined in the nodding. Manny made sense. With the tide swung his way, Manny pressed home his advantage.

"I don't think the upper storey should cover the whole length of the building … maybe only half, or even a little less. Apart from a functions room and the centre's management office, perhaps a couple of extra rental spaces could be included for the right kind of businesses or offices. Simply adding a bit on the top will not cost anywhere near what you might expect."

Robinson ran his hand through his hair and then asked the question. "Well, what does everyone think? Do we ask the architect to add a partial second storey or not?"

There was unanimous support for the idea. For another half an hour, the group discussed the second storey. Then all except Manny departed. Geoff and Manny spent a couple of hours brainstorming the addition to the building to enable Geoff to take firm ideas back to the architect.

From his experience with other developments, Geoff knew firm deadlines needed establishment at the outset. Failure to do so could see a project crawl along far longer than it should, chewing up funds while it was about it. The architect, the construction firm's site manager and Rick Winston all knew the beginning of April was the date set for the opening of the new shopping complex. There would be no deviation from that date. There needed to be a grand opening to bring in shoppers as soon as the doors opened and to lift the spirits of the town. This meant finalising the design as soon as possible … and that meant a probable difficult meeting with the architect to explain that he now wanted a couple of changes made, not the least of which was the addition of a partial second storey.

Believing the plans finished, the architect called Robinson for a meeting to go over the final drawings. He was disappointed when Geoff showed little enthusiasm.

After apologising in advance for the changes he was about to request, Geoff outlined the requirements in terms of an 'upstairs' storey. He still wasn't convinced about what should occupy the upstairs area other than it was a good place for the centre's management office. They agreed that the second storey should have movable partitioning for configuration later to suit requirements.

"Right; what about the ground floor design, is that okay?" the architect asked a little tersely.

"Yes, I like what you've done. It is in line with the brief I gave you. However, one thing I didn't have in mind when we discussed the initial brief is something I now want included. There needs to be a good restaurant in there somewhere," he stated, with a sweeping gesture across the plan. "A restaurant with a view out over the water, and one that maybe lends itself to a bit of outdoor dining."

The architect rubbed his chin and pondered the new request for a moment before taking up his pencil and a blank sheet of paper. He drew the footprint of the building as it existed on his plans. Then he drew in a semicircular protrusion about half way along the rear wall of the building. This, he explained to Geoff, would be a glassed in area where people could sit and look out across the water. Next, he sketched in the rough outline of a wide overhanging roof that ran the full length of the rear of the building. The roof provided almost a skillion effect. He explained that this area would provide for outdoor dining, not only for this new proposed restaurant but also for any other eateries that might eventuate along that wall. The overhanging eaves along the front and ends of the building would provide a covered walkway for customers. The architect admitted to being surprised at this late stage request to include a restaurant in the plans. As far as he knew, there hadn't been any enquiries from potential restaurateurs to set up in the new complex.

"The make-up of the future community will demand a top-notch place to eat. The pub's food is fine, if you're hungry, but there's not much else to recommend it as the best eatery in town. I intend to remedy that situation."

La Boulangerie

Oyster Point gradually came back to life during January. The community rolled up its sleeves, assessed the damage and got on with getting its lives back on track. Some distance inland from the coast and unscathed by the cyclone, work began on the new mine site. Geoff Robinson's makeshift supermarket continued to experience strong trade, but the other part of his dream for Oyster Point was another story. Concerns centred on the gamble of establishing a new shopping complex. Geoff counted on the future expansion of the community and attracting businesses into the new complex. The end of January saw the first flickers of interest by potential tenants. Some of that interest originated a long way from Oyster Point.

"Why can I not stay in Brisbane?" Cecile wailed. "I have my work ... my friends ... everything is here. I love our city apartment."

"I am going to be working up there all the time soon. It's not going to be as it has been, with me commuting, but spending most of my time here. Construction is about to begin. I need to be there," her husband replied. He expected a hard battle, but was determined to win. He continued to press his argument. "You only work two, sometimes three days a week. What do you do with the rest of your time?"

"Well, there is always housework and meeting up with my friends ... and looking after you, of course."

"What about when I'm not here, when you don't have to cook for me or look after me? There is little housework in an inner city apartment this size." He had made plans but he wanted some preliminary discussion before he told her what they were. He sighed. It was obvious meaningful discussion about their future was not going to occur, so he took a hard line.

"Cecile, I have made airline bookings for tomorrow. We are flying up to have a look at the place. You will be on the plane with me in the morning. There is no point arguing any longer. I am going back to the office now to pick up some papers to take with me. I'll be back soon."

He did need to go to his office, but he also knew Cecile would sulk for the rest of the evening. It was as well to give her some time to adjust to the idea of tomorrow's trip. It only took a few minutes to gather up the papers he wanted, but he needed to waste more time before returning home.

He knew how his wife reacted. Right now, she was angry and argumentative; a spitfire. Then the tears would come, followed by the silent treatment for the rest of the night. Better to let the first and second stages pass before going home. He opened the bottom drawer of his desk, took out the bottle of single malt and a glass and poured himself a good measure. With his feet on the desk and drink in hand, he let his mind wander back to when he met Cecile.

John Munroe and Cecile Baudin met on the French Riviera almost 12 years ago. John, an engineer, had completed two years in South Africa working for an international mining company. With quite a bit of leave accumulated, he decided to go home to England to spend time with family and friends he hadn't seen since leaving for South Africa. After only a couple of weeks back home, he realised he could not stand much more of the rounds of visiting and visitors, and being fussed over by his mother. Two months was a long time in purgatory. He needed something else to do; somewhere else to go – somewhere that would be a real holiday.

It was almost the end of the season. Finding accommodation on the French Riviera wasn't a problem. His bank balance was healthy. He booked for two weeks and, three days later, began his real holiday. The first night there, he decided to try out a recommended restaurant. Without an exact address, he set off down the street, reading signage on the fronts of the buildings as he went. Because he was looking up at the buildings, he didn't see the dark haired young woman coming towards him. She was reading a leaflet and hadn't been looking where she went either. They collided rather heavily. The young woman ended up on the pavement. No real harm done, but the petite brunette was always going to come off second best against the solidly built 190cm blue-eyed blonde.

Cecile Baudin and her best friend talked for years about a holiday on the Riviera. With their careers now established, that holiday was to become a reality. They planned ten days of sheer pleasure, taking in the sun and good restaurants. Just before the holiday, her friend acquired the latest of hot fashion accessories: a new Vespa scooter. Then, two days before they were due to leave Paris, she came off the scooter, breaking a leg and sustaining various other minor injuries. Cecile went on holiday alone. It hadn't worked out as she'd hoped. Not sharing the experience with someone special wasn't nearly as good. At her hotel, she picked up a leaflet advertising a well-known local musician providing live entertainment at one of the area's leading restaurants. Leaflet in hand, she set off in search of the restaurant, coincidentally, the same restaurant as John was looking for.

After they finished apologising to one another, and discovered they were both heading for the same restaurant, they agreed to find the place and have dinner together. They enjoyed each other's company and arranged to meet again the next day. Cecile only had seven days of her holiday remaining. The pair spent those days together and, when Cecile returned to Paris, John went with her. It took only a couple of weeks in Paris, to realise this was more than a holiday friendship. They had something special.

John remembered all the telephone calls and emails over the next 12 months until they married. Following the wedding, Cecile remained in Paris for a couple of months while John returned to South Africa to finish up there. Then the couple moved to Australia, where John was to work at a new mine. That was 10 years ago now. They saw a bit of Australia as the company moved him from one mine to another. About four years ago, his work brought them to Queensland, but the company suffered the same fate as many other miners. Mines closed and staff, including John, became unemployed. For a brief moment, his future look grim, but a week after he became unemployed, another company hired him to work on plans for a new mine.

Although working out of the company's Brisbane office initially, in more recent times, he found himself commuting between Brisbane and the proposed mine site. When the project finally received Government approval, he realised he would be spending his time on both the development of the mine and the new port sites. All opportunity for him to return to Brisbane, even for an occasional day, would disappear. He needed to move north, and establish his life at Oyster Point.

He understood Cecile's reluctance to leave Brisbane. They were happy here, and she developed something akin to a Parisian lifestyle. A trained chef, who then trained as a baker, she put her career on hold when they married. A chance discovery of a great little bakery close to their apartment led to a meeting with its owner, Pierre, and subsequent part-time work for him. Perhaps that was the answer to making the move north work for her. She might settle down if she could continue with her love of baking.

Ah well, that was an issue for another day he told himself. It was getting late. He needed to go home and pack a bag for the early morning flight – and face whatever stage his wife's mood had reached. He knew from experience that, if he made it clear a certain course of action would occur, his wife would comply, but not necessarily with good grace. When he arrived home, he found his wife had moved into the spare bedroom, but he was relieved to find she had packed a bag.

The flight was uneventful if somewhat silent. On arrival, he collected a hire car and drove to Oyster Point… an hour-long boring drive, with virtually nothing of interest to see along the way. John groaned inwardly as they drove into Oyster Point. It did not present an appealing picture so soon after the cyclone. He found himself explaining at length why it looked as it did and how wonderful it would be when the reconstruction was complete. Their first challenge was to locate the office of real estate agent, Rick Winston. A phone call found him at the construction site of the new shopping complex, so they drove along Main Street to what looked like the right place.

Conspicuous as the only person on the site not in work clothes, the real estate agent was easy to find. Introductions over, Winston suggested they move to one of the tables along The Esplanade and away from the noisy construction site. John got straight to the point: he was looking to buy a house and outlined what he wanted. He also was interested in the new shopping complex and suggested they might have a chat about it again after they looked at houses. It was lunchtime, so they arranged to meet Winston again after lunching at the hotel.

There were three houses to inspect, one close to the centre of town and two others in a upmarket gated community. Cecile remained sullen throughout the inspections, but John thought he detected a flicker of interest in the last house in the gated community. He knew better than to push for a comment then, but would ask for her thoughts over dinner that evening. As they completed that last inspection, John suggested they take advantage of the poolside furniture to sit and discuss the shopping complex. Winston laid out the complex's floor plan on the small table before launching into his sales pitch.

"I know the place doesn't look much at the moment and it's hard to imagine what it will become but, mark my words, within the next few months this whole place will become a throbbing multicultural town as construction workers from the mine, the haul road and the port take up residence. The shopping complex will become the dynamic centre of town. We are keen to entice new and exciting businesses into the complex to meet the needs of those new residents. The precinct will be a vital part of the town and will support and add to the supermarket development next door. By selecting a space off the plan at this early stage, potential lessees have the opportunity to pick their preferred location within the building. We expect the sites to be snapped up quickly, so we ask for firm expressions of interest at the earliest opportunity."

Cecile could maintain her silence no longer. She definitely did not like this real estate man. "John, why are we looking at these plans? We are not shopkeepers. You work for the mining company. What does it matter what the shopping centre will look like?"

"I have some ideas, Cecile. You obviously are not interested in them, so perhaps you should have another look around the house and the gardens while I speak with Mr Winston."

She stomped off into the house, realising she had crossed the line in being so rude in front of the real estate agent. As she admired the beautiful mass of ferns, cycads, bromeliads and other tropical plants occupying a large part of the backyard of the property, John came to say they were leaving. Time had allowed her to assess her situation. She realised her sulk had persisted long enough. She knew that, if she didn't smarten her attitude, she was likely to find herself receiving a stern rebuke from John. She smiled sweetly at him and asked, "Where are we going next? What else do we have to look at today?"

Thank God, the storm is over John thought, and he returned her smile as he answered. "I don't think there's much else to do today. Maybe have a bit of a drive around before heading for our accommodation at Arkana Beach. What do you think?"

She nodded, and they walked back to the pool to say goodbye to Rick Winston who was fighting the breeze as he rolled up his plans. Their drive around the town, taking in the destruction and the reconstruction work, took little time and they soon were booking into their hotel at Arkana. It was still early, so they took a stroll down the main street, enjoying the cool afternoon breeze and calling in to all the boutiques, bistros and bars to soak up the colour and flavour of the place, before returning to their hotel to freshen up for dinner. Dinner in the hotel's restaurant was unexpectedly excellent: wonderful food and great service. Even Cecile commented on it.

While they waited for their dessert to arrive, John launched into the difficult conversation they had to have. "Which of the three houses we looked at today did you prefer?" He asked casually.

"None."

"Was there anything you liked about any of the houses?"

"Nothing; not a thing. John, I am French. I come from Paris. I do not belong … how do you say … in the bush."

Let the battle begin he thought as he struggled to maintain a straight face and normal voice. "Cecile, this is nonsense. We talked about this when the downturn in the mining industry first occurred. You knew we would have to move, possibly even leave Australia, so what is all this nonsense about? You are acting like a spoilt child. Tomorrow I will be signing a contract for one of those houses. Tonight is your opportunity to have some input into that decision."

"Tomorrow?! No, no. Why can't I stay in Brisbane in our apartment? …Or perhaps we could find something here at Arkana. I saw some beautiful houses up on the hills this afternoon. Maybe one of those is for sale."

"Here's how it's going to be, Cecile. For the next 18 months or so, most days I will be able to come home at night and sleep in my own bed. If you wish to remain in Brisbane, that is up to you, but I will not commute. My work here will require long days I suspect, and I do not want to have to drive for another hour or so after I finish work in order to sleep in my bed at Arkana. I *will be* signing a contract on a house tomorrow, and I will be living in it. What you choose to do is up to you, but I would prefer you chose to live there with me."

Cecile bit her lip. She knew John well enough to know there was no room to move on this issue. "If I have to put up with any of them in order to be living with you, then I think the last house we looked at is preferable," she snapped at him.

"That is good. Thank you for your comment. I preferred that one. Tomorrow we will talk to Rick Winston about how soon we can sign a contract."

"I do not like that real estate man."

"I don't like him much either, but I'm not buying him. I'm buying a house, and he happens to be the person handling the sale."

"Why all the fuss about the shopping complex? What is this 'idea' you spoke of?"

"It bothers me that, for most of our marriage, you put your career on hold to follow me wherever my work took me. I see our move to Oyster Point as an opportunity for you to return to your career, but also to assist the many European families that will come to settle in Oyster Point. It is an opportunity for you to establish your own boulangerie, and to provide all those wonderful treats those families wouldn't have been able to get in Australia."

"You want me to work full time now?" she asked incredulously.

"Well, what else would you do? You said yourself there was nothing to interest you at Oyster Point. Already, the team of people I work with include a Swiss, a German, an Italian and one I think is French. They all will move their families to Oyster Point. These are just examples of the people who would welcome the wonderful fare you make."

Cecile did not respond. Conversation lapsed for their desserts arrival. They did not return to the subject again that evening, but John noticed Cecile became quiet and appeared to be weighing something up in her mind.

Before leaving the hotel the next morning, John changed their flight to the following day and arranged to spend an extra night at the hotel. That done, they drove back to Oyster Point to meet with Rick Winston again. The house presented no problems. He could have the contract ready for signature that afternoon. With that matter dealt with, John asked for another look at the shopping complex plan. This time, Cecile showed a little more interest. Even went so far as to indicate a good location for a bakery.

The real estate agent fancied himself as charming. He had worked out that interest in the complex had something to do with this lady, and having reached this conclusion, he directed his attention – and his imagined charm – to Cecile. "Please, call me Rick. Now, my dear, tell me what your requirements might be so we can work out whether this space would be suitable for your bakery."

"Mr Winston, I am not *your dear*, and I would need to think about the layout and other things before I give you that kind of information. I imagine my husband's thinking merely is to lodge an expression of interest," she replied condescendingly. "If we should decide to proceed, that is the space I want."

John fought back a smile. No one else he knew could put someone down with such finesse as Cecile. She left the other person in no doubt about where they stood, just as she had done now with Winston. However, he thought it better to step in and save the situation before it deteriorated and everything might be lost.

"Right then, as my wife indicated, we will put in a formal expression of interest on that particular shop space. Please have whatever necessary documents drawn up as well, and I will follow up on the expression of interest when the building is nearing completion."

They lunched at the hotel again and then filled in time looking over the area, including the new port site, until the house contract was ready for signature. The day's business completed, they drove back to Arkana Beach. John noted the atmosphere between them had improved, and it improved further after they spent a lazy hour or two by the hotel pool, before again spoiling themselves in the hotel restaurant.

On the flight back to Brisbane, Cecile lowered her tray table. When John glanced over, he felt a tingle of excitement. With the dimensions of the shop space scrawled across the top of the page, she was scratching out rough layout plans. She had chosen an excellent location, and he felt confident she had warmed to the idea of her own bakery.

John collected their mail on the way up to their apartment and threw it onto the hall table as they took their bags through to the bedroom. It was later, while Cecile made coffee that he sorted the mail. "You seem to have scored the lion's share of the mail," he called through to the kitchen. "There's a couple of very official letters from France."

Cecile rushed through to the sitting room, slopping the coffee as she plonked the tray down on a table and snatched up her mail.

"I'll take these through to the balcony then, shall I?" John suggested but received no response. He had just set the tray down on the small glass-topped table when he heard his wife cry out.

"*Mon Dieu.* No, no; this cannot be true."

"What is it? What's wrong?" he asked, rushing back into the sitting room.

His wife stood beside her opened mail. A roughly torn envelope lay on top of everything. Cecile, looking shocked and pale, held what he presumed were the contents of the torn envelope. With his arm around her shoulders, he steered her towards a chair. "Sit," he commanded. "Come on, sit down. You look like you've seen a ghost. What has upset you so much?"

"My grandmother … How do you say it? …My mother's mother was from

Australia."

"Okay; so your maternal grandmother was Australian. I don't suppose the world will end because of it," he said with an encouraging grin. "Where's the problem in that?"

"But we are *French*. How can this be? There must be some mistake."

"Come on, ma Cherie, tell me the story -- right from the beginning – so I can understand how you came to get this piece of paper – certificate or whatever it is – that's upset you."

She swallowed hard to regain composure before speaking. "My friends, Therese and Mimi, kept talking about their research and the little discoveries they made. They told me they were tracing their family history. At first, it was boring listening to them. I wasn't interested. Then I started thinking about my family and how little I knew about them."

"Your mother only died about five years ago. Didn't she talk about them? You get my lot together and it's not long before they're banging on over many cups of tea about some ancient relative or long lost ancestor."

"No. I don't think she knew too much. Like me, she was an only child. I didn't really know my grandmother. My father's being in the diplomatic service, meant we lived in many different counties until I was about 15."

"Yes. That's when he scored that plum job back in Paris. You moved back there and that's where you stayed, until I came along and swept you off your feet."

His attempts to lighten the moment were working. A hint of a smile tugged the corners of her mouth. "My grandmother died while we lived away from France. I think my mother went home for the funeral, but I don't know anything else."

"Well, it seems that, if you want to know more, you will have to keep researching."

"Yes, but I don't know how to research in Australia. I will talk to Adel. She knows how to do this and maybe she will help me. How much longer will we remain in Brisbane? How long before I have to move to Oyster Bay?"

"Umm, a month, maybe six weeks... who is Adel?"

"The woman in the apartment below us; I often have coffee with her."

"I thought her name was Adelaide."

"She prefers Adel. I will call her. See if we can talk tomorrow."

Armed with freshly made strawberry tarts and the documents from France, Cecile joined Adel for coffee the next morning. After explaining the Australian system of registering births, deaths and marriages – and the variations across the States – Adel drew up a research plan for Cecile's to follow, and offered to take her to the Genealogical Society's rooms that afternoon to get started. From the Parish Register entries from France, they knew her grandmother was born in Queensland, thereby narrowing the research area.

While the indexes provided a few useful leads, frustratingly, not the information Cecile expected. Adel noted her companion's disappointment and explained that their research could provide only basic information; the clues. To get all the details she wanted, they needed to obtain certificates. Cecile remained despondent. Adel realised her friend found researching outside her home country overwhelming.

"You might not think so, but we gathered a lot of information today. Let me do the next part of the research for you. That way you'll be free to get on with planning your new shop. You can pay me for whatever it costs afterwards. What do you think?"

Cecile pondered the offer for a few moments before replying. "Y-e-s; that would be wonderful, but how long is it likely to take?"

"It doesn't take long. I'm leaving tomorrow to visit my daughter in Sydney for a few days. I'll make a start on it next week. Don't look so worried. We will have it sorted out before you leave."

John came home that evening to find papers scattered all over the table. On his way through to the kitchen, he casually glanced at the paperwork and his spirits soared when he realised Cecile had been planning her shop. There were lists of equipment and potential products to sell, sketches of possible layout, and other stuff that he didn't understand. Cecile's excited update on her thoughts for the new shop dominated conversation over dinner. It so dominated her thinking, she forgot to mention her family history research until later in the evening when they were relaxing with a drink.

She sat up in bed scribbling in her notebook while John read a magazine. When he was ready to turn his light off, he casually asked, "So, should I confirm our interest in that shop in the new complex and have a contract drawn up?"

"*Mais certainment,* I am not doing all this work for nothing. Of course we are going to have my *boulangerie.*"

Over the next few weeks, there were many discussions with Pierre about equipment and layout, and what lines Australians most preferred. She also picked his brain for all the information on the Queensland rules and regulations applying to food handling and setting up a commercial kitchen. Both their post box and their inbox contained more mail than usual as quotes and catalogues for all manner of stuff arrived. What brand of oven to buy? Could she have gas ovens and cooktops? What competition was likely in the complex? John volunteered to contact Rick Winston, the real estate agent. He thought it best if he made the enquiries rather than let the excitable Cecile deal with the man. It involved several calls to Mr Winston over the next few days. Confirmation of delivery dates for orders already placed – fortunately – was not required until closer to when the shop was ready for occupancy.

The weeks flew past. Staff at Pierre's requiring leave took it while Cecile was still there. This had Cecile working virtually full time to cover the staff absences. John, now away for days at a time on the mine site, was at Oyster Point on settlement day for the house. He rang that night from a small motel he booked into on the highway not far from Oyster Point.

"We own our new house," he announced. "Settlement was today, so you need to think about how soon you and all our belongings will relocate to here. The apartment goes on the market this weekend. Whenever I can, I check on the shopping complex progress. Rick Winston says the walls of your shop will be up by this weekend. He would like to see your plans next week so they can complete any internal structures."

"Oh, everything is happening so quickly. I only have sketches. I don't have plans that I can give to anyone."

"That's okay. I can work from your sketches to produce plans over the weekend. I've also located a firm that will install all the kitchen equipment when it arrives. I'll be home some time on Friday. See you then."

Cecile went to bed late but couldn't sleep. Her mind occupied with all the things she still needed to do, she started questioning what she already had done. She gave up on sleep, got out of bed and started lists of required actions: one for the shop and one for the apartment/new house. Then she turned both lists into one combined timeline and noted those things already completed. By the time she allocated potential 'action dates' for the outstanding items, she was ready to try for sleep again.

Over breakfast the next morning, she reviewed her timeline amending and adjusting as she thought necessary. With the day to herself, she decided to spend it making a start on cleaning out the apartment's cupboards in readiness for the removalists. Around lunchtime, while sitting on the floor sorting through a box of files from the hall cupboard, she came to the concertina file of her family history papers. Shaking her head in disbelief, she thought, I have been so busy I have done nothing more of this. Then the memory of her last conversation with Adel thundered back.

"Adel!" she exclaimed aloud. "Oh dear, I haven't even been to see her." She jumped up and rang Adel.

A croaky Adel eventually answered. "I'm sorry, Cecile, I only arrived home from Sydney last night. Just before I was due to come home, I went down with that wretched flu that's doing the rounds down there. It flattened me for ten days. I promise I will send for your certificates tomorrow."

Although disappointed, Cecile insisted it wasn't urgent. Adel should only do it when she felt up to it, but Cecile suspected her family history research would not progress further before she left Brisbane. She consoled herself with the thought that there were too many other things to do and think about to worry about family history.

The couple spent most of the weekend finalising Cecile's vision for her bakery. True to his word, John produced a series of plans for the real estate agent as well as the company installing the kitchen. Cecile flew north with John on Monday for another look at her space and to discuss her plans. The next time she saw it, all of the structures would be in place, the painting and floor coverings completed. That night she told John she would organise removalists as soon as she returned to Brisbane and – hopefully – she would be at Oyster Point and moved into their house by the end of the following week.

Tuesday lunchtime, she was back at their apartment and making arrangements for the move. The earliest the removalists could come was next Tuesday. That gave Cecile a few more days to do things. Next, she rang Pierre to explain the timing of her departure from Brisbane and, unless it was essential, she would not be in to work again. There were friends she needed to say goodbye to, and arranging lunches or coffee with them took quite a bit of time. Mimi insisted that, as Cecile wouldn't leave Brisbane until Thursday next week, she should stay with Mimi after the removalists came on Tuesday.

Cecile was looking up professional cleaners in the phone book when the phone rang. It was the Brisbane real estate agent asking to show a potential buyer through the apartment at lunchtime on Wednesday. No, that didn't suit. She had friends coming for lunch on Wednesday. They agreed an inspection for Thursday lunchtime. The rest of Tuesday afternoon was spent identifying things the removalists should not pack, as John would take them in their car when he drove to Oyster Point.

Early on Wednesday morning, when she was up to her elbows in preparing lunch for her guests, Adel came up to the apartment. She brought a couple of friends with her and apologetically asked if they might have a quick look around the apartment. They were interested in buying and, although Adel told them Cecile's apartment was the same as hers, they still wanted a quick look. Cecile, unhappy about showing the place in its present state, reluctantly agreed. They didn't stay long.

Lunch was wonderful. It was fun but also sad. After a long lunch, Cecile's three friends left, vowing to keep in touch. She was stacking the dishwasher when the phone rang. It was the Brisbane real estate agent. A couple had signed a provisional contract on the apartment. They hadn't even wanted an inspection. When the agent mentioned their name, Cecile knew exactly who they were. They were Adel's unexpected visitors from this morning.

Thursday seemed to disappear in a whirl of coffee and food. John arrived home on Friday and, after signing various papers for the sale of the apartment – now under an unconditional contract – he settled down to help sort out what would go north in their car. They spent an emotional weekend together, saying goodbye to everything they loved about Brisbane. Sunday night, they packed the car, went out to dinner, and had an early night. Early Monday morning, John set off on the two-day drive north to Oyster Point. Soon after John left, the reality of the situation descended upon her, and Cecile dissolved into uncontrollable tears. The sobbing and tears lasted quite a while, eventually giving way to sniffling and a headache. She gave herself a stern talking to… there were things to do and tomorrow the removalists would come. The thought of the removalists almost precipitated another flood of tears.

As arranged, the removalists came and the apartment was empty except for Cecile's suitcase and her laptop. She fought back the tears again as she locked the door and left for Mimi's apartment. The cleaners came on Wednesday morning and, until they were finished, Cecile spent the morning with Adel talking over old times and each other's plans for the future. With her keys handed in to the real estate agent, Cecile went back to Mimi's apartment for dinner with a large group of friends before catching the flight out the following morning.

All their belongings arrived at the new house late Wednesday afternoon. Nothing was unpacked when she arrived on Thursday. However, the coffee machine, groceries and a few other things that came by car were in the kitchen. Unpacking took forever. There were so many decisions to make about where to put things – not the big things, but which cupboard or drawer for the small things. Cecile became impatient. Once the more important stuff was unpacked, she wanted to see how her shop looked. John insisted they spend the whole day unpacking. There was plenty of time tomorrow to see the shop. By the end of the day, Cecile was petulant. Dinner that night was a stony affair.

John insisted on a leisurely breakfast on Friday morning. Cecile was almost at explosion point, when finally he said they should go to look at the shop. After a small tantrum about having to wait so long, and a tirade of unprintable French, they drove to the new shopping complex. John planned to keep Cecile away from the shop until a few things were completed. The plan worked. She gasped and clapped her hands to her mouth at the sight of her new bakery. The display counters and bread racks were in place. A considerable racket came from the kitchen area. The tradesmen John hired were installing acres of stainless steel on benches. Other tradesmen would arrive on Monday to install the ovens and cooktops.

Cecile spent the morning checking every minor detail of the work already completed, before turning her attention to the rest of the complex. The place was no longer an empty shell. Walls dividing the various shop spaces were in place. Across the aisle from her shop, a group of elderly people appeared focused on setting up their own premises. Cecile ambled across and introduced herself to Gloria, who had just started explaining about their shop when Gordon wandered up and introduced himself. More introductions followed as Gordon took her on a tour of *Busy Fingers.*

John interrupted her chat with her new acquaintances when he reminded her they agreed to have lunch at the hotel across the road.

"Goodness, I forgot the time," she apologised. Then, looking at the group around her, she said, "Everyone, this is my husband John. We are going to the hotel for lunch. Would you like to join us?"

Invitation accepted, they were a group of ten on their way to the hotel for lunch. They all got on so well, and lunch stretched on for so long that, by the time they left the hotel, they were firm friends. John smiled to himself as he trailed the group back to the complex. He hadn't seen Cecile look so happy and excited in quite a while. His trepidation about moving to Oyster Point disappeared. The drama was over.

As promised, another bunch of tradesmen arrived on Monday morning. It took Cecile some time to convince them where the ovens and cooktops would go and why they had to go where she said they had to go. They soon learned that Cecile was not someone with whom you argued. With everything apparently under control in the kitchen, Cecile felt superfluous to requirements but determined to hang around to keep an eye on things. After wandering out into the main aisle, she overcame the temptation to visit Busy Fingers. They were busy getting set up and didn't need her interrupting them. Instead, for want of somewhere better to sit, she wandered a short distance along and perched on an abandoned carpenter's sawhorse.

A few moments later, Rick Winston and the construction foreman came in. Winston carried three long wooden things. They stopped outside Busy Fingers. Winston gave the foreman one of the wooden things and pointed to an area above the shop's door. Not wanting to have to deal with Winston, Cecile retreated to her kitchen. Emerging a short while later, she found Winston gone, and the foreman now wandering around with a tradesman. One of those wooden things Winston had carried leant against the front wall of her shop. She turned it over and felt a sudden surge of pride: *La Boulangerie.* It was the sign to go above her shop's door. Still having nothing to do, she went back to perching on the sawhorse.

After a while, Gordon Bailey and Anthony Newton from Busy Fingers came in carrying a collapsible card table and a number of folding chairs. Jane Peters, who followed them in, plonked a heavy looking milk crate on the table. While Jane and Anthony fussed about setting up the chairs, Gordon disappeared and returned moments later carrying a Tupperware cake carrier. Cecile strolled up to the group. "Good morning. You all look so busy. Can I help?"

"Definitely," replied Gordon, removing the top of the cake carrier with a flourish. "You can help us demolished this."

Eyes wide in alarm at the sight of the unveiled cheesecake, Cecile asked. "There is already somewhere here where you can buy such a cheesecake?"

The group gathered around the table dissolved into laughter at Cecile's obvious concern about the origins of the cheesecake.

"No, Gordon is our resident cook. When he is here, he plies us with morning tea treats," Jane said.

"I just like to bake," Gordon said as he handed her a slice of cheesecake. "There is no point in baking just for one. This way, I get to bake, and we all get to enjoy."

"*C'est magnifique,*" Cecile purred after the first mouthful. "…So fortunate to have such an excellent baker in your midst, no?"

"He keeps our waistlines in constant peril," commented Lois Riley.

*Morning tea was enjoyable: great conversation, excellent cheesecake and good cof*fee. Gordon 'acquired' the large thermos flasks from the former boarding school where the group were domiciled since the cyclone, and they proved most useful. With their conversations punctuated by the sound of the tradesman's drill, by the time they packed the relics of morning tea into the milk crate, both shops had their name boards attached above their doors. The table and chairs remained in the aisle, but Gordon and Jane disappeared, while Anthony got busy lending a hand in the shop. By lunchtime, all Cecile's cooking equipment was ready for use. Someone was connecting plumbing to the sinks, while an electrician worked out how to connect all of the electrical equipment in the front of the shop.

Again, Cecile found herself with nothing to do and was debating whether to go home or cross the road to the hotel for lunch. A flurry of activity in the aisle drew her out of her shop. This time they brought various containers, and the familiar milk crate. Jane went into Busy Fingers and rounded up everyone. Gordon and Anthony standing by the table beckoned Cecile to join them. Lunch was a quiche and salad, accompanied liberally by lively conversation.

"Tomorrow, morning tea and lunch are on me," Cecile announced. "But I do not have the table and chairs, so may we use these again tomorrow? Is there anything people can't eat or don't like?"

Having committed herself to producing food for the next day, Cecile needed to acquaint herself with the makeshift supermarket. Before they left for the day, Gordon told her not to worry about the coffee, as he would bring the thermos flasks again. After spending quite a bit of the afternoon worrying about what to make for the group, she finally decided it all depended on what she found in the supermarket. She harboured some doubts about the range of products they might have. However, she was pleasantly surprised, and only needed to adjust one of her recipes when one of the ingredients wasn't available. In amongst thinking about the menu for the following day, she spent a bit of time wondering about how to keep everything cold. Before closing the shop that afternoon, the solution dawned on her. Her refrigerated display cases were connected. She needed to test everything before the tradesman finally disappeared. She switched on one of the display cases to allow it to get cold overnight.

Up early the next morning, she had food to prepare. Having made the pastry the night before, she made raspberry tarts (frozen berries of course) with mascarpone cream topping for morning tea. Lunch was to be Moroccan flavoured chicken pieces with salad and fresh baguette. It was as well John now had a company vehicle she thought as she carefully loaded the food into the back of their SUV. Unlike Brisbane, Oyster Point was devoid of public transport. She would need their vehicle to commute between home and shop every day. When she arrived at the shop, the only people around were tradesmen working in other parts of the building.

Cecile tested the temperature of the display case – perfect – before transferring today's food carefully from car to display case. The previous night, she spent quite a bit of time rummaging in cupboards looking for an old picnic basket she knew she stashed somewhere. It now occupied one of the kitchen benches and held disposable plates, cutlery and napkins.

Only a couple of tradesmen came to the shop that day to finish the remaining work. The grey-haired brigade from across the aisle arrived late. They delayed leaving their units until after the post office opened to collect parcels on their way in. With the parcels deposited in the shop, the unanimous decision was for morning tea before commencing work. Cecile saw Gordon bring the milk crate in and realised it was morning teatime. She watched in delight as eyes glazed over when they tucked into her raspberry tarts. There was almost no conversation until the tart disappeared. Good, she thought, I haven't lost my touch. Lunch went down equally well, with conversation mainly centred on the forthcoming official opening of the complex.

Cecile noticed increased activity in some of the other shop spaces so far devoid of name boards. The third name board installed the previous day was for a large space at the end of one of the aisles. She queried the group over lunch about what The Academy was. Gordon explained that the Council had leased it as a community space where various groups or individuals could run workshops or classes, hold meetings and mount exhibitions.

That afternoon, she was anxious to get home to share with John the success of her day. He arrived home before her, having left the port site early. After he kissed her and handed her a glass of white wine, John indicated the mail he had dumped on the coffee table. "There are a couple of big envelopes there for you."

It was a surprise to get mail at their new address so soon. Her excitement rose when she saw one of the envelopes was from Adel. She ripped it open and tipped its contents onto the table. A quick scan of Adel's note indicated she had done a little more than originally discussed as she felt it might get Cecile to a point where she wanted to progress with it herself.

Adel had obtained several of the certificates they identified from the indexes. They related to her grandmother's siblings' births, and included the certificate for her great-grandparents' marriage. That was all they found in the indexes. Her grandmother's birth was too recent to appear in the index but, as Adel pointed out, by obtaining a couple of the siblings' certificates, they would be able to determine where the family might be living at the time grandma was born. Once they had that information, coupled with known details of grandma's name and age, they could apply for her birth certificate.

John looked up in alarm as Cecile squealed. "No, no. This can't be true. I don't believe it. There's been a mistake. Adel must have done something wrong."

As John sat down beside her, he noticed her hand holding that last certificate shook. "What is it? Show me the certificate. Surely it can't be that bad."

Without speaking, Cecile handed him the certificate. He scanned it quickly. "Hmmm, it looks like your grandmother's birth certificate. What's wrong with it? I thought you wanted this information."

"Yes, I wanted the information, but I did not think it would be like this."

"Well, it can't be all that bad and, whatever it is, it all happened a long time ago. So, what's the problem?"

"My great-grandparents were married here in Oyster Point. My grandmother and her brothers and sisters were born here too. Here … at Oyster Point … all those years ago… and now I have returned here. What do you make of that? Is that a sign – an omen – or something?"

"I wouldn't think so. A coincidence: yes. An omen: no."

Cecile threw the certificates in a heap on top of their envelope and sat brooding about their information. John picked up the other large envelope and, turning it over in his hands, tried to lighten her mood.

"This other envelope looks like it's from France. Maybe it brings better news. Were you expecting something?"

As she tore open the envelope and retrieved its contents, she explained to John, "I wrote to the Parish Priest again. I could not find a birth certificate for my mother, so I asked him to check the Parish Register for her baptism. It looks like he has sent me several copies from the register. Hmmm, what does he say…?" She took a few moments to read the Priest's letter, and then shook her head in disbelief. "My whole life is not as I believed. What I know about my mother is not true."

"No, that's not how it works. Your father sometimes can be open to speculation, but your mother is your mother. There's never any question about that … unless you're adopted of course."

"Don't be silly, John. Of course I'm not adopted."

"Okay, so what is this latest revelation about your mother?"

"You know my mother's maiden name was Lefeuvre. The priest could not find a baptism for her under that name, but he did find a baptism under her mother's maiden name. He then searched forward through the register and found my grandmother's marriage to my grandfather Lefeuvre. My mother was nearly three years old when my grandmother married. My mother was illegitimate. The Priest's letter says he believes they changed the child's name to Lefeuvre sometime after the marriage."

"Well, there's always been a lot of that about … and it doesn't change who you are, or who your mother was. You cannot judge what happened back then. You don't know what the circumstances were. What you do know is that two people who loved your mother very much brought her up. I think that's all that matters."

It was cold comfort, but Cecile accepted the truth in what he said. However, she resolved to apply again for her mother's birth certificate, but this time using the surname probably used when registering the birth.

Cecile didn't leave early for the shop on Wednesday. With all work now completed, there would be no workmen coming in today. By the time she arrived at the complex, Busy Fingers was a hive of activity, as was the shop on one side of hers. She learned it was to be a coffee shop and, the one on the other side, a brasserie. Soon after her arrival, the grey-haired brigade began setting up the table and chairs for morning tea. Gordon arrived carrying a large plastic container, which he triumphantly set down in the middle of the table before beckoning everyone for morning tea. They complied and took their places at the table.

Concern registered on Rose's face as she surveyed the gathering. "Where's Anthony? It's not like him to miss morning tea, and I knew he was coming this morning." Rose barely finished speaking when Anthony, sweating profusely, rushed in.

Anthony hurriedly explained his tardiness. "The blasted police have blocked off the road a couple of blocks from here because a big crane is working there. I had to park the car and walk the rest of the way. It's hot out there this morning and, not wanting to miss morning tea today, I hurried."

Vera, sitting next to Cecile, saw Cecile's eyebrows climb almost to her hairline at the site of Anthony. He did present something of a spectacle. His exertions left him with a glowing red face above a bilious green and yellow striped bow tie, coupled with a sunflower yellow shirt. Vera elbowed Cecile in the ribs and whispered, "Nothing a good woman couldn't fix," and added with a knowing nod of her head, "… and Edith believes she's just the girl for the job."

Anthony and Gordon, sitting next to each other, provided different examples of sartorial elegance. In contrast to Anthony's bright plumage, Gordon was wearing an 'I love New York' tee shirt over well-worn jeans.

Cecile discovered it was Edith's birthday. Gordon produced a large cake appropriately decorated for the occasion. Everyone clapped as he unveiled the cake and then burst into a rowdy rendition of *Happy Birthday*. As he doled out large wedges of the cake, Gordon informed them, "It's a new recipe: red velvet. It looked all right when it came out of the tin. I hope it tastes as good." He had no reason for concern. Everyone was soon murmuring approval.

A lull in conversation gave Grace Morrison the opportunity to speak to Cecile. "How are you settling in, Cecile? The town still doesn't look too great, but it will improve. It must be a radical change from Brisbane for you."

That led to Cecile's telling them about her family connection to the town, and how she only learned of it the previous night.

"What was the family's name?" Grace enquired. "Maybe there are some family connections still in the area."

"No, I don't think that is possible. I am not sure what happened, but it appears that at least some of the family moved to France."

"I see, but perhaps one – or another branch of the family – remained here. What was the surname?" Grace persisted.

"Simon," Cecile answered, pronouncing the name as 'See-mon'. "It appears that my great grandfather was French, and he took the family back to France at some point in time. Although what he was doing here in the first place is a mystery to me."

"Simon. Simon. Why does that name ring a bell with me?" Gordon asked no one in particular.

"It sounds familiar to me also," Anthony added. "I have a feeling you might have mentioned it some time ago. Could it have been when you were looking at doing something on early families of the town?"

"Geez, you could be right, Anthony. I'll go back through my research." Gordon produced a notebook from his pocket and scribbled himself a note. He pondered the situation for a moment then, seeing everyone watching him expectantly he commented further.

"I've ordered a new computer and I'm off to the big city tomorrow to collect it. I've packed up my existing machine to take with me. They're going to transfer all my files across to the new computer. I'll be away a couple of days. As soon as I return, I'll look through my research. There is definitely a story about the early Simon family in there somewhere."

Grace beamed across the table at Cecile. "There you are! You are not a stranger in this part of the world after all. I'm sure you will discover your family's connection to Oyster Point."

Busy Fingers

The friendship between Cecile and the Busy Fingers retirees deepened. As friends do, they shared their stories. I remember one occasion when Cecile and Gordon cleaned up after morning tea. They drew up a couple of chairs. Gordon leant back, closed his eyes and related the story of how Busy Fingers began.

"Grace, did I see your daughter here on the weekend? What's her name… Dorothy?"

"Not Dorothy, Edith, her name is Deidre," Grace corrected her friend. "Yes, she was here, briefly. She didn't stay with me."

"Ah yes, Deidre, that's it. Good of her to come and check on how her mother was," Edith added with an audible sniff that made no secret of what she thought of Deidre.

"It's a pity she couldn't stay with you. She was here for such a short time," Rose added.

"Where was she going to stay? She could hardly stay here, locked up as we are like schoolgirls in our dormitory, with barely enough space in our rooms for ourselves and a scant few bits and pieces. She had to stay somewhere. The hotel doesn't have any accommodation available at the moment."

Edith had made it clear she did not consider the makeshift accommodation in the former private school's boarding facility appropriate. The main administration building and some of the cottages in the grounds of their retirement village sustained varying degrees of damage in the recent cyclone. Their block of units escaped unscathed, but the repair works – so much noise and dust from dawn until dark – would make life unbearable.

"I know it's not five-star accommodation, but we couldn't stay in our units while the work went on. We're lucky we stay here at no cost. It's a shame the church closed this boarding school, but being privately owned made it expensive. They struggled to maintain student numbers for a few years, before closing the place down at the end of last year. Has anyone heard what they plan to do with the place?" Rose asked.

Vera shook her head as she replied. "I don't think anyone knows. It has remained empty since last November. It's good they allowed its use as an emergency shelter during and after the cyclone. We were lucky our units didn't sustain any damage. However, it would be difficult for us to move out of our units while work went on at the retirement complex if the church hadn't made this school available."

"At least we have one building to ourselves – all of us from the units, I

"

mean. Most of the residents from the damaged cottages at the retirement com-plex moved away to stay with family elsewhere. Those who stayed at Oyster Point are in one of the dormitories. They are probably going to be here a lot longer than we are," Jane added.

There was consensus that, while it wasn't as comfortable as being in their units, it wasn't too bad. However, Edith remained unconvinced.

Grace returned to the original conversation and said with some emphasis, hoping to end any further speculation about her relationship with her daughter, "She stayed at one of the Arkana Beach hotels. There was some sort of street party on Saturday night she wanted to attend and she wanted to check out all the boutiques to see what they sold. She always looks for sales opportunities."

"She was lucky to get a room with that festival that's on there at the mo-ment," Rose observed. "As Edith said, it was good of her to visit, what with the busy life I'm sure she's made for herself down south. Where is she now, is she still in Sydney?"

"No, no. She moved to Melbourne about 18 months ago; transferred with the same firm on promotion. Now she's a buyer working out of their head office. She sources merchandise for the firm's chain of boutiques."

"I don't know how those working in the fashion industry keep up with it all. Every few months, everyone is raving about a new trend. It's usually even uglier than the previous one." Lois looked around the group for agreement and found some comfort in the fact that most were nodding.

Vera looked over the rim of her cup and sighed, "Maybe it's got something to do with us being so old and the fashionistas – is that what they call them – being young. I can remember when we were young. Some of the fashions we thought were cool horrified our parents."

"It was good of her to visit," Lois agreed. "You are lucky to have a good relationship with your daughter, Grace. Have you always been really close?"

Grace managed a wan smile as she tried to think of an appropriate reply. Edith's quick response saved her the effort.

"Does anyone ever have a really close relationship with their daughters – especially when they're teenagers? From my observations, that's when the rot sets in and it never seems to right itself completely after that."

Edith only ever had one son who went off the rails at an early age, got into strife with the Police and eventually killed himself in a stolen car when he was about 15. She was in denial about his behaviour: always maintained it was someone else's fault. Her husband tried to pull him into line, but Edith always defended him and intervened. Eventually her husband walked out and left her to it.

Close relationship with my daughter, Grace thought to herself, chance would be a fine thing. Gordon's flustered arrival interrupted her thoughts. Nobody thought to tell Gordon coffee this morning was outside instead of in the tiny sitting room as usual.

"I couldn't figure out how to work the blasted stove in that kitchen … and then I couldn't find you. Better late than never; I did finally get a batch of scones made."

While everyone oohed and aahed over Gordon's scones and tucked in with gusto, Grace found herself slipping into rewind mode. Her thoughts turned to Deidre's visit and their conversation. Close…! No, that was not how she would describe their relationship, not since Deidre was a little girl. For years, Grace tried convincing herself that Deidre's father's vanishing act was to blame for the way her daughter turned out: selfish, self-centred, opportunistic, a real user. However, in moments when Grace was honest with herself, she acknowledged she was responsible for what Deidre became. She tried to compensate for what she thought the child missed, only to end up overindulging her.

Deidre hadn't bothered to enquire why they moved out of the retirement village or if anyone was hurt. Her visit was for a specific purpose and that was all they spoke about. The memory of their conversation saddened her. Grace really thought Deidre's visit was out of concern for her mother, and greeted her excitedly. Maybe their relationship was improving.

It's Dee Dee, Mum. It's Dee Dee now, not Deidre. How often do I have to remind you? The memory of the reprimand still stung. Grace's heart sank. No, nothing had changed.

At that point, a passing shower rudely interrupted morning tea. Everyone picked up their coffee – and the scones – and headed inside to the small sitting room. They barely settled before Anthony burst into the room.

"Oh, there you all are. You weren't here when I looked before." He pulled the remaining unoccupied chair closer to the table and flopped into it, ending up with his knees almost under his chin. It was unoccupied because the springs had gone in it. The chair looked okay until you sat in it. Then, it became a sagging void to engulf the unfortunate occupant. "So what have I missed?" Anthony asked as he struggled to regain some dignity – and be able to see over the table without craning his neck.

"We were talking about Grace's daughter's visit on the weekend," Rose volunteered.

"Oh, yes, I saw her arrive. Didn't stay long, I don't think. Jolly good of her to visit though …"

"Argh, don't start that again. It wasn't good of her to visit. She never even asked how we were. No. She came because she wanted something. Why else would she come?" Grace barked as she glared around the table. The group provided comic relief. Her outburst froze most of them with a mug or scone half way to their mouth. Embarrassed, Grace apologised for her outburst. "I'm sorry. Her visit left me in a quandary. She's going to ring me for my answer on a proposition she put to me while she was here. It will probably lead to another argument."

"Is there anything we can help you with, Old Thing?" Anthony asked sincerely. "That's what friends are for you know. Of course, we wouldn't dream of intruding if it is personal…"

"No, it's not personal," Grace sighed. "You're right. Maybe talking it through will help me sort out what I'm going to say when she rings."

They sat up expectantly, prepared to give her their full attention … and why not? This was the first hint of anything interesting happening since their move to the school.

"Okay, here goes. Deidre is just back from an overseas trip looking at what's happening in the fashion world over there. What's new over there this season will be new here next season. The new big thing apparently is hand-knitted scarves, beanies, mittens and things in brightly coloured patterns. She wants me to design and knit a range of these for her to peddle to various boutiques for next season. Of course, the patterns will need to be changed so they appeal to the Australian market."

"It sounds like a very big job, especially if you have to do the design work as well," Rose commented.

"Knitting something from a pattern is one thing, but having to do the design work is something else. Would you be able to do that?" Lois queried.

"Well, possibly, but as I told her, it's a long time since I've done anything like that. Times were tough after her father left us. I used to make all her clothes to help make ends meet. As she was growing up, all her friends had the latest fashions. I didn't want her to miss out or be embarrassed because we couldn't afford those things. I was working – I worked two jobs most of the time – but there still wasn't any spare cash to spend on clothes. So, I bought things from the second-hand clothing stores and cut them up or unpicked them to make into new things for her. Even knitted items would get unravelled and knitted it into something else for her. It was cheaper than buying new wool, and I had to design everything from scratch, as I couldn't afford to buy patterns. Like I said though, it was all a long time ago."

Jane voiced her concern. "If she's looking to supply this stuff to the boutiques, she's going to need a fair quantity. There would be no point in having just half a dozen of each item, would there? How does she expect you to provide her with sufficient stock?"

"I tried explaining that I couldn't produce enough for what she wants to do, and buying the wool would be expensive. I could try bulk buying some of the more common colours, but it would still be an expensive outlay to begin with."

"I don't suppose she offered to fund setting up the operation," Edith commented acidly.

"No, she would have no idea of the cost. The problem is, when she gets one of her bright ideas, she doesn't listen to objections or obstacles put forward. You try talking to her but, in the end, you have to let it run its course – let her get to the point where she thinks all the ground work has been laid out – and then try reasoning with her. She didn't listen to anything I said the other day. I don't know what to say when she rings for my answer later in the week. How do I explain that I can't do it so that there is no doubt about that outcome?"

"My limited knowledge of the girl tells me she will not accept no for an answer without a fight," Vera commented.

Everyone nodded in agreement. Grace felt disheartened and wondered why she thought talking about it would help.

"If it's just the making of everything that is a worry, we could all help with that," Rose volunteered.

"Rose is right," Lois agreed. "We all enjoy knitting – spend most of our time knitting – but we are a bit limited by what we can knit to give away. There's not much call for woollen stuff up here. It would be good to have something different to do and somewhere to get rid of it … not to mention maybe being paid for it."

"We certainly would need to be reimbursed -- at least for any outlay," Edith added.

Anthony appeared deep in thought throughout the discussion. A lull in conversation provided him the opportunity to pose a critical question.

"Exactly how was this arrangement going to work? After all, it is a commercial venture we are talking about here. So, how was the stock to be paid for, and what of the sales income… basically, who gets what out of the deal?"

"I'm not sure," Grace replied feebly. "I didn't go into all the details. I couldn't see how I could do it, so there was no point in worrying about financial aspects. All I took away from the conversation was that I would design and make the stuff she asked for and she would sell it. Er, now that I think back on it, she would sell it. She didn't mention the firm she works for being involved. Maybe I was meant to understand that the firm would buy the finished articles, and she would deal with me on behalf of the firm."

"Doesn't seem like you are too sure about that," Edith observed.

Gordon examined his fingertips as he sat with his hands clasped firmly on the table in front of him. Without looking up, he quietly joined the conversation. "It sounds to me like this could be developed as a worthwhile commercial proposition. What do you think, Anthony? Is there an opportunity to put a slightly different spin on this that could make it a viable enterprise for these good ladies?"

Anthony cleared his throat and adjusted his blue spotted maroon bow tie, giving himself a moment to think before answering. "Well, in my opinion, the original proposal, as Grace tells it, definitely is not a viable option. It's a bit too loose. It might be a good thing for Deidre, but it could end up costing Grace plenty. However, as a group, a knitting co-operative type arrangement could work… as long as the selling side of it was tied up properly."

"I can see all sorts of possibilities for us if we worked as a group," Jane said.

"I agree," Vera said. "It could work and be fun as well, as long as two things were in place. The first being that Grace was able and willing to do the design work required. The second is a little more complicated I suspect. If we are to form some sort of knitting group, why don't we market our own products? Why do we need Deidre – or her firm – involved? How hard can it be?"

"Oh dear, I've never been involved in anything like that before. I can knit just about anything, but I have never done any marketing or selling. Wouldn't there be a lot involved in that?" Rose questioned nervously.

"Yes, there is a bit in setting it up to ensure it operates properly," Anthony admitted. "However, as a retired accountant, I am quite familiar with what is required. It could be my contribution, that and looking after the administrative side of things in the future."

"Right," announced Vera, "It's down to you then Grace. What do we know about these designs she wants, and do you feel up to the job?"

"I don't really know what Deidre had in mind. She took photographs while she was overseas and said she would send them to give me an idea of what she wanted. I did get the impression the designs she saw were quite European. You know, snowflakes, pine trees, reindeers and the like, not very Australian. That's why she suggested the designs would have to be 'Australianised' to suit our market."

"Hmmm, but do you think you could manage the design work," Jane asked.

"Well, I don't know. I don't have any materials for drawing up the designs. I would have to buy some stuff, and I still don't know how complicated the work might be."

Gordon sat up, pushed his glasses up his nose and took over the meeting. "Okay, ladies and gentleman, from what I'm hearing, all the ladies are keen to get involved in producing the product. Anthony assures us it isn't too arduous setting up a proper arrangement to manage the making and selling. The only thing we are uncertain about is what you will make. Here's how I think we should progress. Grace, I believe you expect Deidre to call later this week."

Grace nodded but did not interrupt.

"Right, when she calls, you need to get all the details you can about the designs (ask her if she sent the photos yet?), and how her proposal deals with the selling and marketing." Gordon saw the scepticism on Grace's face. "Don't worry, Grace. We'll give you a list of questions to ask. Once we have all the answers, we'll know how to proceed."

"So, in effect, I'll just be stalling her for a bit longer when she calls," Grace said, starting to feeling a bit more comfortable with the situation.

Gordon nodded. "That's right. You need to make it clear you can't make a decision until you have all the information."

"Any idea when she might call?" Lois asked.

"Not really, but I gathered it might be around the middle of the week."

The room went quiet, each member lost in their own thoughts for a time. Gordon scraped his chair across the tiles and stood up. "My coffee's cold," he announced. "I'm going to make a fresh brew. Anyone else interested?"

This caused everyone to peer into their cups – as if that would tell whether it was hot or cold! Nevertheless, there was unanimous support for his idea, and Gordon disappeared into the kitchen. He emerged shortly carrying a tray with a fresh pot of coffee and clean mugs for everyone. Once they settled back into coffee and scones mode, Gordon tentatively cleared his throat in preparation for disrupting their tranquillity once more.

"At the risk of being out of order, I took the liberty of making a phone call while waiting for the coffee. While you are wrestling with the idea of some sort of knitting co-operative, here's something else for you to consider. I spoke to that real estate chap looking after occupancies in that new shopping complex. There's an opportunity to open a shop, but we would have to put in an expression of interest fairly soon."

"A *shop*?" Lois echoed. "Why would we be interested in a shop? We don't even know if we're going to be in business yet."

"Even if we haven't made a decision about a business, we could still put in a tentative expression of interest for one of the shops. I don't think it's going to take us long to work out what we are going to do and, if we decide not to progress with anything, we just withdraw the expression of interest."

"Yes, we could, but what's the advantage in having a shop?" questioned Edith.

"We could buy supplies at wholesale prices – much cheaper than you can now – and what we don't use ourselves, we sell to the public. We could stock other craft supplies as well, and possibly some art supplies. We could sell anything we make, and possibly sell for others on consignment."

While a degree of caution lingered, everyone seemed keen to know more, and Gordon happily obliged. He outlined what might be involved in a lease agreement, including indicative costs. A long session of questions and answers ensued, with Anthony's expertise called upon frequently. As Gordon commented later, by the time morning tea was over, a definite air of restrained excitement existed. At this point, it all depended on what Grace found out. Both Anthony and Gordon agreed they could be in for disappointment before the end of the week.

Morning tea on Tuesday saw the group eagerly awaiting Grace's arrival. She was late joining them, so unlike her. Before joining the others, Grace checked her emails. She knew they would want to know if there was anything more from Deidre. Her daughter hadn't rung so there was nothing new to tell the group, but perhaps she emailed the promised photos. It would only take a couple of minutes, and it was worth being a bit late if there was something to share with them over coffee.

Disappointment waited in her inbox: there was nothing from Deidre. A quick scan of the new emails found nothing urgent or exciting. As Grace was about to log off, another email pinged into her inbox.

"I don't believe it," Grace exclaimed aloud. "I can't believe she has come through just when I needed her to." Deidre's message was short and abrupt, but the attachments were huge. The promised photos had arrived. They took a while to print, but they were going to morning tea even if it made her late.

By the time Grace joined them, everyone was into the coffee and one of Gordon's excellent teacakes. No grand entrance; Grace simply took her place at the table (with the folder on her lap), said good morning to everyone and accepted a slice of cake. All eyes were on Grace, but nobody spoke. The silence was deafening. She enjoyed the suspense but relented and ended their misery.

"Oh, I almost forgot. I brought something to share with you." With that, she produced the folder, placed it on the table, opened it and spread out the photos. Uproar erupted.

"You sly thing, you," Gordon exclaimed as he beamed at her. "You knew we would be waiting to see if you received anything."

Silence reigned, punctuated only by the shuffling of photos passed around the table. Edith reignited conversation when, with a loud sniff, she declared, "Not very elegant or refined are they?"

"They're meant for the young," Rose countered. "It's the young that follow fashion, and this is the sort of stuff they like. It's not meant to appeal to us oldies."

"The young aren't normally tied down with mortgage payments and other commitments. That leaves much of their disposable income available for indulgence in fashion trends … and they want exciting, different, *controversial* changes each season. Just like these," Anthony concluded, and waved the photo he was holding in the air.

Always the pacifier, Rose continued thoughtfully, "Perhaps we could do two lines: a bright colourful one for the young and a sophisticated, refined line for the more mature. The second line could concentrate on quieter colours and rely on fancy stitch patterns rather than bright designs."

"That's an idea," Lois said. "Grace, we could use some of that variegated wool we were playing with last winter. Done properly and in the right colours it could work well."

"Oh, yes, it knitted up beautifully. That's a good idea."

Vera deliberately placed her photos on the table and looked around the group. "Right, let's have your comments, thoughts, whatever, on what we're seeing. Do we like it? Could we modify it to suit our market? Could we make it?"

Animated discussion lasted quite a while, with questions or negative comments quickly dealt with. When it finally quietened down, Vera took charge again.

"Okay, a fair bit of discussion but I think mostly it was positive. However, we need to establish a clear consensus on how we should proceed with this idea. Should we: set up a business to create knitted articles for sale, and take on marketing our product ourselves. Can I have your votes now, please?"

Voting was swift and straight forward, with both issues supported unanimously. Anthony, scribbling feverishly throughout the meeting, deliberately put down his pen and cleared his throat. "There is one other issue to consider: do we want to establish this group as a business entity? We need to vote on whether to go ahead and establish a business or not. If we are, we can decide on a name a bit later. Right now, we just need clear indication of how the group wishes to proceed."

"What's with all the writing, Anthony?" Jane asked, eyeing his notebook suspiciously.

"I'm recording the minutes of this meeting," Anthony replied a little condescendingly. "If we are going to proceed with any of it, there needs to be formal record of the processes involved and the decisions taken."

"Well done. Just as well one of us is thinking ahead – saves us having to cook up the minutes later," Gordon commented.

Vera continued to drive discussion. "Now, what about a shop: are we going to proceed with an expression of interest?"

Nothing heard for a moment or two as people shuffled in their seats and indecision prevailed. Gordon, realising the lack of information made a decision difficult, took the initiative.

"Why don't a carload of us take a trip to Arkana Beach? We can check out what the boutiques there are selling, what their pricing is like, how they set up their shops, all that sort of stuff."

"How will that help?" Edith snorted. They have cheap beach type stuff for backpackers and the like."

"No, that's not strictly true, Edith," Lois corrected her. "Arkana caters for everything from backpackers to five-star executives. Some of those large hotels include very upmarket stores. I think your idea is a good one, Gordon. The sooner we get information, the sooner we can make a decision."

"We could take a drive today. I'll take my car and three others can come too. Grace needs to come. Who else wants to come?" Gordon asked.

"Vera, are you right to go?" Lois queried.

"No, I can't. Jane and I are going to visit a friend in hospital this afternoon. I think you should go, Lois. It would be good to have you and Gordon cast your artistic eyes over everything."

"If you're available, Edith, it would be good to have you along. Your past experience working with figures and costings will be useful in making assessments," Grace suggested.

"So, do we go this afternoon – straight after lunch perhaps?" Lois asked.

Gordon looked surprised. "No, why don't we go now? It only takes an hour or so to get there, and we could have lunch somewhere when we arrive."

As they got up to leave, Vera called Grace aside. "Remember those couple of Lotto entries we put in just before Christmas? There's been nowhere to check them since the cyclone. Would you mind taking them into a newsagent or somewhere at Arkana to see if we won anything? We probably haven't won a cent, but at least I'll be able to bin them."

No time wasted setting off, the trip seemed to pass quickly as they discussed all manner of possibilities for a future business and shop. After a salad lunch at the sailing club, Gordon parked in the main street and they embarked on a fact-finding mission. After establishing what art materials Gordon could give her, Grace purchased a few other bits and pieces from a newsagent. While waiting to pay, she remembered the Lotto entries Vera gave her. The lass behind the counter ran them through the machine to see if they won anything.

There was a short delay while they waited for another girl to finish using the machine. Gordon wandered over to Grace's side as she waited, and almost had to support her when the sales assistant announced that one entry had won a significant prize.

"What do you mean by a *significant prize*? How much is that?" Grace stammered.

The girl explained, "When it's a significant amount of money, the machine doesn't show how much. It just shows a row of stars instead of the dollar value. We have to ring the Lotto office for more information. If you will come with me now, I'll take you through to the office to make that phone call."

Grace felt a bit weak-kneed and looked at Gordon in disbelief.

"I'll come with you. Go on; go make the call. The others can wait while you do," Gordon said reassuringly.

It turned out to be an uncomplicated exercise, and Grace gasped at the news that one of their joint entries had won $20,000. Gordon hugged her exuberantly, and they made a pact not to say anything about the win until after she told Vera. For Grace, the rest of the visit to Arkana was a blur. The trip home was noisy. They discussed in detail everything seen during their visit. Still too dumbfounded to think of anything but the news she would share with Vera, only Grace remained silent.

The other retirees eagerly awaited their return. In a break with tradition, they gathered again in the small sitting room for afternoon tea and feedback on the Arkana trip. Grace and Vera were late joining the group. On her return, Grace went directly to Vera's room and the two women spent a few minutes trying to get their heads around their windfall. They agreed not to share the news with the others yet, as they needed time to comprehend it.

The information brought back from Arkana was enough to clinch the deal. They would look into setting up a shop. Gordon left the room briefly to make a phone call. When he returned, he announced that the new shopping complex was having an open day for prospective shop owners on Friday. He explained that the building's shell was finished, but completion of the actual partitions, walls, and general layout would be in accordance with each new shop owner's requirements. The project foreman would be available at 9:30am on Friday to explain a few things to prospective lessees, and they could inspect the place until about 2:30pm. They agreed they would all go on Friday to see the place and to determine the best location for their shop.

Friday arrived soon enough. They obtained permission to take some chairs and a table along so they could sit and discuss any issues that arose. Gordon, up early on the day, made a batch of brownies, and discovered a couple of large thermos flasks in the kitchen. The cavalcade set off for the precinct loaded with folding chairs, a card table, and a hamper containing flasks of coffee, mugs and a batch of Gordon's mouth-watering gooey brownies.

They traipsed into the precinct, leaving everything in the cars. After the foreman's spiel, they were free to wander the precinct as they chose. As they moved off, Rose whispered to Gordon, "He must be new to this. He didn't seem very comfortable at all; seemed very concerned actually."

Gordon chuckled. The man hadn't been too impressed with his audience, that much was obvious. "It was the sight of so much grey hair that terrified him," he confided to Rose.

There was only one other person in the group listening to the foreman, and when the other retirees moved off to inspect the place, she and Grace remained behind. In the belief that it pays to know your opposition, Grace struck up a conversation with the stranger who seemed uncertain about what to do next. "I'm Grace. Are you looking at setting up on your own?" Grace asked as she extended her hand. "The mob that just went charging off is a group of fellow retirees. We're still in the process of deciding whether we want to open a shop or not. What sort of shop were you thinking about?"

"Good to meet you. I'm Gloria. I'm looking at stocking fabrics, patterns, all sorts of dressmaking and sewing bits and pieces. I used to work for a large store down south, and it seems like home dressmaking is coming back into vogue. I thought I might also try to stock a brand of sewing machines and maybe overlockers to sell as well. What is your group interested in?"

"We are looking at craft and art supplies, but also selling knitted articles and possibly craftwork from the community to sell on commission. The planning's still a bit loose as we're trying to get our heads around what it will involve and how we can manage it."

The two women headed off together slowly making their way down the main aisle. The walls were already up on three shops with temporary signs indicating what sort of shops they would be. The new lessees apparently reserved their spaces from the plans. When they reached the intersecting corridor, Grace could see her mob further along and, preferring to carry on with just Gloria, she suggested they carry in a different direction. About half way along the corridor, another shop was already established. It was to be a coffee shop extending across two standard shop spaces.

"A coffee shop, eh…" mused Grace. "This could be a good place to open a shop," she said indicating the shop spaces marked out on the opposite side of the aisle to the coffee shop. "That looks like the supermarket end entrance to the precinct and, with the coffee shop here, there is likely to be a fair bit of traffic through this part of the building."

Gloria stood nodding as she surveyed the general area. "I think you're right. Just across here would be an ideal place to open a shop. Plenty of passing traffic, while not too far from the front entrance from Main Street."

The retiree mob, finally reaching that section of the building, rudely interrupted their quiet contemplation of the site. After a brief discussion of where they had been and what they saw, Gordon suggested they should get the table and chairs to discuss their findings in comfort. They disappeared off to the cars leaving Grace and Gloria alone again. "If you think you can put up with that rowdy mob, you're more than welcome to join us for morning tea. There's coffee and brownies as temptation if that helps sway you," Grace offered.

Now a chair short, Gordon perched on an empty drum left lying around, as Grace introduced Gloria. The two women put forward their ideas about locating their respective businesses opposite the coffee shop. After some discussion, Grace's group endorsed her suggestion and promptly launched discussions about its set up. Anthony, sitting quietly through the discussions, seemed to be mentally wrestling with some major problem.

"My major concern at this stage," Grace began, "Is how we are going to run this shop? If we're all busy knitting articles to sell, who will have time to man the shop?"

"Well, I wouldn't be knitting," Gordon stated. "So, logically, I would be busy in the shop."

"That's a very good point you make, Grace," Anthony chimed in. "Who is going to run the shop? Yes, Gordon could run it a lot of the time, but he also goes away a lot. Unless he is planning on changing his ways, it just wouldn't work as a long-term arrangement."

Gordon, a journalist before deciding to retire -- well, semi-retire -- still worked as a freelance, and often made trips away to cover various events for articles in a range of magazines and, from time to time, had feature pieces in major publications. "No, I wasn't planning on giving up writing just yet. So, yes, I see how that might create a problem."

Anthony turned his attention to Gloria. "Are you going into business alone, my dear? How will you manage on your own, or were you planning to employ someone – even on a part-time basis?"

"I seem to have the same problem at the moment. I really didn't want to employ someone, at least not until I saw how the business was going, but I suspect I will run into problems if I try to go it alone. Nevertheless, I thought I'd put in an expression of interest now, and try to work something out over the next couple of weeks before the deadline to firm up on the deal."

It was time to go. Grace and Gloria exchanged contact information while the others gathered up their belongings. A bond already was developing between the women. Grace noticed Anthony watching them intently as she pocketed Gloria's information.

On arriving back at the school, they disappeared to their own rooms to digest the information gained from the morning's activity. As if summoned by some biological call, one by one, they straggled out at three o'clock to gather in the sitting room. Consensus was that a shop was a good idea, but how to run it was a major problem yet to be resolved. Anthony bided his time until discussion ceased. They sat dejectedly drinking their tea or coffee. Satisfied they were about to throw in the towel, he played what he considered his trump card.

"Why does it have to be only craft and art related products? Why can't we extend the repertoire to include other 'compatible' lines … like fabrics for instance?"

"How does that help?" demanded Edith a little too vehemently. "We still don't have anybody to run the shop on a full time basis."

"Oh, but we might do," Anthony replied with a knowing tap on the side of his nose. "There could be another option." Everyone focused on the speaker who fiddled with his rather ghastly yellow bow tie. "What if we were to include fabrics and dressmaking paraphernalia? We …"

Before he could continue, Grace cut in. "Oh, yes. Yes, I see where this is going. That would work – if she were interested, of course. You know, I think she might be persuaded."

"You leave the persuading to me, my dear. I believe the lady to be highly intelligent and probably immediately will see the merit of the proposal. Grace, perhaps you might care to enlighten everyone about our thinking."

Grace looked around the table. Oh dear, Edith was glaring at Anthony. Everyone knew they were sweet on one another, but neither was making a move to do anything about it … and the rest of them were supposed to be blissfully unaware of it all. Pair of old fools, she thought to herself, and then launched into describing a proposition to put to Gloria about joining forces with their group to open one (larger) combined shop.

"That would work," Vera said enthusiastically. "Gloria could run the shop, and Gordon could help out when he was around. That way, if things were quiet, they could schedule themselves some time off. On the other hand, if things got busy, whether Gordon was around or not, one or some of us could help for an hour or two when needed. I think it's a great idea, Anthony. All we have to do now is convince Gloria."

Convincing Gloria fell to Anthony. There was every confidence the old smooth talker would charm her into it. As they left the sitting room, Anthony drew Grace aside.

"I believe you might have Gloria's contact details. Would you care to pass them on so I can get to work on the lady?"

"How did you know? Oh, of course, you were watching when we swapped information. Hand me your pen and notebook and I'll copy it out for you."

Anthony contacted Gloria on Friday evening and they arranged to meet the next morning to discuss his proposal. In Anthony's mind, the meeting went well. It ended with Gloria promising him her answer by Sunday evening. Although quietly confident, Anthony endured an anxious wait until Gloria phoned just before lunch on Sunday. He knew the moment he heard her voice that he had succeeded, her excitement clear in their brief conversation. She spoke to her husband the night before and they agreed that Anthony's proposal solved the one remaining problem for everyone. Elated, Anthony summoned the group to a meeting at afternoon teatime to share the good news. While they excitedly discussed the future, Anthony quietly rang Gloria and asked her to join them for coffee – and some preliminary planning.

Things seem to happen in a whirl after that. First thing Monday morning, Gordon confirmed their expression of interest but explained that now they required a shop across two spaces. Gloria withdrew her individual expression of interest. After speaking to the real estate bloke herself, Edith came up with some indicative costs to set up the shop, and suggested a figure for acquisition of craft and art supplies. Gloria would organise her own stock.

Anthony initiated registration of their business, and a long period of quibbling over an appropriate name for the business ensued. As Anthony's patience was about to run out, there was agreement the business would be called *In Stitches*. It took them even longer to agree on a name for the shop, but eventually settled on *Busy Fingers*. Keeping the accounts straight would be a complicated affair, as not all of the group were sufficiently financially secure to invest in setting up the shop. Ultimately, it was Grace, Vera, Lois, Gordon, Anthony and Gloria who put up the capital, Grace and Vera using sizable chunks of their recent Lotto winnings. Keeping the finances sorted out fell to Edith and Anthony.

Walls went up, fittings arrived and were installed, and their computerised cash register almost created nervous breakdowns for all. On paper, the machine seemed ideal. You simply keyed in the relevant information about the purchases. It calculated the cost, totalled it and told you how much change was required when you entered the amount the customer tendered. It also would link to the credit card facility when they finally got that sorted out with the bank -- an all-round wonderful system that required a mathematical genius to operate it.

After much nagging and haranguing, the supplier sent a technician for a day of free training. Having decided almost from the outset that the operator's manual was an excellent volume *if you knew how to use the machine before reading the manual*, Anthony chose not to participate in hands-on training. He sat quietly documenting the technician's every word on the step-by-step-operation of the beast.

The women busily knitted their usual lines, stock was due to arrive the following week and the official opening of the new complex was less than three weeks away. Grace didn't knit much during the last week or so. There were queries about it over coffee one morning. "You haven't been to our knitting sessions for a while, Grace," Edith commented with an edge to her voice.

"Probably like the rest of us, she's been too busy to go out, so hasn't got any gossip to bring to the knitting sessions," Jane observed. "There's no need for us to get together to knit. We can do just as well in our rooms. We only gather together to drink coffee and keep up with the gossip … oh, and eat Gordon's baking."

"It's about company and interaction and conversation, aspects of life that must be maintained at our age," Edith argued.

Grace realised her absence was being judged as 'slacking off' instead of assisting with the task in hand. She wondered how to explain tactfully that she had been doing her bit: some preliminary design work. She waited for a break in the banter between Edith and Jane to state her case, but Gordon's arrival with a plate of cupcakes saved her. He waited until Anthony joined the group and everyone was fully engrossed in cake and coffee before delivering his news.

"I've just had a call from the lovely Mrs Jenner – remember her, our wonderful complex manager."

"Wonderful? Lovely? Are you sure you remember Mrs Jenner?" Lois asked incredulously as she recalled the sour-faced cantankerous retirement complex manager.

"As I was saying," Gordon continued, "our wonderful complex manager rang and asked me …"

"What makes you so special?" Edith demanded. "She has never bothered to ring any of the rest of us." She looked around to table for endorsement and was satisfied to see gently shaking heads.

"Well, Edith dear, if you kept your phones with you, turned on and charged, she would have spoken to several of you before she spoke to me. Now, if I may continue …" Everyone nodded encouragement, so he began again.

"Mrs Jenner rang to say the expected completion of work at the retirement complex is Thursday, with the last of the contractors and equipment exiting the site on Friday. We could move back on Friday, but the place might still be a bit congested. She suggests leaving it until the weekend. After trying several of your phones without success, she was a bit exasperated by the time she spoke to me. She asked me to pass on the information as she wasn't going to waste any more time trying to ring the rest of you." He finished with a wide smile at everyone.

A loud cheer went up from around the table, followed – predictably – by grumbling about having to move back when they are already so busy with knitting and setting up the shop and getting ready for the opening.

"Oh, for goodness sake, how much do we have to shift? We only took the bare essentials with us, so it won't take long to move back," Vera said.

"… And I almost forgot to tell you, Jim, the gardener, is back and is cleaning up the site after the contractors and, Mrs Jenner said she is making 'young Jimmy' available to assist us with moving our things," Gordon added. Everyone erupted in laughter. 'Young Jimmy' was 60 years old if he was a day.

Deidre's call shocked Grace, only over two weeks later than expected. With everything happening, she totally forgot about her daughter's promise to call her. Panic set in. Oh God, what do I to say to her, she thought. While answering the phone with one hand, thanking her daughter for the photos and making small talk, Grace scratched around in the desk drawer with her free hand. Where was that damned list of questions she was to put to Deidre? Then it occurred to her. There wasn't any need for those questions. They were now redundant. What Deidre might or might not have planned was no longer of any consequence.

"Yes dear, they are lovely and I'm sure they will appeal to the young. Yes, I agree that more Australian oriented designs would work better. In fact, I am working on some design ideas. We should start making things soon … Oh, I meant to tell you, the other ladies here will all be involved in the knitting."

"I didn't think you could produce enough on your own for what I think the market will be," Deidre snapped. "So when is the first of the stuff likely to arriving here? Send it to my home address."

Grace took a deep breath. Enough was enough. "Why would you expect to receive anything, Deidre dear? You haven't bought anything. Our business fills orders as soon as possible after their receipt. If you are interested, send us an order. There's an order form on our website … that's our *Busy Fingers* website."

Deidre slammed down the receiver. Although stunned by the ending, Grace felt good. It felt good to deal with Deidre like that. Should have done it years ago, she told herself.

The group migration back to their units on Saturday morning was uneventful and, although there wasn't need for young Jimmy, there was no sign of him anyway. It wasn't until Sunday morning that the group convened again in the small courtyard outside Gordon's unit. Once they all assembled, Gordon told them the real estate chap rang during the move the previous day.

"He said the 'community space' was available and what did we want done with it. I had no idea what he was on about, but he said we needed to sort it out quickly so it would be ready in time for the opening. Anyone got any clues?"

Vera and Jane exchanged a look. Vera hesitantly took the lead. "Er, we might know something. When our friend Gladys was in hospital, she shared a room with Muriel. Through visiting Gladys, we also became friendly with Muriel So, after Gladys was discharged and moved south to live with her daughter, we continued to visit Muriel. Muriel just happens to be the mother of our local Mayor, who we've met a couple times at the hospital. During our last visit with Muriel, the Mayor arrived for the last bit of visiting hours. Muriel insisted we tell her daughter all about our plans."

Jane took over the story. "I got carried away in the midst of it all, and went on about how great an extra space would be for running classes and workshops, and to use as a gallery for periodic art exhibitions. Caroline, the Mayor, thought it a great initiative to rejuvenate the community after the cyclone and to provide an interest for all the women new to the town. I guess I kept banging on about the benefits of such a community space and how there were a couple of shops in the new precinct not yet taken up."

"You think the Mayor has stepped in? Done a deal of some sort?" Lois asked.

Vera and Jane both shrugged. It seemed unlikely, but maybe …

"All will be revealed tomorrow – hopefully – when I go to meet the man," Gordon suggested. Vera and Jane volunteered to accompany him.

On Monday, with the mystery solved, the trio rushed back to the retirement complex for morning tea and to share their news. The Mayor had convinced all those involved that the two empty shop spaces at the far end of the northern corridor should become a community space. The prospect of drawing in more people on a regular basis had a certain appeal that helped sell the idea. She negotiated a considerably reduced rental. Council would pay the first three months' rental of the space as a trial, with a view to negotiating something with the Busy Fingers group. Gordon explained that they took the liberty of asking for a few things, which the Council also agreed to pay for.

"One end of the double space will be closed off as storage area. The Council is donating a number of folding tables and chairs that stack on trolleys for ease of movement. Installation by Council of some sturdy shelving will allow Gloria to store a few sewing machines for her sewing classes. Storage of a few artists' easels, if we can afford them, will be in that area when not in use. The latest in gallery hanging systems is being obtained for around the walls."

All were dumbstruck for a few heartbeats before everyone started speaking at once.

"Will the hanging system be up in time for the opening?" Lois asked. Gordon nodded. "We must have an exhibition in there for the official opening of the complex; make a good impression from the start."

Gordon and Lois had a few reasonable pieces of artwork between them. They could rustle up a few of the more artistic knitted pieces left over from last winter, and Grace and Lois had felted cloche hats and bags. Yes, there would be a half-decent exhibition – 'half decent' being the key words – and it provided Busy Fingers an opportunity to advertise its wares. A schedule of classes was agreed, and Gordon was to write copy for flyers. In the end, it didn't matter. A better alternative presented itself.

All shops closed by six o'clock the afternoon before the official opening so precinct management could add some final touches. Some grumbled, but all complied. There really wasn't much to do, but they kept fiddling. About mid-afternoon, Gordon disappeared.

They hadn't met all the other storekeepers as they had been too busy, and the other store owners were the same. Rose lamented the fact that, although they now could link people to their respective shops, they had met only some of their fellow tenants.

Just before six o'clock, noise at the junction of the corridors caught everyone's attention. Workmen set up a table and a number of chairs. People took this as the signal to close up and be gone, and duly complied. As the last sets of shutters closed, the real estate agent marched in carrying a tub of ice sprouting several bottles of bubbly. Following closely was Gordon wheeling a tea trolley laden with quiche, cheese straws, a selection of vol-au-vents and a platter of antipasto. Everyone entered into the spirit of the evening. People no longer remained strangers.

Vera and Grace sidled up to Gordon. "Brilliant move, Gordon, look at how it has brought everyone together," Vera said.

"Wonderful gesture, but it must have cost you a packet," Grace added.

"It needed something to get us all in the mood for tomorrow … and it didn't really cost a packet. I leant on the real estate chap to fork out for the drinks. I have been writing a fair bit of copy over the last couple of months for both the developer and the real estate agency. I've done very well out of it, so it's only fair I donate some back."

As they drove up the next morning, a huge sign out front of building welcomed them. The new shopping complex now had a name, and the guessing game over what it would be was over.

Artists' View

*Work progressed at the end of Main Street while the rest of Oyster Point strug-
gled to regain some semblance of normality. For some, returning to their favourite pastimes and sharing the company of like-minded colleagues helped the
healing process. As usual, once the Festive Season was over, a group of artists
eagerly anticipated their first get-together for the year. This year was different.*

"This is the earliest in the year we have ever met, isn't it?" enquired Diana.

"It is early and so soon after the cyclone. Everyone is so busy. The entire
community is almost hyperactive," Bronwyn added, "The entire town assisted
with cleaning up, while helping get the temporary supermarket operational
and making Christmas for their families. We deserve a break from all that for
a few hours."

A small sub-group of Oyster Point Art Society, Diana, Gladdy, Bronwyn,
Bella and Suzie, tried to get together every Wednesday to spend time on their
artworks, and to inspire and encourage each other.

"… And then that awful thing happening to Mr Green, and we had his
funeral to attend," Bella added. Ted Green's death hit her hard. She photo-
graphed Mr and Mrs Green the week before the cyclone. It was during the
installation of their new cold-room. Gordon Bailey, the semi-retired journalist
she often worked with, had a commission lined up for a series of stories about
people in the north. He asked to use her photographs in his project. Bella
swallowed down a half-sob. "The new cold-room wasn't even commissioned
before the shop was destroyed. Ted Green was a friendly soul, a great community asset. What happened to them was so unfair."

From an upstairs window of his apartment in the big old house, his family's home for five generations, Dr Rex Holmwood, now retired, watched the
art group set up in the shade of the big old mango trees along his yard's rear
boundary. It was good to see them making an effort to re-establish their lives.
Then, As he indulged in his customary afternoon scotch and soda, he idled
away the time thinking back on his life in this house – currently owned by his
son -- and his memories of the town. Now nearing the end of his life, cyclones
weren't overly concerning. He experienced quite a few over his 88 years,
most while living in this house.

He took another sip of his afternoon tipple. His gaze drifted to the block
across the street, taking in the old warehouse building, which sustained only a
cracked window in the cyclone, and the now vacant old Queenslander's block.

It was as well the developer demolished the old house. If the developer, or the white ants, hadn't done so, the cyclone would have blown it to pieces causing immeasurable damage to everything around it. Thinking of that house brought back other distant memories.

The Simons, one of the pioneering families -- someone told him they were French -- built that old Queenslander. During the 1950s-60s, the Bradley-Bells, with their horrible son, Gerald, owned the house. My God, the grief that boy caused the rest of us was legendary. Ah well, the house was gone now, and so was Gerald, although he still owned the place until the developer bought it. Over the years, there had been many sad stories about its past occupants. I suppose we will never know how true they were after all these years, he thought.

Bronwyn's unmistakable laugh floated up from the backyard, jolting Rex out of his reverie. He returned his attention to the art group. There is a lot of talking but not much artwork happening down there, he observed.

The group worked solidly for quite a while before taking a break. Current events dominated conversation: the new Oyster Point shopping centre, and the new mine's likely impact on the town.

"I've heard there will be a café and a restaurant, and plans for outdoor dining. Good opportunities for some interesting drawings, and we won't have to cart these flasks and food around with us. I can't wait," Gladdy said enthusiastically. "We'll be able to make the shopping complex our first port of call each week."

"We won't have to cart our chairs either," Bronwyn added, "Only art gear."

"Right, let's drag ourselves back to the present. Are we going to keep working after lunch, or going home?" asked Suzie.

They agreed on an early day, but they should discuss the group's focus for this year's work before they left. Several ideas were forthcoming, all relating to either the cyclone or its impact on Oyster Point. Although vigorous discussion occurred, frequently interspersed with fits of laughter, no resolution emerged. Bella sat quietly throughout most of the discussion. When silence descended, she tentatively voiced her idea.

"Immediately after the cyclone, I raced around taking photos of the damage, not just to the town centre, but everywhere. I came yesterday and took some of that area where they are stockpiling all the gear. One of the men confirmed they were going to construct a shopping complex, with work starting next week."

"Well that's one bit of gossip that's turned out to be true," Diana interrupted.

"It got me thinking," Bella continued. "Maybe I should take a series of photos of restoration of the town and of new buildings as they progress, like a pictorial record of the recovery of Oyster Point. While we discussed the coming year, it occurred to me that we should think about sketching and painting what happens as it happens, particularly down this end of the street. We might base an exhibition on it later, once everyone has recovered or, perhaps, after the shopping centre opens."

"I think that has possibilities," Bronwyn agreed.

Bella elaborated on her ideas. "The man I spoke to said the shopping centre was expected to open around April. After that, we could continue with whatever project we choose for the rest of the year. What do you think? I'm going to take photos anyway. Maybe Gordon Bailey will do a feature article on it and use my photos. I also thought maybe we could base some artworks on the photos I have taken so that we get a complete record, and not just what happens from now."

Interest grew until finally there was agreement they would follow Bella's suggestion. That triggered a long discussion on how the project should proceed.

"Has anyone heard what they are going to call the shopping centre?" Gladdy asked. The somewhat gossipy member of the group, who worked part-time as a receptionist at a local motel, prided herself on being ahead of the pack in knowing what was going on around town. She claimed it was important so she could keep motel guests well informed.

"We've been waiting for you to tell us, Gladdy. Don't tell us your sources have let you down," Bronwyn chided her.

"It's not that," Gladdy responded. "At least four people have given me different names, with each person swearing they have inside information that the name they gave me is the one."

"I wouldn't be surprised if they keep the name under wraps until the opening," Bronwyn said thoughtfully. "Everyone will be kept guessing up to the last minute. It will help keep interest alive."

"Bella, you've been photographing things, has there been much progress thus far?" asked Suzie.

"To date, I've observed outdoor meetings of self-important bigwigs in white hardhats, then rat walls and foundations were dug, and now materials and more equipment are arriving onsite."

"We should have started today," Bronwyn commented ruefully. "But, how about next week, we set up opposite the project and start recording progress? Better late than never, eh? We can move over to the new supermarket site when work starts there. Bella, I imagine you will take photographs every day."

"I'd be crazy not to. The construction site is only a few hundred meters from my house. So far, I have some great shots taken at sunrise and the just before sunset. I haven't stored my camera in its backpack since before the cyclone," Bella admitted.

"I like the idea of putting it all together in an exhibition," Gladdy said. "The town would appreciate that. Maybe we can promote it along the lines of 'phoenix rising from the ashes' or, more appropriately in our case, an albatross, as the harbinger of good fortune, unfurling its wings over the ruins." After more discussion, they agreed an exhibition along those lines would work.

The following week, the group settled themselves around one of the picnic tables beside The Esplanade and focused their attention on the construction site. Concrete trucks arrived several at a time. Bronwyn, with paper and graphite pencils in hand, wandered over to the safety fencing. When she reached the barrier, a bloke in a hardhat with a blue site supervisor sticker on it strolled up. Her ploy to get his attention worked. She noticed him frequently gazing in their direction since their arrival.

"Can I help you with anything?" he enquired.

Well that's a good start, thought Bronwyn; a nice bloke, it seems. "Yes, perhaps you can. We wanted to tell someone official that we'll be hanging around from time to time." She went on to explain what they intended doing and that any one of them could turn up to sketch on any given day. "We are *au fait* with occupational safety requirements, so we guarantee not be a nuisance."

"You've already had someone here most mornings since last week, haven't you?"

"Yes. One of our members is also a photographer. You've probably seen her roaming around with her camera. Hang on a minute, I'll introduce you."

Later that morning, the group moved to set up beside the old warehouse parking area. One painted, while the others sketched. Their presence attracted onlookers who stopped to enquire about what they were doing. Most were keen for a chat and were happy to share their recent cyclone experiences. Their stories helped identify potential concepts for artworks, as well as providing an opportunity to put the idea of an exhibition out there for comment.

People came and went all morning. It was a busy day for the supermarket. During the morning, the artists chatted with quite a few locals, many they hadn't seen since the cyclone. They noticed a few newcomers as well.

"Nothing like a bit of publicity to draw visitors in for a look-see, is there? It's a pity the tourists are not here this early in the year. They don't usually arrive before May when it starts to cool down a bit," reflected Suzie. "Still, it would be good if they were here to see our exhibition." There were nods all round.

"It's lunch time," said Bella. "Let's go back across to The Esplanade where there's a bit of shade."

Once they settled with their flasks and sandwiches, Diana revisited their conversation from last week regarding potential art projects for the coming year.

"I have another project I've been thinking of working on. It's about women -- and blending the past with the present -- but I would need a model for some of the works I envisage. I'll need a body to sketch, not just a face. How do you fancy our chances of finding a nude model in Oyster Point?"

"Funny you should mention that. Just the other day I thought it would be good to do some life drawing, but where would we find a model? As I drove along the road beside the ocean at the time, it occurred to me that the local nudist beach could be the place to find someone who might help. Has anyone been around to that secluded cove lately?" asked Bronwyn, tongue-in-cheek."

The nudist beach, not intended as a tourist attraction, is for serious naturists only. Casual sightseers are not encouraged and, as a result, the secluded cove doesn't offer the easiest of access. After parking on the street, access to the isolated strip of coastline is by foot along a rough dirt track.

"Thank goodness you are only joking," said Bella. "I'm afraid I wouldn't be much help showing up round there on a recruiting mission."

Suzie nodded in agreement. "Even if it were of interest to me, I'm not showing my after-baby body to anyone." The three older artists looked at one another, peered down at their cuddly shapes, shook their heads and grinned wryly.

"Why the sudden interest in the nudists' beach as a potential source of models anyway?" queried Gladdy. "Why would a naturist be more likely than the average beachgoer, to become a life-drawing model? I wouldn't have thought they were any different from people who kept their bathers on." Gladdy paused for breath, and thought through the remaining comment she wanted to make before finishing. "It doesn't necessarily follow that they'd want their image displayed in public any more than the next person does."

"No, you're absolutely right, but you all know that it's nigh on impossible to find life-drawing models around here." Bronwyn agreed. I thought that, if we could find someone who is comfortable with nudity to start with, we might be able to entice them with the lure of a few extra dollars."

A few weeks later, when they met again across the street from the construction site, Diana said, "Only about a month to go, or so I heard. There's supposed to be a grand opening the first weekend in April."

Gladdy looked up from her sketching. "How'd you hear that?" She was just a touch put out by Diana's being ahead in the information gathering game.

"Paige was cutting my hair. You know Paige, whose salon used to be on the other side of town, in that old commercial building that was sold out from under the tenants noses." Diana started to explain.

"Yes, she's been operating out of her own home for months now," said Bronwyn, "And I hear she is over that arrangement. She has no privacy and gets phone calls even on Sundays for appointments. I go to her myself but I haven't been for a while." She ran her fingers through her thick wavy mop. "Holy smokes. I'd better make an appointment. I just realised I haven't been since last October."

Diana continued with her news. "Well, she's going to set up a salon in the new complex and she's calling it *Waves*. Paige said there's a big event planned for the opening, including some special meal at the restaurant on the opening night. Bet there will be no mere mortals like us invited to that."

After some thought, Diana remembered more of the information she gleaned from Paige. "The owner of a boutique that is setting up in the new complex is planning to hold an open-air fashion parade as part of the opening celebrations, and wants others to get involved if possible. She is a firm believer in that sort of collaboration between businesses – particularly in situations like the new complex – as being good for trade all round. She talked about some initiative she was developing to offer shoppers a discount when they bought from two or more stores in the complex … some sort of discount voucher system, or something."

"Sounds like this boutique person might be a bit of a go-getter," Suzie commented. "Oyster Point could do with a few like that to get it going again."

"Anyway, getting back to Paige," Diana continued. "Paige's new salon is doing the hair and make-up for the parade. She asked me if I would model some of the clothes. It was suggested to Paige that she might ask a few people on whom she could create some special hairstyles to be a part of the parade and, if they modelled hairstyles, it would be good if they modelled clothes at the same time."

"So, did she have something special lined up for you?" Gladdy asked.

Diana rewound her conversation with Paige before replying. "This was how she put it, 'your hair is a great base shade; it will work wonderfully with some really innovative colouring'. What," said I, "You want to tint my hair? I don't want a tint. It'll give me a regrowth problem. She told me she planned to work with foils and that she had some really nice copper, gold, bright aubergine and bronze colours."

"Oh, I can't wait to see this," Bella smirked. "What did you say?"

"She knew what buttons to press. Being a retired hairdresser myself, and a good friend to boot, she thought she could talk me into letting her do something exotic, and gave me the big sales pitch about my great cheekbones, how I look a million dollars in my clothes, and how I would be just the candidate for an interesting style."

"So, come on, what did you say after a promotional package like that?" Bronwyn asked with a giggle.

Diana shook her head in disgust and gave a wry smile. "Do you reckon I was being set up? Of course, I was. I couldn't believe myself when I opened my mouth again. In a moment of weakness, I squeaked, 'yes, okay'. Was I mad, or what?" The group dissolved into laughter and Diana came in for a generous dose of ribbing about being so easily 'buttered up'.

Those who agreed to model for the fashion parade met at Patsy Evans' place that Friday night for a few drinks and to begin choosing outfits from the boutique's stock arriving daily. Patsy has a large house on the waterfront. Her husband died leaving her well provided for. Although most of the time she found the house too large, she couldn't part with it. Patsy and Diana's friendship went way back. Their daughters grew up together, and later they both lost their only daughters around the same time in tragic accidents. Diana's daughter was killed in a skiing accident while she was living overseas, and Patsy's daughter by a hit-run driver while attending a southern university. The tragedies forged an even stronger bond between the women.

In a similar way, Patsy formed a friendship with Mariah Obrin. While still young, both women lost the husbands they adored. In Patsy's case, sometime after the death of her daughter, she remarried but now found herself widowed again. Mariah's daughter, Alexia, deeply traumatised by her father's death, caused Mariah go to great lengths – including moving to Oyster Point –to heal her daughter. After her father's death, Patsy's daughter also became a troubled soul. Patsy daughter had suffered in the same way and was just starting to get her life back together when she died. These shared similarities were the essence of Mariah and Patsy's bond of friendship.

It came as no surprise when Patsy offered her friend, Mariah Obrin, the owner of the new boutique, the use of several rooms to store her stock until the two new shops were ready. Mariah's daughter, Alexia, would manage *Embellish*, her mother's second shop in the new complex. Diana often dropped in for a chat with Patsy, so she was familiar with the size of house and knew that Mariah would find the offer to store the stock there in the interim a godsend.

On the Friday night, after they'd chosen and tried on some outfits, the models adjourned to the pool deck for drinks. This was a large area dotted with small tables and chairs. Patsy's late husband, due to the nature of his business, hosted many gatherings, including pool parties, so the property was well set up.

As they were enjoying their drinks, Patsy came up quietly behind Diana and said, "Come and sit over on that end of the deck, away from the crowd, I want to talk to you about something." Seated and sipping their drinks, Patsy said softly, "Don't look directly at them, but who is that blonde talking to Grace and Vera from the retirement village?"

Diana did her best impression of idly scanning the party and languidly slid her gaze around the crowd, allowing her eyes to linger briefly on the trio Patsy mentioned. "Beautiful view, Patsy, at this time of night …," and then more quietly, "that's Moira Whitlock. Why do you ask?"

"Well, I was sitting with friends drinking coffee the other day when I saw her leaving the nudists' beach carrying a towel and other sunbaking paraphernalia. You told me you were desperate to find a life-drawing model. It occurred to me that she looks like someone who would be comfortable about herself and her body. I wondered if it might be worth asking her."

"That's interesting, Patsy, thanks," said Diana. "I tend to agree. I think you just gave me a worthwhile tip."

After a pleasant half-hour of relaxing and chatting, the women agreed to congregate at Patsy's house again the following Friday night to look at that week's new stock and finalise their outfits for the parade. Moira was one of the first to leave.

Diana noted Moira's impending departure and, responding to a sudden idea, asked her friend to help. "Patsy, I'm heading off now too. I'm going to wander off after Moira to see if I can catch her for a private chat. Could you do me a favour? Follow me to the top of the stairs and keep the next group who are leaving chatting for a few minutes before letting them leave."

As Diana followed Moira down the stairs, she heard Patsy say, "Ladies, before any more of you leave, can you help me out? I just realised we haven't found Mariah a size 18 model yet. Does anyone have any suggestions? Surely someone knows somebody we could approach."

Damn, thought Diana, why isn't that new coffee shop open yet? I could ask Moira to come for a cuppa with me. "Hey, Moira, wait up," she called. "Can I talk to you about something? Come for a walk along The Esplanade. It won't take long, and it's still early," Diana suggested.

"Okay, I'm still a bit too wide awake. If I go home now, I'll take ages to get to sleep. Maybe I should have had another glass of wine before I left."

Diana decided the direct approach might be best. She took a deep breath and got on with it. "I wanted to chat about models for life drawing for our little art group. You do the odd bit of nude sunbathing, I believe."

"What?" Moira spluttered. "How did you know that? Who told you?"

"Someone saw you the other day, coming down the track from the nudists' beach."

"Who was it?"

"That doesn't matter, Moira, she's not about to tell the world."

"She'd better not."

"Hey, hang on a bit. Be fair, Moira, It wasn't her leaving the nudist beach in broad daylight. If you don't want people to know you're a naturist, you'd better save your jaunts for out of town where no one knows you. Anyway, what's so shameful about it? There are lots of people who enjoy that harmless activity."

"Hmm, okay, point taken. So what is it? What did you want to ask me?"

"There are five women in our art group. You know most of us I think. We need a nude or partially nude model. If it's more comforting for you, we're more interested in painting body shapes than recognisable faces."

"What's wrong with my face?"

Diana was starting to get a good feeling about things in spite of Moira's show of resistance. "Nothing, you've got a lovely face. It's just my way of telling you that no-one needs know who the model is, if you don't want them to."

"Hmm … and where would this modelling happen?"

"Not sure yet, but somewhere private; we don't want an audience any more than you do. It affects our concentration."

"What are you paying? If I was interested, I'd want $25 an hour."

"You're prepared to model for us?"

"Yeah, I suppose so. Okay. I'm out of work just now. The money will come in handy."

"Done," said Diana. "Let's shake on it." She couldn't believe her luck. The group was prepared to offer $35 an hour -- and still might if Moira worked out okay. "Would you like to meet the group?" Moira shrugged and then nodded. "Good, turn up at ten o'clock next Wednesday. We meet at the picnic table on The Esplanade across from the shopping complex."

The following Wednesday, Diana, excited about her news, barely managed to wait until they all settled before telling them. "Girls, we have a model and – wait for it – she'll be here in an hour to meet you. However, I've been thinking, it's getting close to the opening of the new complex. I suppose we should concentrate our efforts on sketching and painting what's happening over there, and leave the life drawing until after the opening of the new place. Still, it will be good to have Moira on board and ready to go once we start working on other stuff."

"I think you're right," Bronwyn said. "We've come this far with recording all the work down this end of town, I think we should concentrate on that to ensure a complete record." The others simply nodded their agreement. "However, it is good for Moira to meet and get to know us before we need her to start modelling. When she sees we are serious about our art, it might make her more comfortable if she has any lingering doubts."

"I agree. Good work on your part, Diana, finding someone so quickly," Bella added.

Diana smiled wryly. "Thanks for the compliment, but it's down to Patsy that we are talking to Moira."

The meeting with Moira went well. The group spent some time outlining their proposed project and how Moira, as their model, would be involved.

Moira understood how busy they were with their current project, and was happy to wait until after the opening. What really impressed the group were the questions Moira asked and the comments she made regarding their proposed project.

"She's not just a pretty face -- and a good body," Bronwyn commented after Moira left. "I think she knows a bit more about art than I expected. Some of her comments about our project are worth considering. It could give the concept extra depth. We should keep her involved as much as possible until we need her to model, even if it's just to have coffee with us occasionally."

Next morning, Bella arrived at the construction site early. She wanted some shots as they lowered the big skylights into position on the roof of the complex. She wasn't the only onlooker there that morning. Gordon Bailey also came to watch. He told Bella that, once the skylights were in place, the shopkeepers could access the complex to begin organising their shops. Gordon quizzed her about what she and her art group were doing as he had noticed them around the site since construction began.

After explaining their project, she added that she also was producing a photographic record. Gordon interrupted with questions several times as she detailed the extent of their work. Bella finished her explanation with a thought that occurred to her as they spoke.

"It would be good if we could do some sketching inside the complex before it opens," Bella told him, "To illustrate those final touches and the shopkeepers' activities in the lead up to the opening. I don't suppose they would let us in, but it would allow us to create a few good 'end of project' images."

"I'll have a word to the construction foreman to see if we can get you access and Rick Winston if necessary. He seems to have some say in what goes on. Tell me more about your project. How's it going? What's planned for the work you're producing?" Gordon enquired thoughtfully.

A bit perplexed, Bella looked at him for a moment before answering. She thought her explanation covered everything but apparently, it wasn't enough. Choosing her words carefully, she answered. "It's coming along okay. We haven't taken stock of what we've done so far, but we have many finished works. I don't suppose we've given much thought to what to do with the works other than maybe having an exhibition at some time. We thought it would be good for the locals, and to give newcomers a bit of an insight into the cyclone damage and what's risen from the debris. There hasn't been any discussion about when or where such an exhibition might happen."

"Do you think you will have your works completed by the opening, which I believe is the second weekend in April?"

"The *second* weekend…? We understood the opening was to be the first weekend in April."

"Yeah, it was set down for the first weekend before people realised that is the Easter weekend this year. Those waiting to open shops received letters advising them they postponed the opening a week. It avoided commercial suicide by having the opening over Easter."

"None of us thought about it being Easter. A week's postponement is a good move. Now about our work …" Bella thought for a moment before continuing. "I suppose we could have enough works if we put in a concerted effort between now and the opening, particularly with that extra week available. We don't have a timetable but, yes, I think we could have enough by then. Why do you ask?"

"I don't know if you're aware… actually, I don't think it is public knowledge yet, but there is a 'community space' in the complex. It's intended for the community's use for workshops, classes, meetings, whatever, but it's also being set up with a good hanging system for exhibitions."

"No, we didn't know. I suppose that's not surprising, as little about the new complex is common knowledge. I guess it's a ploy to keep the community guessing and have everyone turn up for the opening to satisfy their curiosity. The only thing we've heard about is Paige Matthews opening a new salon in there."

Gordon nodded. "I think there is much to sort out, but I can tell you there will be a community space in the building. The Council leased the space and asked us, Lois and I that is, to look after bookings for the use of the space. They asked our gang to mount an exhibition in there for the opening. It's been causing us some concern as all we have is conventional craft, and we don't feel it's appropriate for a major opening exhibition. It seems your group's material would be ideal for the opening exhibition, and the theme suits."

She gave it some thought. "Our stuff would fit perfectly, and it gives us the deadline we need to prod us along. I'll talk to the others, but I think they'll agree."

"Could I have a look at some of your work beforehand? It seems I might be creating some advertising material for the opening. I could include something about your exhibition. I assume some of your photographs will be in the show."

"Yes. It's strange though, because originally I intended the photographs for a quite different purpose. Apart from the fact that I can't leave my camera alone, I started taking the photos with the idea that, at some time, you might write a feature or something on the 'resurrection' of the town after the cyclone."

Gordon's eyebrows shot up and he nodded sagely. "We should give more thought to your idea for a collaborative article once the complex is up and running. I think we could knock up a first rate feature article." As she had all the photos she needed that day, Bella drove home to make phone calls.

When she proposed producing an exhibition in accordance with Gordon's suggestion, initially Bella received the responses she expected from the group. We haven't enough time; are our works good enough; will the public be interested? Bella left them to think it over after reminding them she needed to tell Gordon whether they were interested or not within the next day or two.

She knew her group well. Within a day, they all rang to support the idea, although some nervousness remained. Only then did Bella advise Gordon the group would mount an exhibition for the opening. Gordon took advantage of the phone call to tell her that the construction foreman gave approval for them enter the building to sketch during the week prior to the opening. Bella called the group together to pass on the information.

They agreed to set aside some time each morning for sketching the interior of the complex and, of course, Bella should bring her camera. For the week and a half prior to accessing into the building, there was little time to think about anything other than getting as much of their work finished as possible.

On their first day in the building, Bella sought out Gordon to arrange an inspection of the exhibition space so they could calculate how many artworks were required and to inspect the new hanging system. "That system is fantastic," Bronwyn cooed. "It gives us all the flexibility we could want to show off our works to their best advantage. …And the lighting! Perfect, couldn't be better."

Everyone worked at a frenzied pace producing more works while still completing other pieces at home. Gladdy and Diana somehow managed to complete their works well ahead of the others. As their 'reward', they got the job of creating the text panels for each of the works. If this was to look a truly professional exhibition, there needed to be an exhibition catalogue. The task of working with Gordon to produce one fell to the same two women.

During the trio's deliberations over the catalogue's design, the question of whether to sell their work or not arose and needed settling prior to completing the catalogue layout. Protracted discussion amongst the members resulted in the majority of the works being for sale, with the exception of one or two pieces to which their creators had some strong attachment. They also agreed that, for this inaugural exhibition, the artists would recoup only their costs for each work, with any additional money going towards purchasing equipment for *The Academy*. The board above the door indicated that was the official name for the community space.

In that brief week of sketching prior to the opening, the art group members got to know the shop owners. Several proprietors often got together for morning tea. In no time, the art group became part of those gatherings. Apart from the new friendships formed, the interaction with the shop owners also brought a bit of paid work to the group.

It began with restaurant owner, Arturo Santana and his chef, Bruce, asking them to produce designs for the restaurant's menus. The two men knew what they *didn't* want, but weren't sure how the menus should look. After discussion went round in circles for some time, Gordon, who had joined them, tried to give it some direction.

"As I understand discussions so far, three menu designs are required." He sought confirmation from Arturo and Bruce. They nodded in unison. "Good. Now, perhaps the most critical one is a souvenir menu for the official dinner to mark the opening of the complex. The other designs required are for menus for everyday operations: one for lunchtime and the other for dinner. Is that right?"

After a further short burst of discussion, the art group were alone to ponder their situation. It was an exciting opportunity, but time was short. They had little time to think about it, let alone produce something. An immediate start required; they commandeered the table and chairs.

This is where, sometime later, they sat looking glum and dispirited when Gordon spotted them as he stacked some of the shelves in Busy Fingers. He thought strategic intervention might help and sauntered over to them.

"I noticed you sitting here with faces as long as a wet weekend. What's gone wrong? You were so excited and enthusiastic earlier this morning."

Bella responded. "It's this great offer of some work – *paid* work ..."

"Well, that's great, isn't it?" Gordon interjected.

"Yes, it would be if we even knew where to start, and had time to think about it, before coming up with some ideas. On top of that, we haven't a clue about how to charge for that sort of work," Bronwyn explained.

"I might be able to help there. How about you take some of that time you say you haven't got to tell me about the job. What do you see as being involved and how do you see it – the job – progressing?"

Gordon made notes, interrupting periodically to ask questions or suggest ideas. As Gordon scribbled the last of his notes, the women spoke quietly amongst themselves.

"Did you notice things seemed a bit tense between Arturo and Bruce ... or did I just imagine it?" Diana asked.

"Only a bit tense...?" said Gladdy rolling her eyes. "They couldn't even look at one another. I suppose it's the stress of the opening and that big dinner."

"There is an even bigger problem as I see it," Bella said quietly. "Even if we do come up with designs they like, our work will look like sketches or paintings. The menus need to look professional. They need to be proper reproductions, and none of us has the skills to produce that. That requires … uhmm, what do you call them? Oh, yeah, it needs a graphic designer to produce the sort of work printers require."

Now finished with his notes, Gordon re-entered the conversation. "How about you come up with the designs and have them approved. I'll worry about having them graphically rendered. The only real problem I see is, to have them ready for the opening, the designs need approval by the end of tomorrow at the latest. "

An audible gasp came from a couple of the women, and a collective groan went up from the rest of the group as the reality of the timeframe dawned on them. Gordon remained upbeat and encouraging. He took the lead and began directing discussions. Soon they were making real progress.

Diana, sitting quietly since their meeting with the restaurant people, finally clarified her thoughts sufficiently to make a suggestion. She cleared her throat to get their attention. "I was thinking about the design for the official dinner menu, and have an image in mind. It might incorporate a line drawing, or similar, of the complex itself. As this is the new dawning of shopping in Oyster Point, can we use that as the basis of a concept?"

Diana's comments started the creative juices flowing. Ideas for colours and composition soon came thick and fast. Gordon sat back and listened with a satisfied grin on his face. Within about fifteen minutes, the women agreed on two variations of the same basic idea. The task of producing the souvenir menu artwork based on their agreed ideas fell to Diana and Suzie.

"Okay. That was relatively painless. Now, let's look at the other two menus you have to design," Gordon urged them.

Gladdy started speaking tentatively, as though she was thinking aloud. "I've been thinking about the name they've given the restaurant, *The Quarterdeck*. Imagine sitting there on the quarterdeck looking out to sea. What would I see?"

"Well, it probably would depend on when you were sitting there," Bronwyn responded. "I imagine the view would change depending on the time of day or night."

That was all it took for ideas to flow again. Within half an hour, they had two ideas for the menus based on what might be visible from a ship's quarterdeck during the day, and what the scene might be at night. They decided on the colours for each one and the design components for inclusion in each design. This time, the task of producing the artwork fell to Bronwyn and Bella.

Gordon reminded them of the deadline for the artwork, and that they needed to present the designs to the restaurant people first thing the next morning.

Bronwyn arranged a meeting for nine o'clock the following morning to present their designs. As she did so, she hoped she sounded more confident than she felt about having something to present at such short notice.

As they gathered up their things to leave, Diana's phone rang: Patsy inviting her to lunch. "I'm just on my way home now, Patsy. Is it okay if I come straight round?"

When she rang the bell, Patsy's voice floated down to her. "The door's unlocked. Come in. I'm in the kitchen."

Diana found her parked on an office chair in the kitchen, and with a foot swathed in bandages up on a kitchen chair.

"What have you done to yourself," Diana demanded.

"I was walking on the beach yesterday and sliced my foot open on some glass in the sand. Anyway, many stiches later, I now can't walk for possibly two or three weeks."

"So, make the most of it -- read a book; watch TV. Is there something else? You seem very down."

"It couldn't happen at a worse time. Mariah's two shops are ready for us to move her stock in. She's picking up a load tonight ready for the morning. I was to move the remaining stock tomorrow while she and Alexia priced and hung everything. Now I can't do anything. I thought of asking you to help. I know how busy you are with your art stuff, but I can't think of anyone else."

"Hmm, maybe there is someone. Someone who is unemployed at the moment might help … but they might want some cash in return."

"Not a problem. I'll pay them, of course. Who …?"

"Moira Whitlock. I'll give her a call now."

Diana reported that Moira would arrive at eight o'clock the next morning, but she only had a small car and it probably would require many trips to move all the stock."

"She can use my big SUV. With the back seats down, there's heaps of room in the back. Oh, this is wonderful."

"Have you told Mariah about your foot?"

"No, I didn't want to bother her. She is worried. Alexia has descended into one of her dark places again. Mariah is concerned about her."

"We all have our problems. Come on, it's a quick lunch today. I'm going to be burning the midnight oil as it is to meet my deadlines." As soon as they had eaten, Diana rushed off.

Bella went home and started work. She completed her designs that afternoon and asked Gordon over to look at them. He arrived just after five o'clock. Her two design variations were impressive. Gordon indicated his preference and asked her to scan and email them so he would have electronic copies from which to produce their graphic counterparts. After Gordon left,

Bella rang to tell Bronwyn of her progress. Bronwyn, her designs almost finished, would email them to Gordon as well.

Gordon spent a very late night -- early morning really – using graphic software to reproduce the emailed images, focusing firstly on the concepts he thought most likely to receive approval. Next morning, Gordon added his digital renditions of the designs to the bundle of paper taken to the restaurant meeting. The women, suitably impressed and buoyed by Gordon's artwork, were on a high as they traipsed off to their meeting.

The meeting went well and the group emerged from the restaurant about twenty minutes later. However, their faces told Gordon there was another problem. They explained that Arturo loved their work and made his selections. His choice of designs for the lunchtime and evening menus agreed with Gordon's preferences. That's a relief, Gordon thought. It only leaves the graphic reproduction of the souvenir menu design and some tarting up of these other two to complete.

"So, why the long faces again?" Gordon asked. "They liked the designs. We can have them ready on time. Where's the problem?"

"They want a firm quote on the job, and we have no idea how to do that," Bronwyn responded. "We don't know how to price our time for that kind of work, and the price has to cover your work as well as the printing, if that is our responsibility."

"I see, but it's not really a problem. Each of you needs to tell me how long it took you to produce your designs. I'll add in a bit of time to cover the meetings you had. I'll cost out my work. Then, I'll ring my mate who has a small printery at Arkana Beach to get a price from him … and lean on him to get the job done at short notice. Any other problems? No? Okay, here's my notebook, write down your design times."

They did as requested, and were still thanking Gordon when Jason from the new brasserie, ambled past checking on the various stores' progress. The restaurant's artwork spread out on the table caught his eye. He came over for a closer look.

"That's pretty impressive stuff," Jason said. "It appears you guys know what you're about when it comes to art. That gives me an idea. The Brasserie already has menus printed, but our intention is to put a 'daily specials' board up on one of the walls. We wanted a chalkboard… easy to clean off at the close of each day, ready to write up the next day's specials. I hesitated about it because of concerns about how it would look. I didn't want anything as plain and ugly as a dark rectangular panel. Now that I've seen this …," Jason added as he flicked through the artwork on the table, "Maybe you guys could paint an appropriate border around the board so that it wouldn't end up the eyesore I imagined it might."

"They'd be happy to do something for you, mate," Gordon replied be-fore the women could think about it. "I suppose you'll need this before the opening?" he added. "Have you any ideas about what you want, a design or anything? How big is this board going to be anyway?"

"Er, no I hadn't thought about it. This artwork made me revisit the idea. I suppose, in keeping with the location of the place, the theme should be something nautical … or marine." Without any clear ideas, Jason was wrong-footed by the whole thing. "I don't know how big the board will be. I haven't bought one yet."

"Well, you had better get yourself organised if you want it up by the opening. Come on, Lad, get moving. Get yourself a board, and these ladies will get it sorted out in time for the opening," Gordon assured Jason.

Last thing that afternoon, Jason dropped a chalkboard into Gordon at Busy Fingers for him to pass on for decoration.

"Happy to oblige, my friend, and it will only cost you a meal and a couple of drinks for each of the ladies … and me."

The artists were at Bella's when Gordon delivered the board that evening. Having worked on potential design ideas after leaving the shopping complex, they were ready to begin. Late on Wednesday night, the job was finished and, by lunchtime on Thursday, it was dry enough for Gordon to deliver to Jason.

For the women, it was a relief to see an end to their commercial ventures. They had an exhibition to hang, and it was quite late on Thursday night before they finally were satisfied with the way it looked.

The Mayor was thrilled with the souvenir menu, and impressed with their work for others in the complex as well as their exhibition. She invited them to the official dinner. Gordon, as a shop owner, already had an invite. So much for their earlier predictions of hobnobs only being on the guest list.

After locking the door on their exhibition in The Academy that night, Suzie arched her back and stretched, before suggesting, "I move that we tell Moira that there will be a delay of a week or so before we start our next project. I, for one, am exhausted after this last couple of weeks."

Her suggestion met with weary, but contented, nods all round.

The Quarterdeck

The run up to the opening of the complex proved a long and complex journey for some. While others experienced a shorter but drama plagued interlude. Disaster can appear imminent before any major event, and that is how it was for one establishment.

Gordon Bailey collected the daily specials board just before lunchtime on Thursday. The art group members produced a good design for the borders of the blackboard to display The Brasserie's daily specials. Now the paint was dry, Gordon was anxious to deliver the board to Jason, The Brasserie owner, to get it up on the wall ready for the official opening the next day. As Gordon loaded the board into his car, he received some good-natured advice from the art group. "You better take some tools with you," Bronwyn shouted as he slammed the car boot closed. "Jason is a chef. He is not likely to have tools, and is probably useless when it comes to drilling and screwing."

The Plaza was a hive of activity when he arrived. Shopkeepers put the final touches to their windows and primped their displays. Jason was at the counter discussing something with Ginger, The Brasserie's barman. They both turned to greet Gordon as he entered the shop.

'Ginger', as he became known to friends and associates a long time ago was Michael Ginger. The common practice of putting surnames first when listing names, saw him frequently recorded as 'Ginger, Michael'. Too much temptation for Australian jokers, he became known as 'Ginger Mick', and more commonly referred to by the shortened version. Anyone who didn't know his full name found this confusing. There was not a hint of ginger in his swarthy good looks.

"It's dry and ready to go up. What do you think?" Gordon asked as he held the board up for inspection.

"Yeah, good," Ginger responded in his usual economical way.

"They've done a great job," Jason added as he scrutinised the board.

"Okay, where does it go?" Gordon asked, looking around the shop. There weren't many options: lots of glass but only one long solid wall.

"I thought we'd put it up here," Jason replied, pointing to a space on the wall near the counter, "Just inside the door where they'll see it as they come in."

Ginger's trunk-like tattooed arms held the board aloft against the wall while Jason and Gordon gave directions: down a bit; left a bit; no, too far;

right hand up a bit; perfect – hold it there.

Gordon grabbed a pencil and marked the corner positions on the wall. Arturo Santana rushed in and barged up to Jason, interrupting the trio. "Jason, I need your help," He croaked. "You wouldn't happen to know any chefs who might get at short notice?"

Stunned, Jason recovered quickly and replied slowly as he pondered the question. "What do you mean by 'short notice'? When would you want them to start and for how long? Oh, and how many do you want … uh, need?"

"Now, today; I only need one … but I'll need him for tomorrow night's dinner and until I can find a permanent head chef."

"Geez, Art, you don't want much! The tourist season is not in full swing yet, so there might be someone from Arkana who could help out – might only be for the weekend though. I could make some phone calls, but I can't promise I'll do any good." Jason did not look convincing as he weighed up Art's request. "I thought you had a chef. Isn't Bruce your head chef?" Like others, Jason also suspected everything was not well between the restaurant owner and his head chef.

"Things haven't been going well with Bruce," Art admitted. "They weren't good from the beginning. In fact, I was beginning to wonder if he was a chef. Comments by the kitchen staff suggest they also don't think he is much of a chef."

"Oi, you lot, I'm not going to stand here all day holding this board up in the air," Ginger announced.

"Oh, sorry Ginger. Gordon, if have finished marking, Ginger can put the board down. We'll have another go at putting it up later, after we've sorted out Art's problem," Jason said. "…So, Art, what has happened with Bruce? The Plaza opening's official dinner is tomorrow night. Are you telling us you haven't got a chef?"

"Bruce came in late this morning, only stayed a little while, and then he and Sharon disappeared."

"Who is Sharon?" Gordon enquired.

"She was the maître d' – or whatever you call that person who runs the front of house. She had designs on Bruce from the moment she arrived, and it looks like it paid off. I think they've had a bit of a thing going the last couple of weeks. Anyway, they disappeared together this morning and only returned just on lunchtime. I was coming back from the supermarket and saw them drive into the car park. I went to ask where they were all morning. We had a blazing row in the car park. Bruce was none too complimentary. I don't suppose I was either. I started to walk off, thinking that was the best thing to do. I glanced into the car as I walked past. The car was packed. They were going to shoot through. So, I told him to bugger off."

"Hmm, sounds like he was going anyway. The bottom line now, however, is that you don't have a chef – and that could be very embarrassing come tomorrow night," Jason mused.

"Yeah, I think he realised that the job – or at least tomorrow night – was beyond him. Of course, his new girlfriend, Sharon, had to have her say as well, and announced she would be going with him."

Jason heaved a sigh of resignation, "Okay. I'll go and make some calls, but I don't know that I'm going to get any worthwhile chef to come striding through your door anytime soon."

The conversation was between Jason and Art and, not wanting to intrude, Gordon stood slightly apart from the two men as he watched people coming and going along The Esplanade. Suddenly, his eyes lit up, and he spun round to face the other two men. Ginger, now back behind the bar, looked up in surprise.

"Don't do anything just yet," Gordon requested. "Just give me a moment. You two guys sit down and have a drink or something until I come back." With that, Gordon strode out of The Brasserie heading for The Esplanade.

The two men exchanged glances and Jason shrugged. "I don't know what it's all about, but I suppose we should take his advice and wait for him to return."

As they watched, Gordon approached a young couple walking along The Esplanade towards the supermarket. A lively conversation took place, punctuated by the young couple's occasional glances towards the Plaza. Then, all three turned towards the complex and Gordon, standing slightly behind the other two, spread his arms wide and herded the couple across the grass verge towards The Brasserie. As the trio approached, Jason and Art dismounted their stools and moved towards the doorway.

Gordon beamed widely as he led the young couple in to meet Art and Jason. "Art, let me introduce a solution to all your problems," Gordon announced expansively. "This is Beppe Antonelli and his partner Elene Metaxas. They're living on their boat in the Marina at present. Beppe is a chef, and Elene is a front of house expert." After everyone shook hands, Gordon continued. "I met them the other morning when I came in early. They were sailing up the coast when their boat developed some problems with its motor. They managed to limp into Oyster Bay. They did ask me if there was any work available. I knew you had all your kitchen staff, so I suggested they wait until after the opening before making enquiries at the restaurant. Anyway Art, they are looking for work. It's over to you now. Perhaps you'd like to show them the restaurant and have a bit of a chat with them."

In the short time they knew him, Jason and Gordon had never seen Art lost for words, but apparently there is a first for everything. When he found his voice again, he stammered, "Come, the restaurant is this way. It's called *The*

Quarterdeck." Those in The Brasserie heard him stepping up his sales pitch as he led his prospective employees through the complex.

"I don't know about you, Gordon, but I am anxiously awaiting the outcome of that meeting," Jason said, jerking his head to indicate the retreating trio. "It might mean the difference between scrambled eggs or something decent at tomorrow night's dinner."

"Well, I thought I might just sit here for a bit to see if any of them venture back this way to tell us how things went," Gordon replied.

With a mixture of pride and apprehension, Arturo showed the young couple into his restaurant. Disappointingly, Beppe didn't show much enthusiasm for the dining area, although he said it was 'very nice'. Elene was more impressed but stopped short of raptures. However, the kitchen generated something approaching raptures for Beppe, and he waxed lyrical about it for a few moments before Arturo dragged them back into the dining area. As they sat at one of the tables, Beppe voiced a couple of concerns.

"Arturo, you didn't introduce us to any of the other staff. Do they know about Bruce?"

"No, I haven't told them yet. I thought I would wait until we had a chat, and then I would be able to tell them the whole story."

"I am a bit concerned. With the opening tomorrow night, I expected the staff would be busy preparing. At what stage are preparations?"

"To tell the truth, Beppe, I don't know." Arturo grabbed one of the souvenir menus for the dinner and thrust it towards Beppe. "This is the menu for the dinner, but I don't know what's been done – if anything – towards preparing it."

"You said you had a second chef. Wouldn't he take over in Bruce's absence?"

"Sam is very good, but he's young and doesn't have a lot of experience. He could hold the fort on a regular night, but he couldn't handle tomorrow night's affair."

"I see. Have the kitchen staff been given the recipes for this menu?"

Arturo shrugged, admitted that he didn't know, went back to the kitchen, and returned with a handful of paper. He placed it on the table for Beppe who scanned each sheet before slumping back in his chair.

Beppe took a deep breath and exhaled it through pursed lips. "Arturo, the menu is great. The recipes are *crap*."

"Ah, that explains some of the comments I heard in the kitchen earlier today. Can it be fixed in time?"

"Yes. I can give them decent recipes for most of the dishes right now, but I don't have a couple of the recipes in my head. I need to get them from the boat. Elene, would you go back to the boat and collect my portable hard drive while I sort some of the other recipes for the kitchen staff? Arturo, I'll need that computer, and I'll need to have a look at what ingredients we have on hand to be sure we can use my recipes. Perhaps Sam and I could go through what's in stock." Elene nodded and said she would go as soon as she had a good look around the dining area.

The tour of inspection with Sam only a few minutes. Beppe returned to Arturo waiting in the dining room. "There are a couple of ingredients we don't have. I could adjust the recipes to do without them, but the dishes would be much better if we had the proper ingredients. I haven't seen the stuff I need in the supermarket and, only being new to the area, I'd don't know where we might be able to buy the stuff I need at short notice."

Arturo held his hands out palm upwards shrugged. "Don't ask me. Maybe Jason will know."

Elene finished inspecting the dining area and came over to the two men. "While you guys talk to Jason, I'll go back to the boat. Arturo, I'm hoping some of that herd of people in the kitchen are front of house staff. We need to get this dining area set up properly. Even though the restaurant won't open to the public tomorrow, with that glass frontage, people walking through the complex need to get a great impression of what this place will be like. After I get back from the boat, I want to spend the rest of the day with the front of house staff setting up the dining area and going over their duties with them. Is that okay? Oh, and we'll need flowers for the tables."

"Okay, go ahead and do whatever needs doing," Arturo replied nodding enthusiastically. "Go to the florist's for whatever flowers you need. Tell them I'll pay for them later."

"Okay. Just one question though: where is the florist?" Elene asked.

"Eh? Oh, I forgot; you're new to Oyster Point. It's in the next block. Go past the hotel and then it's about half way along the block."

With that, the trio headed out of the restaurant: Elene to the boat, and Beppe and Arturo to talk to Jason.

When the two men arrived at The Brasserie, they found Jason, Gordon and Ginger standing back admiring the daily specials board now affixed to the wall. The board looked good, and Beppe and Arturo commented accordingly before Arturo explained their ingredients problem. Jason thought the only place they might get what they needed in a hurry was from one of the hotel restaurants at Arkana Beach. He disappeared to make phone calls and soon returned grinning triumphantly. One of the restaurants would give them some from their stock on the understanding that Beppe replaced it when his supply arrived.

"Well, Arturo, it looks like you're going for a drive to Arkana Beach. You're the only one that's not busy at the moment." Then another thought occurred to Beppe. "By the way, shouldn't we do something about contracts before much longer?"

"Can we talk about contracts when I get back? I think it is more important to get these ingredients for you. I promise the contract will not be a problem. I'm grateful."

"Name your price, mate," Gordon advised Beppe in a stage whisper and added an exaggerated wink and a nod.

Arturo took off immediately for Arkana, leaving Beppe standing in The Brasserie. He gave the others a wry smile and said, "In the absence of anyone else to do it, it looks like I now have to introduce myself to the other staff and tell them what's happening." Laughter greeted his lament.

Everything in the kitchen went relatively smoothly for the rest of the day. Beppe felt a bit of a prat when he introduced himself as the new head chef. He noticed the staff's depressed mood when he was in the kitchen earlier in the day. It even bordered on hostile. His announcement didn't improve things. He felt his optimism ebbing. Chin up he told himself, we have to get down to business. His request for a progress report produced only a couple of mono-syllabic responses, but they were enough to indicate little or no progress so far. He made one final announcement.

"I've had a look at the recipes. Rubbish! I'm going to print off some new ones for you. It should take just a few minutes. In the meantime, here's a list of what you can start on while you are waiting." He took some comfort from what appeared to be a degree of renewed interest.

Elene returned with his hard drive. Before he started on the recipes, Beppe took her into the kitchen, introduced her, explaining she was the new maître d', and asked the front of house staff to go with Elene to start setting up the dining area. There was a bit of shuffling of feet, but no one moved. All of the staff stood looking at him. Some were scowling. Sam broke the silence.

"Look, Beppe, thanks for taking over, but we are all still in the dark as to what has happened. Are Bruce and Sharon coming back? Were they sacked … are you pair just filling in for tomorrow night, or what?" Sam asked quietly. "Things haven't been real good since we started. It would help if we knew what was going on."

Beppe explained he hoped Arturo would brief them on everything that happened, but that wasn't possible because he sent Arturo to Arkana to collect some additional ingredients they needed for a couple of the dishes. "I know this hasn't been handled as well as it should but, we have a very important dinner to prepare for tomorrow night. The future of The Quarterdeck – and jobs as well probably – depend on how well we do our jobs tomorrow night and over the coming weekend. First impressions stick, so how about we get on with it? Anyone with something to get off their chest should talk to me while I organise the recipes for you."

No one came to talk to him. He noticed the noise from the front of house staff increased in keeping with their rising excitement as they rearranged *t*ables and other furniture. After running them through their paces to ensure their service skills were up to scratch, Elene talked uniforms and who would do what, before asking for suggestions for flowers for the tables. By the time Arturo returned, the place looked like a restaurant and the mood in the kitchen was buoyant. Arturo gave the ingredients to Sam, as he could see Beppe was busy explaining something to a kitchen hand.

The rest of the afternoon disappeared in a blur of activity. As soon as she allocated tasks to keep the wait staff busy, Elene went to organise flowers. She hoped she had allowed enough time for the florist to produce all the arrangements she needed.

Elene found Marilyn, the florist, operated out of a tiny shop that looked as though it might once have been a café or milk bar. Inside was dark and dingy. Elene felt her heart sink as she walked through the door and peered around the shop. She did not hold out much hope of getting what she wanted from here. First impressions are not always accurate however. Closer inspection showed the wide variety of flowers available was top quality and the arrangements on display were breathtaking. Perhaps I will want a long-term relationship with this business after all, Elene reassured herself.

The artificial arrangements for use every day on the tables presented no problems and were finalised quickly. The fresh flower arrangements for the tables for the opening night dinner proved more complicated. Elene had a clear idea of what she wanted, and the wait staff agreed with her. Perhaps they were just being polite, but they seemed to like her ideas. Now Marilyn was telling her she couldn't have what she wanted.

"I know those flowers you want do look lovely and are readily available in Melbourne, even during summer, but they do like the southern climes better than up here. They're very delicate and don't travel well, and they don't last long in our heat, even in air-conditioning. I don't even try to use them up here. Maybe we can come up with something else. Tell me what your idea is based on." Marilyn finished speaking and pulled over a couple of stools so they could sit while discussing how to get around the problem.

"I thought those flowers would be good because they don't have long stems and would sit low on the table while making a good show. The souvenir menus are in delicate dawn-like colours – apricots, pinks, crimson and gold. I was looking to keep the colour theme going on the tables," Elene explained.

Marilyn thought for a moment. "So, we are looking at those colours and low unobtrusive arrangements. I might have something that will do the trick. I brought in some new stock this morning but haven't put it out in the cabinets yet. Come through to the back with me and I'll show you. Can you describe the colours you want a bit more clearly?"

Elene tried to think of the right descriptive words as they walked through to the workshop area. A number of buckets and other containers filled with orchid blooms sat on a low bench along the back wall of the workshop. Elene started trying to describe the colours she wanted. "Well the main colour is kind of a soft apricot -- or maybe you would call it salmon -- it's a bit hard to ... oh, goodness. There, that's the exact colour I'm looking for," Elene gasped as she pointed to a bucket containing long sprays of orchids. "... And look, those ones over there also are the right colour to go with those apricots ones."

Marilyn pulled from the buckets one spray of each of the orchids Elene indicated and picked out a couple of others. She spread them on the workbench and grabbed a pair of shears. A few snips later, she had arranged a beautiful small low example of a table arrangement. "Just perfect," Elene sighed. They discussed the number required and prices. Elene was about to leave when she remembered she planned having two large displays in the dining area as well. It took only a moment to describe what she wanted. She left confident Marilyn would produce something perfect.

By the time Arturo announced they were closing and herded everyone out of the place, things were well on track for the official opening dinner. As Arturo, Beppe and Elene walked out of the restaurant together, they met Gordon on his way back from checking the hanging of the exhibition in The Academy.

"How did the day finish up?" Gordon enquired. "There seemed to be a flurry of activity in there when I walked past earlier."

"Well ..." Beppe began, but stopped when he spotted Jason standing in the doorway of The Brasserie. He wanted to thank both Gordon and Jason and didn't feel like having to tell the story twice. "If you are on your way out too, come with us to The Brasserie. I need to let Jason know how things went as well."

The quartet strolled to The Brasserie, admiring each shop as they passed. When they arrived, Jason remained in the doorway waiting for Ginger to finish doing something before locking up for the night. He used the time to appreciate the transformation that turned an empty space into his brasserie. Although he needed no excuse, the arrival of his four visitors was his incentive to announce a pre-opening happy hour.

Beppe insisted he wanted to buy them all champagne as a thank you. Jason argued that he didn't have to buy it, but Beppe insisted. "Besides," he announced with a wink to Gordon, "with the contract Arturo is writing for me, I can afford it."

"That might be the case, mate, but the cash register is not turned on and is empty at the moment, so you can't buy anything," Jason advised, and indicated to Ginger to retrieve a bottle from the refrigerated cabinet. "I see you haven't wiped the smile off Art's face yet. He dropped in here when he got back from Arkana. Grinning from ear to ear he was, like he'd just had a private audience with Santa Claus."

Ginger joined them in a celebratory glass of bubbly. Conversation flowed easily between them. Each shop's representative at the table spoke about their state of preparedness for the next day and the highlights – and low lights – of achieving it. Eventually, the group's curiosity swung conversation back to Beppe and Elene. Jason voiced the question the others were too polite to ask.

"Gordon told us how you just managed to make it into Oyster Point with a sick boat. Where were you heading, and what happens now that you're stuck here for a while?"

"Well, it's a bit of a long story," Beppe said slowly. "We weren't really heading anywhere in particular."

"It must be great to be footloose and fancy free. Able to head off to wherever your fancy takes you," Jason responded.

"Oh, for goodness sake, Beppe, tell it like it is," Elene rebuked him. "We ran away."

"Eh, running away…? From what…?" Gordon asked incredulously.

Elene gave a half-hearted shrug and replied, "Our families."

"I accept that rebellious teenagers sometimes run away from home but, I'm sorry, you two don't look like teenagers," Gordon said.

"No, we're no longer teenagers, but we are 'ethnics'." Beppe's response caused the group to exchange glances.

Gordon used his hand to encourage Beppe. "Okay, come on. Come on don't leave us dangling like this. Tell us the story. It doesn't matter that it's long; we've still got half a bottle of champagne left."

Beppe took a moment to compose his thoughts before beginning. "Both Elene and I came to Australia as very young kids. We grew up here – well, in Melbourne. We grew up as Aussie kids. Unfortunately, our parents couldn't let go of all of the old traditional ways. Our mothers still don't speak very good English, even after all these years. Anyway, the one tradition that caused all the problems was the old practice of finding a spouse for your children."

"God, does that really still happen … here in Australia?" Jason blurted out.

"I don't think it is common practice," Arturo replied, "But, yes, I believe it still happens in some families."

Beppe continued the story. "My family arranged a 'suitable bride' for me while I was still at primary school and, since I turned 21, they have hammered me about getting married to the chosen girl. I stalled them using my apprenticeship as an excuse but, as soon as I was qualified, they stepped up the pressure for me to honour their agreement with the other family. Eventually, I argued that I needed to get my career firmly established before I could even think of getting married and supporting a family and, besides, I had never even met the girl. Then, a couple of years ago, just before Christmas when we were really busy in the restaurant, this girl turned up at home to spend a couple of weeks with us – with her mother in tow. Fortunately, I was too busy to spend much time with her – or her mother – and I think the relationship between my family and hers became a bit strained after the visit. In a bid to placate matters, I claimed I was saving up to buy a place of my own to be financially independent when I finally married."

Beppe stopped for breath and Elene continued the story. "My situation was much the same. The family picked out a husband for me when I was still very young. By the time I turned 20, they pressured me to get married. Our families don't recognise any of this nonsense about people no longer being minors when they reach 18, or even 21 for that matter. They expect their children to remain obedient to the end. Like Beppe, I had never met my intended husband. He was a fair bit older and, when I was about 15, my family was devastated when my intended spouse died in a motorbike accident. Undeterred, they set about finding me another husband before I became too old for anyone to be interested, and soon entered into a new agreement with another family, but this time the man was a widower and twice my age. There was no way I was going to marry him. So, like Beppe, I came up with all sorts of excuses to delay a wedding."

Gordon was shaking his head in disbelief. Jason, sitting with his mouth hanging open in dismay throughout the story, finally found his voice. "I can't believe people still do this in Australia. Why come here if you just want to live the life you used to have rather than accepting the new world you've come to? I'm sorry, that was a rhetorical question. Please go on."

"Anyway, to cut a long story a bit shorter," Beppe picked up the story again, "Shortly after that visit, Elene came to work at the restaurant I was managing. We clicked from the word go, but were very careful to keep our relationship from our families. Then a few months ago, someone saw us together and told Elene's father. She was beaten. She didn't tell me initially but, after the third time, when she was fairly badly injured, I found out about it. A real brawl took place between Elene's parents and mine, and it all went downhill from there. Elene had paint thrown over her car, and she was spat on walking down the street. Another old crone of a woman came into the restaurant and spat on her. I used to ride a motorbike to work and came out one night to find the tyres slashed. A few nights later, I was walking home when a couple of blokes attacked me. I was lucky a patrol car happened to come by during the attack and rescued me. I only ended up with a couple of broken ribs and a black eye. That crystallised it for us. We weren't going to give in, but the only way we would survive was to get away. It took a bit careful planning but, in less than a week, we secretly moved everything we were taking with us on board my boat. I'd owned the boat for about 12 months, but nobody knew about it."

"It's almost unbelievable that a father would treat his daughter that way. You hear about these arranged marriages in other parts of the world, but you don't for one moment think it's going on in Australia," Gordon said in disgust. "Was it just because you weren't honouring the agreements they'd made with your respective intended spouses' families?"

"No, not really. I suppose there is more to it than that. You see, Elene's family are Greek Cypriots, and mine are Sicilian. There seems to be a convention that children should marry within their own 'tribe'. That's partly why these arrangements are made when the kids are young, so it's all tied up snugly and according to the rules."

"Geez, mate, you guys were lucky to get away. I dread to think what might have happen if your families got wind of what you were doing before you left," Jason said.

"Yeah, it took a bit careful planning. I think I was still hyperventilating when we were halfway up the New South Wales coast," Elene said with a laugh.

"Should I be concerned?" Arturo asked Beppe.

"Concerned about what?"

"…Your families coming to wreck my restaurant – or worse! How long do you think you will stay here, or are you suddenly going to do a midnight flit and leave me in the lurch?"

Everyone had a giggle at Arturo's questions, and then dissolved into laughter when they saw the very real concern on his face.

"No one is going to come looking for us. Both families have disowned us," Beppe reassured Arturo. "As for how long we might stay, you might be pleased to see the back of us after tomorrow night," he teased.

"Anyway, what are you fussing about, Art? I would have thought you would understand all this sort of stuff. Don't your lot carry on like that too?" Jason queried.

"What do you mean: *my lot?*"

"Your ethnic tribe … Arturo *Santana*: what's that, Spanish or something?" Jason continued.

"Possibly originally, but my family are from South America. I am Australian. I was born here."

"I don't know which suburb your accent comes from then," Jason continued to goad Arturo.

"Ignore him, Art," Gordon advised. "He's just winding you up to see if he can wipe that smile off your face. If you weren't one of us, he wouldn't be ribbing you like he is."

Arturo, finally realising Jason was having a go at him, laughed along with the others. "I think it's time to stop talking and put some more of that stuff in these glasses," Arturo said as he gestured towards their glasses on the table. "They have been empty for too long and we will die of thirst if they are not refilled soon."

With the glasses refilled, and the bottle emptied, Gordon proposed a toast. "Here's to a successful opening tomorrow and being overwhelmed by community support all weekend." Some general discussion regarding the opening and speculation on likely crowd numbers followed until the glasses again were empty. They waited for Ginger and Jason to clear away and lock up before walking out together.

As they started along The Esplanade towards the marina, Elene suddenly stopped. The couple had been walking hand-in-hand, and her sudden stop jerked Beppe around so that he was facing back the way they had come. "What's up? What happened – what are you stopping for?" Beppe asked in surprise.

"Remember this morning; we were on our way to the supermarket for groceries. We still haven't got those groceries and, even if we could survive tonight and tomorrow morning, we won't have time tomorrow to shop."

Beppe slapped his hand against his forehead. "I forgot about the groceries. We don't even have milk for breakfast. You are right. We won't have time tomorrow. We should that now. There's just enough time before they close."

With each of them carrying a bag of groceries, they set off once more for the marina. They walked in silence for a couple of minutes, before Elene took a deep breath and exhaled slowly. "What a day today turned out to be. It started out like any other day, but look at how it's ended," she said wistfully.

"What? With the two of us carrying groceries…?" Beppe goaded her.

"No, don't be smart. I mean, the gods must've been smiling on us today when you consider all that happened; new friends, new job. You know, I think I'm really going to like Oyster Point." Beppe smiled as he reached down and took her free hand, and they walked the rest of the way to the boat in silence.

That evening they were both preoccupied, their minds galloping as each one silently went over their plans for the next day. Although they went to bed later than usual, and experienced a restless night, they both rose early. Beppe made coffee and went up on deck to watch the sunrise. About five minutes later, Elene slipped onto a chair beside him. They sat in silence until their mugs were empty. Then, Beppe stretched and stood up, picked up both empty mugs and started towards the galley, asking over his shoulder, "What time are you going to work today?"

"The florist said she would bring some of the arrangements between 8.00 and 830 this morning, and the ones for tonight's tables would be ready by five o'clock. She will try to deliver those in the afternoon, but will ring if that isn't possible. If she can't bring them to the restaurant, Arturo will have to collect them. To answer your question, I'll need to be at work by eight o'clock."

"In that case, we can walk in together. I planned to be there just before eight o'clock. Jason said he would be there to let me in, since we haven't got a key yet."

Beppe's mobile rang just after seven o'clock: Arturo. "I think I forgot to mention yesterday that there is a breakfast at the hotel this morning for all the shop owners," he apologised. "It's at 7.30 in the hotel's dining room. I think they are going to give us the run down on the day's program of events."

"That's nice, but we are not shop owners," Beppe responded.

"No, but you are managing the place. The chef and maître d' were invited. If you can make it, I'll see you there at 7.30."

Not wanting to miss it, the pair quickly dressed, grabbed their bags and jogged The Esplanade to join the last stragglers arriving for the breakfast. Geoff Robinson, the complex developer, laid on quite a spread. Full English breakfast for those so inclined, or croissants and fruit for others. Not wanting to appear aloof, the couple indulged in croissants and very good coffee as they mingled and chatted. Both kept one eye on the time. After a couple of brief speeches, they received copies of the weekend's opening program. With the formalities out of the way, at eight o'clock, the couple quietly slipped away.

As they stepped off the footpath to cross the road to the complex, Elene looked up and exclaimed, "Something has changed … I think."

"What?"

"Has that sign always been there? I hadn't noticed it before."

"Huh, no, that's new. I wonder if anyone won the sweepstakes."

"What do you mean: 'sweepstakes'?"

"I heard there was a guessing game going on about what the new complex would be called, and then one of the local bookies started taking bets on the name."

Installed sometime during the night, a sign now stood in front of the building. The concrete footings protected by a safety fence for the last week or so now supported a huge elevated sign. After months of speculation, the complex now had a name.

Jason jogged after them to let them. Most of the restaurant staff were already milling around waiting to get in. As Jason unlocked the door and held it open for everyone to enter, the florist's van arrived. Elene waved the front of house staff over to help carry in the table arrangements. Keen for a sneak peek at the restaurant, the florist insisted on carrying in a couple of the arrangements herself.

"These are the everyday arrangements," Elene explained. "We will have these on the tables today so the place looks 'finished' to shoppers passing by.

We'll swap them for the other fresh arrangements for the dinner when you bring them this afternoon. We were told the place will close at 5.00pm today – earlier than normal – so I might need Arturo to let you in or, alternatively, I could send him to collect the arrangements."

Marilyn was not going to miss seeing her orchid arrangements on the tables that evening. She would deliver them. Apart from the artificial 'everyday' arrangements, the florist also brought two massive arrangements in faux antique urns. Elene placed one on a side table about half way along the dining area, and the other she placed on the end of the bar next to the wall. As she placed this last arrangement, she realised she hadn't mentioned something. "I forgot to mention it yesterday, but it might be a good idea to put a card advertising your business next to that arrangement on the bar."

"Can't hurt to advertise," Marilyn said. "I'll bring something when I deliver the other arrangements this afternoon. The whole place looks wonderful. It makes my shop look a bit of a dump by comparison."

"I think there are still a couple of vacant shops …," Elene suggested.

After the arrangements were on the tables, Elene showed the staff how she wanted the napkins folded. While most of the staff folded napkins, a couple of the girls polished the last of the glasses and the cutlery. One of the girls was late, and arrived about nine o'clock. Although they were only setting up the dining area, Elene asked that they wear their black uniforms. She didn't think girls in skimpy tops and shorts or jeans gave the passing public the best impression of the restaurant. The late arrival wore her black uniform as requested but the sight of her stopped Elene dead in her tracks. The rather well-endowed girl wore a see-through blouse with nothing underneath. Elene's conversation off to one side with the girl did not go well.

Elene carefully explained to the girl that her attire was inappropriate and suggested she go home to change her blouse and not come back until the afternoon shift began at four o'clock. In spite of Elene's diplomatic approach, the girl became argumentative and abusive.

"This is what I wore at the hotel I worked at before and they didn't complain," the girl spat at Elene.

"Well yes, it probably is okay for a girlie bar, but it is not acceptable for this restaurant," Elene countered.

The girl made a few abusive comments before Elene delivered the final word. "By all means, you may wear that outfit anywhere else you choose, but not here. Go home now and don't bother coming back. You will be paid until 11 o'clock which is when the morning shift is due to finish."

"You're sacking me?" the girl gasped.

"That is correct. Now leave the restaurant please."

The girl grabbed her bag from the table where she dropped it and rushed out the door, bumping heavily into Arturo on her way out and showering him with expletives. Arturo stopped, stunned for a moment, and then approached Elene.

"What's going on with the girl with the big … er, uhmm … the girl who just left?"

"I've just sacked her," Elene replied. "Her 'big er uhmms' on display did not create the right impression for this restaurant, and she refused to go home and change." Arturo was still digesting what happened as Elene continued. "You mentioned yesterday that your family owned hotels and restaurants and that you had quite a bit of experience in restaurants."

"Yes, that is true. My family owned quite a few restaurants over the years and we all worked in them."

"Good. You'll be managing the bar tonight."

"The bar? Why will I be working the bar? You have plenty of staff."

"All my staff will be waiting tables. First impressions count. I want tonight's diners to spread the word not only about the great food but also about the excellent service. We had just enough staff for tonight but now with one less, I need you to manage the bar. Are you up to the job, or not?"

"Of course I know how to run the bar."

"Excellent. Be back here appropriately dressed by five o'clock." With that, Elene stalked off to check on the napkin folding.

Still reeling, Arturo made his way to the kitchen in a bit of a daze. Beppe, at the far end of the kitchen explaining something to one of the kitchen hands, didn't notice Arturo enter the kitchen. Sam called to Beppe to come and check on something and, when Beppe turned around, he spotted Arturo peering over the bench at what Sam was preparing.

"Hey, Arturo, out! You can't just wander in here. This is a food preparation area. You can only come in here if you are wearing the appropriate gear."

"What? It is my restaurant. I can go where I like."

"You are right. You can go where you like … and I still don't have a contract, so I am not the food safety officer. In fact, I'm not sure I even work here."

"Geez, Beppe, what are you on about?"

"If a health inspector comes through that door right now, all the breaches he immediately sees will close this kitchen, cost you a massive fine, and my career will be down the toilet. So, either you go outside and suit up appropriately, or I slip out the back door now *and have never worked here. Capice?* What's it to be?"

Arturo, shaking his head in disbelief, slowly made his way out of the kitchen. Beppe started to follow him to explain more fully the health regulations relating to food preparation areas, but decided against it. He would let Arturo think about it for a while and see what eventuated.

Sam's voice brought Beppe back to reality. "Beppe, in case you've forgotten, you were coming over to see me about something before you were side-tracked."

"Sorry, Sam, what's the problem?"

"It's the alcohol called for in this recipe; we don't have any. We don't have any in our kitchen stocks and there's none in the bar. Can we substitute something else?"

"Y-e-s, we could, but it wouldn't be as good. I think we might send Arturo shopping."

Arturo sat watching the staff folding napkins, and a more dejected sight Beppe hadn't seen in a long time. "Hey, Arturo, I need your help." That had the desired effect. Arturo bounced up and came across to the kitchen door. Beppe wrote what he needed on a slip of paper and handed it to Arturo. "We need this for one of our dishes but we don't have any. Would you mind asking if they have a bottle at The Brasserie? If they can't help, maybe see if the hotel sells it."

Like all the shops, The Brasserie remained closed. As the complex didn't open that day until ten o'clock, all the shops would stay closed until just before opening time. Arturo knocked on the door to get Ginger's attention. He waved Beppe's note under Ginger's nose as soon as the door opened.

"Do you have any of this and can I buy a bottle?"

Jason wandered out of the kitchen to see what was going on. Arturo explained the restaurant's current crisis. Jason raised his eyebrows in question at Ginger who held aloft a bottle.

"We have another," Ginger reassured Jason.

"There you go, Arturo. You can go back and keep them happy. It's good to see they have you working, Art. I'd hate to think we were all busy and you were sitting around doing nothing," Jason said with a grin. "Ginger, maybe you should start an account for the restaurant. They could become one of our best customers if Beppe is going to be using lashings of alcohol in his cooking."

Arturo mumbled something that Jason couldn't hear. "What's wrong Art? Today is the big day we've all worked towards. Your new staff has rescued tonight's dinner. Why the long face? Why so grumpy?" Jason asked.

"I'm like the hired help in my own restaurant: drive to Arkana, find the alcohol, manage the bar tonight, can't go in the kitchen. They just order me around … and she has already sacked one girl."

"Beppe and Elene are the managers you hired for your restaurant. To me, it sounds like they have everything under control and I am looking forward to the dinner. Ask yourself, are they doing a good job? You've a decision to make, Art … and you have two choices…. do you want to be the big boss, or do you want a damn good restaurant? The owner and the manager are two different roles. You need to accept that you are the owner: you put up the money to establish the restaurant. They are the managers: they protect your investment and help it make a profit for the owner. The choice is pretty simple when you come right down to it."

"You are right. I am feeling just a bit unimportant -- uhmm, unnecessary – at the moment."

"*Superfluous* is the word you're looking for, mate … and you are – at least until you have to manage the bar tonight. Today, and probably from here on in, everything depends on your managers. Now, I suggest you get this alcohol back to the kitchen before your delay spoils the dish I'm supposed to eat tonight. Oh, and if you're going to be managing the bar tonight, shouldn't you be practising your cocktail shaker moves today?"

Arturo laughed. "You are right … about everything. I am just not used to not being the big boss. I can see I may have to visit this establishment every day for a while for a daily dose of therapy."

"Better start a personal account for Arturo as well," Jason called to Ginger.

All three men laughed, and Arturo saluted The Brasserie with the bottle as he departed.

In line with the lessons learned that day, Arturo didn't take the bottle into the kitchen. He stopped at the door and knocked. Sam looked up and Arturo waved the bottle at him. "You found some …" Sam said in surprise as he came over to collect it.

Beppe, some distance away, hadn't heard Arturo knock but Sam alerted him to Arturo's presence. He joined Sam and Arturo at the kitchen doorway. "I wasn't confident you would find any in town. Well done; where did you get it?"

"The Brasserie; they have another bottle so they let us have this one … well, they sold us this one. The restaurant now has an account at The Brasserie," Arturo informed him.

As Beppe discovered, in spite of the best intentions, things do not always go according to plan. His elation at having the right alcohol for Sam's dish soon disappeared. He decided to test one of the Bavarian cream bavarois prepared the previous day. The dessert that night was to be a vanilla bavarois surrounded by passionfruit coulis with a pile of tropical fruit salad on the side. It was critical that the Bavarian cream component was perfect. They made more than they needed, so there was no concern about 'wasting' one to ensure they were up to standard.

The moment the bavarois came out of the mould and landed on the plate, Beppe knew there was a problem. He picked it up and tested its texture with his fingertips. He called over the staff member who made them and thrust the plate with the bavarois at the staff member. "You made these yesterday?" The lad took the plate and nodded confirmation. "Watch this," Beppe demanded as he picked up the bavarois and bounced it on the bench top. Then he bounced it off the floor. The young lad watched in amazement as the bavarois bounced off surfaces like a rubber ball. "I think we have a small problem here, don't you? We have about 100 bavarois that nobody can eat. Tell me what ingredients you used."

"I followed your recipe exactly – and multiplied it by the right number to make 100."

"Show me the recipe you used."

The lad fetched the recipe sheet, now with his calculations scrawled on the bottom of it. Beppe wasn't concerned about the recipe – he knew that was okay – but quickly scanned the lad's calculations.

"Where did you get this figure from?" Beppe demanded jabbing at the figure for amount of gelatine to use in the mixture.

"I multiplied the amount of gelatine in the recipe by the number of bavarois we were making. See, there's the calculation."

"You mean this '200 grams' that you multiplied?" Beppe queried as he pointed to the figures.

"Yes, in the same way as I did for all the other ingredients."

"Read the recipe out to me, please." The lad started reading from the list of ingredients. Beppe stopped him when he read out the amount of gelatine. "20 grams of gelatine… not 200 grams," Beppe barked. "Empty those moulds and clean them for me while I make a new batch."

Red-faced and visibly upset, the lad retrieved the trays from the fridge and set about preparing them for Beppe's new batch.

Beppe looked up from preparing the replacement dessert. Sam standing hands on hips, looked perplexed as he peered into a fridge.

"Do we have a problem, Sam?" Beppe asked.

"N-o-o … well, I'm not sure really."

"Okay, what's bothering you?

"We seem to be preparing a lot of food for 90 people. I mean, *a lot* – like way too much for that number of diners."

"Good lad; well spotted. It's actually 92 diners at the last count but, you are right, we are preparing an excessive amount."

"Are you expecting a lot more to be added to the list by the time we are ready to start plating up?"

"Relax. No, I don't think it likely we will have any more to feed. Don't worry amount the amount of food. There is a good reason we're preparing so much. All will be revealed later." Sam shrugged and went back to work with his curiosity well roused.

Around mid-afternoon, Arturo was surprised when Beppe asked him to come into the kitchen. Dreading to think what new disaster might have befallen them, Arturo looked around apprehensively as he entered the kitchen. All of the kitchen staff gathered around one of the benches adorned by a large platter of cupcakes and a myriad of coffee mugs. The hum of chatter interspersed with bursts of laughter greeted him.

"Everyone has been flat out. I thought we all needed a break. Join us for cake and coffee, Arturo," Beppe said.

Smiling widely and nodding to everyone, Arturo took his place at the bench. Yes, the transition from being the owner and lord of his domain to being one of the workers would take some getting used to, but it was worthwhile. The mood in the kitchen had improved. It was now positively jumping. Engaging Beppe and Elene must be the best move I've made in a long time, he told himself as he helped himself to a feather-light cupcake.

The rest of the day went by without further drama. Pity the same couldn't be said for the dinner.

The Opening

Weeks, even months, of preparation and anticipation rolled by before the 'big day' finally arrived. Some experienced feelings of exhilaration and achievement. Others had a different response. Those feeling, coupled with events during that first week or so, shaped tenants' views of the future.

Everyone noticed the sign as they left the shopkeepers' breakfast. Concrete footings surrounded by safety fencing for the last few weeks now supported an impressive sign, the top of which was as high as the top of the first floor of the complex. It announced the complex's new name to the world: Harbour Plaza. Everyone going to the complex after the breakfast paused out front to scrutinise this new addition.

Most considered the name appropriate, if not particularly creative. Some questioned the process used to choose it. The more sceptical among the shopkeepers wondered whether 'Harbour Plaza' wasn't the developer's intended name from the outset.

"Well, that didn't take much thought," Edith said dismissively as the group of retirees from Busy Fingers stood admiring the new sign. "But I suppose it is better than some of the way-out suggestions I heard recently."

"I think it's appropriate; logical," Rose replied.

"Surely they wouldn't reward anyone for coming up with *that* name … but, I suppose you're right. It is logical -- and inoffensive," Edith continued.

"The sign makes the place seem more 'finished' somehow, doesn't it?" Grace commented. "Up until now, the whole thing felt like something to occupy our time. That sign brings us back to reality. This is it; we are in business … for whatever that brings."

"Come on ladies – and gentleman – we have work to do before the place is open for business. Anthony, could you give me a hand to carry some stuff in from my car, please?" Gordon Bailey asked.

The sign wasn't the only new addition to appear overnight. Every tenant paused on entering the complex that morning. The place looked transformed. It now hosted much greenery. Large tubs containing various plants and ferns occupied strategic positions under the roof skylights. Wrought iron and timber park benches alternated between the planters. These effectively divided each aisle into two 'lanes'. A jungle of planters occupied the T-junction of the aisles, just some distance out from the entrance to The Quarterdeck restaurant.

The Busy Fingers group halted as they entered the supermarket end door.

"Oh, hasn't that changed the look of the place!" Rose gasped at the sight of the greenery. "Funny how little touches like those make the place seem more inviting."

Anthony urged them forward. "Let's get into the shop. These packets of stuff Gordon gave me are heavy. Grace, would you go ahead and unlock for us, please?"

"That looks like where all the action will be this morning," Vera commented, pointing to a roped off area.

Bollards and rope fenced off a small area in front of the massed planters at the junction of the aisles. Vera was right. This was where the official business of the day would happen. A lectern and microphone occupying the enclosure suggested the official opening ceremony would involve a much speech making. A 'cutting of the ribbon' ceremony would happen prior to opening the doors, but the set-up inside suggested more official action once the public came in.

A further new overnight addition met with the unanimous approval of the shopkeepers. A stores' directory helped shoppers find their way through the complex. The wooden signpost stood in front of the plants at the junction of the aisles, although now partly hidden by the temporary lectern and microphone arrangement. Stained to match the bench seats, the post had many arms, each one pointing in the direction of the shop whose name it bore. A myriad of ferns surrounding the base of the post helped it blend in.

The top storey was incomplete. It remained a shell, a work in progress at present. While it would eventually house a number of spaces, the developer's primary objective remained to open the shopping component of the complex on time.

Work on the new centre management's office remained unfinished. The tower at the rear of the building, which housed the lift and escalators to the top floor, remained firmly closed. It would remain locked for some time to come to prevent the public from venturing upstairs where work continued.

Once inside their shop, the Busy Fingers crew noticed lights already in The Quarterdeck and The Brasserie. They waved at Cecile as she let herself into La Boulangerie. Gordon opened the first of the parcels he and Anthony dumped on the staffroom table. He called the rest of the crew to the staffroom. "In the time we have before opening this morning, I thought we might get ourselves a bit organised," he suggested.

"Organised…! What do you think we have been doing for the last how many weeks?" Edith retorted. Gordon ignored her.

"These are flyers to advertise our planned program of craft workshops. I thought we might place one in every carry bag so everyone purchasing something also walks out of the place with a flyer. If we do this now, we won't have to remember to shove one in the bag every time we serve someone."

"Good thinking, Gordon," Jane exclaimed. "Let's get started. There seems to be a lot in these parcels. Do we have to put all of this in bags before we open?"

"No, just what we think will be enough for today. Then, whenever we have spare time, we prepare more bags for future trading. Not all of the parcels contain flyers. Some contain the vouchers for that discount initiative we agreed to participate in."

"Let's be optimistic about today and prepare a lot of bags," Lois suggested with a wry grin. "While we're about it, someone should tell me again how this voucher thing is supposed to work."

Anthony sighed patiently and began to speak. Gordon cut him off. "Explain while you work, Anthony," he commanded.

"Thank you, Gordon -- see, shoving things in bags while explaining. Right then, the voucher program… As you will remember, most of the stores, with the exception of the restaurant and brasserie, agreed to participate in a discount voucher program during the first week of trading. If it proves successful, we might extend it for the first month."

Anthony glanced around the table as the group nodded knowingly. "Good. What it means for Busy Fingers is that anyone who spends more than $30 receives a $5 discount voucher to use at any of the participating businesses in the complex, including ours if they wish to make future purchases. Likewise, those other businesses will issue vouchers according to whatever they set as their trigger point."

"What do you mean by 'trigger point'?" Rose queried.

"We have set more than $30 as our trigger point, but others set different amounts. For example, Alexia at Embellish set $50, while her mother set more than $80 as the trigger at the fashion boutique."

"So, what happens to these vouchers after they are handed out?" Rose asked.

"If someone presents a voucher, we apply the $5 discount. Then, at the end of the week, all the participating storeowners will gather to 'balance the books' so to speak … that is, to find out who owes what to whom. Everyone clear on that now?"

Anthony gradually raised his voice throughout the explanation, ending up a little hoarse. "What the hell is that racket coming from upstairs?" he demanded. "Surely they're not working up there today. That noise is not a great welcome for shoppers."

"I guess that's for others to know and for us to wonder about," Gordon replied sagely.

The Quarterdeck staff worked until ten o'clock on setting up the dining area to ensure it looked impressive to passers-by during the day. Then Elene sent them to take-in the official opening function, before they went home for the rest of the day -- on the clear understanding they would be back by five o'clock. With her staff gone, there was only Arturo in the dining area … and he was busy fluffing around with his bar in readiness for tonight's dinner. Elene decided to see if she could do to help in the kitchen.

Only Beppe, Sam and a couple of kitchen hands were in this morning. All kitchen personnel would come later in the afternoon to ensure the first course plates hit the tables right on seven o'clock.

"We don't need a hand with anything at the moment, thanks. If you're looking for something to do -- and don't want to go back to the boat for the rest of the day – you could have a look over those menus I've prepared for the next month. If they look all right, type them up ready for printing. You might also show them to Arturo and encourage him to come up with some stunning new drinks to accompany them."

She and Beppe had discussed the long term running of the bar. Both agreed with keeping Arturo on for as long as they could. It felt good having the restaurant owner involved, but not actually meddling in running the place. Elene would discuss that with Arturo sometime in the future, but not today.

A few minutes before ten o'clock, soft piped music floated through the complex; Mozart. Nice, Beppe thought. If they stick with that sort of music, it will work well for our future lunchtime diners. He was so busy he hadn't followed up a thought that occurred to him periodically – usually when he was in the middle of doing something. Prompted by the music, that thought now screamed for attention. He rushed out to the dining area.

"Hey, guys, do you reckon we could find some musicians at such short notice?"

"Don't ask us; we're new in town," Elene replied as she and Arturo shrugged at each other, "But I don't like your chances. Why not ask Gordon…? He might know somebody." Beppe strode off and banged on the door of Busy Fingers.

Gordon closed the door after letting Beppe in. "What's the problem, mate? You look a bit agitated."

"Musicians, Gordon; do you know any who might be available for tonight?"

"Hmm, maybe, but you better tell me what you have in mind."

"I thought maybe just a couple of musicians to play soft music while guests are eating; nothing loud or dance music, you understand. Just music to create the soft ambiance you don't get with recorded music. They would play during the pre-dinner drinks and while people eat – not during the speeches of course – and we would pay them and feed them afterwards. It won't go late I don't think; probably be all over before ten o'clock."

"Just so happens I do know a couple; classically trained. They live in a cottage at the retirement complex. She plays keyboard and he plays a number of instruments, but usually the violin. If they are interested, they should be available. It's unlikely they have anything else on tonight. I'll go and ask if they are interested. If so, they should come and chat to you. Okay?"

"Thank you. I owe you again."

"Yes, and your debt just about amounts to a meal at the restaurant," Gordon replied with a grin.

"…And a bottle of wine to go with it," Beppe added.

After advising he would be missing for a while, Gordon drove to the retirement complex. Ruth invited him in. They were having morning tea. Over a cuppa with Ruth and her husband, Lionel, Gordon explained the reason for his visit.

"Some Schubert and Vivaldi …" Ruth asked her husband. "What do you think?"

"Y-e-s, I think so. Chopin might be too heavy."

"So, you are interesting in playing at the dinner tonight?" Gordon asked.

"Of course," Lionel replied emphatically. "Any opportunity to play for an audience is wonderful. We do need to talk to this chap beforehand though. What did you say his name was?"

"Beppe … if you like, I could take you there now."

Gordon banged on the back door of the restaurant and Sam let in the trio. Leaving the musicians to their discussions with Beppe, Gordon wandered out to fill in time by annoying Arturo. Their discussions took only a few minutes, and Beppe and the musicians soon joined Gordon and Arturo. Beppe grimaced as he posed his question to Elene.

"Where do you think we should locate our musicians tonight? I know you have planned tonight's layout, but could it be altered a bit to fit them in?"

She gave him an eye roll then laughed. "I've been thinking about it since you mentioned musicians. I think we could set them up over there." She indicated a corner near the bar. "There are power outlets if they need them. They wouldn't be in the way of the wait staff and they will be far enough away from all the diners to be heard but not intrusive." She turned to Ruth and Lionel and asked, "How does that sound?"

Everyone was happy with Elene's suggestion. Ruth said they would need only a couple of comfortable chairs and maybe a small side table to hold any bits and pieces they might bring. They arranged to come back around five o'clock to set up. Gordon drove the couple back to the retirement complex where they planned to work on their evening's repertoire. When Gordon returned to Busy Fingers, the Plaza was open for business and most of the shops were dealing with their first customers.

"Good of you to remember us," Anthony hissed as Gordon joined him behind the counter. There appeared to be a break between customers, so Gordon chose to pursue Anthony's comment rather than ignore it.

"I've been busy organising something to make tonight's dinner even more enjoyable for everyone. … and, while I was about it, I found out what created all the noise above our heads this morning."

"Whatever it was, it stopped just before the opening ceremony," Anthony responded.

"A large plastic banner now wrapped around the upper storey announces to the world in very large letters that we are open. The noise we heard was the workmen installing the banner."

"It's a shame you missed the opening while you were away. Your friend Bella took photos of everything though," Rose informed Gordon. "We didn't see what happened outside the front door. However, it only took a few minutes. Someone said the only thing was the mayor cut the ribbon. Then they opened one side of the big doors so people had to file through no more than two abreast. The cleaners, the security guard and that bloke Winston handed each person a lucky number ticket as they came in. Apparently, there are a few prizes to be won, with the winners being drawn at the end of the fashion parade … which, by the look of things, is about to start."

"Thanks, Rose, but I don't think I'll lose too much sleep over having missed all the speeches. Fashion parades also don't hold much appeal for Anthony or me. So, why don't we look after the shop while you ladies take yourselves off to watch the parade?"

Anthony opened his mouth to complain, but a hard look from Gordon silenced his protest. Happy to leave the men in charge, the women joined the crowd watching the parade. A gaggle of potential customers entered the shop as the women left. Apparently, there were others also unexcited by a fashion parade.

Diana Jacobson sat with her eyes firmly closed as hairdresser Paige Mathews coaxed a few obstinate strands into place around Diana's face before applying a mega dose of hairspray to the new hairdo. It felt like she had been sitting in Waves Salon for most of the morning – most of the time with her eyes closed -- for make-up and a new hairstyle. Her mind kept drifting back to that conversation a few weeks ago when Paige insisted Diana's hair looked jaded and needed 'jazzing up' a bit. "Your hair is a great base shade. It will work wonderfully with some innovative colouring," Paige insisted.

The prospect of dealing with regrowth as the colour grew out did not appeal, and Diana strenuously resisted the move. Paige persisted, going to great lengths to convince Diana she wouldn't have a regrowth problem. "Don't be silly. I'll work with foils just to give you highlights she insisted."

Paige, knowing all the right buttons to press, slowly wore down Diana's reluctance. Diana gave in, but not before Paige agreed to change from a permanent colour to a semi-permanent product. Still questioning her own sanity, the previous evening Diana went to Paige's home salon to be 'jazzed up'. The colour application took ages. It was quite late by the time they finished. Both women were tired. Diana left with her hair still wet rather than spend more time having her hair dried. Paige wasn't concerned. Diana was a hairdresser and could do it herself.

As Diana walked into her home, she caught sight of her hair in the hall mirror. She gasped in horror. "My God, what has she done to me?" Her thick thatch now resembled a patchwork quilt. All she could see was splodges of colour randomly scattered all over her head. "Well, Paige will have to work miracles to make something presentable of this mess tomorrow," she informed the mirror.

Waves Salon, Paige's new salon in the Plaza, was doing all the models' hair and make-up for Mariah Obrin's fashion parade. Diana had the last appointment before the parade. With more than a little reluctance, she arrived on time for her appointment and sat stonily, rejecting Paige's attempts at conversation throughout the whole procedure.

Paige's voice brought her back from her reverie and her sulk. "All done; what do you think of the back?" Paige asked as she angled a mirror behind Diana's head so she could see the back of her hairdo.

Diana's eyes snapped open and she stared at the wall mirror. Is that really me, she asked herself. What a transformation … the hair is amazing. The moment was lost when Patsy Evans clomped into the salon on her crutches, her gashed foot still heavily bandaged.

"Oh, God, you look stunning," Patsy gasped and then stood transfixed by Diana's transformation.

"You wanted something, Patsy?" Paige asked.

"Eh? Oh yes; Diana, Mariah is frantic you haven't your first outfit on yet. She's a little tetchy. Do you think you could hurry it up a bit?"

Diana checked the clock on the wall high above the basins. "Geez, I'm late. It won't take me a minute to change," she added over her shoulder as she headed for Mariah's boutique nextdoor.

She changed into the glamorous after-five outfit and Patsy zipped it up. Then Diana slipped on the pair of killer heels that went with the outfit. Realising there was now only one ahead of her in the line-up of models to go out, Diana rushed over as best she could to take her place in the queue. She spent a bit of time over the last few days getting used to the very high stilettoes, but still didn't feel confident walking in them.

There it was: her cue. Filled with trepidation, she sashayed out onto the makeshift 'catwalk' for the long trek down the undercover area at the rear of the Plaza, in through the supermarket end doors and down the main aisle of the complex to return to the boutique. As soon as she was safely back in the boutique and out of sight by the public, Diana slipped off the shoes and padded across to her change area in stockinged feet.

Despite a few wobbles along the way, she made it back to the boutique without falling off the heels and breaking an ankle, or having something else equally undignified occur. She only had two outfits to model. The second one was a casual outfit of slacks and matching top teamed with a lovely pair of colourful *flat* sandals and an eye-catching tote bag. She changed quickly, strapped on the sandals and grabbed the tote bag Patsy handed to her. In a much lighter frame of mind, she took her place once again in the line-up of models awaiting their cues to show off their outfits.

Gordon Bailey looked up from serving a customer to see the parade's final model go past on her way back to the boutique. Busy Fingers received a steady stream of customers despite the distraction of the fashion parade. Anthony was not impressed that only the two men were there to deal with them. Gordon also found himself struggling when a woman asked questions about the suitability of a particular fabric for her next sewing project. But they had managed and, with the parade now over, the women would return.

During the fashion parade, the cleaners rearranged the bollards to create a smaller roped-off area around the lectern. A few minutes after the parade ended, the public address system urged everyone to make their way to the roped-off area for the lucky door prize draws. Geoff Robinson had the microphone. When he believed most shoppers had gathered around, he introduced the local magistrate who tumbled the barrel and the local top cop who drew out the winning numbers.

The draw took longer than expected. It turned into a rowdy affair punctuated by much clapping and shrieks of delight that echoed through the complex. Finally, all prizes were drawn and Geoff took the winners off to the makeshift centre management office – currently occupying space in the cleaners' area – to complete paperwork and collect their vouchers. Prizes included a weekend for two at an Arkana Beach resort, dinner for two at The Quarterdeck, and a number of vouchers of varying amounts for use against purchases from Plaza stores.

By the time the women returned after the parade, it was lunchtime. They agreed to go for lunch in pairs while the rest remained 'on duty' to deal with customers. Edith and Jane were first to take a lunch break but, by then, it was already after one o'clock.

Plonking herself down at the table with her lunch, Jane sighed. "Hasn't today been exhilarating? I know we've been so busy because it's the opening and it won't be like this every day but, so far, it has been exciting."

"I can't wait for five o'clock," Edith snarled. "I've been on my feet since the breakfast, and there hasn't been any let up all day."

"Oh, I'm sorry. I forgot; you're a glass half-empty type of person. Of course it wouldn't excite you that what we've been working for so hard over the last month or so has gone so well today."

"There's no need to be like that," Edith retorted as Jane put her lunch back in the fridge and slammed its door. "I'm old. I shouldn't have to be doing things like this at my age. It's unfair to expect me to be standing around all day," she whined.

"*Old* is a state of mind, Edith, and for the record, you're six months younger than I am. That makes you youngest in our group. You didn't have to become part of Busy Fingers but you chose to … and, no doubt, you'll be only too happy to hold your hand out for your share of any profits."

"I beg your pardon. How dare you ….?"

"How dare I speak to you like that? Let me tell you. I've had it with your negativity. We put up with it because that's how you are. People have worked hard to make this business happen and it has given them a new interest, almost a new lease on life. The least you can do is not kill it for them. So, if you can't be positive about it, just shut up. Oh, and while I have the floor, nobody expects any of us to be here all day every day. Today is an exception to the way we will operate – as you well know."

With that, Jane stormed out of the staffroom, leaving a stunned Edith with a sandwich halfway to her mouth. Storming out to the front of the store, Jane asked, "Who is next for lunch? I'm finished." She went to one of the display bins and started tidying it.

"I'll go next," Grace said, raising an eyebrow questioningly at Gordon and Anthony as she walked past. The sight that greeted her as she entered the staffroom alarmed her.

Her half-eaten sandwich abandoned on the table, tears trickled down Edith's cheeks. As she passed the staffroom door earlier, Grace thought she heard raised voices, and it looked like Edith was on the receiving end. There was no mistaking Jane's anger when she emerged from the staffroom.

Oh dear, how do I handle this, Grace asked herself. She walked over and put an arm around Edith's shoulders. "Come on, dry those eyes and get that food into you. This is our big day and we need all the sustenance we can get to see us through to the end of it. Would you like to take a break? Maybe go home for a bit of a rest this afternoon?" Grace asked gently.

Edith shook her head violently. "No, I'm going to do my bit. She was right though … Jane, I mean. She was right. I didn't have to be involved and I don't have to be here … but I want to be."

"That's right. Nobody is forcing you to do anything, and nobody will ask you to do something you don't want to do. From the outset, your designated role was the bookkeeper – and you have done an excellent job. We all have different skills to contribute, and differing amounts of time available to serve here in the store. Keeping track of our finances and knitting and crocheting things for us to sell are your important contribution to the business. They should be your priority."

"But I won't be seen to be pulling my weight if I don't spend as much time in the shop as everyone else does."

"That's rubbish. Think about Gordon. He is only part-time because of the writing he still does, but he will create all our advertising material. And, when he is out of town, he will be collecting information on what others are selling and their prices."

Edith sniffed loudly. "She was right you know …"

"We've just been through all that," Grace exclaimed.

"No, I mean about it being an exciting day. It is. I don't know why I always find something negative to say … but it is exciting to see so many sales today."

"Tell you what, how about we take a long lunch break and go for a quick look at the exhibition?" Grace suggested and, holding up her hand, continued, "No arguments; they can manage without us for a little while. Come on!"

As they emerged from the staffroom, Grace noticed Anthony's concerned expression as he watched Edith. Grace gave him a wink and announced airily, "We'll be back shortly," as she led Edith out of the shop.

They paused as they entered the exhibition. The art group set up a display of Mothers' Day cards just inside the door. All hand painted, they presented a wide range of images. No text impaired the artwork. All text was inside the card, making the card suitable for framing later as a miniature artwork.

A considerable crowd still viewed the exhibition. The two women decided it wasn't the best time to be there and left after a quick look around. Although they spent little time there, they caught enough snatches of viewers' conversations to know that the paintings and photographs were just right for The Academy's opening exhibition. People related the works to their own cyclone experiences, which they discussed with others viewers. This exhibition might just manage to contribute to the healing process.

Returning to Busy Fingers, Grace watched Jane draw Edith aside and walk off to the staffroom with her, and she noted the relieved look on Anthony's face when both women later emerged from the staffroom laughing.

Five o'clock arrived with amazing speed and it was with a sigh of relief that Busy Fingers closed its doors. The crew wasted no time in returning to the retirement complex to get ready for the official dinner. Gordon took Grace, Rose and Vera in his car, while Edith, Jane and Lois went with Anthony. Silence reigned in Gordon's car for some distance before he spoke.

"Has everyone gone to sleep? It's awfully quiet in here."

"I was trying to work out how much rest I could fit in before having to tart myself up for tonight," Grace admitted with a giggle. "It's different for you blokes. You just have to throw on a shirt and suit and you're right to go."

"Don't forget about the shower and shave, shoes and socks and combing the curls," Gordon added.

They all laughed and Rose gasped, "Ooh, don't make me laugh, I'm too exhausted."

"Aren't we all?" Vera added. "I hope none of us expires during the dinner tonight."

"Well ladies, tomorrow we have to do it again – probably for the whole weekend. I reckon it'll be Monday before things quieten down a bit. What do you think about asking the others over dinner tonight how they feel about rostering on half the gang for half a day at a time?" There was unanimous support for the idea, and they believed there would be no argument from the others.

Ruth and Lionel pulled into the carpark just on five o'clock. Elene summoned some of her staff to help carry the musicians' gear to the restaurant. Her phone rang about ten minutes later. It was Marilyn, the florist. She was about to leave for the Plaza. Elene rounded up her staff again and led them to the supermarket-end doors in readiness to assist with bringing in the table arrangements.

The florist's van parked beside the doors. There was a collective gasp from the staff when Marilyn opened the van's rear doors. The stunning live table arrangements filled the special rack in the rear of the van. Marilyn handed an arrangement to each staff member who, under her watchful eye, carried it carefully back to the restaurant while she and Elene trailed along behind the procession. Each staff member placed her arrangement in the centre of a table she would look after that night.

The musicians set up in their little alcove. Lionel decided dress for tonight should be black tie, while Ruth wore a simple full-length black gown. She set up her keyboard and Lionel had his cello in its stand and his violin on the table. Elene felt justifiably satisfied as she stood back and surveyed her domain while Marilyn placed the last arrangement on a table. Marilyn came to stand beside her. "The place looks absolutely amazing," Marilyn whispered, as if in some holy place. "Oyster Point has never seen the likes of this before. It's breathtaking."

Elene smiled but did a double take when she glanced at Arturo. He grinned so broadly with pride, Elene was afraid his face might split. Just then, Beppe came out to investigate all the fuss. On entering the dining area, he stopped dead and looked around. "Very impressive," he said economically before returning to the kitchen, but Elene saw his eyes light up in appreciation. For her, there was no greater accolade.

At 6.25pm, Connor unlocked the supermarket-end doors, leaving them closed, and then took up his position just inside the doors ready to admit guests on their arrival. It was decided to do this rather than leave the doors open and run the risk of having uninvited members of the public wander in. Within a couple of minutes, the first guests arrived. They came in a rush and were all in the restaurant, drinks in hand, in no time.

As Connor closed the doors after the last guest on the list's arrival, he chuckled to himself at a less than charitable thought. It appeared to him everybody rushed in early to make the most of the half hour of free drinks before the dinner began. The last guest to arrive was Rick Winston. Connor felt a little uneasy as he watched Winston make his way to the restaurant. After admitting Winston, Connor waited by the door for a couple of minutes in case of any late additions to the guest list he wasn't aware. After no further arrivals, he made his way back to his room from where he would monitor the Plaza until after everyone left and he could set the alarm and the lock up for the night.

Two of the wait staff greeted guests as they arrived and handed each guest their name badge. Staff circulated with drinks trays and Arturo was busy behind the bar keeping glasses filled and taking care of special requests. Elene adopted a watching brief near the bar from where she could see all of the drinks area and be ready to jump in to assist with any situation if needed. Rick Winston was last to arrive and trailed the other guests by a minute or so. By the time he arrived, one of the girls handing out name badges had gone to help with drinks, leaving only one lass at the badge table.

She greeted Winston and asked his name. She was required to ask each guest their name before handing them their badge and, although only one badge remained on the table, she applied the same procedure to Winston as everyone else. Winston didn't answer when asked his name, and simply held out his hand for his badge. The girl asked his name again… still no answer. Winston made a grab for the badge on the table, but the girl was quicker. A split second before Winston tried to grab the badge, she picked it up and held it in her hand, but was unsure what to do next.

Elene witnessed the scene and moved to intervene. As she approached, she saw Winston make a grab for the badge. "Mr Winston! What do you think you're doing?" Elene hissed as she arrived beside him. "You are no different from every other guest at this function. They all had to state their names before receiving their badges. She asked politely for your name -- twice. Please answer the staff member or leave."

Winston rounded on Elene ready for an argument, but one look at an angry Elene was enough. He backed down. Elene took the badge from the girl and handed it to Winston, giving him a warning as she did so. "Your behaviour will be closely monitored this evening. I strongly advise you to behave yourself or I will have you ejected." Winston snatched the badge and moved off into the crowd. After a few soothing words to the girl, Elene moved back to the bar.

"Everything all right…?" Arturo enquired.

"For the moment … but we need to watch him. There is a strong smell of alcohol about him already." Elene was unaware, but Geoff Robinson, engaged in a conversation with a group of dignitaries from which he could not extricate himself, had watched the whole Rick Winston episode with growing distaste.

Shortly after, guests moved to the dining area and wait staff busied themselves with settling their guests at the tables. Then, right on seven o'clock, a procession of wait staff bearing the first course emerged from the kitchen. As everyone began eating, the previous buzz of conversation died, replaced by murmurs of approval. The musicians continued playing as they did throughout the drinks period.

The musicians were a great idea," Arturo confided to Elene.

"Yes, their music is just beautiful; perfect for a restaurant, and they know what they are doing," she observed as they stopped playing.

Ruth noticed the master of ceremonies rise and make his way to the microphone; the musicians' cue that speeches were to follow. The rest of the evening went smoothly. The few speeches for the evening interspersed the delivery or courses and the removal of plates … and the musicians continued to serenade diners at all the appropriate times. Finally, they served the last course and delivered the closing speeches. A spare table set up to one side held cheese platters and glasses of port for those who wished to partake before leaving.

Many of the guests left immediately after the final course. However, a few opted to linger over port for continued conversations and networking. Rick Winston was one of those who chose to stay. Elene watched him make his way to the table. Apart from being surly all night, he had behaved himself reasonably well. She became concerned now though. He was decidedly unsteady on his feet. Would he make a spectacle of himself by falling over or, worse still, by spilling a glass of port over another guest?

Winston was the acting plaza manager. All the guests knew of his association with the place. Geoff Robinson in particular, and probably anyone else with a stake in the future of the plaza would not be pleased to see Winston create an embarrassing situation. Elene relaxed a little. Everything seemed to be going okay. However, all was well for only a few minutes, before a nasty situation began developing in the midst of the remaining guests.

Winston initiated a conversation with one of the male guests. He became agitated, and the conversation quickly became heated. The man skilfully inched his way through the other guests and away from the crowd. Winston remained glued to his quarry as they ended up in an unoccupied space near the bar. Along the way, Winston became louder and more offensive. Elene realised the guest was trying to manoeuvre Winston out of the restaurant. It didn't work. Winston took up a position between the man and the door. By then, Winston was shouting and peppering his tirade with obscenities.

The man tried to diffuse the situation with comments like 'don't make a scene', 'stay calm' but, if anything, his efforts further inflamed the situation.

Hand me the phone please, Arturo," Elene demanded. Earlier in the evening, when things were busy, Arturo shoved the phone under the bar. It took him a moment to locate it.

Winston began jabbing his finger towards the man as he ranted. Gordon Bailey came to stand beside Elene. "Should I intervene?" he asked quietly. By the time Gordon asked his question, Winston had progressed to prodding the man in the chest.

"No, I don't want anyone getting hurt. Who is that man, do you know?"

"He's a Councillor … uhmm, Reynolds, I think his name is. He has the Town Planning portfolio in Council."

Connor was on his way back to the restaurant to check how many guests remained and how much longer they were likely to stay when he heard the shouting. He quickened his pace.

The guest managed to slide a couple of paces away from his unsteady adversary, resulting in Winston's next prod missing its mark. Winston almost fell on his face when it didn't connect. Further enraged, he attempted to punch the guest. His attack was halted mid-swing by a well-muscled arm tightly encircling his neck. Winston was powerless against Connor's grip and slid along on his heels as Connor dragged him backwards out of the restaurant.

Elene had hit the speed dial number for Connor just as he appeared in the restaurant. She killed the call and stood watching as Connor dragged Winston down the main aisle and out of sight from the restaurant. Confident they were out of sight, Connor spun his quarry around, bringing Winston's arm up behind his back. He propelled him through the doors, tumbling him out onto the bitumen. Winston landed on all fours. He struggled to his feet and made to rush back in, but changed his mind at the sight of the huge man standing poised with knees flexed and hands on hips.

"I'll call you a cab if you like," Connor offered. "It would not be wise to drive home. The top cop is inside and his officers are checking everyone leaving the dinner." His offer met with a string of obscenities.

Winston staggered off to his car and, with some difficulty, managed to get his bloated body into it. Because he was last to arrive for the dinner, he was parked well back in the carpark. Many other vehicles had left by then, leaving a clear space around Winston's car. Connor pulled out his phone as he heard Winston's car start after a couple of attempts. Connor, speaking on his phone, thought he heard Winston scrape something as he exited via the carpark entrance. The red and blue flashing lights and single brief shrill of the police siren happened before Winston travelled more than 100 metres along Main Street.

Connor stood for a moment before returning inside. When he was halfway back to the restaurant, Geoff Robinson met him in the aisle. "…Everything all right?" Geoff asked.

"Depends what you mean by 'all right'. Your plaza manager was just arrested for drink driving."

"Thanks for your intervention, Connor; well done. If you should happen to get any trouble from Winston, I want to know about it immediately. That's not a suggestion, it's an order. Understood?"

"Sir …" Connor replied and dropped him a mock salute.

Over the next few minutes, the remaining guests traipsed out. Beppe brought on his surprise. All of the staff, including the musicians, sat down to exactly the same meal as the guests had enjoyed. "It's my way of saying thank you," he told them, "And to celebrate the opening of The Quarterdeck."

Vera checked her watch. It was nearly 10.00am. She wanted to duck down to Bedecked & Bedazzled to see if that top she liked was still there. If she went now, she would be back to cover the shop by the time the rest of the gang went for morning tea. As she passed Embellish, she noticed there were about three customers in the shop. The Plaza had been busy since it opened on Saturday morning and the crowd seemed to be growing by the hour.

The blouse she lusted after was still on the rack. She told Mariah, the boutique owner, "If it hasn't sold by the end of the weekend, please put it away for me and I'll pick it up and pay for it on Monday." Her errand completed, Vera headed back towards Busy Fingers, checking out the shops as she went. There were customers in Embellish again – this time, she could see four – but she couldn't see Alexia.

Something wasn't right, so she went in. No Alexia. Unsure what was happening, but aware people can't just wander around in an unattended shop, Vera offered to assist customers. She was finalising a cash sale for one customer, when she heard the shop's toilet flush. Alexia came out, her face ashen. Alexia dealt with the next customer who paid for several items by credit card, while Vera dealt with the other two customers. Both were single item cash sales, and Vera put them through quickly. She completed the last sale at the same time as Alexia finished packing all the other customer's items into a carry bag. As the three customers left the shop, Vera asked Alexia if she was all right – although obviously she wasn't.

"It must be something I've eaten," Alexia replied. "I was more or less okay this morning, but it's gotten worse as the day went on. I'll probably be all right for the rest of the day. Oops, sorry; I've got to go again."

Vera followed her as far as the stock room and heard her throwing up in the toilet. When Alexia returned to the shop, Vera noted that she looked even worse than before. Alexia assured Vera she was fine, and Vera walked out of the shop. She didn't go back to Busy Fingers. Once outside Embellish, Vera turned on her heel and headed back to Bedazzled. She found Mariah tidying a rack at the far end of the shop, and alerted her to Alexia's condition.

"Good Lord," Mariah exclaimed. "Today of all days. I noticed she was off-colour all week. I even asked her at one stage if she was pregnant. That didn't win me any compliments. What am I going to do?"

"Well, I'm sorry Mariah, she really should go home. She is not going to be much use to you today, and you really can't have people wandering round unsupervised in the shop. They could walk off with half your stock."

"Yes, I know, but I can't leave this shop to take her home," Mariah answered.

While Vera and Mariah were discussing Alexia, Moira Whitlock emerged from one of the fitting rooms with a number of garments draped over her arm. "For goodness sake, Mariah, what's more important?" Moira demanded. "Go and take the girl home. I can hold the fort here until you get back. I'm no stranger to retail, and I know enough about fashion to be able to assist customers."

"Go, Mariah," Vera urged the boutique owner. "I can look after Embellish – well, for a while anyway. How much time I can give will depend on how busy we are in our shop and how many of the gang turn up today."

"Thank you, ladies. I'll be back soon as I can." With that, Mariah was on her way across to her daughter.

There were already three customers at Embellish when Vera arrived, and more checking out the window display. They kept her busy for quite a while but, as soon as she had a quiet moment, she rang Busy Fingers to let them know what happened and to make sure they could manage without her.

True to her word, Mariah was not gone long. When she returned, she went firstly to Embellish to thank Vera, before returning to her boutique. Mariah knew Vera needed to be back in her own shop, so she asked Moira if she would go across to look after Embellish. Moira was happy to oblige.

Alexia only appeared at the Plaza on a few brief occasions during the following week. However, on the Friday, she announced she was going to Arkana Beach for the weekend with a couple of friends. She assured her mother she felt much better and probably would spend the weekend just lying by the pool. She arranged for Moira to look after Embellish in her absence. Planned long ago, she wasn't going to miss this weekend. A fierce argument occurred over Alexia's trip away for the weekend when she had been so ill all week. However, when Mariah returned home on Friday evening, Alexia had gone, leaving a note saying she would return on Sunday evening.

Not long after opening on Sunday morning, Mariah was adding new stock to one of the racks, when one of Alexia's friends came into the shop. She nervously approached Mariah, but before she could speak, Mariah realised she was one of the friends who accompanied Alexia to Arkana Beach. With her heart beating wildly, Mariah rushed to meet the girl, and felt herself go weak at the knees when the girl told her what happened. They had taken Alexia to Emergency at the local hospital. The other friend who was with her at Arkana stayed at the hospital with Alexia.

Alexia, not well on Friday night, became worse on Saturday. By Saturday night, her friends were concerned and pressured her to let them take her to the medical centre. Alexia refused to go, but became very ill during the night. By Sunday morning, she was unable to move and lapsing in and out of consciousness. Her two friends enlisted the aid of a couple of men from the neighbouring unit to help carry Alexia out to the car. They left for home with Alexia lying strapped to the back seat. She was in no fit state to argue when they took her directly to Oyster Point hospital.

Mariah grabbed her bag and ran towards Embellish. She wanted Moira to close that shop and go across to look after the boutique. However, as Mariah was about to go into Embellish, she saw Vera wandering back from chatting to Meagan at the coffee shop. Mariah grabbed Vera, pulled her into Embellish and asked her to look after that shop while Moira managed the boutique. She gave the two women minimal details regarding Alexia, but enough for them to understand that this was an emergency and that Alexia was seriously ill.

The other two girls and Mariah waited in an area outside Alexia's treatment area. When they still hadn't received any news of Alexia's condition, Mariah suggested the two girls go home, telling them that she would ring them as soon as she knew more. The waiting seemed to drag on forever. It was lunchtime before a doctor came out to speak to Mariah.

"You're Alexia's mother?" Receiving a confirmation nod from Mariah he continued. "I'm sorry to have to tell you, Mrs Obrin, your daughter is critically ill. Has she been unwell at all lately?"

Mariah explained how Alexia seemed to have suffered varying degrees of illness over the last couple of weeks but, last Friday, she said she was feeling much better – well enough to go to Arkana for the weekend. She demanded to know what was wrong with Alexia.

The doctor studied his hands for moment before answering. "Your daughter had appendicitis. Sometime over the weekend her appendix ruptured, peritonitis set in, followed by septicaemia. I have to tell you we are doing everything we can to save her, but her situation is grave. It is all we can do to keep her alive, and it doesn't appear we're winning the battle. I need to go back in there to help with your daughter, but I felt you needed to know." He left Mariah shocked and numb in the waiting area.

As usual, most of the Plaza shops closed at two o'clock on Sunday afternoon. Moira collected the keys and takings from Vera, and adding them to her own, drove to the hospital. She found the correct waiting area but Mariah wasn't there. Thinking they might have moved, Moira was about to leave when Mariah staggered out of the treatment room and leant against the wall. She was sobbing uncontrollably, tears streaming down her face. A nurse followed her out of the room, put an arm around Mariah and shepherded her to a seat. She spoke quietly to Mariah and then, realising Moira was there to comfort Mariah, left the two women together.

Mariah's deep heartbreaking sobs brought on a coughing fit. Moira crossed the room to the drinking fountain and brought her a cup of water. A few moments later, in between sobs and sniffles, Mariah delivered the tragic news. "She is dead. There was nothing they could do. My little girl died a few minutes ago."

Moira fought back her own tears as she held Mariah tightly. After checking with the nurse that it was okay to leave, Moira drove Mariah home in Mariah's car. Mariah's neighbour came over to investigate. When she heard the story, she told Moira to go, as she would spend the night with Mariah. Shortly after, Vera pulled up in front of Mariah's house. Moira's phone call to Vera briefly explained the situation. She asked Vera to take her back to the hospital so she could collect her own car. On the way, she told Vera that Mariah asked if they could keep both shops open, and only close them on the day of the funeral. She didn't know when the funeral would be, as there probably would be an autopsy before they released Alexia's body, and there could be a further delay if her grandparents wanted to come from the States.

Either Moira or Vera went to see Mariah every evening. On one such visit, she opened up to Moira. "Alexia always had her demons, right from when she was a little thing. She battled them all her life -- whatever ones they were at the time. She adored her father, so that was another demon she battled."

Moira was puzzled and asked, "What happened with Alexia's father?"

"Oh, I've never spoken about it, have I? My husband, Alexia's father, was a marine killed in Iraq in 2003. Yes, she was always a troubled child – and her father's death only made things worse – but she was my little girl, and now she's gone." Both women sat in silence for a few moments before Mariah continued. "All of her grandparents are coming over. There'll be a cremation after they arrive. Then they will take Alexia's ashes back to the States for burial with her father. I'll probably go back with them for a couple of weeks. So, I'm hoping you and Vera will continue to manage the shops until I get on top of all of this."

Moira assured her it was the least they could do, and that Mariah shouldn't bother herself about the shops. As Moira walked out to her car, she phoned Vera. It looked like they both were going to be working full-time for a while.

Caffeine Heaven

From the very day Oyster Point became a settlement, life here was never without its dramas. This new shopping complex mirrored that history perfectly. As is always the case, some fulfil their dreams while others' dreams are shattered... often accompanied by much drama.

"Do you think Meagan is all right?" Grace, asked Vera as she opened Busy Fingers for the day. "She looks haggard lately. I know the coffee shop has been busy. Maybe it's just the workload and the long hours taking their toll, but I am concerned she looks this bad so soon after we opened."

"Yes, I noticed she didn't look great lately. Like you, I assumed she was just a bit tired. I hoped she would pick up once things settled down. Mind you, I think Mick has the better deal. He starts early, but he works fewer hours than Meagan."

The Busy Fingers women were not the only ones concerned about their fellow shopkeeper's well-being. Cecile Baudin also held concerns for Meagan. Cecile's shop, La Boulangerie, was nextdoor to Caffeine Heaven. A few days ago, the thin dividing wall hadn't muffled the ferocious argument between Caffeine Heaven shopkeepers, Mick and Meagan Maguire. Although she couldn't hear exactly what they said, there was no mistaking the vitriol in the young couple's argument.

Stressed and embarrassed by what filtered through to her, Cecile busied herself in her kitchen, making as much noise as possible. The argument occurred after the lunchtime rush, when there were no customers, and just before Mick left for the day. The intensity of the argument shook Cecile. She liked Meagan, who toiled long hours in the shop. Her personality and service made her popular with customers. Cecile was more ambivalent about Mick. There was nothing specific, just something about him made her feel a little uneasy.

As they often did, Cecile and Meagan spoke briefly that evening as they closed up. Meagan's red eyes were obvious. Cecile enquired again if everything was okay. She asked the same question a few times over the last couple of weeks, but today the question stemmed from deeper concern than usual. As usual, Megan fobbed off Cecile's question and concern. Using the excuse that all marriages have their moments, Megan denied anything serious is amiss.

"It's a bit quiet at the moment. Are you available for coffee?" Cecile called to Meagan from the entrance to Caffeine Heaven. Meagan responded with a resigned nod. It had become a ritual. During the lull that often occurred late in the afternoon, the two women indulged in coffee and chat in La Boulangerie. It was a few days since Cecile overheard the Maguires' row, but she noticed the tension remained between her nextdoor neighbours. Meagan usually responded to an invitation for coffee with a wide smile and an enthusiastic 'yes please'. There was no enthusiasm today.

It was different in other ways too. After a hesitant beginning, Meagan began to open up. "Thanks for the coffee invitation, Cecile. I need a break. A few minutes to myself to relax and pretend I'm normal."

"I am not going to press you, but we are concerned for you. If you need someone to talk to, I am here. I will listen. I might not be able to fix anything, but I will listen. Tell me, is the business getting too much for you?"

"I suppose the business is climbing on top of me, but that's not the real problem. I suppose it's a combination of everything: the business, the marriage – life in general."

"Is there any way I can help … or that anyone can help? Would it help if you had someone to assist in the shop?"

"No; I don't think anyone can help. This is something only we can work out. We've stopped talking. Mick and I just don't talk any more. I know we're both working long hours and we're both tired. In addition, there's the stress of the debt we went into to set up the business. I suppose I shouldn't expect things to be any different given our situation."

"No! No, *Mon ami,* it shouldn't be like that. At times like this – tough times -- that's when partners support each other. It's a shared situation. It is not just one partner's fault. One partner shouldn't take it out on the other just because they find life difficult. You are entitled to expect more from your marriage. If I am honest, I don't think Michael is working long hours. I think you are the one working long hours."

"Yes, I do work long hours, but Mick does too. He starts early every morning, so he has to get up very early. It can't be fun getting up in the dark every day. I must admit though, sometimes I do find myself resenting the fact that I'm here all day and then I still have to do the housework and get dinner. Aargh, don't worry about me. I'm just tired and feeling sorry for myself."

Meagan ended the discussion, disappointing Cecile. She felt getting Meagan to talk about her situation was good for Meagan, but she clammed up again. Cecile secretly hoped a future opportunity might arise to continue this discussion. The social interlude ended when a customer came into La Boulangerie.

It was over a week later before opportunity presented for another discussion with Meagan. No improvement in the Maguires' relationship was obvious. Raised voices came from the shop next door on several occasions, albeit less intense than that first row. Megan looked increasingly haggard, and Cecile observed her frequently sporting red eyes and nose.

At another coffee break together a couple of weeks later, Meagan again confided in Cecile. After some general chat, she blurted out what was on her mind. "I think Mick is having an affair."

"*Mon Deiu*, Meagan, you need to have something – some evidence – before you torture yourself with such ideas. If you do not, you will send yourself mad thinking about it. Why do you think he is unfaithful?"

"Oh, you probably think I'm silly -- imagining things -- but he is not himself. Lately, he is not being Mick."

"How do you mean 'he is not being Mick'? I am sorry, but I do not understand. Please explain to me what is different."

"It's hard to explain. It is little things … like when I arrive home from work; he's often not there. Because he starts at 4.00am, he finishes work early every day, usually between two and three o'clock, to get some sleep. He used to be asleep when I got home in the evening. Most days over the last couple of weeks, he wasn't there when I arrived home. He insisted on dinner by seven thirty at the latest. He wakes up, has dinner and watches TV until maybe ten o'clock before going back to bed. After I arrive home, I do housework before making dinner. He was always there – asleep – when I got home."

"Oui, I agree there is a change. Have you enquired about where he goes or what he does?"

"Oooh, yes, and that caused another row. When he wasn't there, I noticed his bike was missing from the garage. I plucked up courage and asked him about it. He said he had taken to going for long rides in the late afternoon."

"So, this is a reasonable explanation, n'est pas? It is good he is getting some exercise. It is a pity he is not getting some exercise helping you with the housework."

"Mick is not a fitness fanatic, never has been. Long bike rides are out of character for him. I challenged him about it. He says it helps him unwind. Discussing it usually results in another row. I asked when I got time to unwind. He told me I ride my bike home from work every day, surely that should help me unwind if I needed to!"

Cecile felt extreme disquiet at Meagan's revelations. Meagan's assessment of Mick's behaviour was right. His behaviour was out of character, but there was nothing to suggest it was anything other than what he claimed. Going for long bike rides didn't automatically equate to having an affair. Realising she probably shared more than she intended, Meagan abruptly ended the discussion by changing the subject.

Other shopkeepers in the Plaza discussed what they termed 'a bit of tension' in the coffee shop. Aware of the coffee breaks Cecile and Meagan shared, Grace and Gordon from Busy Fingers wandered across to La Boulangerie to chat to Cecile. They all agreed Meagan's appearance looked worse than ever. Mindful of her role of confidante, Cecile shared nothing of her conversations with Meagan.

One morning the following week, the coffee shop was late opening. It was only a few minutes past the usual opening time of 6.30am, but regular early-morning customers waited outside. A couple came in and enquired of Cecile about the situation nextdoor. She couldn't help them but felt her stomach constrict with concern.

The early-morning silence of the Plaza suddenly was shattered. Mick roughly flung up the shutters at Caffeine Heaven as Meagan rushed through the Plaza to the shop. In that brief moment as Mick opened the shutters, Cecile glimpsed his face: dark and belligerent. Customers hesitated before filing into the shop. Meagan threw down her bag and took her place behind the counter.

The rest of the day was quiet, but not so quiet that Mick should leave work early. Cecile was alarmed when she observed Mick storm out and drive off during the lunchtime rush. The afternoon continued quietly. By four o'clock, neither Caffeine Heaven nor La Boulangerie had customers. With two mugs of coffee in hand, Cecile marched into Caffeine Heaven.

"You definitely need this," she announced, thrusting a mug into Meagan's hand. "Look at you! What is going on? You are never late to work. What has happened?" Cecile demanded. "I am so worried about you. Please, tell me what is happening. Maybe there is some way I can help."

"No o o," Meagan wailed as she burst into tears. "No one can help. I think my marriage is over. I don't know what to do."

After settling her down, Cecile persuaded Meagan to talk. Cecile guessed there probably was nothing she could do to help, but just getting Meagan to talk might be a help in itself. With gentle encouragement, Meagan began to share the events of the previous night.

"A couple of nights ago, we had a terrible row, the worst one yet. I suppose it was my fault. Since Mick has been going for these 'long bike rides', I never know what time he will come home. A couple of times it was almost nine o'clock. Of course, dinner was ruined by then. He refused to eat it. He claimed it was my fault he went without dinner. I tried explaining, but he would have none of it. Then, two nights ago, he got home just on seven thirty – and I didn't have dinner ready. I explained that I didn't know what time to expect him, and that dinner would only take another ten or fifteen minutes to finish cooking.

I suggested he take a shower while he waited. That's when the colossal row erupted and he pointed out how useless I was at everything."

Cecile refrained from voicing her anger and disgust and quietly encouraged Meagan to continue. After a brief hesitation, the young woman continued.

"After the row, he took his pillow and slept on the sofa. That's not new. Whenever he gets the sulks or whatever, he sleeps on the sofa for a night or two. Our apartment is tiny with only one bedroom. I thought he might sleep on the sofa again last night, as things remained icy between us. He left work early yesterday. When I got home, the car was in the driveway. I thought it strange, as he always puts it in the garage when he gets home. I couldn't put my bike away. He locked the garage. I went inside to get a garage key, but both of them were missing from the key rack. So, I let myself into the garage from inside the apartment."

Another flood of tears and a few moments delay while she regained some semblance of composure before continuing. "I just stood there. I couldn't believe my eyes. He set the garage up as a ... as a camp. He'd set up the camp stretcher and the camping stove and cooking gear. I heard him come back from his ride, but he let himself into the garage and didn't come into the apartment. I waited thinking he might come in after a while. He didn't. At about ten o'clock, I accepted he wasn't coming in and went to bed. I couldn't sleep so, after about an hour or so, I decided to confront him."

More tears and a couple of minutes of sniffling before she was able to continue. Finally, Meagan took a deep breath, cleared her throat and continued.

"He wouldn't even talk to me … just pushed me out of the garage and shut the door behind me. I couldn't get to sleep. I remember seeing four o'clock come round. Then I must have dozed off. I woke up with a start and instantly knew I was going to be late opening up. Of course, Mick wasn't impressed with me. He never said a word – still hasn't– but he let me know anyway. Today he left work even before the lunchtime rush was over."

Cecile nodded sympathetically. "Yes, I saw him leave. How did you manage on your own?"

"Not very well; I can't be in two places at once. I can't be out front dealing with customers and in the kitchen making toasted sandwiches at the same time. In the end, I had to make the excuse there was something wrong with some of the kitchen equipment and, we wouldn't be able to toast or cook anything. If he doesn't do his share, I don't know how we are going to keep going."

"Have you thought about employing someone -- maybe a young girl -- to help out?" Cecile asked, although certain Meagan must have considered it. "It might take some load off you and allow you to reduce your hours."

"We can't afford to pay someone else. I think our debt is part of our problems. Opening this shop looked like a dream opportunity. We knew we needed to borrow to start up. The bank loan we negotiated was good, but then two things happened that I hadn't foreseen: Mick went on a gambling spree, and we had to pay rental on our new premises for so many weeks before the Plaza opened."

"Mick is a gambler?" Cecile asked incredulously. "He would do that knowing it could put your future in jeopardy?"

"Oh, he's not a regular gambler; not a big time gambler," Meagan defended him. "I think he was treating himself to a night at the casino before we tied ourselves down to the shop. However, it ran away with him, and he ended up losing about $7,000. It was bad, but we thought we could work around it. I suppose we might have been a bit short-sighted about how long we would be paying rent on the shop before we opened. I knew it would be some time. I took that into account when calculating how much we needed, but I hadn't allowed for five weeks of rent before we started bringing in any money."

"Can you not talk to the bank? Maybe they can do something to help."

"I tried that a couple of weeks ago, but they didn't want to talk to us. After approval of our loan, we arranged to pay interest only for six months to allow us to get on our feet a bit before we started paying off the debt. When we first came to Oyster Point, we lived in a cabin at the caravan park. It was cheap. However, there is some rule that allows a maximum of three-months' stay. We hadn't been there three months, but they told us to leave. I think it was because the mine company leaned on the park owners to free up the cabins for mine employees. We rented the cheapest apartment we could find. It's a dump, but it still costs a lot more than the caravan park."

"There must be some way your friends here in the Plaza can help you through this," Cecile said as she tried to think of how. "We care about you and want to see you keep going. Think about it. Talk to me about it. I'm sure we can come up with some ideas."

"Thanks, Cecile, but I don't think there is anything that can be done. Anyway, in Mick's present mood, he wouldn't discuss it … and probably would go ballistic if he knew I spoke to anyone about our situation."

"That will not be a problem. He will not find out from me, but think about what I have said."

Dark circles became a permanent feature on Meagan's face and she lost considerable weight. Her clothes hung off her bony frame. Caffeine Heaven customers noticed … and commented on it to other shopkeepers in the Plaza. On an increasingly regular basis, Cecile, Grace and Gordon discussed their concern for their colleague.

It was a couple of weeks after her last conversation with Meagan, when Cecile received an unexpected phone call from a former workmate in Brisbane. Home alone, and exhausted after a busy day, Cecile sat sipping wine while pondering Meagan's situation. The phone call from Angela lifted her spirits and they chatted on for quite some time about mutual acquaintances and about Cecile's new business. As conversation ran out, she asked Angela a question gnawing at the back of her mind throughout the whole Maguire saga.

"Angela, this is going to sound really strange, but I have been trying to think about someone we used to know. Do you remember that good-looking young chef who worked in Giacomo's restaurant for a while some time ago? I think he worked in some other kitchens too and then disappeared. I don't really mean 'disappeared'. I mean, I don't think I saw him again after a while."

"Uhmm, yeah, I think I know the one you mean," Angela responded, and proceeded to give a physical description of the man she thought Cecile asked about. "Is that the one you're talking about?"

"*Oui*, ah *bon,* that is the person I was thinking about. Do you remember his name or what happened to him?"

"Why on earth would you be thinking about him? Is there a story here that I don't know about?"

"*Non!* I will tell you … but do you remember his name?"

"Okay, I was just stalling until I remembered: Michael. Yes, that was his name and I think his surname also started with M – but I'm not sure what that was."

"Maybe it was 'Maguire' do you think?"

"Yes; yes, that was it, and a right piece of work he was too."

"I don't understand; why was he a 'piece of work'? What does that mean?"

"Ah, I see, you didn't encounter him at close quarters, or you would under-stand what I mean. He tried it on with everyone he worked with. He was even stupid enough to get Giacomo's daughter pregnant. He was lucky to get out of that place alive. After that, he worked part-time at a number of different restaurants, but a leopard can't change its spots and apparently, he couldn't change his ways. Eventually, fewer and fewer places would employ him as he preyed on all the female staff. I think finally he got the message and left town … reputedly leaving a few offspring behind."

"He was good-looking and pleasant enough, but I am surprised he managed to seduce so many females."

"Oh, he was smooth, but you didn't get caught alone with him in the pantry or the cold room. He seemed to develop at least six hands that he couldn't con-trol, or maybe he could control them perfectly -- to achieve his intentions."

"Why are you asking about him? I forgot all about him until you asked."

"Oh, it was not for any important reason. Er… uhmm, I saw someone recently who looked a bit like him. I tried to remember his name but could not." Cecile hoped her lie was convincing.

Angela's call ended, Cecile sat nursing her empty wine glass and reflecting on their conversation. She doubted Meagan knew anything of Mick's extramarital activities. Sometime early in their friendship, Meagan told her Mick went to work at the mines when the financial downturn hit the hospitality industry and jobs in it became scarce. Meagan said the money was much better and, once the good money started coming in, they began planning their dream coffee shop.

"Meagan's suspicions about her husband having an affair might be closer to the truth than I thought," Cecile confessed aloud to the empty room. Knowing about Mick's past didn't help, and the knowledge caused Cecile a restless night.

Cecile wasn't the only one not sleeping well. Meagan had not slept well for days. That night was no different. She tossed and turned, unable to get to sleep until after midnight, before falling into a light disturbed sleep. It seemed she barely closed her eyes before a noise woke her. It was a familiar noise. One she heard every morning for the last few days.

She lay still, straining her ears to catch every sound. It was Mick going off to work. Soon she heard the car start, crunch down the driveway and out of the yard. She knew the time. There was no need to check the clock but she did anyway. As she knew it would be, it was 3.00am. This had been Mick's routine for a few days now. He used to get up at 4.00am to bake the sweet treats for the day's trading. Now he went in an hour earlier, but the range of fare had diminished. It diminished in quantity of choices but also in quality.

After closing Busy Fingers for the day, Grace and Vera caught up with Cecile as they walked to their cars. Grace brought up the subject of the coffee shop. "I am starting to worry about how much longer the Maguires will remain in business. Customers are commenting on the place going downhill. I know Meagan is doing her best, but the range of food they offer now is poor compared to when they first opened. And Meagan's appearance certainly doesn't entice people in."

"Yes, it must be bad," Vera added. "Gordon went to get something for morning tea and came back with nothing. He commented there wasn't anything worth buying. Gordon is a good cook himself, so you probably have to take his criticism with a grain of salt. However, it must be bad for him not to find something to bring back."

Cecile, her hand on the door handle of her car, paused for a moment before speaking. "I do not think the future looks good. I am so worried about Meagan all the time. There is so much happening. So many different things are putting the business in danger of collapse. I think, *peut-être*, some of those things Meagan still does not know about," she ventured, recalling her conversation with Angela. "It is sad and distressing to watch, but I don't know what we can do."

A few days later, Meagan was awake when she heard Mick leaving for work. It occurred to her that, when he slept beside her, she never heard him get up or leave every morning. Now, since such poor sleep became her norm, she heard him leaving at the earlier hour every day. Conditioned to it, she awoke in time to listen for it. Despair won out again, and the tears flowed once more.

"Stop it! This is ridiculous," she admonished herself aloud. "This cannot go on. I'm going to have it out with him today – regardless of the outcome," she announced.

It took only a few moments to get dressed and be on her bike. She pedalled furiously towards the Plaza, her heart thumping wildly: not from exertion, but with apprehension. The Plaza was in darkness, no sign of their car in any of the carparks. Meagan let herself into the shop. No Mick, and no sign he'd been there since she left the place yesterday evening. She stood in the kitchen. Bewilderment precluded any action for a time. She didn't know how long she stood there, her world stood still and time was irrelevant.

She sluggishly made her way out of the shop, locked up behind her, and retrieved her bike from where she left it. Dazed by everything, coherent thinking eluded her. She wheeled her bike across to The Esplanade. With no clear purpose or plan in mind, she went to a bench under some trees. After leaning her bike against one of the trees, she plonked down on the bench and dissolved into uncontrollable sobbing.

On the verge of making herself sick, and having run out of tissues, she stood up, intending to go home. What else was there to do? She didn't know where Mick was, but he certainly wasn't where he was supposed to be. As she retrieved her bike, car headlights came along Main Street and turned into the Plaza's parking lot. Her heart missed a beat. Perhaps it was Mick. She would go and challenge him about his whereabouts since 3.00am.

The driver of the car strolled to the Plaza building and went in, turning on the lights inside as they entered. A shaft of light shone out through the open door illuminating the car outside. It was not Mick's car. Megan recognised it as belonging to Annie, one of the cleaners. If a cleaner had arrived, it must be 4.00am. That's when the cleaners started every morning. Mick will probably arrive any minute now, she told herself, and when he does, I'll want to know where he's been for the last hour. Her anger building, she leant the bike back against the tree and sat back down to wait. As she waited in the damp night air, Meagan's emotions became more tumultuous. Her anger competed with her concern for Mick's welfare. Her concern was winning.

Just after five o'clock, Mick arrived and hurried into the Plaza. By the time he arrived, Meagan's concern completely outstripped her anger. She felt over-whelming relief that he was okay. However, she found that her resolve to have it out with him waned and her courage evaporated. She sat for a few moments, totally confused as to what to do, before finally deciding to go home, change her damp clothes and go into work as usual.

She arrived at the Plaza in time to open the shop at 6.30am and welcomed a couple of customers who followed her in for their regular morning breakfast. Today, they only wanted coffee. Megan was relieved. No fresh baking was in the display cabinet. They drank their coffee and departed, but unlike only a couple of weeks ago, no other customers immediately replaced them. The sight of the empty cakes cabinet rekindled her anger. Meagan took advantage of the lack of customers. She stormed into the kitchen to confront Mick who was removing a tray of muffins from the oven.

"Why haven't you finished the baking? When are we going to have something to sell?" she demanded.

"Right now," he barked in response, and slammed a tray of muffins onto a cooling rack. "There has been a bit of a problem; things are a bit slow."

"Is that all were going to have to sell?" She asked incredulously, gesturing at the morning's baking cooling on the bench.

"Yes! That's all we have to sell. I'm trying to cut back on the range we offer to cut costs. We're not making any progress with our debt. It's climbing on top of us. I'm sick of being broke and wondering how much longer it will be before we lose the business."

"Well, if you hadn't indulged yourself at the casino to the tune of $7000, we might be better off," she spat back at him.

Fists clenched and eyes blazing, Mick turned slowly to face her. For a moment, she wasn't sure what would happen. Then luck intervened. Through the small one-way glass panel, Meagan saw customers entering the shop. She rushed from the kitchen to serve them … without appreciating the significance of the words Mick had flung at her. They might have been hostile, but they were the first words he had spoken to her in many days.

Mick's words about their rotten situation gnawed at Meagan all day. It didn't help when he left work at one o'clock again that afternoon. Customer numbers were down again. She arrived home that evening emotionally rather than physically exhausted. Meagan had stopped making dinner. It was days since Mick came looking for dinner. She confined herself to fixing something for herself if she was hungry, or not bothering at all. She tried watching the evening news, but couldn't concentrate and turned TV off. Perhaps it was due to having been up so early that morning – or the emotional strain – when just after seven o'clock and still in her work clothes, she fell asleep on the sofa.

The sound of the car reversing down the driveway woke her. Meagan moved quickly to the window and watched it go, expecting it to follow Mick's usual practice of pausing at the end of the driveway before crossing the street and turning right to head towards the Plaza. She was stunned. There was an almost imperceptible hesitation at the end of the driveway before Mick turned left and drove off in the opposite direction. Confused, Meagan remained there, staring at the road and trying to comprehend what had happened. Perhaps he was going to pick up someone to take them to work. No, that can't be. Only the cleaners started work so early. She realised she still wore her watch and checked the time: 2.58am. He left even earlier this morning.

Clear thinking slowly returned. With no idea where Mick went, Meagan assumed that, at some point in time, he would drive back to the Plaza to start work. She contemplated the route he might take. There were only two ways to the Plaza. The street running past their apartment that became Main Street was the most direct route. An alternate approach came from a different part of town and joined Main Street on the side opposite the shopping precinct. Which route would Mick take this morning?

She cast her mind back to the wee hours of the previous morning when she sat beside The Esplanade waiting for Mick to arrive at work. In her mind, she visualised the various cars arriving at the Plaza. The last one she watched was Mick's. Which way had it come? The memory of their car coming along Main Street came into focus. Mick had not used the alternate route. He would have driven past their apartment. For want of any other clues, she assumed he would do the same again today.

Meagan drew a chair over to the window. If Mick took this route into work this morning, she would maintain a vigil from this window until she saw him go past. At least it was drier and warmer than sitting beside The Esplanade. After about half an hour, she felt drowsy and yawned. Coffee, that's what she needed. Without turning on any lights that might alert Mick to the fact that she was awake, she relied on the glow from the various LEDs in the room and the nearby streetlight.

Armed with a long strong coffee, she resumed her vigil. The street was devoid of traffic all morning until, at just after four o'clock, headlights appeared in the distance. Meagan sat upright and blinked herself back to alertness, only to be disappointed. One of the council's garbage trucks rumbled past on the start of its early morning collection run. The wait was taking its toll. Her eyes became heavier. She succumbed to temptation. With her head resting on her arms on the windowsill, Meagan reassured herself she would hear any car that came past even if she dozed off.

The sound of a vehicle woke her. She thought she'd only been dozing for a few minutes, but a quick check of her watch showed it was now just before five o'clock. She blinked repeatedly to get her eyes to focus as the headlights drew closer … and then sped past. It was their car. Mick appeared to be on his way to the Plaza. Her fleeting glimpse confirmed he was alone.

Meagan's mind was in hyperdrive as it tried to rationalise the situation. She showered. It worked a minor miracle. Her mind cleared. Logical thinking returned. Regardless of the consequences, she resolved to confront Mick. She dressed for work and pedalled off to the Plaza.

It was only a bit after six o'clock when she arrived at Caffeine Heaven. Mick didn't hear her arrive. There was so much noise coming from the kitchen … and he wasn't expecting Meagan at this hour. She stowed her bag under the counter and stormed into the kitchen. This was confrontation time. The kitchen was a scene of chaos. Mick was rushing around like a lunatic. It seemed like every piece of equipment was in use but, not surprisingly, nothing fresh was ready for sale.

Meagan walked over and turned off all of the mixers. She didn't care what this might do to the products Mick was preparing. They would sort this out now, and she wasn't going to yell above that noise.

The din in the kitchen receded. Mick spun round to face her. She read the changing expressions that crossed his face: surprise, guilt, anger. Meagan pulled herself up to her full 164 centimetre height and faced him defiantly. Whatever happens, I will not back down, she told herself. She fired the opening salvo.

"Right, Mick, this is cards on the table time. I want an explanation … an honest explanation … of what's going on. You won't fob me off, and I can tell you that, whatever is going on, it's not going to continue. I have put up with your nonsense for long enough. I have worked my backside off in this place. You seem to have chosen to work gentlemen's hours. Don't tell me about our debt and how broke we are, I already know. I am doing my damnedest to improve the situation. You, on the other hand, seem determined to drive away the custom we've built up. What we offered customers over the last week is downright embarrassing. Customers express their dissatisfaction by staying away in droves."

She let him know she was aware he left the house earlier than normal every morning, and that he wasn't arriving at work until too late to produce anything worthwhile for them to sell. She demanded an explanation of where he went in the mornings, and what he did after work – particularly as the latter seemed to require him to leave work in the middle of the lunch rush hour. It did not lead to a pretty scene … and didn't produce any explanations. Mick's strategy was one of attack. He accused her of spying on him, of not paying him any attention, and acquainted her with a long list of her shortcomings as a wife. It ended with him screaming 'get out' and roughly pushing her out of the kitchen.

Ashen and shaking, Meagan tried to compose herself as she saw the first of their customers enter the Plaza. Somehow, she managed to get through the day until lunchtime. The air remained electric between them. She operated in a daze. Then the lunchtime crowd started arriving. The usual orders for toasted sandwiches and grilled fingers came in. Things went well initially, but the last order she took to the kitchen was a long time materialising. She apologised to the customer for the delay as she made her way to the kitchen with another customer's order.

She stopped dead as she entered the kitchen. Mick was stuffing his apron and jacket into his backpack. The smell coming from the grill caught her attention. She rushed over in time to save the customer's lunch. Turning back to Mick, she watched in disbelief as he picked up his backpack and made to leave.

"What the hell do you think you're doing?" Meagan demanded. "We're not even halfway through the lunch period yet. You're not leaving…? What about our regulars who come in over the next hour for lunch? How am I supposed to make their lunch and serve customers as well?"

Mick pushed past her roughly and headed for the back door. With his hand on the doorknob, he turned and gave her a disgusted look before yanking open the door and leaving. Meagan rushed across and partially opened the door. She watched him march across to the car and drive off. Stunned, she closed the back door and stood for a moment trying to make sense of it all. Then she remembered the customer's order still clenched in her hand.

The fridge held a range of prepared sandwiches. Before lunch every day, a range of regularly ordered lunchtime sandwiches were prepared and stored in the fridge in readiness. If a customer wanted one toasted, the unsliced sandwich went into the sandwich press. She grabbed a ham, cheese and tomato pre-made sandwich, put it in the sandwich press and set the timer. Then, remembering the grilled fingers, she added a sprig of parsley to the plate and rushed out to the long-suffering customer, apologising once again for the delay. A couple of other customers came in but only wanted coffee. As she finished making the second coffee, she heard the timer on the sandwich press ring, announcing her toasted sandwich was ready. A quick trip to the kitchen to retrieve the toasted sandwich, and she was back behind the counter feeling as though she had things under control -- at least for the moment. Another couple of customers walked in together, but they only wanted coffee and muffins; something she could manage easily from behind the counter.

She survived the rest of the day, although it did involve a few trips to the kitchen before the lunch rush ended. By five o'clock, she felt as though she couldn't spend another minute in the place. Quickly bringing in the outside tables and chairs and closing the front shutters, she turned off the lights and let herself out of the back door. Torn between her work ethic and her need to escape, she hesitated briefly before pedalling off home with as much energy as she could muster.

Their car was in the driveway. After letting the self in to the apartment, she knocked on the door that opened into the garage. There was no response. Mick's bike was missing. He probably was on one of his 'long bike rides'. That might be a good thing. It might help reduce the anger levels and allow them to talk more rationally. If he followed his current practice, it would be much later before he returned home. With nothing else to do, she sat down to watch TV and soon dropped off to sleep. Her stomach rumbling woke her. She decided there was no point in dying of starvation over Mick Maguire.

Again, concern for her husband's well-being began to override her anger. Sometime after nine o'clock, it got the better of her. She took the car and drove to the Plaza to see if he went back to work. The Plaza was in darkness at that hour and there was no sign of Mick. Meagan drove home again to spend the next hour and a half alternating between trying to watch TV and pacing the floor. When Mick still hadn't come home by eleven o'clock, she decided to risk looking a fool and rang the police to see if any accidents had occurred that night: no accidents reported. As a last desperate move, she rang the hospital to see if he had ended up there: another negative response.

She poured herself a large Scotch and sat down by the window. A few drinks and many tears later, the remnants of common sense prevailed. After turning off the last of the lights, she headed down the darkened hallway to the bedroom. It was now 1.30am. Without turning on the bedroom light, she grabbed the bedclothes and flung them back a little more energetically than necessary, sending the pillows flying. There was a strange sound. Something flew off the bed and hit the opposite wall. She stood stock still for a moment before deciding it probably was safe to move, and groped around in the darkness for the bedside light.

There was nothing obvious. She cautiously made her way around to the other side of the bed. A large envelope, with one of its corners crumpled from hitting the wall, lay on the floor. After staring at it for a few moments, Meagan bent down and gingerly picked it up... just 'Meagan' in Mick's handwriting on its front. Her stomach tightened and she felt the bile burn her throat. She sat looking at it for a few heartbeats before her need to know what it contained energised her. In her heart, she knew what it was.

Mick's note was brief and to the point. He was sick of everything, had found someone else and was leaving to start a new life. He signed his half of the business over to her, and added the comment, 'it's all yours now; do what you want with it'. Enclosed was a copy of the legal document signing over the business. His note closed with the comment that, by the time she read his note he would be gone and would not be coming back. He wished her 'good luck' and told her not to try contacting him or looking for him.

So..., that's how a marriage and a life planned together ends, she thought as she sat on the edge of the bed shaking her head in disbelief. How long she sat there, she didn't know. There were no more tears to shed. She felt numb emotionally and cold all over. Sometime later, she must have toppled onto the bed and fallen asleep, because she woke with a start with the sun shining in through the window. It was 8.00am. By now, she should have been at work and all her early-morning customers served their usual breakfast fare. She shrugged. Who cares? *My life is over, my world destroyed.*

Clear thinking slowly returned. She still had a business to run. It was her business now, and that meant it was up to her to make something of it -- or get rid of it. More out of habit than any definite purpose, she dressed for work and enjoyed the luxury of being able to drive to the Plaza instead of riding her bike. It was ten o'clock by the time she let herself in through Caffeine Heaven's back door. She didn't open the front shutters. Today she couldn't face customers, and perhaps she never could again. Meagan noticed a sheet of paper taped to the outside of the shutters. Curious about it, but not wanting to go out in the Plaza, she chose to ignore it.

Cecile's anxiety for her colleague heightened when she noticed Meagan leaving early the previous afternoon. When the coffee shop hadn't opened this morning, she knew things were bad. She knew that the previous day, Meagan explained away delays by blaming it on 'problems in the kitchen'. No doubt, she intended customers to interpret that as problems with the equipment, and not problems with the chef. In a bid to help save her friend's business, on a sheet of paper Cecile scribbled that the coffee shop would not open due to technical problems, and taped it to the coffee shop's shutters.

Worry gnawed at Cecile all morning. As soon as she had a quiet period, she knocked on the back door of the coffee shop. Megan was slow to answer. Cecile started to walk away when the lock rattled. The door opened just a few inches. The sight of her colleague shocked Cecile.

"*Mon Dieu, mon ami!* What has happened? Please, let me come in. Talk to me; tell me what has happened."

With a bit of gentle persuasion, Meagan unburdened herself to Cecile. She recounted how Mick broke the news to her that it was over. A check of their bank account revealed he took most of their savings as well. She shared details of their debt, how she couldn't afford to employ someone to help her, but was unable to manage on her own. The bank agreed to the interest only arrangement for six months to allow them to build up their savings again, but now Mick had taken virtually all they managed to save. Before returning to her own shop, Cecile reassured Meagan that not opening the coffee shop today was the best thing to do.

During the morning, Cecile noticed passers-by – shoppers and shopkeepers alike – glancing at the closed coffee shop and raising their eyebrows in surprise. Back in her own shop, Cecile wrestled with the problem of how to help her friend. When Gordon wandered over from Busy Fingers to buy a loaf of sourdough bread, she decided to confide in him. Gordon had heard stories about Mick's philandering at Oyster Point. In fact, a 'reliable source' confided that Mick considered the Plaza a rich hunting ground.

After telling Cecile he would give the matter some thought, Gordon went back to discuss an idea he was developing with the other members of the Busy Fingers crew. They agreed that Gordon should help at the coffee shop. They could manage Busy Fingers without him. It wouldn't be a long-term arrangement, just until Meagan organised a permanent alternative. Assured of his colleagues' support, Gordon refined his idea, before running his plan past Cecile.

That afternoon, Gordon and Cecile took their plan to Meagan. Gordon would work in the kitchen during the lunchtime rush. He would come in a bit beforehand to prepare sandwiches and would leave once the rush was over. For a while initially, he would come in at 6.00am each day to do some baking to use up the stocks of ingredients in the kitchen to produce much the same as he baked for the oldies for their morning teas: scones, muffins, cupcakes, etc. Bread, bagels, croissants and the like, Cecile would supply at cost price.

As expected, Meagan argued strenuously against the plan, even after they explained that Gordon's services were free. That only made her more determined. She wasn't a charity case. None too gently, Cecile acquainted her with the fact that she was indeed almost a charity case, and that their plan wasn't an indefinite arrangement … just until Meagan got herself sorted out. Strong talking eventually won over Meagan. The decider was Gordon explaining that, when the stock of ingredients ran out, he would only come in for the lunch time session. After that, the coffee shop would get all its bakery lines from Cecile.

The plan went into operation the next day. By the end of the first week, business began picking up. Former customers returned. Gordon's baking wooed them back. More importantly, he enjoyed himself in the kitchen, although he knew he did not want to do this forever. There were other projects to pursue, and he felt guilty about his absence from Busy Fingers.

Towards the end of that first week, Moira Whitlock tentatively approached Meagan. Unsure how Meagan would respond to her approach, but it went well. Moira's ancient aunt lived alone in a large old house. Some years ago, the aunt converted a part of the house into a small bed-sit where Moira lived for some time. Nobody occupied it after Moira moved out. The aunt missed having someone around, and Moira was concerned about her aunt being on her own.

Moira explained that, if Meagan moved in, she would be company for Aunt Alice, and keep an eye on her. They would eat and watch TV together in the evenings and Meagan could help with the housework when she had time. She would have her own self-contained bedroom and sitting room, all for a pepper-corn rental. Meagan's face lit up and she hugged Moira. They arranged to visit Aunt Alice after work that evening.

Their apartment held too many memories. Meagan wanted out of it. Apart from that, the influx of people to the town pushed rents higher. The rent on the apartment was about to increase. After meeting Aunt Alice and discovering that they really clicked, Meagan arranged to vacate the apartment the following week. She thought to herself, maybe life has turned a corner and luck has found me.

Half way through the second week after Mick's disappearance, a uniformed police officer and a detective came to speak to Meagan. She took them through to the kitchen. Their presence alarmed Gordon. "It is okay, Gordon. Please look after the counter while I talk to these men."

Gordon left, alerting the detective to Meagan's fragile state as he passed. After only a couple of minutes, he heard Meagan shriek. He rushed back to find her slumped on a stool and propped up against a bench. Gordon spun round to face the police officers.

"She's just heard some news that shocked her," the detective apologised. "We believe her husband left town with Jenny Fenton, one of the cleaners employed here. We found Fenton's husband murdered in the house he shared with his wife. Do you know anything of Mr Maguire's relationship with Mrs Fenton?"

"Not really, but I heard from the other cleaners a couple of days ago that he had an affair with Jenny for a few weeks before he left."

They asked Meagan a few more questions while Gordon supported her with his arm around her shoulders. She showed them Mick's farewell note that she still carried around in her bag, and told them of his strange behaviour over the last weeks. This wasn't simply a midnight flit. Signing the business over to her took time, the couple's departure well planned.

A couple of weeks later, newspapers' front pages carried stories of the couple's arrest in Western Australia. It would be some months before full details of the crime emerged.

The Bazaar

Foreigners took up residence in the community. Some were mine personnel. Others became Harbour Plaza tenants. In the case of the latter, the new skills and abilities they brought amazed me.

Today was shaping up to be another tense day. Amina Badisi's stomach tightened as the morning progressed. She knew the signs. Her partner, Jacque Champeau, was at explosion point. The frustration and anger building for days could not go on like this for much longer.

Lured north from Melbourne, the couple saw opportunities at Oyster Point of achieving their dream: to establish their own charcuterie. They had their shop, but that was a tiny part of the dream. By the time they arrived at Oyster Point, many of the shops in the new shopping complex were taken. Only three or four remained unallocated. They were smaller than the couple wanted. However, at this time, a larger shop would not solve their main problem.

Jacque, a trained charcutier, wanted to produce his own delicatessen lines. The place he worked at in Melbourne purchased all their processed meats from a factory in another part of the state, producing little of their own. Jacque was French, and dreamed of opening his own charcuterie in the true French style. The problem was, that required a smokehouse, which was proving more difficult to achieve than a decent sized shop. After their arrival, they lived in a cabin in the caravan park while trying to establish the shop, find a house, and find somewhere to establish a smokehouse.

Adding to the frustration was the larger neighbouring shop continued to remain empty. On several occasions, even before the Plaza opened, Jacque approached the real estate agent, Rick Winston, about the shop's availability. The local farmers' cooperative earmarked that space as an outlet for their produce. Winston's excuse for it remaining empty for so long was that farmers were busy getting their farms back on track after the cyclone and in time for their main production season. They didn't have time to worry about the shop. Although Jacque knew harvesting had been in progress for at least two weeks, still no produce appeared in the shop. No fittings installed – nothing done to ready the shop for business.

Without a smokehouse, Jacque had to buy his processed meats from a factory near Brisbane. This did not sit well. He felt the product he served his customers was not as fresh as it should be, and not always the best quality.

While business was slow initially, it had picked up and, although not rushed off their feet, they were doing okay.

"I don't know how I'm going to fit in these new spices," Amina thought aloud, and then bit her lip. Comments like that wouldn't improve things right now. She immediately segued to another topic. "I need to find a local source for vegetables. The last lot of carrots and tomatoes were tired looking when they arrived." The new topic only added to the mounting frustration.

Jacque heaved a sign and was about to launch into another tirade about their situation when he spotted Rick Winston strolling through the Plaza. "Be back in a moment," he called to Amina as he left the shop. "I am going to ask the helpful Mr Winston if he can point us in the direction of a good supplier for your vegetables." He caught up with Winston in front of La Boulangerie.

"No, I don't have anything new to tell you about a bigger shop…," Winston began defensively when Jacque caught up with him.

"Huh, I wasn't even going to mention the shop," Jacque retorted hotly. "I came to ask you where we might buy some good vegetables locally. I imagined a local like you would have some idea of where to go."

Winston looked around, and appeared to give the request some thought. Then his eyes lit up. He took Jacque by the elbow. "Come with me. I see just the bloke you need to talk to over there in The Brasserie. His name is Jack Walker. He is one of the local growers, and the two blokes having a drink with him are also growers I think." Winston made his way over to the table as the three men were finishing their drinks. "Jack, this fella runs the deli and he is looking to buy some local vegetables. I thought you might be just the bloke to help him out with where to get them."

"Well now, you might have come to the right place, mate. Jack Walker…," the man said as he extended his hand. "I'm the chairman of the local farmers' cooperative so, I reckon I could tell you a thing or two about buying vegetables, and so could these two here with me. We are all local growers." Jack introduced his two mates, and asked, "What sort of veggies are you looking for, and how much of them do you need?"

Jacque explained about their shop and the types of vegetables they were looking for in regular small quantities.

"Hmmm, limited range, small quantities regularly; sounds like you should be buying directly from a packing shed. What do you reckon guys, is that the best way to go?" The other two farmers nodded their agreement, and Jack continued. "Whereabouts are you living? I suppose it would be best if we found you somewhere close by so you don't have to go out of your way to get the stuff." At that point, Jack's drinking mates said they had to go, but assured Jacque that Jack would be to one to sort it out for him.

Jacque found himself somewhat embarrassed at having to admit they were still living in a cabin in the caravan park after all these weeks. "We really haven't had time to look for something suitable," Jacque explained. "Now that I think about it, ideally we should look for something outside the urban area – probably something with a bit of spare ground."

"What do you want spare ground for? …You planning on growing your own vegetables or something?" Jack asked with a hint of concern in his voice.

"No, no. I am a charcutier. I need a smokehouse." Jacque saw the other man's confused expression and explained as simply as he could what that meant. "I don't seem able to get anything useful out of that real estate fellow, and I haven't got time to go looking for something myself, so we are still in the caravan park."

"Well now, laddie, I just might be able to help you with that too. Suppose you tell me exactly what you want – or, better still, what you *need* – and I'll see what I can do. That bloke Winston is too busy feathering his own nest at the moment." Jack saw the blank look spread across Jacque's face, and hastened to explain. "He was only supposed to be a big noise around here during construction. Then the developer was to appoint a centre manager. Winston remains on the job until a manager is appointed. Secretly, he's hoping they forget about appointing a manger and leave him in charge. That way he gets a free office, free phone – free everything – to do this job and run his real estate business on the side," Jack ended with a knowing tap on the side of his nose and checked the time before continuing.

"How about you come to my place and have a look around? What about this afternoon, what time do you shut up?"

"We closed the shop at six o'clock, but we could close early today. Yes, I think we could close at five o'clock and come to your place straight afterwards."

"Yeah, that would be good. That gives us plenty of time for a look around. The packing shed will be working until about seven o'clock tonight. There's been a lot of picking today. I'll give you a bit of a mud map so you know how to find the place. It's a big place just the other side of the river; you can't miss it."

"Oh yes, I think I know the place. I have seen the big shed."

Jack sketched a map on the back of a coaster anyway. Both men stood and shook hands ready to leave. "Oops, I told Amina I would only be a few moments. I don't think she will be impressed I have been gone so long."

"Don't worry about it, mate. Just tell you've had a very productive meeting and that should square it," Jack said with a knowing wink.

Jacque found himself at a loss on several occasions during his conversation with Jack. His upbringing was bilingual. He believed he spoke English very well, had never encountered any problems with the language in Melbourne, but talking to Jack had him mystified on occasions. Maybe it was like dialects. Perhaps Queensland English was a different dialect from that spoken in Melbourne.

Amina wasn't impressed Jacque was gone so long, and even less impressed when he said they were closing early. After he explained his meeting with Jack Walker, she calmed down, but had endless questions Jacque couldn't answer. The rest of the day seemed to pass quickly, and it was time to drive to Jack Walker's property.

Jack waited at the packing shed. "Good on ya; right on time. ...So, this must be the little lady. Pleased to meet ya. I'm Jack." Turning to Jacque, he carried on, "I've been thinking about our conversation this morning, and I think I could have something that might be right up your alley. I think we should go and have a look at that while it's still light, and then we can come back here to the shed."

Jacque and Amina exchanged glances but agreed and soon found themselves bumping across Jack's property in his dusty old Land Rover. They pulled up on top of a small ridge near a boundary of the property that overlooked the river. In a cleared area stood a small cottage, three outbuildings of varying sizes, and a number of fruit trees.

"This used to be my place," Jack enlightened them. "My parents built it for me and my new bride just before we got married. She was a city girl – a teacher – and never are really took to life on the farm. I thought it might work out okay living down here, away from everything else that was going on, but apparently not. In the end, she ran off a bloke from the packing shed. He was some sort of merchant banker from England out here on a working holiday. Anyway, she must have worked out he had something better to offer than I did, and she took off with him. Damn shame too; he was one of my best packers that season."

"Judging by all the buildings, there seems to have been a bit happening here. What were all the sheds used for ... and is that some sort of stockyard I can see over there through the trees?" Amina asked.

"Yeah, we tried a few things here. She didn't want to continue teaching after we got married, but had all these fancy ideas about how to fill in her time. She went to some cheese-making workshop and decided she would be a cheesemaker. We already had a couple of cows. She pestered me to get a few goats. ...So, we had to have a dairy to handle the milking and all that, and then we had to have a proper kitchen – or whatever you call it – where she could make the cheese. It had to have a special temperature controlled room and everything. She did make a bit of cheese that wasn't too bad, but the fad didn't last long."

"I see you have a few pomegranate trees with fruit on them," Amina observed.

"Yeah, that was another fad. She got into all this new-fangled cooking and flavours and stuff. She claimed pomegranates were important to her cooking and she couldn't buy any locally, so we got some plants. They were just about to produce the first crop when she took off, so nothing has been done with them since."

"The trees need a bit of attention," Amina admitted, "But they are in good condition in spite of everything, and the fruit looks good. If you're not doing anything with the fruit, could I buy some from you for the shop?"

"No, you can't buy it. Take it. It's only going to fall off the trees and rot here. If you can do something with it, take it. I'd be happy to see it put to some use. Now, do you want to have a look around inside the house?"

"Uhmm, could we have a look in there, first?" Jacque asked pointing to the largest outbuilding.

"What … in that kitchen building? Yeah, okay. Follow me." Jack unlocked the door and they followed him in.

"It is huge. From outside, I didn't realise it was so big," Amina said. "It's beautiful."

"No, it's *perfect,*" Jacque corrected her.

"Yes, well, my wife had big intentions. This is how she wanted it, so this is how we built it. Are you ready to look at the house yet?"

"Yes, please," Amina answered, "but could we have a look at the dairy on our way over to the house?" Jacque shot her a quizzical look, but she ignored the question it asked.

Happy to oblige, Jack opened the dairy and waited outside while the young couple took a quick detour through the place. Amina looked excited when they returned.

"I noticed a separator and a churn of some sort in there."

"Yeah, that was another one of my wife's big ideas. Any milk she didn't use for cheese making, she was going to turn into butter. I don't think any of that equipment in there's ever been used."

"Do you still have the cows and the goats?" Amina asked.

"They are over in the next paddock. That block is not much good for growing anything, so it was a good place to put the animals. I had to build a bit of a compound arrangement for the goats. They kept wandering over into the veggies, and my father was threatening to shoot the lot of them."

"So what do you do with all the milk now that there is no butter or cheese making going on?" Amina persisted with the questioning.

"Well, I use a bit and I keep the packers accommodation stocked with fresh milk, but mostly I just feed it to the pigs."

"Pigs! You have *pigs?*" Jacque exclaimed.

"I've got a bit of a piggery on that next-door property I bought. Don't know why I started with them. It must have seemed a good idea at the time. "

"So, now that you've got the piggery, what happens to the pigs? What do you do with them?" An excited Jacque asked.

"Send them to the meat works. Oh, there is a travelling butcher comes around – he's fully qualified and everything and it's all legal. He will slaughter a beast on your property for your own use. I get him to knock over a cow or a pig occasionally just for me and maybe to put on a barbecue for the workers."

"Mon Dieu, I think I have died and gone to heaven. If you can give me a positive answer to one more question, Jack, I'll know that is true."

Jack looked a bit perplexed but replied, "Well, ask your question, and we'll all find out whether you're still alive or not."

"I was wondering … could I build a smokehouse here, say, over there on that clear bit of ground?"

"I don't really know what a smokehouse is but, as long as you build it and you don't burn the place down, I can't see any problem with it. You'd better sit him down, Amina. He's looking a bit shell-shocked. You still haven't seen the house. Do you want to see inside or not?"

"Yes, of course we want to see inside. Can we look now? I'm sure it will be just fine. We are not looking for a palace. With the shop, we spend so little time at home anyway," Amina assured him.

The house was small and compact, with two bedrooms, a small office and an open plan living area, but surprisingly modern and well laid out. Painted throughout in a cream colour, it already had a stove, fridge and washing machine installed. The floors were ceramic tiled in a rich brown colour. There was no question about whether it was suitable. They could not have hoped to find anything better. The big question that remained was how much leasing all of this would cost. Prepared for the worst, Jacque asked the question.

After a few moments thought, Jack replied. "Let's see now, you be doing me a bit of a favour if you moved in here." He saw the confusion spread across the young couple's faces and hastened to explain. "A few of the properties around here have had problems with squatters taking over unoccupied buildings. They seem to delight in causing a fair bit of damage and spraying graffiti everywhere. I've been lucky so far. No one's been near this place, but I make a point of coming down to check just about every day. I think we can come up with a reasonable price … and, of course, you'd pay for your own smokehouse. I could give it some thought and let you know within the next couple of days, if that's okay."

What was there to object to? The hard part was going to be waiting to see what the price would be. They agreed they would wait to hear from him.

"Right then, let's go back and have a look at the packing shed and see if we can get you some of those vegetables you want."

The packing shed was impressive, the vegetables were good quality and freshly picked. Amina selected and paid for tomatoes, carrots, lettuce and capsicums, and added them to the box Jack gave her for the pomegranates. They said their farewells and took their leave. Neither of them spoke on their way back to the caravan park, each lost in their own thoughts of the future unfolding from their brief visit with Jack Walker. However, once they were back at their cabin, the talk started and continued well into the night.

Just before closing time the following day, Jack Walker strode into the shop with a large envelope in his hand. "Have a look at this and see what you think," he said as he handed the envelope to Jacque.

With trepidation, Jacque opened the envelope and withdrew the lease contract. Amina, standing behind him on tiptoes read over his shoulder. She let out a squeal of delight, and her eyes filled with tears.

"We'll take it," Jacque almost shouted. "Are you sure you are okay with this, Jack? We are not looking to take advantage of you." The price Jack asked was unbelievably low and something they could manage easily, even if the business didn't increase further.

"I think it's a fair thing," Jack said, "And I'll be really happy to have you pair living down there on the property."

"How soon could we move in?" Amina asked timidly, not wanting to push their luck.

"Well, you don't have to wait for anyone to move out. Move in as soon as you like. It's up to you, but I imagine you'd be happy to get out of that cabin you're living in, and I fancy Jacque here wants to get started on his smokehouse."

As he was leaving the building, Gordon Bailey, a Justice of the Peace, witnessed the signatures on the contract. They asked Jack to join them in a celebratory drink at The Brasserie, but he declined as he had something to attend to at the farm. Gordon, however, wasn't in any rush to leave, and he was more than happy to join them for a drink. They closed the shop in a daze and adjourned to The Brasserie, adding Cecile to the group along the way as she was in no hurry to go home either since her husband, John, would not be home that night.

Everything they owned, was in storage in Melbourne, so first thing the next morning, Amina called to have everything brought north at the earliest opportunity. Its earliest arrival was the coming Friday afternoon. One of them supervised the unloading and they moved in after their usual early closing on Sunday. Jacque rang Jack to suggest that, the next time Jack was in town and had a few minutes to spare, Jacque would like a meeting.

A couple of days later, the two men took over a table at the coffee shop for their meeting. Jacque was anxious to get an agreement in place for the supply of fresh vegetables. He wasn't necessarily looking to Jack for the supply but, as Jack was chairman of the local farmers' cooperative, he seemed the right person to approach. Apart from that, Jacque also wanted to talk about the possibility of buying pork from Jack for processing into products for his charcuterie. While the opportunity presented itself, Jacque made the bold move of questioning Jack about the future of the proposed farmers' market store.

"Eh? Nothing is happening – nor is going to happen. The cooperative put in an expression of interest –back in February, I think – but, sometime towards the end of March, we withdrew it. It seemed like a good idea to have a local outlet for our produce but, when we looked into it, it didn't make any sense. At best, we only harvest between May and September, after that it gets too hot to be picking good stuff, and people want to shop for their fruit and vegetables at the one place. They don't want to have to go from shop to shop. So, if they were going to buy their fresh veggies from us, they'd be looking to buy their apples and oranges from us as well. We don't grow those things. We would have to bring them up from down south. That involves having an agent to go to all the markets, paying the freight, and maybe not having the best quality or the freshest product when it finally arrived … and when we weren't harvesting, even the vegies would come up from down south. It all looked too hard, and we decided we should stick to what we do best: running the farm."

"So why am I having so much trouble getting that real estate man to let me move into your space? He keeps telling me that your lot are going to set up in there but there are just a few delays."

"I don't know what he's on about, but I can tell you that there is no farmers' market going to happen. I suspect the sleazy Mr Winston has some secret agenda, some racket he's trying to pull off. Your best bet, laddie, is to have a quiet word with the developer who owns this place. He's in town now. I saw him go into The Brasserie a few minutes ago. We should wander down and I'll introduce you to him."

Geoff Robinson, the developer, sat alone with a drink and a newspaper. Jack made the introductions as promised, gave the developer a bit of a clue as to the problem, then took his leave and left Jacque to get on with presenting his case. Not sure what reception he would get, Jacque kept it straightforward and unemotional. He needn't have worried. The developer was interested in what he had to say. He suggested Jacque be patient a bit longer until he sorted it all out. Jacque, only mildly optimistic, walked back to The Bazaar.

Robinson, intending to walk across to the supermarket, impulsively turned left instead of right as he walked out of The Brasserie. He walked into Busy Fingers and asked for Mr Bailey. Gordon, working in the stock room, heard his name mentioned and came out to see who was looking for him.

"Mr Robinson, what brings you to our establishment and, more importantly, what causes you to utter my name?"

"Mr Bailey, I have a little job for you. Oh, let's stop buggering about, mate, and get down to business. I need an advert done to go in the paper and maybe the same info on a few flyers to put up around the place. Do you reckon you could knock something together for me?"

The two men had become friends over the last few months. "Not a problem, Geoff. What's the ad for?"

"A Plaza manager."

"O-o-h, I thought Rick Winston had that job in the bag."

"So did he."

"Okay, details please: how long do you want applications to stay open for? I'll need to check when the paper can run it and calculate the closing date from there."

"A week … I don't want to waste time."

"Right. So, when would you want this person to start?"

"Yesterday preferably."

"Oh, good; no pressure then, just some degree of urgency. Hmm, I might know …."

"Do you know someone who might be interested? I'm in town until tomorrow night if they want to talk to me about the job. I need someone good though."

"I'll give you a call. Let me ask a few questions first."

"Thanks, Gordon. I'll owe you if you can find me someone quickly."

Gordon went back to the stockroom. It was worth a call he decided, took out his phone and punched in the number. "Eileen, this is Gordon Bailey. I know this is your early finish day. Are you likely to be coming into town?"

"I never get to finish on time, but I am just about to leave, and I was coming into town. What's up?"

"Could you come straight to Busy Fingers, please? I have something I want to talk to you about."

"Great, I love a mystery. I'll see you in about ten minutes … but, if you're planning to ask me to marry you, don't bother. I've sworn off men."

"You should be so lucky. See you shortly."

Right on time, Eileen Bennett, the retirement complex assistant manager, walked into Busy Fingers. Gordon showed her through to the small staffroom and launched into his mission. "First off, I'd like your opinion, Eileen. As a management-type person, how would a job as Plaza manager here rate?"

"It would depend on a number of things of course – hours of work, responsibility, salary but, generally speaking, it would be a *d r e a m job*. Why do you ask? What's this all about, are you thinking of applying for a job?" She cocked her head on one side and looked at him expectantly.

"No, it's nothing like that. Look, it might be none of my business, but I've noticed you're not exactly happy in your current job. No surprises there; how anyone could be happy working with Mrs Jenner defeats me. So, how would you feel about applying for the Plaza manager's job here?"

"I doubt I'd stand a chance. I'm sure they'll bring in some big name from down south but, if they were calling for applications, I probably put my hand up anyway. You never know your luck if you don't have a go."

"My sentiments exactly; just sit tight for a moment while I make a phone call." Gordon made the call while they sat there. Eileen heard only one side of the intriguing conversation. "Hey, Geoff … Gordon Bailey; remember I said I would give you a call. This is *that call. W*here are you at the moment?"

Geoff Robinson was stunned. "I'm having a look around the supermarket. Why do you ask? Don't tell me you have someone interested in the position?"

"Well, since you're so close by, would you like us to maybe go over to the hotel or somewhere else for a chat?" Gordon asked.

"You have someone there now? Don't worry about going over to the hotel. I know just the place for a private meeting. Give you a call back in a few minutes."

Gordon spent the next few minutes chatting to Eileen about the Plaza and the various businesses so that she had some background knowledge before she met with Geoff. Eileen felt herself becoming more nervous by the minute but the wait wasn't long and Geoff rang Gordon about ten minutes later.

"Sorry about the delay," Geoff said. "I had to extricate Winston's fat arse from the manager's office. The coast is now clear. It would be good if you brought your person along and introduced us."

Gordon ended the call and smiled across at Eileen. "Showtime – come on, let's go. I'll take you for your interview."

On weak legs, Eileen followed Gordon down to the Plaza manager's office. Gordon knocked once before entering and making the basic introductions. "Geoff, this is Eileen Bennett. She is currently the assistant manager at the retirement complex. Eileen, this is Geoff Robinson, the bloke who is responsible for all of this …"

"… And the supermarket," Eileen added as she extended her hand to Geoff.

"Right, you don't need me. I'll leave the two of you to get acquainted," Gordon said as he backed out of the room.

The meeting – or so-called interview – between Geoff and Eileen carried on for some time. Geoff liked what he saw in the young woman. He was aware it was getting late and, as they had covered everything he could possibly want to know, there was little point in prolonging the meeting. Almost as an afterthought, he realised he should ask to see the woman's qualifications and CV. "I don't suppose you brought any of your certificates, or references or anything with you."

"No I didn't. I didn't know I was going to have an interview until Gordon brought me down to this office. I could go home now and get them for you, but it might be a bit late by the time I get back, and I think most of the Plaza closes at six o'clock. What would you like me to do about getting them to you?"

Geoff thought about it briefly, before suggesting she go home to collect them before meeting him again on the terrace at the hotel. He suggested they meet at 6:30pm, and that he might invite Gordon to join them there for dinner at seven o'clock. Eileen agreed and, relieved that the interview process was over, rushed home to get ready.

For Geoff, checking Eileen's credentials was simply a matter of process, which only took a few minutes. That left the remainder of the half-hour before Gordon joined them to finalise details of Eileen's contract. By the time Gordon arrived, Eileen almost had recovered from the shock of it all. Gordon joined them and ordered a drink, before Geoff made the big announcement.

"Gordon, let me introduce you to the new Harbour Plaza manager, Eileen Bennett. She will be on the job from the start of next week."

"Please don't say anything back at the complex just yet, Gordon," Eileen pleaded. "I'll give notice in the morning. I've got a fair bit of leave owing, so basically I'll finish up at the complex tomorrow afternoon and then be on leave for the rest of the week before starting at the Plaza next week."

Gordon, congratulating her enthusiastically added, "I know you're going to be a lot happier in this new job – and you'll do well in it too – but you will be missed at the complex. However, my lips are sealed until such time as you're prepared to let people know what's happening."

As arranged, the new Plaza manager commenced the following Monday. Late that afternoon, she called into The Bazaar and spoke to Jacque. Amina wandered over to see what was going on, as Eileen finished introducing herself.

"I am introducing myself to all the shopkeepers in the Plaza, but I particularly wanted to talk to you first. I noticed amongst the paperwork in the office several requests from you to move into the bigger space next door. I couldn't find any response to those requests, so I'm assuming there hasn't been one. First off, I'd like to apologise for that oversight for whatever reason it occurred. I've looked through all the records, and I can't see any reason why you can't move into that space if you're still interested. Of course it would require a new contract, and it is a bigger space so the rent would be higher but, if you're still interested, I could have a new contract drawn up for you to look at by tomorrow evening."

"Yes, we are definitely still interested. We understand about the higher rental, and would be happy to look at the new contract," Jacque responded. Then, turning to Amina, he added, "This will add so much more to what we already have to do, but I can't wait for it to happen."

Life looked rosy for the couple. They moved into their house, the smokehouse was almost complete. Jacque negotiated supply arrangements with the small salt works a few kilometres from Oyster Point for salt, and with a sugar mill a bit further south for the supply of raw sugar, the basic brine ingredients for his smoked meat. All he needed now for the smokehouse to become operational was a good supply of the right sort of sawdust. This last issue was a problem. He resolved to ask Jack Walker the next time they met if he knew of anywhere close where Jacque might be able to source appropriate sawdust. A few days later, Jack was in the Plaza and Jacque explained his problem.

Rubbing his stubbly chin, Jack pondered the problem for a moment before answering. "I can't really help you with that one," he started off tentatively, "But I think one of our growers, Joe Lombardi, has a mate somewhere around here who has something to do with sawmilling. I'll have a word to Joe for you, and we'll see where it goes from there." The next day, Jack rang to say Joe Lombardi's mate had a small sawmilling operation about 60 kilometres from Oyster Point. Joe would take Jacque to meet him as soon as Jacque could organise some time away from the shop.

Apart from Joe nearly talking his ear off, the trip proved worthwhile. Jacque organised supplies of everything he needed and at a good price. They loaded as much of the various types of sawdust as possible into the tray of Joe's Land Rover before leaving the sawmill. Jacque already had made salamis from pork from Jack's piggery. Now he could start producing his smoked meats.

"Have you forgotten something?" Cecile called after Amina as she exited La Boulangerie. Amina bought a loaf of bread, but the bread and her change remained on the counter.

"Oh, I'm sorry. My mind was elsewhere," Amina apologised as she returned to collect the bread and money. "I can't seem to concentrate on anything at the moment. There's just too much going on in my head."

Cecile studied her friend for a moment before commenting. "I thought everything was good for you and Jacque."

"Yes. Yes, it is. It's unbelievable the way things have turned out, but you know how life is. Just when you think everything is wonderful, something else comes along to wreck things."

"We have a little time before you open. How about a coffee…? And maybe it would help if you talk about whatever the problem is." Once settled with their coffees in La Boulangerie's kitchen, Cecile again gently encouraged Amina to open up. "So, do you want to talk about it, this thing that is worrying you so much?"

Amina sighed as she thought about where to start her story. "It's my mother ... No, she is not ill or anything like that. Maybe I need to tell you the long boring story so you understand. We came to Australia when I was about ten and settled in Sydney. I had a normal Australian upbringing, except my mother held on to some of her Moroccan ways. Just after I finished my second year exams at university, my father died in an accident at work. I was devastated. I didn't want to go back to university but my mother insisted my father would want it."

"I agree with your mother. She did the right thing, urging you to go back."

"Well, I went back and, after graduation, a girlfriend and I decided to reward ourselves with an overseas trip. I had a part-time job through my high school and university years. I thought I would have to pay my own student fees after dad died but the Workers' Compensation payout covered them, so I had a bit of money saved up. I was at university in Melbourne. In reality, I already had made a break from home and from Sydney. Am I boring you so far?"

"Not at all; I am waiting to hear where the problem lies."

"Well, we went to England first. We were there a couple of months when my mother wrote to say she had remarried. He was Lebanese. I had met once. I was happy for her. Now there was someone to look after her. Not long after that, my girlfriend moved in with a man she'd met. I went across to the continent, and travelled around a bit before ending up in Morocco visiting my relatives. It was there that I met Jacque and went back to France with him. About five years ago, we came to Australia. We travelled around a bit before visiting my mother in Sydney. I couldn't believe the change in her. She had gone completely 'old country' in her dress, in her way of life -- in every way." Amina stopped for a moment to draw breath and gently shook her head at the recollection of that visit.

"I understand it must have been a shock to see her like that. Was this something her husband imposed?"

"She said it wasn't. I could never work out how it happened, but she was happy. He seemed fond of her and was a good provider. He was a successful businessman with a beautiful home. We only stayed a couple of days before moving to Melbourne. Then, last December, we thought that, once the Christmas-New Year rush was over, we would visit her again. Before we finally decided about it, Mum rang to say they were going overseas and would be away for about six months. They spent Christmas in Lebanon with his elderly parents, and then attended a family wedding and a few other events over the following couple of months. She hoped there would be some time for her to visit her family in Morocco before they returned to Australia."

"Maybe you were disappointed you couldn't visit her as planned, but I sense your visit was out of duty. Not something you really wanted to do."

"Yes, you're right. I wasn't looking forward to it. Then, just as we were busy in the week before the opening of the Plaza, she wrote me that her husband had died at the end of February and, according to his wishes, was buried in his hometown in Lebanon. Rather than risk leaving their Sydney home empty, they leased it out for six months, so she was going to continue with her holiday, visiting Morocco and her sister in London, until the lease expired. Cecile, the lease ends next week. I don't know how my mother will handle going back to that house alone, but I can't get away to be with her. I feel I should ask her to come and spend some time here with me, but I have so little free time, and I don't think she would fit in here at all. Our house is only small. What if she decides she wants to stay for a long time?"

"If you do not ask her, you will struggle with your conscience for a long time. Maybe you should ask her to come, but explain what your situation is and what it might be like for her when she gets here," Cecile counselled.

Amina took Cecile's advice. Her mother agreed to visit after dealing with a few things in Sydney. No, she did not want Amina to book airline tickets. She was coming by train. It would be more convenient for Amina to collect her from the Oyster Point railway station. Everything went according to plan but, on the big day as Amina drove to the railway station, she realised she was no more comfortable with the impending visit than she was when they arranged it.

The train was at the platform when Amina parked the car. Not wanting to leave her mother standing around on her own, she jogged onto the platform. Judging by their clothes, most of those alighting from the train were work-men, probably workers on the new mine being established in the hinterland. Amina scanned the small crowd gathered around the porter's trolley collecting their luggage. There wasn't a headscarf or long dark dress in sight. She felt her stomach tighten: what had gone wrong? Had her mother gotten off at a different town? Was she still on the train, not realising this was her destination? Amina could see a guard further down the platform and started running towards him.

As she passed the crowd collecting their luggage, she heard her name called; her mother's voice. She scanned the faces of the crowd for a familiar one: there was none -- and there was no headscarf there either. Then Amina's eyes alighted on a tall, elegant woman coming towards her. "Mother? Mum! My God, it is you. You look … *amazing*."

Samira Buttuta wore an elegantly cut biscuit coloured pantsuit over a collarless blouse of some silky fabric with a paisley design in shades of apricot, blue, brown and gold. She teamed this with tan high wedge platform soled sandals. Her hair and what little make-up she wore were immaculate. As she hugged her mother, Amina became aware of her own appearance that morning: crumpled tee shirt and jeans teamed with scuffed red ballet flats. Amina trundled her mother's suitcase to the car as she outlined the day's plan. Firstly, they would go to the house, where Jacque would be waiting for the car to go in and open up the shop. Amina would spend the day at home with her mother.

"Nonsense! No, you cannot do this. You have a business to run. You must go into the shop as you do every day. Besides, I don't want to stay at the house today. I want to come into town with you. I want to see the shop, to see the place – to talk to people."

Unable to persuade Samira otherwise, they all went into town. Things went reasonably smoothly for a while but, by mid-morning, the two women were starting to get on each other's nerves. Amina suggested her mother go for a walk through the Plaza to see the shops and, while she was about it, she might buy a loaf of bread from Cecile. It was only a short walk to La Boulangerie, and the smell of freshly baked bread was so enticing, Samira called there first.

The shop was empty. After introducing herself to Cecile, the two women began chatting. Gordon interrupted them when he wandered in from Busy Fingers. Cecile introduced her visitors and explained to Samira that Gordon and all the others involved with Busy Fingers, with the exception of Gloria, lived at the retirement complex. They chatted together for a while. Then, as Gordon was leaving, Cecile suggested he take Samira to Busy Fingers to introduce her to the other ladies.

Once outside Cecile's shop, Samira touched Gordon's arm and said, "Before we go over to meet the other women, could I speak to you for a moment please?" Gordon indicated he was happy to oblige and Samira asked her first question. "Is there any public transport in Oyster Point?"

"No, not now; there used to be a taxi service, but the man's house was severely damaged in the cyclone. He's had some sort of breakdown – bit like shellshock I suppose – and hasn't worked since. Is there somewhere you need to go? I know Amina's busy. Maybe I could drive you," Gordon offered.

"Cecile said you live at the retirement complex." Gordon nodded. "Would that be the Dunes Retirement Village?" Samira enquired tentatively.

"Yes, that's the one. Do you know of it?" Gordon asked in surprise. He thought it strange someone just arrived in town had heard of the place.

"I need to go there, and I'm wondering if, maybe some time soon, you might be able to give me a lift to the village … only if it is convenient of course."

"That's not a problem," Gordon replied. "I have to go back there after morning tea to pick up something I forgot this morning. You could come with me then. In fact, it's almost morning teatime now. Why don't you join us for morning tea, and then we can go afterwards?"

"Thank you. That is kind of you. However, I'd prefer Amina didn't know what I was doing at this stage. The business I have at the village might take me a few minutes, would that be inconvenient for you?"

"It would not be inconvenient. Okay, here's what you're going to do. You are going to tell Amina that you are having morning tea with all the oldies at Busy Fingers and then you are going for a drive around the place. No need to tell her you're going with me – just in case she gets nervous about you being alone with a strange man."

Samira laughed and thanked him as they continued to Busy Fingers. After a brief introduction to the women in the craft shop, Samira returned to The Bazaar to tell Amina of her plans. Then, having delivered her message to Amina, Samira enjoyed the lively conversation that accompanied morning tea with the grey-haired brigade, before accompanying Gordon to the retirement complex.

Gordon showed Samira where his unit was located before taking her to meet Mrs Jenner. He left them to deal with their business and went back to his unit, where he would wait for Samira. Mrs Jenner grabbed a rolled up plan and led Samira across to one of the cottages. After inspecting it, Samira announced that it met with her approval, but she wanted it repainted, the carpets removed and all floors ceramic tiled.

They returned to Mrs Jenner's office where the manager produced paint colour charts and tile samples. Samira knew what she wanted: off-white paint throughout and sand coloured tiles on all floors. Mrs Jenner agreed to give her a call as soon as she knew the anticipated completion of the work. After Samira noted the bank account details for the transfer of the purchase money, her business at the village then completed, she went to find Gordon.

As they drove back to the Plaza, Samira asked, "I haven't seen any car dealerships. Is there anyone at Oyster Point who sells new cars?"

"Not at Oyster Point," Gordon replied, "But there are a couple in the town south of here. Is there anything you need some help with?"

"I want to buy a small car. I know exactly what I want. I just need someone to sell me one."

"Okay, when we get back to the Plaza, we'll have a look in the phone book to see which dealership sells what you're looking for and get their phone number. I have some business to take care of in that town next Wednesday if you want to come with me. Am I right in thinking Amira doesn't need to know about this either?" Gordon asked with a lift of an eyebrow.

"No, Amina doesn't need to know. She worries – fusses too much. When we work out whom to see about a car, I will give them a ring and organise everything. That way, when we go there, I only need to complete the sale and then drive it home."

Gordon considered his next question for a moment but decided to ask it anyway. "I don't mean to be rude, but will you need to organise finance to purchase the car?"

Samira laughed aloud. "Oh, Gordon, thank you for your concern. My two husbands left me very comfortable. It might not be obvious, but I am really quite well off. I will simply give the dealer a bank cheque on the day."

Everything went according to plan. They sorted out which car dealer and Samira arranged for her new car to be ready for her when she arrived. The day she was to collect the car, Grace from Busy Fingers also accompanied them. She wanted to have a sneak peek in a craft shop at the other town. It was a pleasant drive, and all three were in high spirits. The only down side to the day for Samira was the time it took to process all the necessary paperwork before she could actually drive her new car out of the showroom. The three of them met up again for lunch at a local bistro before seeing Samira safely off on her way back to Oyster Point.

The hour-long drive home allowed Samira to be comfortable with her new car by the time she parked in the Plaza's staff car park. It wasn't until closing time that Samira revealed her new purchase. It had been a busy day for Amina and Jacque, and they both looked weary by the end of it. After they locked up, Samira accompanied the couple out to the car park but, at the last moment, made a detour to her own car. "See you at the house," she called out as she unlocked the car.

The surprise element was not wasted. Amina and Jacque stood gaping in disbelief.

"Mum, can you drive? Do you have a driver's licence?" Amina asked, concern audible in her voice.

"Of course I can drive. I've had a licence since you were a little girl. I just didn't need to drive. I bought this car this morning and drove it back, so now I am independent and you don't have to worry about me." … And I'm going to be even more independent in a couple of days' time when my cottage becomes available, Samira thought, but that's a surprise for another day.

As promised, Mrs Jenner advised the expected completion of all work was Friday. Samira could move in as soon as she liked after that. Her belongings coming from Sydney were due to arrive on Friday afternoon. If the workmen hadn't finished by then, the removalists could unload everything into the cottage's lock-up garage.

Samira was at the cottage when the removalists arrived. The workmen still cleaned up around the place, but work inside was finished. She supervised the positioning of furniture in all the rooms and then made sure the right boxes went into the correct rooms ready for unpacking. Last thing before leaving, she turned on the fridge. The next day, after helping Amina and Jacque open up, Samira purchased groceries from the supermarket, before spending most of the weekend unpacking and setting up her new home.

She tried to behave normally on Monday morning. After helping open up and announcing she would be gone for the rest of the day, Samira invited the couple out for dinner that night. After giving directions on where to go for dinner, she left the shop. Samira always believed it best to tell Amina about things after they happened. Telling her beforehand only brought an avalanche of questions and objections – and fuss and worry. Monday night's dinner at Samira's new cottage was a perfect surprise, and made for a delightful evening once they got over the shock. During dinner, she told them she had moved out of their house, they were once again free to live their lives without her hanging around, but that she hoped they would remain close.

A few days later, Samira's next dinner party was for newfound friends from Busy Fingers, who also lived at the retirement complex. There were two additional guests, Cecile and Gloria. Cecile stayed behind after the others left to help clean up and pack the dishwasher. Samira took the opportunity to question her about something that nagged her almost since her arrival.

Gordon told her he was helping Meagan with the coffee shop. Samira thought it a strange arrangement. When she asked about it, Gordon fobbed her off, saying that Meagan had experienced a bit of 'an upset'. He was just help-ing her. She questioned Cecile about the nature of the 'upset' and the arrange-ment with Gordon. Reluctantly, Cecile told her how Meagan's husband left, leaving Meagan with a considerable debt that she didn't know how she was going to meet and no one to help out in the shop, particularly in the kitchen. Cecile also added that Meagan now considered giving up the shop and return-ing to live with her parents before she went bankrupt.

"It sounds to me as though she needs an investor, an investor who would pay off the debt and also assist in the shop, perhaps a partner," Samira sug-gested.

"Yes, that would be the miracle Meagan needs, but I do not think there are many miracles like that in Oyster Point," Cecile replied.

"Ah, but you only need one such miracle to save the coffee shop … and maybe, even at Oyster Point, such a miracle is not impossible to find," Samira added with a knowing wink.

Surprises

Oh, what a time this was. Things happened ... stress levels rose ... people had secrets ... it was all there and so much fun to watch.

In the weeks following the opening, the anticipated slow-down in trading didn't occur, but the frantic buying and selling of that first week settled down. Customers remained plentiful and regular. By now, most shops had set their routines. The Plaza's family – its business operators and the centre manager – established a secondary routine. They came together after close of business every Friday night to unwind and review the week.

One of the first things plaza manager, Eileen Bennett, did after moving into the new manager's office upstairs was establish a small rooftop garden. This was partly for aesthetic reasons. The view from her office window of a vast expanse of bare concrete was glary and ugly. Her secondary motive was to create a place where the plaza's operators could gather to relax, and discuss operations and future initiatives. She witnessed these weekly gatherings strengthen friendships and mutual support among the operators, and it allowed her to establish a closer relationship with the lessees.

A few of the operators were feeling the strain of stopgap arrangements in place since soon after the opening. As the somewhat diminished Busy Fingers crew tidied up after closing, Rose wondered aloud, "It would be good to know when we might have all our people back again."

"With the craft workshops taking off so well, there is no chance for any of us to have a day off. Did anyone else notice how tired Vera is looking? Managing Embellish full-time is starting to take its toll on her," Lois observed.

"I thought all those 'helping out' arrangements were to be short term. It has been a couple of months at least since Vera was available to help here and, if something isn't resolved soon over at Caffeine Heaven, Gordon could find himself helping out there permanently. Has anyone heard what's happening with Mariah Obrin? Is she coming back from the States, or does she expect Vera and Moira to continue running her stores for her indefinitely?" Edith asked a bit tartly.

"I agree we are feeling the strain," Grace murmured. "I suppose we should not whinge too much. Our store has been busy since we opened. Every workshop has filled. We have quite a few regular customers as well as new ones. A couple of days ago, I asked Moira about Mariah. Apparently, she hasn't heard anything for weeks."

"That's all well and good, but what about Gordon?" Edith snapped. "It doesn't look as though Meagan has done anything about recruiting replacement staff since her husband absconded with the cleaner. It's a generous gesture on Gordon's part to help out, but what about us here at Busy Fingers? Is Gordon coming back to the fold, or is there some other attraction keeping him at Caffeine Heaven?"

"Now, now, Edith," Anthony said soothingly. "Meagan's financial position is precarious and it will take her a while to recover from that and the psychological battering from her miserable husband."

Edith continued grumbling to Anthony as they went to their respective cars for the trip back to the retirement complex.

Without any prompting from Edith, the matter of Mariah's extended absence caused considerable speculation at the that Friday night's get-together. "It is a bit remiss of me, but I haven't contacted her," Moira admitted. "I know her daughter's death devastated her. I wanted to allow her time to deal with it without any intrusion from me. I will try emailing her. I'm okay but, for Vera's sake, we can't continue to run Mariah's businesses for her for much longer."

As Moira spoke, Grace noticed Edith, sitting beside her, move forward on her chair in readiness to throw something into the conversation. Grace also noticed that Edith, her jaw firmly set, was looking directly at Gordon. She gently elbowed Edith in the ribs and hissed, "Don't do it! Do not ask Gordon about coming back to Busy Fingers ... well, not in this forum anyway." Edith 'humphed' in response and sat back in her chair, but made it clear this was not her preferred option.

Those operators arriving early on Monday morning received a surprise. They found Mariah Obrin admiring the window display at her Embellish store. "I hope it meets with your approval," Vera chirped as she walked up to Mariah. "Welcome back. We were worried about you and how you were coping."

"... And worried that you might not be coming back," Moira Whitlock added as she joined the two women out front of Embellish.

"I almost didn't -- couldn't. That's why I was away so long. "I'm so grateful for all you have done, but I'm going to have to ask you to bear with me for a few more days until I come up to speed with everything again." Both women assured her that wasn't a problem. Then Mariah and Moira headed for Bedazzled, leaving Vera to open the Embellish store.

Grace popped her head around the door of Embellish. "Was that Mariah I saw here a few minutes ago?" Vera nodded. "That will be a relief for you. How's she going?"

"She looks better than when we last saw her, but still not herself. I'm not sure she will hang around too long. It's only a feeling I have but…," Vera ended with a shrug.

That week was hectic for Mariah as she picked up the reins of her businesses again. She needed several short meetings with Vera and Moira, all after closing time. Vera felt estranged from the Busy Fingers crew. She didn't see them at the Plaza and, getting home so late, she didn't see them at the retirement complex. However, Mariah assured them everything would be normal by the start of the next week. This meant Mariah would take over Bedazzled, Moira would move back to Embellish and Vera could regain her former life and involvement with Busy Fingers.

As the Busy Fingers crew walked to their cars after Friday night's get-together in the rooftop garden, Grace commented to Vera. "I thought Mariah looked brighter tonight. Maybe she is settling back in and will stay." Grace's comment came back to Vera on the following Sunday afternoon during Mariah's final 'hand-over' meeting.

"It's only fair to tell you that I was thinking of selling up everything here and going back to the States permanently. I came back with that firm intention, although I didn't know how long it might take. However, I believe I can now safely say *I am staying. Yes*, I have decided not to sell. I will be staying in Oyster Point. So, Moira, I hope you're happy to continue as long-term manager of Embellish." Her listeners gave a mock cheer and clapped. "Well, Moira, will you stay on?"

Moira hesitated almost imperceptibly as the other two women awaited her reply. "Yes. Yes, of course I'll stay on, if you're happy with that arrangement."

"Are you sure?" Mariah queried. "You seemed a bit hesitant."

"Yes, I'm quite sure. If I hesitated, it was because I was still taking in all you said. Of course I will stay on."

At the retirement complex later that evening, while discussing the meeting with Grace and Gordon, two questions occurred to Vera: what had changed for Mariah during the week, and why had Moira hesitated to answer? Gordon thought he might have some clues about the first question.

"While you ladies were busy supporting Mariah before she took her daughter's ashes back to the States, someone else also provided a strong shoulder to lean on… and I think that support was just as strong during this last week. Maybe 'support' isn't quite the right word for it.…" Gordon suggested, with a shrewd tap on the side of his nose.

"Oh, come on. You can't leave us hanging like that. What do you know?" Grace demanded.

"W-e-l-l, Mariah and a certain bookshop owner seem to spend quite a bit of time together. She's a keen reader, but she would have to be a voracious reader to need to visit the bookshop as often as she does."

"You know, now that you mention it, Mariah visited the bookshop a lot even before Alexia's death," Grace mused.

"I would be delighted if someone gave her comfort – or more. Now that you've mentioned it, however, I'm sure I'll constantly be on the lookout for Mariah entering the Good Companions bookstore. I won't be able to help myself," Vera admitted.

"I don't really care what's going on," Grace said thoughtfully. "I'm pleased something is helping Mariah with her recovery. If that 'something' is Jeremy Sinclaire's support, that's good. If it turns out to be something else, that's even better."

"I admit to being a bit sceptical," Vera admitted. "I don't see how she can slip away from the shop during the day. From next week, when she takes over Bedazzled again, she won't leave the shop unattended while she slips to the bookshop, and that's how it was before she went back to the States."

The other two just shrugged in response, but each knew they would pay particular attention to the bookstore's future coming and goings. Before the others left, it was agreed Vera should take a day or two to relax before returning to Busy Fingers. Edith snorted in disgust when they shared that decision with the rest of the crew.

"… And I suppose the rest of us aren't worn out from having to cover for Gordon and Vera while they were off helping others. We've all been working extra hours. When do we get time off to relax and recover? Anyway, managing those shops couldn't have been too demanding. Moira looks as though she has put on weight lately."

As they learnt to do, everyone treated Edith's outburst with ignore, but she implanted a question in more than one listener's mind." Rose also noticed Moira was looking a little more rounded than usual. "Yes, she is looking well," Rose commented. "It's good to see after she was so sick for all those weeks earlier on."

Good old Rose, Grace thought, she always finds something good to say. It was true. Moira was off colour for a while. She looked terrible but soldiered on in Bedazzled. It's good if she is over it and is putting on a bit of weight again.

"Good morning, ladies," Jack Walker greeted Amina Badisi and her mother, Samira Buttuta, as he strode into The Bazaar. "How's everything with you this morning?"

After the usual pleasantries, Samira asked, "Jack, are you in a hurry this morning, or would you have time for a coffee with me?"

"It's that time of the day and I'm ready for a cuppa. Shall we go across to Caffeine Heaven?"

They chatted aimlessly until their coffees arrived. Then Samira got down to the real reason for her coffee invitation. "You told me how hard this year is for farmers following last December's cyclone. I wondered whether the wives of your farmers' co-operative members are able to help at all."

"Some help out in the packing shed occasionally, but mostly they are confined to doing the domestic stuff and keeping the books. Why the strange question? I didn't know you were interested in the workings of the co-operative."

"Perhaps that's not where my interest lies. I'm more interested in talking about what I think the women could do to help the situation – perhaps only in a small way."

Jack leant forward and propped his chin on his elbow on the table. "This could be a weighty discussion. I think more coffee and something to chew are required." Once the new order arrived, he smiled broadly at Samira and said, "Okay, tell me what's on your mind."

"I think the women – under the umbrella of the co-op of course -- could produce a range of products for sale to assist with the members' cash flows." She had Jack's attention. He sat upright and indicated for her to continue.

"In your packing shed, you showed me what you called 'seconds': produce blemished or misshapen and unsuitable for market but okay to eat. Perhaps that produce could become pickles, chutneys and relishes for sale. There are plenty of fruit trees around. There's a big orchard at the back of your house. They could use the excess fruit to make jams and other spreads."

"I like where you're going with this, Samira. It certainly would use up a lot of stuff that otherwise would be wasted. Most of the wives keep their own kitchen gardens – much too big for the family's needs – but there seems to be something in the culture to do that. You've obviously given this some thought, so tell me how you see it happening."

"First, you would have to put it to your members, then the women need to discuss it to gauge support for the project and how it might work. The co-op could buy salt from the salt works here at Oyster Point and, perhaps, bags of sugar are available from the sugar mill in the next town. Maybe the co-op could arrange special discounted prices from those suppliers. We would need to buy containers and have labels printed. None of that should present any problems. The only problem I see is finding an appropriate commercial kitchen to work in."

"That's not a problem. I know where there is one."

"Yes, I know there is one at the house where Amina lives, but Jacque uses part of that for his meats and Amina uses that other part for her cheese making. It wouldn't work trying to run this project out of there as well."

"I wasn't talking about that kitchen. There's a commercial grade kitchen at my house." Samira's eyebrows almost hit the ceiling. Pleased with himself, Jack continued, "That skillion added to the back of the house was my mother's idea. Her thinking was along the same lines as yours, only she planned to operate the business herself and not as part of the co-op. Anyway, it didn't get off the ground. Oh, she did some preserving or whatever, but it was just for us. She never sold anything. I haven't been into the kitchen for years but it's still all there – steel benches, pots and pans, cookers -- everything. You might have to fight the spiders and geckos that have taken up residence."

"When could I have a look at it?"

"Why don't you come out this afternoon? There's a co-op meeting tomorrow night. We could get your idea planned out so you could present it to the members at the meeting."

They agreed three o'clock for the kitchen inspection and rose to leave. Gordon Bailey came in as they paid their bill. Samira intercepted him on his way to the kitchen. "Gordon, could I have a few minutes of your time soon, please? There's something I've been meaning to talk to you about."

"Sure, how about after work today?"

"Why don't you come for dinner; say, seven o'clock?"

"I'll never turn down one of your dinner invitations. See you tonight."

As they turned to walk out, Jack shot her an enquiring look. Samira ignored it. "I must get back to The Bazaar. I'll see you later." She walked off, leaving Jack wondering what he had missed. Samira resolved not to mention anything to Amina at this time. If the co-op agreed, she would go ahead with her plan. Telling Amina about it in advance would only create hassles. Better to do it and tell her later.

The store was busy after lunch, delaying Samira's departure. It was a few minutes after three o'clock when she arrived at Jack Walker's farm. He was waiting, took her directly around to the back of the house, and stood aside for her to enter.

Samira clapped her hands together and sighed, "Oh, Jack, it's perfect." She spent the next few minutes checking out the contents of the various cupboards, and all the equipment before announcing, "All that's needed is to remove the dust and a few cobwebs and we could be in business. There's even a supply of bottles in one of the cupboards, enough for us to start with. Between now and tomorrow night when we put it to the meeting, you will need to think about how to charge for the use of the place and all the equipment."

"No need to think about it. Use of the place is free. If the co-op agrees, it will pay for electricity and gas, sugar and salt, and any other supplies until the project becomes self-supporting. Then we will look at how it operates after that."

Samira was surprised to find she arrived home in one piece. Her mind so focused on planning her project, she didn't remember anything of the drive from Jack's farm to the retirement complex. Now, she had to set all that aside. Gordon was coming for dinner and she needed to get her head around her conversation with him. He arrived on time with bottle of wine in hand. As they sipped a glass before dinner, she started the discussion she had planned since arriving home from Jack's farm.

"Gordon, I have heard rumours that Caffeine Heaven is in serious financial difficulties and that is why you have helped since her husband left. I realise this is a delicate matter and you might not want to discuss it, but I'm not after gossip. My interest is genuine but I don't want to say too much just yet."

After a few moments consideration, Gordon shared what he knew of Meagan's situation. By the time Gordon left, she had a clear plan to take to Meagan the next day. Samira watched the coffee shop until the lunchtime rush was over. When the place was empty, she wandered up to Caffeine Heaven to arrange a meeting with Meagan.

After closing time seemed the best. Samira was due at the Farmers' Co-operative meeting at six o'clock. Meagan closed up at six o'clock but, by the time she brought in the outdoor furniture and cleaned up, it would be about seven o'clock before she could get away. Sure she would finish at the meeting before seven, Samira asked Meagan to wait at the shop for her in case she ran a bit late.

Jack was a good chairman. The co-op meeting opened dead on six o'clock. He introduced Samira and handed over to her to outline her proposed project. There was silence while she delivered her proposal. Then the questions flowed, all sensible, practical questions. The overall response was positive. Discussion swung round to how the co-op would manage the project. Samira broke into the discussion.

"While it is important for you, the members, to discuss such matters, it is not appropriate for me to be a party to those discussions. As you all seem in favour of seeking input from your 'significant others', if you can suggest a good time for such a meeting, I will leave you to discuss any associated issues."

It was agreed ten o'clock Friday morning was a good time. The meeting would be at Jack's shed. The men would alert their women and Jack would email everyone – just in case someone forgot to mention it to their wife. Samira kept an eye on the time. She became increasingly anxious as the meeting stretched on longer than anticipated. At last, she was free to leave and might just make her appointment with Meagan on time. Samira pulled into the Plaza parking lot at seven o'clock and knocked on Caffeine Heaven's back door a few moments later. As Meagan let her in, Samira told herself the easiest way was to jump straight into the subject. That's what she did as soon as they sat down.

"I have a proposition to put to you. Please don't be offended, but I am aware of your situation. My proposal could change that."

"It would need to be a miracle."

"Perhaps it is. Two husbands left me very well off. I would like to help you out by investing in your coffee shop. My proposal is that I would become a partner by buying a share of the business. You could then use the money to pay off debt. Until the end of this month, I am a bit involved with other things. After that, I should be free to work here. However, until the end of the month, I could work here some days, and that would reduce Gordon's involvement."

Meagan shook her head as she tried to understand Samira's offer. "How would this … this proposal work."

The debt stood at $18,000. The Maguires put in $15,000 of their own money and the bank loan was for $18,000. After the end of the current month, Meagan needed to start paying redemption as well as interest. She hadn't built up enough capital to do that. Samira nodded her understanding at various intervals, as Meagan explained the situation.

"Okay, this is what I propose," Samira began slowly and thoughtfully. "I will put in $15,000 to match your contribution and, in return, I will become an equal partner. We will pay my $15,000 off the debt, leaving only $3,000 plus interest to deal with in the future. It is good to leave a little bit of debt to retain the bank's interested in us."

"That would be incredible, but what will you get out of this arrangement?"

"I will work in the shop and, if I judge things correctly, business has picked up to the point where we both will be able to draw a small wage each week. Who knows, if the business continues to do well, later on you might want to buy me out again."

The proposition seemed almost too good to be true. Caution prevailed. "I imagine there will be a bit involved in setting up and, no doubt, expense to go with it."

"Yes, a bit, but that would be my cost. Think about it. I don't want to rush you into anything but I would appreciate an answer by the end of the week. I'm available if you need to discuss things further."

Their meeting over, Meagan locked up and drove to Aunt Alice's in a daze. It was a lot to think about but, first, she would discuss it with Aunt Alice. The elderly woman had not lost any of her faculties. She was practical and, most importantly, she had a good business head. Alice kept Meagan's dinner warm and joined her with a cup of tea when she sat down to eat. That provided the opportunity for Meagan to explain why she was late and to outline Samira's proposal for Alice.

"You haven't had time to think, but what's your initial reaction to the offer."

Meagan hesitated before answering. "I wanted to shake her hand there and then and start the process tomorrow."

"But now …?"

"Oh, I still feel the same, but I'm scared. I've never made this kind of decision on my own before. I can't afford to get it wrong."

"From what I've heard, I think you'll find Mrs Buttuta is a keen business woman and an all-round 'good guy' who genuinely wants to help you while looking after her own interests as well. You could do worse."

"…Like losing the business? I know it's my decision to make. I'll try to sleep on it and give it more thought tomorrow." However, there wasn't much sleep that night. Meagan's mind kept exploring every possible positive and negative of Samira's proposal.

When Meagan was leaving for work the next morning, Alice noted she looked a lot brighter. As she saw her out the door that Wednesday morning, Alice said quietly, "You've made your decision, haven't you?"

"I think I have. We might be celebrating tonight." After the early morning rush was over and Meagan judged it a reasonable hour to ring people, she called Samira and accepted her offer.

Things happened at warp speed. The earliest appointment with the solicitor was mid-morning on Thursday. Gordon held the fort while Meagan went to attend to 'some business matters'. He minded the shop again the following day when Meagan and Samira signed legal documents making Samira an equal partner in Caffeine Heaven. The women agreed not to discuss it with Gordon until the partnership was a reality. With everything now legal and only bank accounts left to deal with, on their return to the shop, they broke the news to Gordon.

Gordon and Samira agreed a work roster until the end of the month. Samira would work Tuesdays, Thursdays and Saturdays, and Gordon would work Mondays, Wednesdays and Fridays. They each would work alternate Sundays. As he dashed out of the shop, Gordon asked the women to wait there. They exchanged a look; both concerned that the news had upset him. He was gone only a few moments, and returned brandishing a bottle of champagne. They toasted the new partnership and all it entailed.

After sipping one glass, Samira said, "I don't think I should have any more. It has been a heady day without adding too much champagne to it." She told them of her meeting with the Farmers' Co-op wives that morning and the enthusiastic response the project received. They adjourned the meeting to inspect the kitchen at Jack's house before selecting four from their ranks to work with Samira on developing an operational plan and work rosters. A whole gaggle of them was coming on the weekend to clean the kitchen ready for production.

Jack negotiated good deals on salt and sugar. He collected a couple bags of salt from the works and one of the other members collected a couple of bags of sugar. All the bags sat in Jack's foyer in readiness. By lunchtime, when the meeting broke up, they had agreed production would start on Monday, and compiled a list of who would supply which ingredients. Their first products would be strawberry jam and lemon curd.

Meagan and Gordon cheered in unison as Samira finished recounting her morning's activities. "Oh, that reminds me. Gordon, there is one other thing. Now that you might have some spare time, do you think you could design a label for our products, and provide some advice on getting them printed?"

"Nice segue." Gordon's replied.

The only task left for Samira was sharing details of her week's endeavours with her daughter, Amina. Not a task she cherished, Samira decided it could wait a couple of days before she dealt with it. After all, the partnership deal was incomplete until the financials aspects were in place. She transferred her money to Meagan today, but dealing with the loan redemption and setting up a new business account would happen at their appointment with the bank on Monday afternoon. As Samira drifted off to sleep that night, it occurred to her that her life had suddenly become very busy.

Monday provided a prime example of how chaotic life had become. Samira was on the road to Jack Walker's farm by eight o'clock. The other women were not expected to arrive until 9:30, but Samira wanted no hitches today -- no hitches that might dampen enthusiasm. She spent considerable time on Sunday going through her collection of recipes.

Armed with appropriate ones for today's endeavours, she also brought a few others to discuss with the women for possible future production. If not during their coffee break, Samira hoped there would be some other time during the day when they could brainstorm designs for the labels. Gordon and the printers needed to work on producing the labels as soon as possible. Amina would agree to stock their products once there was something to show her… and after she got around to telling her about this new endeavour.

The kitchen sparkled. Saturday's cleaning frenzy worked wonders. Samira busied herself setting up slicers, pans and bowls, and various utensils they would need. She started collecting bottles from the cupboard. They needed cleaning and sterilising. She didn't know how many they would need today but decided 'plenty' was a safe approach. The first batch of bottles was being sterilising by the time the first of the women arrived.

Jack saw Samira arrive and heard her rattling about in the kitchen. He took the opportunity to move the bags of salt and sugar from his foyer to the kitchen and helped Samira empty them into the enormous storage bins. "Is this all the stuff you'll need beside the fruit and vegetables?" he asked.

"No. No, there's a fair bit more stuff to come. Someone is bringing eggs and Marjorie is bringing homemade butter from their dairy. I'll ask Amina to order us a couple of large containers of vinegar – just to get us started – and then we will need to order our own. I know your mother had a good supply of bottles in that cupboard, but we will use all those quickly. We will need to order more and other sizes too."

"You're an amazing woman, Samira Buttuta. You certainly seem to have everything organised in here. I'm off to the shed … don't want to be hanging around here when the petticoat brigade start arriving. You know where to find me if you need me."

"We won't, but thanks. I'm going to pick some lemons that are about to fall off that tree down the back, and I might pick some of the other fruit if they decide to make marmalade later in the week."

A car's arrival ended their conversation. Jack bolted for the shed. Marjorie struggled in with a large plastic container of butter under her arm and her bag over her shoulder. As Samira placed the butter in the small walk-in cold room, Marjorie returned to her car to collect a large box of strawberries. "They are all ripening at once, and that recent bad weather damaged the look of a lot of them. I can't sell them in punnets looking like that but they will be fine for jam," she told Samira.

Others brought containers of strawberries, but none as large as Marjorie's. Sue brought three dozen eggs. After agreeing coffee would be at 10:30, Samira allocated everyone a task to occupy them until coffee time, and then went off with two buckets to pick lemons.

All morning, the kitchen resonated with conversation and light-hearted banter. By lunchtime, the strawberry jam was bottled and the lemon curd almost ready for bottling. They even managed to come up with a basic design for their labels during the coffee break. As Samira drove back to town to meet Meagan for their appointment with the bank, she was elated. The morning achieved much more than expected, and the women were hooked on the project. They scheduled a marmalade-making session for Friday.

Gordon managed the shop while the partners went to the bank. Meagan paid the $15,000 off the loan, and they established a new agreement to pay redemption of $500 plus interest, monthly for the next six months. Meagan was nervous about meeting the repayments, but Samira had checked the books. She knew they could manage the payments. With a new business account established and all the necessary signatures in place, the partnership was complete. All that remained was for Samira to tell Amina about it … and about the co-op women's new venture. The latter was critical, as she had to ask Amina to order the vinegar they needed.

Over coffee after work with Gordon, they finalised the label designs. Gordon would work overnight on proofs of labels. As Samira would be working at Caffeine Heaven the next day, he arranged to bring them for approval after she arrived home from the coffee shop. If they were okay, he would send them to the printer they used for The Quarterdeck menus. He might be able to talk them into having them finished by the end of the week.

The printers excelled themselves. Gordon collected the labels when he was in the area on other business on Thursday. Samira, thinking ahead, also asked for labels for the marmalades they would produce on Friday. These wouldn't be ready until early the next week and would be couriered to Oyster Point.

Samira had a free day on Wednesday. She planned to spend time working on menus for the coffee shop. Her mind drifted back over the previous day, her first day at the coffee shop. After starting work at six o'clock, by the time Meagan arrived just before 6:30, she *almost* had freshly baked fare available for customers. She was putting a cheesecake (Gordon made the base the previous day) in the refrigerated display cabinet when she heard Meagan let herself in through the back door.

"Mmm, that smells wonderful," Meagan greeted her. "What's on the menu so far?"

"I've put a cheesecake in the cabinet. The muffins come out of the oven in about five minutes. There are two batches: one sweet (apple and cinnamon) and one savoury. I hoped to have them ready by the time you opened up, but they're almost done."

By the time Meagan opened up and was taking the first orders for the day, the muffins were out of the oven. The smell greeting customers was intoxicating. All the first few customers ordered a muffin to accompany their coffee. Lunchtime saw no departure from the usual range of fare. Samira worked through until two o'clock and managed to prepare a couple of things for Gordon for the next day. On reflection, the day went well, but Samira's ambition was to introduce a range of new, exciting lunchtime fare and to update the range of sweet treats on offer.

She worked on her ideas until mid-morning when she took a coffee break. As she sipped her coffee, she looked over her list of new dishes. She nodded. Yes, that would do for a start, but she would need to buy some ingredients she required tomorrow. That meant going to the shopping precinct … and that meant not putting off any longer that conversation with Amina.

After purchasing some items from the supermarket, Samira went to The Bazaar for the remainder of the ingredients she needed. Amina was serving a customer when she arrived, so Samira went to the shelves and selected the items she needed. As the customer left the shop, Amina's attention focused on her mother. "What are you planning to do with that much stuff?"

"Ah, good, the shop is empty."

"I don't know that I consider an empty shop 'good'."

"Well, no, but I wanted to speak to you, and part of that conversation is about why I need these items … and something else as well."

The conversation that followed was much as Samira expected. Amina questioned, argued and ridiculed every aspect of both endeavours as her mother explained them. Then there was anger. "Why wasn't I told about all this before now? Why do I have to wait till it's all over before you discuss anything with me?"

Tired of tiptoeing around her daughter's view of life, Samira took a deep breath before quietly answering. "This conversation is exactly why I didn't talk to you earlier. In fact, I put off talking to you for as long as possible to avoid having to go through this."

"What do you mean?"

"I know you see me as an ancient motherly housewife. I'm not and never have been. I have university degrees in economics and business management, I managed your father's and my investments, and I was involved in my second husband's business. Might I remind you, I am your mother, not your child. I do not need your permission or your approval to make decisions. I am independently wealthy and used to managing my own affairs. I came to Oyster Point to be near my only child and to help her if she needed it. I chose not to interfere in your life and I would prefer you didn't try running mine."

Amina was stunned and lost for words. She shook her head as if trying to clear some confusion, and then opened her mouth to speak. Samira cut in before she could utter a word.

"Good, now we've cleared that up, would it be possible for you to order a couple of large containers of vinegar for the co-op project? Oh, and would you be interested in stocking the products they will produce?"

Although her daughter remained somewhat stunned, mother and daughter managed to sort out the vinegar requirements and selling products through The Bazaar. Her business completed, Samira turned to leave. At the door, she stopped and turned back to Amina. "The next time Jacque is here and you can leave him to look after the shop, come and try the new lunch menu at Caffeine Heaven." As she walked to her car, Samira hoped Amina wouldn't take her up on her suggestion for a few days yet – at least not until she had time to implement the new menu properly.

Back at her cottage, Samira decided on a snack for lunch before settling down with a book for the afternoon. The container of strawberries in the fridge caught her eye. These were leftovers from the jam making on Monday.

Nobody wanted them, everyone claiming they had enough of their own at home. They encouraged her to take them and she did, without any idea what she would do with them.

An idea for their future occurred to her as she examined some of the fruit in the container: strawberry tartlets with some sort of topping, cream or meringue perhaps. That gave rise to another idea: lemon meringue tartlets. She would buy a few bottles of the lemon curd the next time she went to Jack's farm. "Oh, I can't," she announced to the empty kitchen. "We haven't set prices for the jam or the curd yet."

That realisation sent her to her computer to look up prices of various sized bottles from likely suppliers. Then there was a call to Jack to get the prices he paid for the sugar and salt. "I still need to add on an amount for usage of equipment, gas and electricity, and labels," she mused aloud. The next half hour or so was spent scribbling on a pad and working her calculator to death. At last, she had worked out prices for both products.

As there was little difference between them, she wondered whether they might be able to standardise the price for all jams and curds sold in that sized bottle. Back at her computer, she drew up a costing sheet and entered details of the costings. She printed off a few copies to take with her to the farm on Friday and, on another blank sheet, started entering costs she worked out in advance for the marmalade they would make on Friday. If its cost fell within the same range as the others, she believed a standard price was justified. Unless she was mistaken, she believed the women would be happier with a standard price than a whole range of prices.

Since all the main ingredients were donations, cost prices were low. This allowed retailers to add a reasonable mark-up and still end up with an inexpensive product on their shelves. Shelves, she thought. Now that's something I hadn't thought of. Maybe I should talk to the women – and Jack – about obtaining some sort of stand on which to display our products. We would need one for Amina's store and one for members to take to the many local markets. Hmmm, probably need to be two different designs … but that's something for someone more technical than I.

Samira felt her excitement rising. She was looking forward to the Friday session with the other women. This project might be good to earn a little extra cash for co-op members, but it was very absorbing. Between the co-op kitchen and Caffeine Heaven, she was in no danger of becoming bored any time soon.

Friday evening, when most of the shop owners gathered in the rooftop garden after closing time, the only ones missing were those from The Quarterdeck and The Brasserie, because those businesses traded until late into the night. These were social get-togethers but they also provided an opportunity for friends and colleagues to share news or seek help with problems. Meagan looked forward all week to tonight's gathering. After the first few minutes of general chatter subsided, she saw her opportunity.

"This evening, I would like to share something with you. Good news for a change … see, I'm smiling. I know I haven't been good company for a while now. As of this week, all that changed. Now, I'm no longer miserable, just nervous. While I have the floor, I would like you to welcome my new business partner. You already know her as a person, but now you also can count her as one of us traders: Samira Buttuta."

A collective gasp greeted Meagan's news. Already aware of the situation, Gordon and Amina just smiled politely. Then the applause broke out and everyone was congratulating the two women. Samira succumbing to Meagan's encouragement, outlined her planned new menu, and her excitement at indulging her passion for cooking. Questions and comments about changes at Caffeine Heaven filled the next few minutes.

Mariah judged it was time for her to share with the group. When a lull again occurred in conversation, she grasped her opportunity. "As we are in a sharing mood, I thought I should confirm what is happening with my shops. Yes, I am back and I'm planning on hanging around for a while." An almost shy little smile tweaked the corners of her mouth. "I will go back to running Bedazzled, and Moira has agreed to take over managing Embellish for me. The other good thing about all this is that Vera has reclaimed her life and is able to join the crew at Busy Fingers again. I have to admit, it hasn't been easy but, with such good friends around me, I know I'll get through it."

More applause greeted Mariah's news, followed by a toast to new beginnings. Light conversation filled the rest of their evening. The only other piece of conversation to attract much interest came from the centre manager, Elaine Bennett. She said she was initiating an advertising campaign to try to fill the remaining vacant shops, and asked if anyone knew of any interest in them. The session didn't go late. Saturday was another working day and a late night would make tomorrow a struggle. As if in response to some unspoken command, they all rose almost simultaneously and started saying their goodnights.

Moira downed the last of her drink before picking up her bag and hauling herself to her feet. Vera watched this performance curiously. Grace noticed the hint of a frown cross Vera's face. She moved to her friend's side. "What's up? You seem a bit concerned about something."

"I'll tell you about it on our way home."

Grace nodded and moved off to join the others now making their way to the stairs. Gordon held the door open them. Grace stopped and stood beside him. Only the three members of the Busy Fingers crew remained in the rooftop area. Elaine Bennett went to her office. She would lock up after everyone left.

"The weather is beautiful at this time of year," Grace commented to Gordon, "Just perfect for spending a couple of hours up here in the evening. I found tonight really relaxing … o-o-h, look at that!"

Gordon followed her gaze and grinned. "Well, I guess that doesn't leave too much to wonder about. We might keep quiet about it though. No point in spoiling some future surprise for the others."

As they watched, the last couple of the group ahead of them reached the bottom of the stairs, exited the stairwell area and entered the shopping plaza through the big doors that they still kept locked during the day. Jeremy Sinclaire had a protective arm across Mariah Obrin's back as he guided her out into the plaza.

"I don't think either of them is going straight home tonight," Grace whispered with a giggle.

"Oh, I don't know," Gordon replied. "One might be going home … the other one might tag along for company."

"What's going on?" Vera enquired as she joined Grace and Gordon at the door. "I hope I didn't hold you up. I couldn't find my car key in my bag. As I'm driving us all back to the retirement complex tonight, I thought it critical that I found it." With that, she held the offending key up by its tag and waved it in front of her two companions. Vera seemed to have forgotten her original question, so the other two left it unanswered.

After arriving back at the retirement complex, the other two waited while Vera locked her car before the three of them made their way together into the building that housed their units. As they crossed the foyer, Vera sighed and said, "There's a very positive vibe about the Plaza at the moment. It's been building for a couple of weeks. Sales are good and improving, and the size of the town is increasing by the day. So many new faces around, so many different nationalities; it gives the place a new 'flavour' somehow. The good news stories tonight were like the icing on the cake. I think the Plaza will become an exciting place to be involved with."

There was murmured agreement as the trio split up to make their way to their individual units. She is right, Grace thought as she inserted the key in her door. There is almost an excited air about the place. If it keeps building like this, we could be in for an exceptional Christmas trading period – and a busy one. I hope all our crew is up to it.

Next morning, as Grace and Vera waited in the foyer for Gordon to join them for the trip to the Plaza, Grace reminded Vera she hadn't spoken about whatever concerned her the night before as they left the rooftop garden. "Come on, you said you would tell me on the way on home. What was it?"

"I didn't want to say anything in front of Gordon. Don't look like that. It's nothing important, just a bit surprising. I noticed Moira was drinking mineral water last night. That's not her usual tipple."

"Do you think she still might not be very well?"

"I'm not sure what I think. There have been a couple of little things – including the mineral water – which are so out of character for Moira."

"Keep your eyes open. Let's see if we spot any other funny things before we rush to conclusions."

The next Friday night, Moira wasn't at the rooftop garden. Mariah was surprised, as Moira had indicated earlier that she would be there. Rose offered her thoughts on the reason. "I spoke to Moira briefly this afternoon. Embellish was busy all day. The warmer weather is bringing customers in for beach gear. Moira looked very tired when I saw her. I commented on it. She said she was so busy all day, she was feeling a bit worn out."

Mariah looked concerned. "I hope she is okay. I'm delighted both my stores are so busy, but I don't want to kill my Embellish manager in the pursuit of sales."

It was the middle of the following week, when a casual comment by Edith caused pause for thought. As Edith entered the Busy Fingers store that morning she announced, "I'd swear Moira has put on more weight. Even her face is starting to look fat."

"I don't know how you can tell," Rose said quietly. "Moira's promoting her new line of casual beach clothing. She has taken to wearing those flowing brightly coloured things Embellish sells. Their design -- loose and baggy – means they are cool for summer. You could be as big as a house and no one would notice if you wore one of those outfits."

Edith's initial comment stopped Grace as she filled the sewing threads stand. For a moment, she stood with her hand poised above the stand. Vera, working nearby, noticed the sudden halt to operations and sidled over to Grace. "What's up?" she whispered as Rose delivered her news about Moira wearing Embellish styles to work.

"Uhmm, I'm not sure. How about we take a coffee break?"

"It's a bit early, isn't it?"

"I thought that, if we had ours now, we could mind the store while the others all went for their break." Vera realised there was more to Grace's suggestion than coffee.

As the two women walked past Edith and Rose fussing with a display stand, Vera announced, "We are taking an early break so we can cover for the rest of you when you go for morning tea."

They barely turned the coffee machine on before Vera couldn't contain herself any longer. "Okay, come on, what's this all about?"

"Well, it is pure speculation on my part, you understand, but I'm beginning to wonder if Moira might continue putting on weight for a bit longer yet. A sort of 'localised' weight gain, if you know what I mean."

"Pregnant? You think she might be pregnant?" Vera's eyes opened wide as she studied Grace's face for clues.

"I don't know, but think about it. If you put it all together, it does suggest that. She was unwell for quite a while, she was drinking mineral water instead of her usual wine, she is wearing baggy outfits … and you noticed her struggling to heave herself out of her chair the last time she was with us at the roof garden."

"Yeah, but some of those chairs are terrible; so low and deep, you almost have to climb out of them. We all try to avoid them because they are too much of a challenge for us oldies."

"…But Moira is a lot younger than we are. She shouldn't struggle as much as she did."

"Hmmm, you might be onto something. At our hand-over meeting with Mariah, when Mariah asked Moira to be full-time manager of Embellish, she hesitated before accepting. The hesitation was only about as long as a heart-beat, but it was there. It was strange and Mariah queried it. Moira's explanation for the hesitation seemed reasonable at the time."

Grace pondered the situation as she carried her coffee to the table. "Like everything else, in itself, that doesn't mean anything. I'm probably just an old woman with an over-active imagination."

"I'm not so sure about that. Is Moira seeing someone? I've never seen her with anyone. I admit I don't know anything about her private life. I wonder who the father is … and how long it will be before she shares the good news."

"It might not be *good* news, particularly as she seems to be keeping it a secret. How long ago was it that we noticed she was unwell?"

A quick trawl through their memories and some rapid arithmetic produced a couple of startling facts. Moira was showing signs of being unwell when she came to help Mariah set up Bedazzled before the Plaza opened. If that were the case, it happened sometime prior to that.

"She must be about five months along," Vera said.

"Yes, that's my reckoning as well," Grace replied. "If we are correct, she's won't be able to keep it a secret much longer. It'll become obvious to all and sundry."

"Just look at us carrying on out here like a pair of old gossips. Maybe we should get back to work… and not share our thinking with anyone?"

"Agreed, but I know I will be watching developments closely in future."

By the end of the month, those new initiatives from early in the month were old news and had become part of the routine of life in the Plaza.

The farmers' co-operative womenfolk now produced an extensive range of jams, curds, pickles, chutneys and relishes. Amina reported good steady sales of their products through The Bazaar, and Jack Walker reported the women were selling quite a bit at the various district markets. Samira did her bit to help by using as many of their products as possible in the new range of food they offered at Caffeine Heaven.

Something of a mutual admiration society developed between Samira and Jack Walker. The frequency of their contact increased significantly once Samira sold the co-op on the idea of the women producing various products using what they were growing. Jack had never met anyone like her before; so driven and so efficient. To Samira, Jack remained something of a mystery – an enigma even. Most people's first impression of Jack was of a local bushie – unrefined and a master of mild Australian vernacular. In a short time after she met Jack, Samira recognised much more than that in the man. This was someone switched on to more than his farm, down to earth, and a very shrewd operator. Someone with whom she could have in-depth meaningful conversations.

Jeremy Sinclaire and Mariah Obrin lunching together failed to attract any attention these days. Clifton Sinclaire, Jeremy's son, managed the Good Companions store while his father lunched with Mariah. At first, Jeremy took lunch to Bedazzled where the couple ate together. However, now that Mariah's best friend, Patsy Evans came in for two or three hours to help every day, Mariah left the store for lunch. The couple often ate at Caffeine Heaven and occasionally at The Brasserie. There is no longer any mystery about why Mariah changed her mind about staying on in Oyster Point. Both she and Jeremy are positively glowing now their relationship has taken off.

While Gordon Bailey remained available to help at Caffeine Heaven if required, Samira's becoming full-time there, freed him up to return to his former life: helping at Busy Fingers and writing those articles he meant to get around to for months. As a semi-retired freelance journalist, he has missed writing, and a couple of publications hounded him for articles.

One particular magazine wanted a follow up on the piece he did early in the year on the devastation and recovery of Oyster Point. He suggested on a couple of occasions that it might be better to wait until the Plaza was open for about six months before writing the follow up article. His hope was to stall things long enough to find time to write something. However, although no longer tied down to Caffeine Heaven, it will take him a while to catch up with his writing. His current priority, is attending the swag of outback festivals in Queensland and the Northern Territory over the end of August and early September.

These always provide a wealth of material for articles written over the following few months. This year, his trip will be a bit different. He will take a carload of products from their Busy Fingers store. Grace will fly out to meet him at a couple of venues and set up a stall to sell their wares. She will then fly back to Oyster Point, leaving Gordon to complete his outback wanderings.

Moira's dramatically changing figure now has everyone's attention. Although obvious, she maintains her secrecy about it and the father's identity. Vera shared her concerns with Grace. "I am going to have to broach the subject of what Moira's plans are for after the baby arrives. Is she going to work on, take extended time off, or become a stay at home mum? I suspect Mariah will ask me to look after Embellish again if Moira is only going to be gone a short while. Since Moira isn't talking about her situation – and certainly hasn't admitted she is pregnant – I'm not sure how to have that conversation."

Grace shrugged. "Maybe you should talk to Mariah. She might know Moira's plans. If not, she will need to find out sometime. Anyway, Mariah might not be planning to ask you back. She might have other ideas, like asking Patsy to manage Embellish. I think you have a right to know at least how it is likely to involve you."

"You're right; I'll talk to Mariah."

"It is so long since life was 'normal' around here, I'm not sure what normal for Harbour Plaza looks like any more," Grace observed.

Connections

Ah, the problems secrets cause… All keepers of secrets struggle with the big question: whether to share their secrets with one or some, or to guard them from everyone. Of course, there are no secrets from me. I know them all. All those Harbour Plaza secrets and the anguish some caused.

".… Yes, yes, we are interested in second hand books …. Yes, even old books …. Well, if you bring them in, we'll have a look at them …. Yes, we would need to have a look at them …. When you say 'a lot', roughly how many? …. Perhaps you could bring a few at a time …. Maybe put a few in a carton or something; just however many you can manage comfortably … Yes, we do need to look at them first …. Okay then, you think about it …. Bye."

Jeremy Sinclaire, sorting stock in the back room, found his son's phone conversation intriguing. He wandered out to the sales area of Good Companions bookstore in time to hear the 'clunk' of the phone being hung up. "Anything good come out of all that?" he asked.

"Some old biddy with a lot of old books wants to know what we will give her for them. I don't know how many times you have to tell people that you need to actually see the books to know whether you want them or not." Clifton Sinclaire vented his frustration.

"Our potential clients are not 'old biddies', Clifton. Appropriate decorum prevails in this establishment. Now tell me the story, please."

"I'd never call her an old biddy to her face. It was… never mind. She called about a lot of old books and wanted me to give her a price unseen. I couldn't determine how many 'a lot' was, but it sounds like a substantial collection. She says some of them are very old and quite yellow."

"They could be worth a look. If there are too many for us, we might be able to offload some to other second-hand stores around the place. Did you get her details? I could have a look at the collection and give her some idea of whether we are interested. It would save her traipsing in here with them."

"I made a note of the caller ID number. She said her name quickly, but I think it sounded something like Tristan."

Jeremy made the call: her name was Grisham. He arranged to call at her house at ten o'clock. She lived a few kilometres up the highway on the northern side of the river. Mrs Grisham reminded him of an old mop: pencil thin and short – barely five feet tall he estimated – and topped by a mop of steely grey hair permed almost to oblivion and with patches of pink skull showing through. She greeted him in a nondescript floral cotton frock topped by a frilled apron teamed with a warm smile, cake and coffee. Social niceties demanded he spend time over the morning tea she provided. It wasn't wasted time, however, as she shared something of her history with him.

Then they moved to the books in a backroom of the cottage. A room in an attic-type space served as a small bedroom for some time before becoming a storage space for junk and other possessions too 'precious' for disposal. "I was born and grew up in this house," Mrs Grisham announced proudly. "I think it was my grandparents' place originally, then my father's and now it's mine. The need for a new roof made me look at what was up in that attic. My grandson helped me sort it out a bit, and bring all these old books down here. I don't know how long they have been here, but they went into that attic more than 70 years ago after it was no longer my bedroom."

Lost for words and with mouth agape, Jeremy surveyed the books. He smiled weakly at Mrs Grisham. "It may take me some time to look through this lot," he said, gesturing around the room. "Is it all right if I stay for a few hours? I could come back another day, if it were more convenient."

"Stay as long as you like. Come back again another day if needed to finish. There's cold chicken and salad for lunch if you're still here. If you don't need me, I'll get on with other things."

Where do I start? Jeremy stood rooted to the spot. Come on, man, get your arse moving, he told himself. It wasn't a large room. Stacks of books – about thigh high – filled more than half the room. He knew there would be very few gems, a few good ones, quite a few that were okay but not particularly interesting, and a lot of rubbish. That's the way it is with collections. He planned his attack: stack any gems and good stuff over there, the okay stuff here, and the rubbish over there on the other side of the room. After a deep breath, he pulled on cotton gloves and walked to the first stack.

Time passed unnoticed. Mrs Grisham startled him when she spoke. "Lunch is ready, if you can tear yourself away. The bathroom is across the hall, if you want to wash up."

Jeremy quickly flicked through remaining books of the current stack before slowly straighten up and stretching his back. He had made good progress. More importantly, if his preliminary assessments were correct, he had identified a staggering number of gems… exciting gems.

After lunch, Jeremy retrieved a number of cardboard cartons from his vehicle before again attacking the stacks of books. He labelled a couple of cartons 'gems' and 'really good' respectively, and packed the appropriate finds into each. It was almost something of a relief to find that one back corner of the room held stacks of old magazines. Some of these might be worth a bit but, with so many good books to deal with, Jeremy had difficulty generating any enthusiasm for the magazines.

Mrs Grisham announced afternoon tea. Jeremy welcomed the break. His back let him know he was no longer young. However, he now felt confident he would finish all the stacks by the end of the afternoon.

It was after five o'clock when he completed the last stack. As he stretched his back yet again, he surveyed his day's work. He had assessed everything except the magazines. Elated with the finds, he found it almost impossible to comprehend the number of books identified as gems. The challenge now was to decide which ones he wanted and how much to offer Mrs Grisham for them. Before leaving, he arranged to return the next day to collect more books and start payment negotiations.

Back at the store, Clifton gave him a sullen welcome. "Nice to see you back. It would have been nice to know you would be gone all day."

Clifton was like this for a few days now and it was beginning to wear thin with his father. Jeremy chose not to respond, instead walking through to the stockroom to retrieve the trolley without a word. As he opened the back door, he called over his shoulder. "You might give me a hand if you're not serving at the moment." Jeremy's tone suggested it was in Clifton's best interest to comply without argument.

"Are you sure we want all these books?" Clifton asked as they wheeled the last cartons into the stockroom. "A lot of these cartons are labelled as gems. Can that be right? You actually found that many gems?"

"Give me a hand to unpack a couple of the cartons onto the sorting table please, Son. I think I will be here until quite late tonight. I want to reassess as many of these as possible before tomorrow so I can get an idea of what we are going to have to pay Mrs Grisham. Perhaps you could give me a hand. We'll slip down to The Brasserie later for a quick meal, if that's okay."

They worked well as a team. While Jeremy examined each book, Clifton entered its details onto a database and checked the internet for any available current buying and selling prices for other copies of the book. At about 7.30pm, they made their way to The Brasserie. Clifton's sullenness had vanished and, over the course of their meal, he chatted animatedly about the books. After dinner, they continued working until about eleven o'clock. By then, only a couple of cartons labelled 'really good' remained unopened.

Jeremy was silent on the drive home. He had printed out the information from Clifton's database and now his mind feverishly tried to calculate how much the reassessed books would cost him. Their cash reserves were good, but there were still more cartons to collect. He knew he had to be discerning or they could deplete their cash reserves. However, he must offer Mrs Grisham a reasonable price.

The following day, he returned to the store by lunchtime. Over lunch with Mariah Obrin, he babbled on excitedly about the treasure trove he acquired.

The books left a large hole in their capital but they were worth every cent of it, and Mrs Grisham was ecstatic about her payment. After lunch, Jeremy told Clifton he would be spending a good deal of time in the stockroom over the next few days, and promptly disappeared.

At closing time, Clifton wondered if his father intended working late again. He was trying to decide whether to interrupt his father or leave it until after closing to ask what plans were for the evening. No decision was required. Jeremy rushed from the stockroom to the front door. On his way out, he called out, "Hold the fort a bit longer, please. I'll be back as soon as I can."

Somehow managing not to run, Jeremy was relieved to find La Boulangerie still open. "Cecile, Cecile, are you here?" he called out as he rushed into the shop and found it deserted. Cecile, looking a little startled, bobbed up from behind the counter.

"Jeremy! What is wrong? What has happened?"

"Oh, there you are. Sorry I shouted; I didn't see you down there. Cecile, I think I have found something that might interest you. Perhaps, after you close up, you might come down to Good Companions so I can show you."

"I am closing now. If you will wait a moment, I will come with you. Can you not give me some clue what this thing is?" Jeremy just laughed and shook his head.

He held the door open for Cecile to enter the bookstore before leading her through to the stockroom. On the way through, he spoke to Clifton. "Close up now please, and then come and join us in the stockroom. You too will be interested in what I have found."

A solitary book lay in a cleared space on the sorting table. Jeremy guided Cecile to the table and, after putting on cotton gloves, picked up the book. He showed Cecile the cover and spine. Clifton noticed a confused look cross Cecile's face. "What's this all about, Dad? Why have you brought Cecile and me to look at this particular book?"

Jeremy placed the book back on the table and carefully opened it to the title page. Cecile gasped. Clifton galloped around the table to peer over his father's shoulder. So there's an inscription, he thought, so what? Cecile's squeak of delight brought him back to reality.

"*Tres magnifique!* There is a date… I must think on this for a moment… Yes, I think maybe it is my grandmother." She explained to her equally excited audience that the inscription, in French, told them the book belonged to Angelique Simon. It was a gift to Angelique on her ninth birthday. The date and age were correct for Cecile's grandmother.

With a soft moan, Cecile clapped her hands to her face and looked up at Jeremy, her eyes brimming with tears. "Soon after I arrived here, I received information that my … how do you say it … my early family … a long time ago … were here in Oyster Point. I thought, *impossible,* and I did not think on this again. I wanted to believe it was wrong. John, my husband, said the certificates would not lie and I should look more at this. I did not want to. We are French, not Australian, I told him.”

“I'm not sure how you feel about finding this. There is more, but this already is a shock. Perhaps we should leave the rest until you work out whether you want to know more.”

“No, no, I do want to know more -- now. I do not want to wait. I want to see whatever it is. How did you know the name Simon was connected to me?”

“Someone I was chatting to in the store one day suggested there might be an early connection. I can't remember who it was. Now, are you sure you want to see what else I have?” She nodded enthusiastically and gestured for him to show her.

With great care, Jeremy turned to the back of the book. There, sandwiched between the end paper and the back cover, was a yellowed, neatly folded sheet of paper. He lifted it out and carefully unfolded it on the table. It was a letter to Angelique from her father. The date on the letter echoed the date of the inscription.

Cecile read the letter quickly and then stepped back from the table to prevent the tears rolling down her cheeks from falling on the document. Surprised by her movement away from the table, Jeremy spun around to look at her. She gestured that she was okay and to give her a moment. Jeremy offered her his handkerchief and she wiped her eyes.

“Mon Dieu, that is so… so beautiful. Her father must have loved this daughter very much. I think I need to sit down, please.” Clifton grabbed a chair and wheeled it around the table. Cecile flopped onto it and Clifton wheeled it in closer to the table. With her head in her hands and her elbows propped on the table, she read the letter again… and again.

“I don't know how Mrs Grisham came to have this book, or if there are any others that belonged to the Simon family, but I will ask her about where these wonderful old books came from,” Jeremy assured Cecile. Then, to Clifton, “I'll give her a ring in the morning to see if I can visit her tomorrow. If it suits her, you could be on your own a while again tomorrow.” As an afterthought, he turned back to Cecile. “May I mention your possible family connection and why I'm interested in the provenance of the collection?”

“Oh, *oui,* maybe she knows something. If she does, I would like very much to meet with her. I must go home and tell John what has happened.”

“We all should go home before it gets any later.” As Cecile stood to leave, Jeremy folded the letter, put it back in the book, placed the book in a book box and handed it to Cecile. “This belongs to you. It would thrill me if you accepted it. Please take it with you.”

That brought a new flood of tears and a half-hearted show of resisting the offer, but there was no way she was leaving Good Companions without that book. With the book firmly clasped to her chest as they walked to their vehicles, she assured Jeremy she was okay to drive home.

John hadn't arrived home yet. Dumping her bag on her way through, Cecile went directly to the office. She dug out the certificates and other family information. That's where John found her when he arrived home, sitting on the floor with bits of paper spread out around her. "What happened? Did you drop a file or something?"

"Non, I am looking again at all that information about my family."

"Great; I always thought it would be good for you to investigate a little further. There could be some interesting stories wrapped up in your family's history. ...But, what prompts you to revisit it now?"

Cecile walked him through to the lounge room where she left the precious book in its box, and explained what happened earlier that afternoon. "So now Jeremy will try to see Mrs Grisham again tomorrow to see if he can find out anything more for me. I am beginning to hope there is some connection and she will be able to tell me more about my Simon family."

"When you first received all that information, didn't Gordon Bailey suggest he was familiar with the Simon name? Perhaps you could have a talk to him again to see if he remembered anything about the name."

"Merci beaucoup; I had forgotten about that. Thank you for reminding me. I will give him a call now."

"Do you think you should? Maybe you could see him at the Plaza tomorrow."

"No, no; I will call him now."

Gordon was apologetic. The matter slipped his mind. He remembered offering to look up his research on the Simon name once he got his new computer up and running, but forgot to do it. Cecile's disappointment was clear. His guilt matched her disappointment. "I'll have a look at what I've got tonight and talk to you tomorrow. There is one thing though; I don't know how much I have or how relevant it might be. Please don't get your hopes up too high."

Don't get my hopes up too high, she thought, how can I not? However, she reassured Gordon that whatever he had would be very welcome. Later, over a glass of wine, John also tried to dampen her enthusiasm without any appreciable success. The phone rang as Cecile was making a move to prepare dinner. It was Gordon: could he come over -- after dinner perhaps?

"N-o-o, come now and eat with us – unless you have other plans for dinner, of course. You have something to show me?" Cecile asked, trying to keep her voice neutral.

"I'll have a shower and see you in about 20 minutes," Gordon replied without answering Cecile's question.

Over her clattering and banging in the kitchen, she told John that Gordon was joining them for dinner. He again advised not getting too excited. Cecile just smiled and nodded as she turned the chicken pieces she was browning. "*Mais certainment.* I know it might be nothing and I should not get excited but, if he is coming tonight instead of waiting until tomorrow, he must have something for me, *n'est pas*?

Twenty minutes felt more like an hour. Cecile's emotions fluctuated between excitement and apprehension. When Gordon arrived, all three gathered briefly in the lounge room before John excused himself to attend to the cooking. He wanted to give Cecile her own space to listen to Gordon, but he would keep an ear open for anything that suggested what she heard was distressing.

From a large envelope, Gordon withdrew a number of printed pages and laid them on the coffee table. "These are my research notes, mainly transcripts of newspaper articles." Cecile made a grab for them. "No, wait please. How committed are you to finding out about the local Simon family? What if it is not all 'good' news?"

"I have thought about this. I decided I want to know -- no, I *must* know, no matter what it is."

Gordon took an audible deep breath as he considered her response. "Okay, I will leave these pages with you to read when you are ready. Then, you might want to talk to me again. Suffice to say their story is interesting and intriguing, but not necessarily the stuff of normal family relationships or happy endings. I suggest you leave reading it until after I've gone and you have a quiet time to yourself. Now, am I still invited to stay for dinner?"

John was relieved to hear Cecile laugh and wandered out from his self-imposed exile in the kitchen, to catch the end of something Cecile was saying.

"…Of course you must stay for dinner, which should be just about ready by now. If you and John entertain yourselves for a few minutes, I will go to dish up."

As he dropped into a chair opposite their guest, John raised his eyebrows in question at Gordon. "Everything go all right?"

"So far, but stay close by when she reads the stuff I gave her. It doesn't exactly tell a pretty story. Although she says she wants to know, I'm not sure how she will react."

Light-hearted conversation accompanied dinner. Cecile joined in and seemed to enjoy the evening, but both men noticed she was distracted. As soon as dinner was over, Gordon took his leave. Aware his wife wanted to escape to read Gordon's information, John volunteered to clean up and pack the dishwasher. Cecile collected Gordon's pages and went to the office to read them alone.

John read the newspaper for a while before deciding to venture into the office. Alarmed at the sight that met him; he rushed over and wrapped an arm around his wife's shoulders. "What is it? What can be so distressing? Give me that stuff." He snatched the pages from Cecile's hand. The silent tears trickling down his wife's face wrenched his heartstrings.

"No, John, give it back please. It is such a sad story. It is not what I expected or hoped for, just very sad. I must talk to Gordon again to see if there is more he can find out about the family. He was right, it is intriguing." He left her alone with the information, which she continued to pore over long after he went to bed. It was unsettling that she wouldn't discuss it. If he knew how the story went, he could be ready for whatever fallout might result. No doubt, there would be a whole truckload of emotional upheaval over the next few days.

The now silent house provided Cecile the solitude she craved at this time. She read Gordon's material again. Absentmindedly, she reached for pen and paper and began scribbling as she read. At the end of the last page, she glanced at her scrawl. She had created her own haphazard record of names, dates and events. After studying her notes for a few moments, she tore off her notes and started a fresh page, this time setting the details out in logical order.

It was almost impossible to comprehend. She had some connection to the incredible story hinted at in the notes. There must be more available somewhere. Gordon's information suggested a more complex story with a tragic ending. It had her hooked. She needed to know the whole story, as ugly as it might prove to be.

Her mind wandered back to events at the Good Companions bookstore, and she ran over everything Jeremy said about Mrs Grisham. What was the woman's connection to the Simon family, and would she agree to a meeting? A worrying thought occurred to Cecile: even if they did meet, the woman might not want to share her story, or might not have any information to share. It was with this lingering doubt that Cecile forced herself to go to bed, although she knew sleep would be elusive.

When John wandered out for breakfast, Cecile was ready to leave for the Plaza. "You're early today aren't you?" he queried. "You don't usually leave for work for another half hour or so."

"I want to get an early start and have everything done so I can have some time to speak with Gordon. I am not sure what to do if Jeremy persuades Mrs Grisham to speak with me. She is an old lady who probably won't want me to visit in the evening. I might have to close early, or shut for some time during the day. It is difficult to organise with no one to help at La Boulangerie."

"Well, if it helps, I'm not going out to the mine site for the next two days. I have meetings here in town this morning and then I'm free all afternoon – or I could work this afternoon and take tomorrow afternoon off instead if that suits you better. I have looked after the shop for you before, so it will be okay. Give me a call when you know what is happening."

Cecile planted a kiss on her husband before dashing out the door. Today is looking better already, she thought. If Jeremy can work some magic with Mrs Grisham and set up a meeting for today, it will be perfect. Good fortune continued when she arrived at the Plaza. Gordon Bailey had arrived as well, and they walked in together. They agreed to meet at La Boulangerie at ten o'clock.

As ten o'clock drew closer, Cecile almost wished the customers would stop coming – just for an hour or so to allow her to talk to Gordon in peace. The shop was empty when Gordon arrived. Cecile called him through to the back where she was making coffee. She caught her breath as Gordon walked in. He carried another large envelope.

"I decided to do a bit more digging," he said as she poured the coffee. "I found a bit more for you. The trouble is, the more I find, the more tantalizing the story becomes. I don't know how much more we can discover, but we are still a long way from knowing the whole story." Cecile slowly withdrew the envelope's contents: another three pages.

While scanning the pages, she handed Gordon a copy of the timeline she created the previous night.

"Is this my copy – can I make notes on it?" he asked. Cecile, engrossed in reading his latest offering simply nodded.

Cecile was at the end of page three when Jeremy called out. She invited him to join them for coffee. "I hope you have brought good news in return for this coffee," she said as she handed him his mug.

"If by 'good news' you mean Mrs Grisham has agreed to meet with you, then yes, I bring good news. She suggested this afternoon. In case she has a nap, I suggested three o'clock. You have an invitation to join her then for afternoon tea. I think she is excited too. Is that okay, or should I call her back and change the arrangement?"

"No, that is perfect. John will mind the store for me. I must call him. Gordon, I will let you know what I learn." The two men took the hint and left her alone to make her call.

John arrived at about 1.30pm to find her dashing about serving customers and looking distracted. He made them both lunch while she served the last customer. In spite of his best efforts, Cecile remained agitated and unsettled until it was time to leave. She gathered her accumulated paperwork and stuffed it into an envelope. After checking Jeremy's map of how to find Mrs Grisham's house, she gave John a quick peck on the cheek and left.

She didn't need Jeremy's map and easily found the address. Mrs Grisham was on the doorstep before Cecile exited the car. Both women were excited, but manners dictated they should enjoy the tea and chocolate cake before getting down to anything more serious. Nevertheless, cake and tea were dispatched swiftly. With crockery and everything else left abandoned on the table, they adjourned to the sitting room and took their places on opposite sides of a long low coffee table. It was time to see where this meeting might take them.

Cecile hoped for maybe an hour of her host's time. Excitement increased as the meeting progressed. By five o'clock, the women were firm friends. While Elsie Grisham had little information to share, Cecile had plenty to give in return. By the end of the meeting, when they both admitted they were suffering information overload, one thing was clear: there was a family connection, albeit distant, convoluted and tenuous, but still a connection. After agreeing to meet again soon, Cecile drove back to the Plaza in a daze.

She rushed through to Busy Fingers in search of Gordon Bailey. He didn't have to ask how her meeting went. Her glittering eyes and the excitement plastered on her face were indications enough. She continued at pace straight up to him and asked breathlessly, "Are you available for dinner tonight?"

"Definitely – shall we say seven o'clock?"

"No, come straight after work, say, 6.30pm. I don't know what we will eat but there will be something." Gordon laughed and agreed to follow her and John home after the stores closed … which would be in a few minutes time, he thought as he checked his watch.

Then she was on her way to La Boulangerie where John had three customers waiting while he tried to assist an elderly woman decide which variety of loaf she wanted. The look of relief that crossed his face as Cecile entered the shop didn't escape notice and caused a giggle among those waiting in line. By the time the last of the customers was on her way out of the store, it was time to close for the day.

While locking up, she remembered to tell John that Gordon would be joining them for dinner again tonight. He suggested steaks on the barbeque accompanied by a couple of salads and headed to the supermarket to get what was necessary. Cecile drove home and organised wine, glasses and nibbles on the deck in time for Gordon and John's arrival. With glasses filled, Cecile began. She was anxious to share her news and the two men were keen to hear it.

"Elsie, Mrs Grisham, was wonderful. She had little information about the family, but it helped understand their story. I put together the family's story from what I now know, or think I know. Henri Simon, the head of the Simon family here at Oyster Point, I think was Elsie's Grandfather … although she doesn't know that and I'm not altogether sure it is correct. If I am right, we share the same ancestor. Her story is a little different from mine, but it is fascinating." From there, the story flowed on. As Cecile unfolded her cobbled together story of the family's history, the men struggled to follow all the players and events.

Henri Simon arrived in Australia from France in the 1870s and ended up at Oyster Point. It was one of the earliest settlements along the coast and became an important port for the surrounding hinterland. Simon saw its potential and, using family money from France, established an 'agency', an import/export operation. He built the large warehouse on part of the area now occupied by stage 2 of the supermarket. He also built a store next to the warehouse, where the old hall used to be, and that old Queenslander that was the family's home on what is now the supermarket carpark.

Once his business was established, the young Henri – now in his early thirties – sent for his bride. Their families arranged the marriage between Henri and Marie when the pair was quite young. Marie's family were becoming concerned that Henri had reneged on the deal and were relieved when the call came for her to join him. Marie was now 23, and it was becoming embarrassing that she was not yet married. Everything was prepared in advance. The couple married in Brisbane two days after Marie arrived in Queensland. The newly-weds then boarded a coastal vessel for the trip north to Oyster point.

Soon after, babies began arriving with monotonous regularity. Quite a tribe amassed despite a number of miscarriages and infant deaths along the way. They might have numbered significantly more if Marie had not become ill. Her illness was serious and progressive. She declined through a number of stages until finally becoming bedridden.

It was at this point in the story that John suggested they light the barbeque, and leave the next instalment until after they had eaten. Gordon and Cecile prepared salads and set the table while John dealt with the steaks. While dinner wasn't rushed, it wasn't a leisurely meal, and it didn't leave Cecile's story on hold for the duration either. Aspects of the story dominated conversation during the abbreviated meal break. Afterwards, comfortably settled in the lounge room, Cecile continued her story.

"Although Marie was so ill, it appears Henri did not want to miss out on the ...uhmm ... how do you say... 'home comforts'. Whether he had grown tired of Marie, or because of her illness, Henri found comfort elsewhere. The relationship he started with a local woman lasted for some time."

Gordon sat upright. "This might be the woman alluded to in those newspaper articles. They never really said there was someone else involved. It was only inferred that something not quite aboveboard went on."

"Yes, I think that was the case. Marie became ill during her last pregnancy and, by the time the baby arrived, she was too ill to care for it herself. Her oldest daughter tried to take over but she was still a child and too young to look after a new baby and the rest of her siblings. Henri employed a housekeeper and shortly after, also a nurse to look after his wife and the new baby."

"I think I can see where that situation was headed," John murmured and raised his eyebrows at Gordon, who nodded his support for the unspoken idea.

"For some time Marie was completely bedridden, then a slow improvement. On good days, she could walk around for brief periods, and on not so good days, she would sit in a lounge chair for a while. There remained days when she could not get out of bed at all. However, because of her improved condition, Henri decided Marie no longer required a nurse. His oldest daughter and the housekeeper could manage everything between them. A short time after that, the story becomes tragic." Cecile paused while she took another sip of coffee.

"I take it this is the time when the newspaper was full of her apparent disappearance," Gordon asked.

"Yes. According to the newspaper, Marie spent the morning sitting on the verandah and then in the sitting room. Some of the children were at school but after lunch, Henri loaded the rest of his children and the housekeeper into his wagon and took them to a nearby beach for the afternoon. Reports say he dropped everyone at the beach with a picnic hamper and returned to work in his office until it was time to collect them again. Something delayed him and it was later than intended when he collected his family. When they arrived home, Marie was not about. Everyone assumed she was in bed. The household was busy after that. There was the hamper to unpack, children to bath and dinner to prepare. Nobody went to check on Marie until dinnertime. She wasn't in her room or anywhere else around the house."

Gordon took up the story. "The newspaper reported Henri raised the alarm after they searched everywhere and realised she was missing. It was late – coming on dark, I think -- but a few people searched the area around the house. There was no sign of her. The conclusion was that, after the family left, she suffered some sort of 'mental lapse' – I think they called it – and wandered off."

"That is correct. Henri and the housekeeper argued that Marie was not strong enough to have wandered off, but people reported seeing her strolling in her garden on occasions. A huge number of men searched with lanterns late into the night. They searched unsuccessfully for the next two days. Stories began to emerge about occasions when Henri, having had too much to drink, was heard shouting at Marie that she disgusted him and that her illness was all in her mind. When questioned about the stories, he claimed that Marie was trying to punish him for taking her away from her beloved France and bringing her to Oyster Point. Her illness was largely feigned and not as serious as she would have people believe."

John was shaking his head in disbelief. "Surely no one believed that story. There must have been a doctor or others who could swear her illness was genuine."

"That might be true today, John," Cecile said. "Henri was a big man in the town – an important man. He claimed he had not gone to the house after dropping his family at the beach and people remembered him at his workplace. Speculation ran rife and continued for many weeks. Then whispers began to circulate about Henri's supposed liaison with another woman."

"I remember this bit of the story," Gordon said and chuckled. "An over-zealous local plod arrested Henri on suspicion of having done away with his wife. He spent a few days in jail, but they didn't have a body or any other evidence of foul play. They had to let him go …. much egg on face for the local copper, and transfer to another town. However, about six months later, based on gossip and sworn statements from some residents, the new officer in charge of the local Police dragged Henri in for questioning on a number of occasions. It must have been apparent to Henri that there was a strong case building against him. He sent the family and the housekeeper off somewhere, didn't he?"

Cecile nodded. "Yes. He told the Police he sent them south for a holiday to avoid having them distressed by what was happening. Then, a few days later, it emerged that Henri also disappeared. From sightings and other information received over some time, the police pieced together a picture of what happened. Residents saw Henri drive a wagon out of town late one evening. Investigations showed he travelled through the night to the next town south of Oyster Point. The next day he sailed for Brisbane where he met his family. Later, they all travelled on to Sydney and boarded a ship for France."

Cecile reached the end of the story and settled back in her chair. The two men looked at her expectantly but she didn't notice. John and Gordon exchanged a look. Gordon shrugged to indicate he didn't know whether that was the end of the story or not. John felt cheated and left dangling by the ending. After the silence stretched on for a couple of minutes, John could contain himself no longer.

"So, what about this other woman, the one you share an ancestor with? Where does she fit into all this?"

"Eh? Oh, I forgot to tell you about that part, didn't I? Well, hers is another story, but I believe it is part of the same tragic story of the Simon family. Where to start? Maybe with Elsie Grisham's Grandmother, I think. Yes …?" Cecile looked from John to Gordon for confirmation. They both nodded and Cecile launched into the next episode of the Simon saga.

"Of course, Elsie knew her grandmother and her 'grandfather', but she doesn't know anything about them. After her mother died, Elsie found her mother's birth certificate amongst her mother's papers. It showed her mother's parents were the two people Elsie knew as her grandparents. Then, about 20 years ago, for some reason she needed to produce a copy of her mother's birth certificate. She presented the document from amongst her mother's papers, but it was rejected. It wasn't a 'proper' certificate. It was not stamped, or certified, or something. I don't understand what the problem was. Whatever the problem, she had to obtain a new copy."

"It was probably only an extract and not a full certificate. They are cheaper but not usually acceptable for legal purposes," Gordon commented.

"Ah, I see. Maybe that was the case. When the new copy arrived, it told a different story. The mother – that is, Elsie's grandmother – was still the same, but there was no father's name. A note in the margin of the certificate showed that the surname of the child – Elsie's mother – changed when she was about five or six to the surname the family used: Elsie's maiden name, Hinchen."

"Elsie's mother was illegitimate. When was she born? Until relatively recent times, if the baby's parents were not married, the baby's registration was under its mother's surname and – regardless of whether the father was known or not – his name would not appear on the certificate. Formal adoption didn't come in until sometime in the 1920s, I think. Before that, if the mother married at some later time, any previous – illegitimate – children simply became known by the new husband's surname." Gordon's explanation of those early practices helped Cecile better understand what happened.

"A-a-h-h, *merci, Gordon. I was not aware of this practice. You are right. This probably is wha*t happened with Elsie's mother. Elsie now accepts that the man she knew as her grandfather was not her mother's biological father. She doesn't know who her real grandfather was and says, although she has tried, she cannot find out."

"It sometimes is difficult to prove beyond any doubt, but there often are ways of getting a reasonably accurate idea of who it could be," Gordon said.

As Cecile's story rolled on, John had reclined his chair and now lay back, hands clasped behind his head, contemplating the ceiling. "Hmm, it's a good story, but that's all it is: a story."

"What are you saying? You think I am making up some … some … fairy tale?" Cecile demanded indignantly.

"No, My Dear. Your story *might be* accurate – or *close* to it – but it is still a story. You have gathered information from a number of sources and rolled it together to come up with a story. There is no real evidence to support that story. How can I put it? What I'm saying is that it probably looks all right, but the story might not be accurate. More real evidence is needed."

"Pfff, of course evidence is needed, but I know I am right. Gordon, you asked when the mother was born. I can't remember the exact date, but it was late in 1901. Everything happening so long ago makes it difficult to check."

"1901…," Gordon mused. "Isn't that the year Marie disappeared and everything went downhill from there for the family? Yes, I am sure she disappeared early in 1901. There will be something in those newspaper extracts I gave you."

"Mais oui, I think this is correct… and I remember it was 1901 when the family went back to France. I must ask Jeremy If I may look at some of those books."

"Did you find out anything about the books?" Gordon asked.

"Not much, but I think there might be more to learn from the books themselves. *Mon Dieu,* I want to know so much more… but where to find it? How to find it?"

"I might be able to help with that…"

"You know how to do this?" Cecile excitedly interrupted Gordon.

"Not really, but I do know someone who does it professionally. She has been a professional genealogy researcher for decades. Her husband is an engineer and was one of the first group to start work on the new mine site. She moved to Oyster Point with him and still does a little research. I'll talk to her about what might be possible. To help her get started, you need to add all the new information to that timeline you drew up, and document everything you learned from Elsie."

"I will do that tonight before I go to bed."

"Oh, good, some of us are going to bed tonight," John commented. "It sounds like I should mind the store for you again tomorrow while you continue your quest for knowledge."

John's comment about bed caused a flurry of 'watch checking'. "God, look at the time," Gordon said. "I've got an early start tomorrow. I'd better be off. I probably won't get a chance to talk to that researcher until about mid-morning. I'll let you know the outcome."

Gordon's departure brought the evening to an abrupt end. After clearing away the last few things, John went to bed and Cecile disappeared into the office.

The morning dragged on. John came in at 12.30pm, freeing Cecile to go in search of Jeremy. She found him lunching with Mariah Obrin in Caffeine Heaven. Not wanting to intrude on Mariah's time, Cecile simply asked if she could look at the other Grisham books at some convenient time. Jeremy suggested straight after lunch, but Cecile was hesitant, as she wanted to leave the afternoon free in case Gordon organised a meeting with the researcher.

Luck prevailed when Gordon sauntered over to their table while they were discussing the matter. He made a tentative appointment with the researcher for three o'clock that afternoon. Cecile agreed, and spent a few moments explaining and apologising to Jeremy before they agreed on five o'clock to look at the Grisham books. Cecile returned to tell John of her afternoon schedule.

The meeting with the researcher went well. Gail Dunbar impressed as being professional and knowledgeable. Cecile handed over copies of everything she knew – or thought she knew – and they agreed the scope of the research to be undertaken.

"She seemed confident there was more to know," Cecile said as they drove back to the Plaza. "I have decided not to talk to Elsie again until I know more. There's no point in both of us worrying ourselves with questions. I will wait until Mrs Dunbar has something new."

After finding John managing okay at La Boulangerie, Cecile went to Good Companions bookstore. It was only a bit after four o'clock but she hoped Jeremy wouldn't mind her arriving so early. Clifton was behind the counter. She asked for Jeremy and was apologising for being early when Clifton cut her off.

"He's not here. I don't know where he is or when he will be back. What did you want anyway?"

Stunned by his attitude, Cecile stammered out the reason for her visit. "Well, if you agreed five o'clock, then I suggest you come back at five o'clock," Clifton replied.

Cecile hurriedly backed out of the store and, still shocked by her reception, slowly made her way back to La Boulangerie. When she was a few metres from her store, Jeremy entered the Plaza and waved to her. She stopped and waited for him.

"I see you're free. Do you want to come and look at those books now?"

She hesitated, not sure what to say. "Uhmm, I'm not sure that's a good idea. I've just come from Good Companions."

"… So, why didn't you go through to look at the books?" Jeremy asked, genuinely puzzled by Cecile's actions and hesitancy.

"Clifton told me to come back at five o'clock as arranged. He said he didn't know where you were or when you would be back."

Jeremy demanded the full story of her encounter with Clifton. He apologised for his son's attitude. "I don't know what's gotten into him. For a while now, he has been so sullen and rude. I tried ignoring it, but this is inexcusable." Despite trepidation about the reception she might receive, Cecile accompanied Jeremy to the bookstore. She needn't have worried. Clifton made no comment, but the look she received spoke volumes.

Together, they systematically examined Elsie's books. Quite a few, although not considered 'gems' by Jeremy, contained inscriptions or names indicating they belonged to members of the Simon family. These were old and mostly children's books, but not necessarily rare. They put them to one side. When they finished, Jeremy packed those they set aside into a couple of cartons and took them to Cecile's car. She would record anything relevant, identify any she might want to buy, and bring the lot back to Jeremy when she was through with them.

By the time they finished, Clifton had closed the store and gone home, as had John. As she drove home, Cecile hoped John had started dinner. Jeremy also wondered whether Clifton was making their dinner. However, he doubted either of them would eat much after the conversation he planned having with his son as soon as he arrived home.

A prepared salad waited on the kitchen bench while Clifton fussed about preparing a couple of steaks. "Thank you for making a start on dinner," Jeremy began, "But please leave it for a few minutes. I want to talk to you."

"Can't it wait until after dinner?"

"No, I want to talk to you now. Let's get a drink and go out on the deck. Clifton scowled at his father, but Jeremy's tone left little room for argument. As soon as they settled, Clifton demanded, "What's so important it can't wait until after we've eaten?"

"Exactly this: your current attitude. You have been sullen, surly and rude to me -- and to others -- for days now. It can't go on. I need to know what's wrong. Maybe there is some way I can help with whatever is the problem."

Clifton snarled a few dismissive remarks in reply. Jeremy persisted, eventually taking a hard line on the issue. He saw Clifton's shoulders sag and knew he had won through. He allowed the lad a few moments to make the next move.

"Dad, what do you know about Claudia Sanders?"

"Claudia Sanders…? Well now, we have her books in the store. They're good sellers. A romance novelist as I recall. She has a strong following locally. I've heard some of her books described as 'racy' – not pornographic or erotic though. Why do you ask? Is there a problem with her works?"

"They do sell well and Claudia earns a nice income from them. There are a couple of things you might not know. Claudia is alive, well and living here in Oyster Point, *and* ... 'she' is not a female."

"No, I didn't know, but I don't think the fact that Claudia is not a female really matters, does it? Surely it is the quality of the work that matters, and I am led to believe she is a very good writer."

"Dad, brace yourself … *Claudia is me* ... or, perhaps more correctly, I am Claudia."

Jeremy struggled to contain his surprise. "I am amazed. Congratulations, that's wonderful, but why the secrecy?"

"Would you buy a 'chick lit' romantic novel written by a bloke?"

"I see your point, but Claudia has many books published. Why is it a problem?"

"A national radio station wants to interview Claudia. With a foghorn voice like mine, there is no way I could pass for female. The marketing exposure such an interview would provide is s-o-o tempting, but I can't see how I can do it."

"You're right. It's too good to pass up. Let me think on it tonight. There has to be a way around this. Now, let's eat. I'm sure I think better after food."

Next morning, when Clifton arrived bleary-eyed for breakfast, Jeremy announced he had come up with an idea. "Claudia needs to email the radio station asking to receive in advance the questions the interviewer intends to ask. This is necessary to allow her to think on appropriate answers before the interview takes place."

"That doesn't alter the fact that I am never going to sound female."

"No, but you won't have to. Once we have the list of questions, you write out the answers you want to give. Then we find a willing female to learn 'her lines' and do the interview in your place."

"Brilliant! That might just work. Who could we enlist to be Claudia?"

"Hmmm, how would you feel about Mariah Obrin posing as you? Her Texan drawl would add another dimension to the charade, don't you think? I'm sure she would be up for it. I could ask her, if you like."

"You're right. Mariah would be up for it and she would relish the deception. She's a good egg, is Mariah."

"I can't tell you how pleased I am to hear you say that. You see, unless you have some strong objection, I am thinking of asking that 'good egg' to join our 'nest'. What do you think?"

"Are you talking about marriage or just shacking up?"

"Good heavens, a man like me has his image to consider, Son. I don't 'shack up'; I get married."

"Good for you. There's just one small problem with that approach. You still have a wife – my mother – albeit long-time estranged and still in the UK. Might not that be an impediment to your plan?"

"Ah, circumstances change. When I realised my feelings for Mariah were becoming serious, I took steps to eliminate that problem. Your parents' divorce was final last week."

They 'clinked' coffee mugs in a toast to the future. The day had started out well.

A couple of weeks later, after most had left the Friday night gathering in the rooftop garden, only a small group remained after Eileen Bennett went to put her office 'to bed' for the night.

Jeremy Sinclaire cleared his throat. "While we are a small intimate group, I wish to share something with you. Sometime ago, a strong connection developed between Mariah Obrin and myself. That connection grew stronger as the year progressed. I realised just how strong while she was overseas for all those weeks. Anyway, long story short…"

"They're the best kind," Clifton chirped.

"Yes, well … as I said, long story short: I have asked Mariah to marry me and she has done me the honour of accepting." A cheer went up from the group as they raised their glasses in salute to the happy couple.

"Speaking of connections…" John began. "You all are aware of recent events that sent Cecile off on a quest to establish her family connections. Perhaps she might share the latest information she received."

"It is fascinating," Cecile began. "I have used two researchers, one here and one in France. I think you all know the story up to when Henri Simon escaped to France with his family in 1901…?" There were nods all round. "We now know that my grandmother was his youngest child born here at Oyster Point not long before his wife, Marie, 'disappeared'. However, there were more Simon children."

"I smell a story here," Clifton murmured.

Cecile nodded and continued. "The housekeeper who took the children away from Oyster Point when things became 'difficult' for Henri travelled to France with the family. Once in France, Henri passed her off as his wife, although it seems they never married. She was a lot younger than Henri, and younger than Marie. Their life together in France produced three more children. I am waiting for information on what happened to all those Simon children. However, there was one more child born here in Oyster Point. The rumour that Henri had a mistress here was true, and the suspicion that he got rid of his wife to be with her also might be correct. In 1901, not long after the family went back to France, his mistress gave birth to a daughter. That girl went on to be Elsie Grisham's mother. So, you see, there are now two people in Oyster Point who can claim a direct connection to the local pioneer, Henri Simon."

While Cecile received comments and congratulations on her discoveries, Mariah leaned over and whispered to Clifton. After a brief hesitation, he shook his head emphatically.

Then it was Gordon Bailey's turn to speak. "I'm sorry to disappoint you, but I don't have any revelations to add to the night's proceedings other than to note that our diligent Centre Manager, one Eileen Bennett, will be back any moment to chuck us out. So, before she does, please charge your glasses for one last toast: Be they intriguing, awkward or delightful, connections enrich our lives. *Here's to connections!*

Wheels & Deals

Incidents during October confirmed residents of Oyster Point are not fools. Astute, quick thinking and courageous, they are capable of compassion and concern for their fellow man... and, when needs be, they can be just a little bit devious. They strengthen my belief that the future of this community is in safe hands.

I'd better get a move on, Meagan thought as she wiped down Caffeine Heaven's outside tables. Sam will pass here in about two minutes. In her peripheral vision, she spotted Sam, approaching from the northern end of The Esplanade, the athlete's demeanour indicative of his competitive spirit. His face thrust forward to meet the headwind and his arms furiously pumping, he kept his racing wheelchair at top speed. Meagan checked her watch. Give him another twelve to fifteen minutes and he'll be finished his workout and ready for breakfast.

Sam Pelham, Oyster Point's racing wheelie, undertook his five kilometre training regime most mornings. Afterwards, he visited the coffee shop for breakfast before heading off to start work at ten o'clock at the gym. Saturday usually meant a slow start to the day, but there was still plenty to do before clients swarmed in for their workouts.

As she straightened up, Meagan heard a shout and spun around towards The Esplanade, in time to see Sam slam on his brakes to avoid colliding with two men. Engrossed in their conversation as they left the marina, they hadn't paused to look before stepping onto The Esplanade, and straight into Sam's flightpath. Sam braked. One side of the racing-chair lifted high off the ground. He threw his weight across to the raised side of the chair to counteract it and bring it squarely back to earth. Wheelchair racing is not for the fainthearted. It can be rough and tumble, but Sam was used to coping with such situations.

Although Sam's actions prevented an accident, Meagan wished she could hear what was happening over there. Sam could be fiery when provoked. Maybe I will get the details when he comes for breakfast. She admired Sam. A nicer bloke you could not find anywhere. A crack sportsman, he was training for an upcoming triathlon when an accident put him in a wheelchair. It never held him back. He was still an athlete and probably was one of the busiest people in Oyster Bay.

The incident over, Sam wriggled his body back into a comfortable racing position. He kicked up the pace a notch for the run to the coffee shop and arrived almost on time. Meagan Maguire watched Aiden Warry, her new employee, hurry across to greet Sam as he parked beside one of the outdoor tables. At the end of August, Samira Buttuta, Meagan's partner in the coffee shop, convinced Meagan their financial situation had improved sufficiently to take on a young part-time employee to help in the shop and allow both of them some time off each week.

Aiden was an apprentice chef at one of the local motels, but only managed to get a few hours work each night. The additional extra hours six days per week at the coffee shop gave him the equivalent of full-time employment. They took turns at everything in the shop. This morning, Samira was the breakfast cook. Meagan and Aiden took care of front of house.

A bit of a gym junkie, Aiden knew Sam well. "You okay, Sam?" he asked. "That was a near miss over there."

"It takes more than them to unseat me." Sam grinned.

"Your usual order won't be long. I think it's almost ready."

Meagan grabbed two coffee mugs and an espresso pot and headed in Sam's direction, hoping to get the details of the incident on The Esplanade. It was good friends like Sam, who helped her through the worst crisis of her life, a crisis that rendered her broken-hearted, penniless, almost bankrupt, and overworked to the point of collapse. Thanks to the support and help of friends, her life now was much brighter.

After refilling mugs on her way, Meagan finally made it to Sam's table. She dumped the two mugs on the table and filled them before flopping onto a chair opposite Sam and opening the conversation. "How's it going, Sam? … Great morning to be out training."

"It's too nice a day to be going to work."

"Right you pair, stop gossiping. Breakfast is served. Samuel, here's your order: Eggs Benedict," Samira said with a smile. "I've been meaning to ask you, Samuel, how come you always order that dish when it's my turn as the breakfast cook?"

Sam winked at Meagan and replied, "It's because I love your cooking, Ms Buttuta – and also since you are the only one other than my mother who calls me Samuel. You make me feel special. Haven't you worked that out yet? Come on; sit down and have a coffee with us. Take a load off before the next mob arrives. I am almost dreading the time when you have young Aiden trained up to take up his share of the cooking duties. I'll really miss the breakfasts you make for me, not to mention the lovely way you say 'Samuel'."

"Plonk yourself down beside Sam, Samira while I get another mug," Meagan said.

Samira was happy for a break after her 6.00am start. While Meagan fetched a mug, Samira frowned at Sam. "You Aussies speak strangely sometimes, Samuel. Meagan says 'plonk yourself down' and means 'sit down', but

Anthony at Busy Fingers explained that cheap liquor is referred to as 'plonk'."

They still giggled over Samira's confusion when Meagan returned. After chatting for about five minutes over coffee, Meagan noticed the coffee shop filling with customers and Aiden needed help. By the time everything was under control again, Samira was back in the kitchen and Sam was on his way to the gym. Damn, she thought. I didn't get to find out about the kerfuffle on The Esplanade this morning.

A while after Sam left and most of the other diners were gone, two men walked in and sat at a table in the far corner. They ordered big breakfasts. Meagan explained that the breakfast menu period was over and breakfast fare was not available at that time of day. The older one became abusive and demanded his order. The younger one was just plain rude.

Although there were few other customers in the shop, the pair caused a scene that was not good for the place's image. Not sure what to do, Meagan made a tactical retreat by saying she would check if the chef was still available to prepare breakfasts. From the kitchen, Samira heard the raised voices and became concerned. As Meagan entered the kitchen, she demanded to know what was happening.

"They want breakfast," Meagan said. "I think we should give them what they want."

"I think we should call Connor Aston, the security Guard, and ask him to remove them."

"No, it's not worth making a scene over. Besides, I think they are the same two blokes Sam had a run in with his morning. If you wouldn't mind making them breakfast, I think it would be for the best." Samira reluctantly agreed, but kept an eye on the pair through the one-way glass panel as she did so.

After dawdling over their breakfasts and a couple of coffee refills, the men left, fortunately before the usual lunchtime rush began. On Samira's insistence, Meagan rang Connor and passed on details of the men and their behaviour. She didn't think they would be a problem for the Plaza, but it roused Connor's interest. He intended keeping an eye out for them.

Trading at the Harbour Plaza was good since it opened but, on odd occasions, stores experienced a quiet hour or two. That particular afternoon, both La Boulangerie and Caffeine Heaven shared one of those rare quiet times. Cecile Baudin from La Boulangerie strolled nextdoor to Caffeine Heaven with a plate of sweet treats and enquired if Meagan and Samira wanted to barter: to trade connoisseur's coffee in exchange for a platter of *beau petit gateaux* and scintillating conversation.

"I see you're as busy as we are. Sit down Cecile, and let's enjoy a coffee break," Meagan said.

Cecile mentioned Sam's near miss earlier in the morning. "I was so glad it wasn't serious."

"What? Samuel nearly had an accident…? He did not mention that to me. What happened?" Samira demanded. Between them, Cecile and Meagan told Samira of Sam's early morning encounter on The Esplanade.

"I saw those two men in the plaza later. Did they come in here?" Cecile asked.

Meagan described her experience with the two men whom she thought were the same ones Sam encountered. Samira could not see them clearly from the kitchen and wanted a description of the men so she would recognize them if they came in again. Neither of her companions could give much of a description. Cecile did not see them clearly and Meagan, rattled by their behaviour, didn't take much notice.

"There are always strangers in the Plaza," Samira commented, "But mostly they are only new people moving into the town, and soon they are no longer strangers. Those two do not sound like they are thinking of becoming residents."

"Now I think about it," Cecile said, "I think I have seen those men before, here in the Plaza. It was a couple of months ago – or was it last month? I'm not sure when, but I think it was same pair. They wandered around the Plaza for several hours, and eventually came into my shop to buy bread. I remember they made me feel uncomfortable."

"In what way…? Did they cause trouble?" Samira asked.

"No, not trouble; they treated me as if I am less intelligent than they are. The first time, I thought it was just how they react to foreigners. I remember now. They have been into my shop twice since we opened. They treat me the same way every time. I have seen them come from the direction of the marina. I think maybe they have a boat there."

"I think you might be right," Meagan answered. "They were coming from that direction this morning when they almost walked into Sam. Today is the first time I have seen them."

"They purchased some of my bread a couple of times. What I did not like was the way they tried to chat to some of the older High School kids in here. Nothing specific; it's just that I don't think adults are usually as persistent when teenagers obviously aren't interested. I wasn't sure it was appropriate behaviour, so I watched closely."

"Did you notice if they hung around the young ones when they were here this time?"

Cecile shook her head. "No, I don't think so. Today, they just wandered about. The teenagers were in the Plaza as they usually are on Saturday mornings – except, the boy with the charming smile wasn't here today. He must be ill or something. He is usually the centre of attention for the rest of the group."

The friends' coffee session ended with the arrival of a group of lady bowlers who came across the road for a cup of coffee while they waited for a competition team from a nearby town to arrive.

"Look at the time," one of the women exclaimed. "That other mob should be here by now."

"Probably held up at those blasted roadworks," one of her companions commented. "They have been ongoing along the highway ever since the cyclone. We were never held up like this when we all travelled by train. The railway is so underutilized these days. Still, I suppose the north can hardly whinge about the 'tyranny of distance' now."

"Is that such a good thing?" a blue-haired matron asked. "Take our ever-increasing drug problem for example. I don't remember drugs being so prevalent when we were a bit more isolated." There was agreement all round.

"Did you hear about the recent fuss at the high school?" one of the women asked Meagan when she brought their coffees. "According to my neighbour, the school expelled one of its students after he was caught supplying other students with drugs. He said he got them from a truck driver."

"Yes, it was on the local TV news," Megan replied. "The Police charged a road transport driver recently with supplying. I don't know if it was the same one the boy was buying from, but I hope so."

The bowlers' gossip session ended with the appearance of another group of lady bowlers. They waved them over to the coffee shop. As Meagan pushed two tables together to accommodate the expanded group, she grimaced as she thought back to when Mick refused to talk to her about what was going on in his life. She thought drugs might be involved. If only they were. That might have been easier to fix. She dismissed her thoughts, smiled and got on with the job. "Good morning ladies. Can I take your orders?"

After breakfast, Sam Pelham went directly to the gym for his usual Saturday shift. It was busy for the first couple of hours. Then he had a 15-minute break between clients, just enough time to fit in a quick lunch break. The phone rang as he gulped down the last of his sandwich. The clank and thump of weights mingled with the incessant jangling of the phone as he rushed to answer it. It was Sam's next client apologising for running about ten minutes late. What a bonus; he would enjoy the extra time to relax.

In an earlier life, the gym was a dress shop. The premises retained it large plate glass display windows. Where once manikins displayed the latest in women's fashion, a selection of fitness gear and home gym equipment now languished in less decorative splendour. An area immediately inside the entrance was now the reception area and provided a quiet lounge for clients and staff to sit and relax. Sam pushed his wheelchair away from the reception desk to an open space in the lounge area. He leant back and idly watched passers-by on the street.

The time passed quickly and Frank, his tardy client, soon arrived looking harassed and uptight. "How's it going, Frank? You're looking a bit stressed. Come on, let's get you started and see if we can't relieve some of that," Sam said as he led Frank through to the machines to begin his workout.

Although focused on Frank, something in the back of Sam's mind niggled at him. It was something to do with what he saw out on the street, but he couldn't recollect seeing anything important. He remembered something vaguely bothered him at the time but, because he was busy with his client, he couldn't concentrate enough to recall what that was. It wasn't until his client was bench-pressing weights that the fog cleared. Sam noticed a new tattoo peeping out from below the sleeve of Frank's tee shirt. That elusive detail from the street scene suddenly hit him.

"That's it; the tattoo!" he yelped.

Frank looked up startled. "What about my tattoo?"

"Eh? Oh no, nothing; your new tattoo just reminded me of something else."

"You're not thinking of getting one yourself?"

"No, they are not my scene. Don't mind them on other people, but not on me."

Bits and pieces of information from his earlier mind-in-neutral observation of the street drifted back. By the time Frank's shortened session ended, it all made sense. Frank was the last client for the day. The gym closed early on Saturday. Most of their clients were involved with sport of some sort in the afternoon. As he saw Frank out and closed up behind him, Sam mulled over what to do. It could be nothing, but somehow he didn't think so. Finding himself beside the reception desk, he picked up the phone.

"Hello, Constable Damian Kelleher speaking."

"Hi Damien, it's Sam. What time do you finish work today?"

"Hey, g'day Pelham. Today it's six o'clock. Why, what are you up to? It's been a while since we got together."

"…Fancy catching up for a drink tonight?"

"That would be great. I have nothing scheduled. See you at 6.30pm at The Brasserie, okay?"

"I'd better come clean though. This is a combination affair: part social and part business. We haven't caught up for ages, and I think something I saw today might interest you − if local gossip is anything to go by."

"Now you have me curious. See you later, *ciao.*"

They ordered a couple of beers and a selection of tapas, and filled in the time taken to demolish the food with chat about what each had done since their last meeting. Then it was down to business. Sam led off.

"I think I have some information that you might want to discuss with your colleagues. I don't know whether there's anything in it or not. It's just that I've seen a couple of things that got me thinking." The arrival of a couple more beers interrupted Sam's prepared story. As soon as the waiter left, he continued.

"This morning when I was training along The Esplanade, two blokes walking from the marina nearly wiped me out. The younger of the two had a unique tattoo." He described the artwork in as much detail as he could remember. "Anyway, cutting a long story short, I don't think they were locals. They didn't seem to know much about Oyster Point."

"If they are from the marina, they probably aren't locals – maybe yachties just stopping over briefly."

"That's what I thought at first, especially as they were in a hire car the next time I saw them. However, if you spotted the one with the tattoo talking to a local young lad through an open car window, would you start to wonder about it? Their conversation was short. You know, hello – goodbye and that's about it sort of thing."

"As we said, if not local, he might have been asking for directions."

"That was my thinking as well. It took me quite a while to work out what bothered me about that meeting. I replayed the whole scenario through my mind and it came back to me. I reckon I saw an envelope and a small package change hands. It happened in a flash… and I couldn't swear to it."

"You're not usually a suspicious bloke, so why do I think there's more to it than that? Go on, what's gnawing at you?"

"This is where it gets tricky. The local lad leaning into the car was young Jayden Struthers. He wore one of those jackets with a front pocket that goes right across the midriff area. You know the type; you can use the pockets as hand muffs in cold weather. Why would he wear such a jacket in October? That's probably what caught my eye in the first place. As I said, the whole thing happened too quickly for me to be positive about what I saw. I know the kid has a questionable history. I might be jumping to conclusions. I was only idly watching the street, but, if I did see a package, why did it disappear so quickly?"

"What makes you think Jayden has a 'questionable history'?"

"A while ago, I heard school students gossiping outside the bakery about the expulsion of one of them for supplying drugs. There was comment about the Police interviewing Jayden in connection with it. They believed that Jayden was his usual charming self and managed to sweet-talk his way out of it. It was obvious the students believed Jayden was in it up to his neck."

"So much for Police interviews being confidential; there's nothing like small town for everyone knowing what's going on."

"Yeah, unfortunately that's the way of it. Anyway, that's it. I thought I should pass on the information. It's up to you what you do with it. If it turns out that the young lad is playing out of his depth, maybe I have done him a favour."

Damien conceded Sam's information was worth investigating, and they returned to general chat as they finished with coffee.

A few days later, when a group of young High School kids came into La Boulangerie, Cecile handed them a bundle of brochures. "You all know Sam Pelham, the wheelie athlete?" she asked. They all nodded.

One girl replied, "Everyone knows him. He's putting our town on the map… and he rocks! So, what's this all about?"

"Sam dropped these leaflets in and asked me to hand them out to local students. I am guessing that is you."

Concerned about what he believed he saw on the street and the possibility of Jayden and maybe other students getting themselves into strife, Sam decided to try a new initiative to occupy the bored youth of the town. Sam's schedule left him with a quiet period after three o'clock every Tuesday. He decided to introduce a 45-minute free workout session choreographed to rap music. He hoped to have the gym filled with teenagers from 3.30pm every Tuesday.

"I think it's a nonsense," Edith declared, accompanying her declaration with a toss of her head. "We're not into that sort of thing here. It's an American thing and it should stay there. Instead of trying to copy everything the Americans do, we would do better to remember we are Australian."

An uncomfortable squirm by those gathered around the table followed her delivery. No one felt inclined to make eye contact with Mariah Obrin, but Mariah was every bit a match for Edith. "Well, Edith, it's swell of you to credit us with inventing All Saints," Mariah's deep Texan drawl responded, "But I think you will find All Saints Day and Halloween celebrations originated somewhere else. We just saw the opportunity to turn something scary into something fun."

Edith, accepting her defeat, scowled and slumped back in her chair. It seemed as though everyone seated around the table began speaking at once. Grace looked pleadingly at Gordon to do something to rescue the situation and ease everyone's embarrassment. He gave her a half-hearted nod, then clapped his hands and called for order. Silence descended on the rooftop garden.

"Thank you. Now, before that little segue, we were discussing Halloween and whether the Plaza should do something to capitalise on the occasion." Gordon paused briefly and glanced around the table. Everyone appeared relatively calm, so he continued. "Maybe we could have a show of hands: those in favour of doing something … and those who think we should ignore it."

Almost every hand shot up in support of doing something. None voted against it and Edith, having made her point previously, elected to abstain from voting. "Good," Gordon resumed "All we have to do now is decide on that 'something'. My thinking is that we should be free to do whatever we fancy in our own shops, but we should come up with suggestions to take to Centre Management regarding what might be done in the general areas of the Plaza."

The regular Friday night gathering looked like running later than usual. With the air now cleared after Edith's outburst, suggestions came thick and fast. Mariah was in constant demand for her appraisal of the suggestions. As the session progressed, suggestions became increasingly creative and enthusiasm for the event ran high.

Suggestions were finalised and the topic exhausted by the time Elaine Bennett, the Centre Manager, wandered out of her office to join them. As Elaine sat sipping her wine, the group outlined their ideas for the Plaza to celebrate Halloween. Suggestions included a costume competition for primary school aged children and face painting for anyone so inclined. Discussion of various appropriate decorations for both the general areas and the stores made it late by the time the evening ended.

Vera, Grace and Lois rode back to the retirement complex with Gordon. "I can't get over Edith's outburst tonight," Vera commented. "She was deliberately nasty to Mariah. Okay, I know how she feels about this whole Halloween thing, but there was no need for that behaviour."

"She always tends to be a bit negative about anything new or different, but she has been particularly prickly and difficult to live with lately," Lois observed.

"I can't help wondering if there is something going on in her life that we don't know about," Grace mused. "It seems she has been offside for ages, but it has only been the last week or so that I noticed it."

"You might be right, Grace," Gordon agreed. "Anthony has been a bit tense this last week or so as well. There could be something going on. I'm concerned now that it might be something unpleasant but, knowing the lady as we do, I don't think we are going to find out unless she wants to tell us." They agreed there was little point in wondering about it further and dropped the subject in favour of discussing how they might decorate their Busy Fingers store for Halloween.

There was agreement that decorations would go up on the following Friday in readiness for Halloween on Saturday. They would forego their usual Friday night get-together to work on decorating their stores. This allowed everyone barely a week to source – or make – decorations. Lois and a couple of ladies from the local art group would run a face painting booth in the Plaza's main aisle throughout Saturday until the Plaza closed at 9.00pm. Moira Whitlock and Mariah Obrin would judge the costume competition. Vera agreed to look after Embellish while Moira was busy with the competition and Mariah persuaded her best friend, Patsy Evans, to mind Bedazzled for her.

How owners planned to decorate their stores remained top secret. After all, there was a bottle of fine French champagne at stake. Behind the scene, Eileen Bennett worked on Geoff Robinson to up the prize a little more for the best decorated store. So far, she had talked him into upping the champagne to a magnum, but she was still working on getting him to add caviar – or strawberries or chocolate -- to the prize.

It proved a busy week for some. Cecile Baudin and the staff at Caffeine Heaven devised and tested their ideas for ghoulish sweets to sell for Halloween. At Caffeine Heaven, Meagan and Aiden were enjoying the preparations. Samira remained a little unsure about it all, but entered into the spirit of things. Over at Busy Fingers, Grace and Rose occupied themselves for much of the week with coloured paper and cardboard producing what they hoped were appropriate decorations to hang on fishing line from the ceiling of the store.

Clifton Sinclaire came up with an idea for the Good Companions bookstore window. He had to produce a reasonably detailed sketch of his proposal before finally convincing his father his idea would work. ...And then the hard part began: sourcing the requisite props. Enthusiasm for the idea increased as the week progressed and, by mid-week, both men were equally excited about their intended window display. However, Clifton felt compelled to swear his father to secrecy. He didn't want anybody knowing their plan before the display's unveiling, and that included Mariah Obrin. "So no loose pillow talk please, Dad," he cautioned Jeremy.

Other issues besides Halloween occupied the minds of some of the retirees from Busy Fingers. Edith's pricklier than normal demeanour continued, causing quite a few ruffled feathers on occasions. After she was overheard being short with a customer, it was agreed she should stay out of the store for a while. How to achieve that without getting her further offside was the problem. Gordon came up with the hint of a strategy. He ran it past some of the others and, together, they fleshed out their approach.

The year was disappearing fast. Soon it would be December, and the anniversary of *that cyclone. Their decision to open a business after the cyclone was without too m*uch research or planning. How had their business fared to date? Did they want to continue with their Busy Fingers store? There was likely to be considerable interest should they decide to sell. While selling should realise a considerable capital windfall, it would also return them to a full-time existence at the retirement complex. They would become 'true' retirees again.

Answers to some of those questions would become clearer only after an investigation of all aspects of their business operation to date. At an impromptu meeting of the group, it was agreed Edith, as the bookkeeper, and Anthony, as their accountant, should take time out from working in the store. They should devote their energies to producing a detailed report on whether the group should continue as is, consider future improvement strategies, or sell out. Anthony and Edith, ecstatic about their task, almost immediately distanced themselves from the group.

While Harbour Plaza's community remained preoccupied with Halloween for most of the week, underneath all the preparations by mid-week, another story was developing. A story that would have its climax embedded in Saturday's Halloween celebrations.

"Hi Damien, have you got the day off?" Meagan asked. She didn't often see Constable Damien Kelleher in the coffee shop at that hour.

"I should be so lucky. I have a few hours to myself. It's a late start for me today," Damien answered. He knew being there for breakfast on a Thursday morning was unusual but he played it down.

In reality, Damien was already 'at work'. After his meeting with Sam, and discussions of Sam's concerns, it was decided to investigate. They began by asking questions at the marina. Sam's description of the distinctive tattoo proved useful. Robert Jensen, the marina manager, identified the men and their boat. He provided the Police with the date of the boat's next reservation of a marina berth.

Jensen's information had the boat arriving late Wednesday afternoon. An officer stationed at the marina from Wednesday morning reported no sign of the boat by the time he was relieved at 6.00pm. His relief spent a long night cooped up in the marina manager's office. Again, it looked like nothing would happen. Concern was that information had leaked to the men in question, resulting in their abandoning their planned stopover at Oyster Point. Continued surveillance paid off.

As the end of his all-night vigil approached, the officer on surveillance duty at the marina struggled to stay awake. That changed at five o'clock when action at the entrance to the marina revived him. A quick scan with his binoculars confirmed the boat's arrival. He was disappointed. His shift ended in less than an hour and he would miss any action that might occur. He rang details of the boat's arrival to Sergeant Yaeger.

Brian Yaeger wasted no time in implementing their plan. A couple of phone calls resulted in Damien Kelleher sauntering into the coffee shop for breakfast while another constable began reading his paper in an unmarked car in the carpark. While waiting for his breakfast, Damien noticed Sam come into the outdoor area for his usual after-training breakfast. Neither man acknowledged the other's presence. Covert operations need to be just that: covert. However, Damien felt, in this instance, Sam needed to be aware things might happen in the area around The Esplanade. For Sam's safety, Sergeant Yaeger approved giving him limited information about the operation. Damien's chat to Sam about it also meant Sam didn't blow things by recognising Damien if they encountered one another.

Damien was half way through his breakfast when the two men from the boat walked into the coffee shop. They selected a corner table, ordered and wasted no time in dispatching their meals. By dawdling over coffee, Damien was able to stretch his time at the coffee shop until the men had almost finished breakfast. After paying for his meal, Damien sauntered out to the carpark. As he donned his sunglasses, Damien nodded to his colleague in the parked car, before driving off in his own vehicle. Game on, he told himself as he made his way to the Police Station.

Nothing happened until late afternoon. The two men from the boat made plenty of phone calls and wandered around until about an hour before the top of the afternoon tide when they went back to their boat. After a spot of fishing, they dined at The Quarterdeck before returning to their boat. When nothing had happened as the end of his shift approached, Steve Lorimar, on surveillance duties at the marina, began thinking the whole thing was a fizzer.

Sergeant Yaeger's gut instinct told him things needed a bit longer yet. He paused briefly to admire the early morning silvery haze drifting across the bay before making his way to Caffeine Heaven. Newly appointed to Oyster Point, he only arrived in the town at the start of the week, and remained unknown to all but his own troops. His phone rang while he waited for his order to arrive. It was Steve Lorimar phoning in his report on last night's surveillance. Brian watched Sam whiz along The Esplanade as Lorimar delivered his report.

"Nothing happened all night until a few minutes ago. They are now heading your way, Sarge. I'll leave them to you. My relief has arrived. I'm off now."

"Right Steve, get plenty of sleep. I think we are going to be busy for a while yet."

While he ate, Brian Yaeger watched the two men enjoying their breakfasts. He used the time to review plans for the day. Damien Kelleher was in the unmarked vehicle. His teammate today was a police photographer borrowed from an Arkana Beach station. The photographer, wearing a gaudy blue shirt with yellow palm trees printed all over it, and his oversized camera bag were aboard a hired moped. Damien would follow the men while the photographer stayed close by. If anything looked like happening, Damien would call the photographer, who would covertly take photos.

Friday started out with a bit more promise. The men from the boat hired a rental car and set off around town. They met with six people over the course of the morning, including a swaggering but tense Jayden Struthers. Some of the others they met were locals, but some were strangers. Young Struthers was their last contact before lunch. When the meeting took place, Damien called the photographer but remained close enough to watch. A swift transaction occurred before Jayden headed off on foot.

After advising the photographer of his intention, Damien pulled out into traffic and, from a considerable way back followed Jayden a short distance from the centre of town to a quiet residential area. Damien knew where the lad was heading. He parked the car and continued on foot. Although some distance back, he kept Jayden in sight, wanting to watch what might happen to the package he saw Jayden slip into his pocket. Soon Jayden turned the corner into a quiet street. Damien quicken his pace The lad wouldn't hear him as he had his iPod firmly attached to his ears.

Damien continued to shorten the gap between them. At the front gate to a house, Damien was close enough to tap the lad on the shoulder. Jayden spun around to face Damien, his jaw dropping when he recognised the police officer.

"Hi Jayden, are mum and dad home today?"

"Yes, it's dad's day off. Why?"

"I think we might go and chat to them."

The swagger disappeared. The lad now more closely resembling a cornered animal. He attempted to make a run for it. Damien, anticipating the move, clamped a firm hand on the lad's shoulder and propelled him in the direction of the front door. "Don't waste both our time by being silly. Let's go to see them, shall we?" although it was a question, Jayden knew it didn't need an answer. He was going to front his parents.

Bill Struthers answered the door. "What the hell is this all about?" he demanded as he glared at his son standing on the porched in the firm grip of a police officer. Damien felt the boy's shoulders sag in defeat. "You better come in and tell me what this is all about." They followed Bill Struthers into the lounge room. "Right Constable, tell me what this is all about. What's he supposed to have done this time?"

"Following our receipt of confidential information, our station initiated a surveillance operation. Young Jayden here dropped into the midst of our operation when he was involved with one of our suspects. I followed him, and here we are. We hate to see our teenagers recruited into something that can quickly become criminal. I'm hoping that, if he's gotten mixed up in something stupid, we can sort him out and get him back on the right track."

"Recruited? What are you talking about?"

Damien turned to the now shivering teenager. "Jayden, there's a package in your pocket. Get it out, please." At that point, Jayden's mother, Colleen Struthers, came to join them in the lounge room.

"Do I have to … here and now?" the lad whimpered. His pleading look almost weakened Damien's resolve.

"Jayden," his mother wailed, "What have you been up to? Why are the Police here?"

"Mrs Struthers," Damien addressed the woman, "Would you have a clean plastic bag in the kitchen we could use, please?" She left and returned a few moments later with a large zip top bag. "Now Jayden, please remove the package from your pocket and place it in this bag."

"What the hell's this about, Jay? What's in the package?" Bill Struthers demanded. Jayden kept his eyes lowered and remained silent.

"Jayden, tell him or I will," Damien said. Jayden shook his head. "Okay. I am sorry Bill, but that package contains drugs, drugs to sell to students."

"Drugs! You mean narcotics -- illegal substances?" Bill struggled to understand. Colleen burst into tears.

Damien slipped on latex gloves and carefully opened the package without taking it out of the plastic bag. A number of tablets rolled out into the bag. Many more remained in the wrappings.

"Surely you aren't using these," his father croaked.

"No, I don't do drugs; never have," Jayden shouted.

"So you're not using, you are just dealing? How stupid can you be, Son?"

His wife sobbed loudly. "Is that what these are: drugs? …And you sell them to other students. How could you? How did you get involved?" she asked between sobs. All the lad could offer in reply was a weak nod of his head. He couldn't lift his eyes from the carpet to face her.

"Let's all stay calm. What was in the envelope you handed over, Jayden?" Damien asked.

"Cash."

"How much?"

"Three hundred bucks."

"Is this the first time you have dealt with these blokes?"

"No."

Bill Struthers couldn't remain silent. "What the hell have you gotten yourself into? Where did you get that sort of money?" His son remained silent and eyes downcast. "What happens next, Constable?"

"We need a few answers from Jayden, and we will need to speak to you all again –down at the station. In the meantime, if I can have an undertaking from each of you that Jayden will not leave this house until I speak to you again, I am prepared not to take him into custody right now."

After receiving solemn promises, Damien took a few moments to ensure Jayden understood the gravity of his situation. Then Constable Kelleher left the family to deal with their shock. He headed back to the Police Station to hand in his evidence, and report his activities to Sergeant Yaeger. He discovered he wasn't the only one who had been busy. Others were digging into the backgrounds of the two men from the marina.

The younger one was the overly indulged son of a wealthy – mega wealthy – businessman and philanthropist presently living in the Cairns region. The luxury cruiser currently moored in the marina was his son's twenty-first birthday present. It appeared relations between father and son became strained during the preceding year. In a bid to pull his son into line, the father reduced his son's allowance to an amount equal to the dole. So far, they hadn't found anything on the other man on the boat.

Late Friday afternoon, Sergeant Brian Yaeger decided he needed a good coffee and knew exactly where to get one. His officer's latest report on the whereabouts of the two men from the boat might have influenced that. After returning to their boat for a couple of hours, the men returned to the shopping precinct. They wandered around in the supermarket for half an hour and checked out its associated specialty stores, before going to Harbour Plaza.

Yaeger ordered coffee and a pastry before selecting a table in the coffee shop's open dining area that extended into the Plaza's main aisle. From there, Yaeger could see most of the Plaza and anyone wandering through it. It wasn't long before he noticed a small gathering forming at the far end near The Academy. He guessed they were High School seniors. At the centre of the group were the two men from the boat.

While sipping his coffee and casually reading a newspaper abandoned on another table, he kept an eye on the far end of the aisle. There was a familiarity between the group and the men. Convinced this was not a once-off chance meeting, he took out his phone and rang his station. It was a short conversation. He hoped everything would be in place in time. Brian abandoned the newspaper and focused on his phone, flicking through emails and appearing to text people.

The group started to disperse. Yaeger rang the police station again. This time his call lasted some minutes. He spoke directly to the officer who fed information to officers stationed at all exits from the Plaza. "Main exit …two girls: one in bright pink top, the other in jeans and denim jacket. Supermarket exit … one blonde girl and two lads in wild looking boardies." He maintained the running commentary as the young group members made their way to the various exits. Yaeger couldn't be sure he saw anything changing hands when they were together, but his officers would pick them up as they left the Plaza. Even if they weren't carrying anything illicit, they would face questioning about their association with the two blokes.

Samira asked if he wanted a refill. As she placed the fresh coffee on his table, the two men exited The Academy and began checking out the various store windows as they slowly made their way through the Plaza. "I hope they do not come in here again," Samira said when she noticed Brian watching them.

"Why, do they cause trouble when they do?"

"Oh, I do apologise. It is most unprofessional of me to speak of our customers. Please ignore what I just said."

"I don't think it is unprofessional. They obviously concern you and I'm interested to know why. Do they create trouble or behave aggressively or abusively?"

"Most of the time, they just make us feel uncomfortable. I don't know why. There is just something about them. Look at them now. They do this often."

"What do you mean?"

"I know I'm being a silly old woman when I say this but, in old movies, they would say people behaving like this were 'casing the joint'." Then Samira excused herself and went to serve a customer waiting at the counter.

My dear lady, I think you could be right, Brian thought as Samira walked away. I think there are two games at play here: drugs and robbery. He snatched up his phone and rang . The two men were heading for the main exit. Monitoring the men's every move would resume.

Stores began closing. There was nothing more for Brian to do here. He went in to pay for his coffee and to apologise to Samira for delaying their closing up. As he entered the shop, he was surprised to see Meagan and Aiden up on ladders. Brian queried Samira about what was happening.

"Tomorrow is Halloween. All the storeowners have agreed to decorate their shops and Plaza management will decorate the general areas. The Plaza will have entertainment – mainly for children but also some live music – and will stay open a little later than usual. Everyone is being encouraged to wear costume tomorrow."

Every officer, except the one on surveillance duties at the marina received a call to a meeting at the station at seven o'clock that night. Damien Kelleher came in early to take care of a couple of things before the meeting. As he walked in, his phone rang.

"Constable Kelleher, this is Bill Struthers. Look, I'm sorry to have to do this but something has happened." There was no mistaking his agitation and he rushed on. "I didn't think I'd get you at this hour but I didn't know what else to do… especially as you were so good about all that stuff with Jayden today."

"That's okay, Bill. Just tell me what the problem is and I'll see what I can do to help."

"Jayden's gone ..."

"Gone where?"

"I don't know. He is frightened about something. He got a phone call about half an hour ago. Afterwards, he just kept pacing around his room, smacking his forehead and carrying on. Whatever the call was about really frightened him. Then he rushed out of the house. I tried to stop him. Anyway, I don't think he intended heading for the town centre. He would walk if that were where he was going. He's taken his bike. I think he's going somewhere further. I didn't know what else to do, so I called you."

"Leave it with me. I'll see what I can do but I'm not making any promises." Damien ended the call and promptly called Steve Lorimar parked in an unmarked car near the entrance to the marina. "Steve, there could be young lad on a bicycle possibly heading in your direction. It will be young Jayden Struthers and I think he is heading for the marina and that boat. If he comes your way, grab the lad and hold him. Who is on surveillance at the marina tonight?"

"Bob is on tonight. Hang on … yeah, I see a kid on a bike at the other end of The Esplanade. These binoculars the Sarge gave us are good."

Damien rang Bob who was in the marina manager's office for the night. He gave Bob the same message as he gave Steve, adding that Steve would try for an intercept. If the kid managed to get into the marina area, Bob was to grab him, if possible without blowing his cover.

It was time for Sergeant Yaeger's team meeting to begin. Damien stuck his head round the door of the meeting room where most of the officers already waited for the meeting to start.

"Damien, are you joining us?" Brian Yaeger asked, interrupting his opening speech to do so.

"Something's going down right now, Sarge… something relevant. I'll be back as soon as I can. You might want to hold the troops until I get back though."

Yaeger nodded and waved him on his way. Damien ran for his car. His phone rang as he turned the key in the ignition. Steve Lorimar's voice floated over the ether. "I have the package in the Plaza carpark. What do you want me to do with him?"

"Hold him; I'm on my way over to you." Call ended, he screeched out of the Police compound and headed for the Harbour Plaza carpark. He parked beside Steve's vehicle. After a short conversation and a quick check of Steve's 'passenger', Steve and Jayden transferred to the rear of Damien's vehicle.

Back at the Police Station, Damien stuck his head into the meeting room again interrupting the Sarge's delivery. "I'm back, Sir, but it'll be a few minutes before we know anything. You might like to join me."

After telling everyone else to stay put, Sergeant Yaeger accompanied Damien to an interview room where Steve waited with Jayden. "I've rung his father. He should be here in a few moments," Steve said as they entered. Brian suggested Steve join the others in the meeting room. As Steve left the room, Bill Struthers arrived.

It only took a few hard words from Damien, backed up by a couple of threats from Yaeger about what could happen to him, to get Jayden talking. The two officers listened, Bill Struthers alternated between rubbing his face and shaking his head, and Jayden talked…and talked. When he finished, it took just a couple of questions to clear up some details before Jayden was led away to spend the night in the cells. The lad's father was upset. Damien escorted him to the carpark. "Bill, a night in the cells will help Jayden understand what lies ahead if he doesn't mend his ways. It also will keep him safe until our operation is over."

After Yaeger's meeting, they knew what tomorrow would bring and their roles in the operation. The meeting broke up, but Brian called Damien back as he was about to join the exodus. "A moment please, Constable. Good work today. We'll talk more once this operation is over." Damien knew tonight's events were the final straw for Jayden's parents and what little he could do wouldn't help much.

"O-o-oh, doesn't the place look incredible," Rose exclaimed as they entered the Plaza on Saturday morning. "I didn't think I was too fussed about this Halloween thing, but seeing all this makes me excited. I think it's going to be a great day… and evening."

Strings of jack-o'-lanterns hung above the aisles. Large black plastic spiders hung strategically from the ceiling, occasionally accompanied by fake webs. Every store window sported decorations. Carved pumpkins, bats, witches hats and brooms, ghostly apparitions, spiders and webs, and tombstones appeared everywhere. Storeowners arrived loaded up with garment bags and various other bit of costume. A small roped-off area for the face painting activities and a small stage appeared in the main aisle overnight. Everyone worked late last night but the effect was well worth the effort.

Good Companions bookstore took out the prize for best display. Clifton's opened grave tableau, complete with opened (cardboard) coffin, tombstone, Grim Reaper looking on and plastic bats and pumpkin lantern, was amazing. Myriads of books with appropriate titles and suitably scary covers spilled out of the open 'coffin', and the pumpkin lantern bathed the whole thing in an eerie glow.

The Plaza was busy. Adults and children alike came in costume and joined in the spirit of the day. Apart from the face painting, Sam ran sitting aerobics sessions throughout the day and members of the art group ran (ghostly) story telling session in the appropriately decorated Academy.

After a busy day, the tempo stepped up a notch in the evening. Although stores weren't particularly busy, the crowd in the Plaza swelled considerably as people enjoyed the atmosphere, a meal or a drink, and the entertainment. Costumes predominated. The supermarket complex remained open until seven o'clock and all businesses there reported increased sales.

Late in the afternoon, Sergeant Yaeger began stationing his officers in and around the Plaza and supermarket complex. He 'borrowed' several officers from the Arkana Beach precinct to augment the small Oyster Point force. Tonight, some remained in uniform but out of sight, while others were in plain clothes. A few, including Damien Kelleher, were in costume. Whether in civvies or costumes, they mingled with the crowd throughout the evening. Connor Aston, the Plaza's security officer, sat with his eyes glued to the numerous monitors in his office. He couldn't help but think that, unless they carried a placard, it would be hard to spot anyone intent on no good in this costumed crowd. …But spot them he did.

At about eight o'clock, one of the cameras caught three people entering an empty shop close to the main entrance. Connor waited a few minutes. No one came out of the empty store. He called Brian Yaeger. Brian, sitting in his favourite coffee shop, called the information through to the officer on duty. He relayed the news to all the officers involved with the Plaza.

Earlier, Brian received a similar call from his officer monitoring the cameras in the supermarket complex. The officer who called it through identified the older of the two men from the boat. The man and two youths entered the men's toilet a few minutes before the complex closed. They never reappeared. Brian didn't think anything would happen until close to nine o'clock when the Plaza was due to close. A tense couple of hours lay ahead for those officers on supermarket complex detail.

After receiving the call from , Damien Kelleher sidled up to Sam Pelham watching the live entertainment in the Plaza. To all around them, it appeared Damien was asking Sam for directions. Damien sauntered off in the direction Sam indicated for the toilets. A few moments later, Sam backed his wheelchair away from the crowd watching a band perform, and aimlessly threaded his way through the Plaza. He knocked and Connor Aston let him into his office. "Damien says you have some images I should have a look at," Sam said.

Connor brought up the tape. Three people slipped into the empty shop. One of those was the younger man from the boat. There was no mistaking that tattoo. Sam also recognised one of the other two people as a local lad. He called Damien Kelleher.

The call was brief. "The young bloke with the tattoo, one local lad and another one I don't recognise. So far, they haven't come out of the shop." Damien relayed the message to . Brian smiled when he received the message. He guessed right. It would be 'Game On' at both locations at about nine o'clock if things panned out the way he expected. His men were ready.

A handful of costumed stragglers made their way out of the Plaza at 8.45pm. They were the last to leave. Some stores already had closed. Brian's men quietly made their way to their appointed posts: the toilets, Caffeine Heaven's kitchen, Busy Fingers' staff room. An eerie silence enveloped the place as lights turned off and the last of the storekeepers departed.

Connor sat glued to the screen showing the empty shop area. Ever so slightly the door moved. A couple of heartbeats later, a tattooed arm held it wide open. Two costumed lads slid out, and the bloke with the tattoo followed them. Connor gave Brian Yaeger in the coffee shop a running commentary on the trio's movements.

Steve Lorimar's contact was Damien Kelleher. Three men emerged from the toilets in the supermarket complex. Damien's phone vibrated. He answered it and handed it across to Brian Yaeger, mouthing 'Steve' as he did so. Brian handed the phone back after a few words. Two officers in a parked car outside the Plaza jumped. Something was happening in the supermarket complex. All the lights suddenly came on and there seemed to be a fair bit of noise. The two men left the car and stationed themselves near the Plaza's supermarket end doors. They exchanged a grin and one said, "Our fun is about to happen."

He was right. A couple of minutes later Sergeant Yaeger gave the command and his men swarmed out of their hiding places. Each of the costumed blokes had selected a store and was now endeavouring to break-in. Before anything could happen, the two lads were on the tiles and handcuffed. The tattooed bloke, more alert than the other two, made a dash for the supermarket end exit. He tried the doors. They were unlocked. He threw his weight against them. The doors swung open and he rushed out… headlong into the arms of the waiting officers. "Going somewhere are we, Sir?" one of the officers asked as he held the man face down on the bitumen while his colleague snapped on the handcuffs.

The paddy wagon would be full tonight, Brian Yaeger mused as he watched the six miscreants loaded aboard. It was a successful night; nothing stolen, no damage done and all of the players rounded up. Yep, his first week on the job at Oyster Point could be classed a success.

Early Sunday morning, everyone received word the shopping precinct would remain closed for the day while Police completed their investigations. I'll never say no to a Sunday off, Gordon Bailey thought to himself as he picked up his computer and his coffee. It was a glorious morning and he fancied writing under the pergola in the garden. Anthony was already there with coffee and a newspaper. Gordon dumped computer and coffee on the opposite side of the table and was about to sit down when Anthony jumped up. As he struggled in the breeze to fold his newspaper, Anthony snarled, "Can't a person get any peace… have any privacy in this place?"

Although realising Anthony didn't expect an answer, Gordon decided to provide one anyway. "No, Anthony, this won't do. I've had enough of this nonsense. I am not aware of having done anything to upset you and nor is anyone else in the group. So, mate, we're fed up, and it's time you explained you unacceptable behaviour."

Anthony stood his ground and looked ready for a row. Then, suddenly crumpled and sat down heavily on the chair he just vacated. "There's a lot on my mind… no, don't ask. I can't talk about it – don't want to talk about it. I am very worried about something and I don't know what I'll do if it happens."

"Maybe we can help somehow…"

"No, no one can help. It's just a waiting game now. I don't mean to be such a pig, but I really would like to be left to myself for a bit."

With that, Anthony walked off. Gordon found himself battling a myriad of different thoughts about what could be causing Anthony such worry. Whatever the cause, it looked certain to remain a mystery for a while yet.

Revelations

November was a month of revelations bringing to an end many secrets and much of the speculation from earlier in the year. However, sometimes the keeper of a secret is determined it should remain just that, as it continues to tantalise others.

Moira's 'secret' was obvious to everyone. She was pregnant, and well advanced. Time slipped by so quickly, Vera still had not spoken to Mariah about Moira's situation. Today's the day, she thought, as she got ready for work. "I will talk to Mariah today," she informed the otherwise empty room. Over the previous few weeks, Vera accepted she would need to pick her time and get straight to the crux of the matter with Mariah. That day, even finding time to speak to Mariah proved difficult.

Early that morning, Mariah persuaded her friend Patsy Evans to mind the store while she attended to some personal matters. As she drove to Harbour Plaza to start the day, Mariah revisited her conversation with Jeremy after they told their closest friends about their intention to marry. Jeremy's usual no-nonsense approach prevailed. As he drove her home that evening, he asked the big question, "When is this marriage going to take place? We really ought to start planning. Setting a date might be the first step."

"By the time December arrives, we will be too busy – hopefully – with the Christmas rush. There are always so many parties on people's calendars right up until after New Year. There isn't time to worry about attending a wedding. I know Patsy is planning an overseas trip for some weeks from sometime in January, but I don't know when she leaves. The wedding needs to be before she leaves or after she returns. I want her to be my matron of honour… or whatever is needed."

While Mariah made coffee, Jeremy sat deep in thought at her kitchen table. Once they were both coffee mugs in hand, Jeremy shared the outcome of his deliberations. "Why do we need to wait? We are free to marry now. We just need to get the paperwork in place to allow it to happen. November seems like a good month for a wedding. It gets it over and done with before the silly season sets in and eliminates problems with Patsy's availability."

"Is it possible at such short notice? There's a lot to put in place; all the arrangements a wedding requires. Still, I suppose it is possible. Just about everything we need to organise is in the Plaza."

Jeremy organised the license for the third week in November, having told Mariah that was ample time to organise their simple wedding. Two things happened immediately: Jeremy shared the date with his son, Clifton, and Mariah hastily organised Gordon Bailey to produce invitations. The invitations collected the previous evening and now enveloped and in a small box on the passenger seat, accompanied Mariah to work.

A few minutes after Patsy arrived to mind the store, Mariah dropped into each business as she made her way through the Plaza. No time was wasted. Her first call was to the Centre Manager's office to check the availability of the rooftop garden – and to share the good news with Eileen Bennett. Then, it was into each of the stores in the Plaza, including The Academy where the art group was hanging a new exhibition. She handed each person their envelope and was gone again with only an additional comment at some places to the effect that she would be back again later.

After checking everything was okay in the store, Mariah retraced her steps through the complex, starting with The Quarterdeck. Beppe would produce a menu for the reception for her approval. Cecile was thrilled to be making the cake and started sketching designs. Ginger Mick at The Brasserie agreed to devise a couple of new cocktails for the occasion. Mariah returned to the art group to aske Bella to be the official photographer before visiting Gordon at Busy Fingers to ask him to chair the reception. When she finally returned to the store, Mariah realised she hadn't given Patsy her invitation.

Patsy tore open the envelope and let out a squeal. "Oh, this is wonderful. I'm so happy for you. What can I do to help?"

"Well, I was rather hoping you would be my matron of honour. It's not going to a formal wedding but we do need a couple of witnesses to sign the register. I'd like you to be my witness."

"Of course, I will, but what else is there to do? There's so much to organise for a wedding. You can't do it all yourself and manage the store as well."

Mariah rattled off everything she had in place, and added, "I will have to sort out what I'm going to wear but, with a store full of clothes to choose from, there must be something here that suits."

"Y-e-s, but it has to be something special. Now, you didn't mention flowers or the honeymoon. Is Jeremy looking after the latter? The flowers are usually the bride's responsibility."

"Honeymoon…? I don't think there will be one of those. We both have stores to run – very busy stores at the moment." Patsy gave her a disapproving look but said nothing. However, the question stayed with Mariah.

While they sat at a table in Caffeine Heaven waiting for their lunch to arrive, Mariah broached the subject with Jeremy. "We aren't having a honeymoon are we?"

"Why ever not? Of course, we are. I've already made a booking."

"How can we get away? We both have stores to run."

"Clifton will run Good Companions in my absence, and I'm sure Patsy would oblige with Bedazzled. …And before you ask, we won't be gone long. We'll be marriage on Wednesday evening, head off on Thursday, and be back here as usual on Monday morning."

"Hmm, I suppose it will be okay. Where are we going?"

"Ah well now, that's a surprise."

In the stockroom at Busy Fingers, Vera and Jane spent the morning unpacking and pricing new arrivals. A radio turned low kept them company. "There it is again!" Vera exclaimed.

Startled, Jane dropped her clipboard. "There what is? I don't see anything. It wasn't a mouse was it?" Jane asked as she looked around nervously.

"What? A mouse…? No; the interview on the radio…"

"What about it?" Jane demanded as she retrieved her clipboard from the floor.

"They are repeating a program I heard a couple of nights ago. What do you reckon about that interview?"

"I wasn't really listening but I think it was an interview with some author."

"Sssshh, listen…!" Vera commanded. Jane stepped closer to the radio to hear the last half of the interview. At the conclusion of the interview, Vera asked again, "Well, what do you think?"

"I'm not sure what I'm supposed to think. I heard the last part of an interview with an author called Claudia Sanders who I think they said was from somewhere around here. I don't know what else…"

"What… about the voice? Didn't you recognise the voice – that deep Texan drawl?"

"Well, yes, she was American, and it probably was a southern drawl. So what…?"

"Who do you know around here that sounds like that?" Jane shook her head and shrugged in confusion. "*Mariah* – that's who."

"Oh, I see. Yes, it did sound a bit like Mariah's drawl, but there's probably quite a few Americans among the newcomers to town; could be any one of them. Anyway, I imagine Mariah is far too busy to be writing novels in her spare time – if she has any these days. Is this … whatever her name is … any good as a writer?"

"I've only read a couple of her books. They're not bad – if you like romantic novels. Apparently, she is a best seller… rakes in squillions from book sales I believe."

"I still think it a wild assumption that it's Mariah."

Vera threw her hands up in despair, but mention of Mariah reminded her of something else. "I intended to have a chat with Mariah today but she spent the morning flitting around the Plaza. When we finish here, I'll duck across to Bedazzled."

It was three o'clock before Vera marched into Bedazzled and thanked her lucky stars there were no customers in the store. "I'd like a chat if you have a moment please, Mariah." Mariah nodded and offered Vera the spare chair behind the counter. "Look, I don't know how best to approach this conversation, so I'm just going to jump right in. Is Moira pregnant?"

Mariah looked a little startled and took a moment to examine the nails on her left hand before answering. "I imagine it is damned obvious to everyone that she is, but she hasn't said anything to me about it. Like you, I'm not sure how to broach the subject with her, but I must soon. Was there a particular reason you asked?"

"I'm sorry, but it sounds like you can't answer the real question. I was wondering what her plans were for when the baby arrives… and whether you might want me to manage Embellish for a while. It's just that it would be a bit difficult for me at the moment, what with Edith and Anthony banished from Busy Fingers to work on something that keeps them away from customers."

"I see your problem. I will have that conversation with Moira in the next day or so, but don't worry about it. If needs be, I will ask Patsy to run Embellish … if we know when, and if Patsy is around at that time." Mariah ended with a wry smile that didn't fill Vera with confidence.

A couple of days later, Mariah poked her head around the door of Busy Fingers and beckoned Vera to come out. "If you can come back to Bedazzled with me, I'll tell you about my meeting with Moira." Vera nodded enthusiastically and the two women hurried back to Bedazzled.

"Don't keep me in suspense, how did it go?" Vera pleaded.

"She wasn't happy about me 'sticking my nose into her business' as she put it but, once I explained my need to know what was happening so I could plan, she calmed down. Yes, she is pregnant, with the baby due mid-January she thinks. She assured me she would be back, but might take a couple of weeks off after the birth. I suggested a month at least, and I think we have agreement on that."

"I see. By January, things might have returned to normal at Busy Fingers. She didn't mention who the father was…?

"I did politely enquire, but there is nothing to report on that issue."

"None of our business anyway I suppose," Vera shrugged. "While I'm here, can you clear up something else for me?" She can only throw me out, Vera thought as she queried the radio interview with Claudia Sanders.

"Good heavens, what makes you think I might be Claudia Sanders? Me? A best-selling romantic novelist…? If only; I wouldn't be worrying about how to manage two stores." Her deep-throated laugh rumbled in reply.

Vera wasn't convinced, but she let the subject drop. As she left the shop, Mariah caught up with her. "Before you go, do you know where there is a florist in town? I know I've seen one somewhere. I'll need to arrange an after-hours appointment to organise flowers for the wedding."

"That would be Marilyn. Her shop's in the next block, not far past the hotel."

After Vera left, Mariah rang Marilyn who said she would call at Bedazzled after she closed up at five o'clock. She arrived at about 5.30pm. "Now, what's all this about a wedding?" she opened with. "What types of arrangements were you thinking about?" Marilyn asked as she fished a notebook out of her bag.

"I don't know really. I don't want a bouquet, but I suppose I have to have some flowers. Then there are buttonholes for the men … oh, and I suppose I need something on the tables for the reception at The Quarterdeck."

"No need to worry about the restaurant. Elene will organise that. Just give me an idea of what you would like and I'll steer her in the right direction when she talks to me. I think you're right about not having a bouquet. How about a spectacular corsage instead? We could colour coordinate it with your frock, and match the men's buttonholes to it."

Mariah felt a twinge of nervousness. It was all happening too easily. "The wedding -- and everything to do with it – is happening here at Harbour Plaza. The ceremony, upstairs in the rooftop garden is at seven o'clock, and everything rolls on from there. What's the latest you can deliver the flowers?"

"Hmm … the ceremony is upstairs, eh. A couple of arrangements up there would be nice; perhaps one on the celebrant's table. Sorry, what else did you ask? Oh yes, delivery won't be a problem. I see word hasn't escaped yet, but I'm moving into Harbour Plaza next week, into that empty shop near the main entrance."

"In that case," Mariah said as she rummaged under the counter and came up with an envelope, "Here's your invitation to the wedding. Bring your significant other with you if he is available." Her last comment seemed to cause a strange reaction from Marilyn but she didn't say anything.

Talk at their Friday night get-togethers in the rooftop garden tended to focus on the forthcoming wedding. During the last one before the wedding, the women dominated conversation as they pursued every detail of the wedding plans and expended much energy in unsuccessfully trying to elicit from Mariah details of her outfit, and from Jeremy, details of the honeymoon destination. However, they did manage to find time in the midst of it all, to welcome Marilyn to the group, and point out that husbands were welcome to attend the

Friday evening sessions. A tight smile and a curt 'thank you' were Marilyn's response.

Rose moved forward in her chair to perch on the front edge. She appeared to be waiting anxiously to say something at the first break in conversation. When the opportunity arrived, she pounced. "Mariah, I've been meaning to ask you something for a while and I keep forgetting." Mariah nodded and gestured for Rose to go ahead. "Thanks; I hope you don't mind, but the other night when I was listening to the radio, there was an interview with a local author. It sounded like you speaking. Well, not exactly like you, but it sounded very much like you? Was it you I heard?"

Vera, who started chuckling about half way through Rose's conversation, now roared laughing, and spilled her drink in the process. "I've already been down that track, Rose; didn't do me any good."

Attention swung from Rose to Vera before all eyes settled on Mariah, who seemed to fidget uncomfortably. She shot a quick pleading glance at Clifton, before beginning to deny any association with the interview.

"No,no ... stop, Mariah. Yes, it was Mariah, and it was my fault," Clifton announced as he help his hands up in surrender.

"How can it be your fault, Dear?" a confused Rose asked.

"I asked Mariah to do the interview for the author ... no, she is not the author. I knew you were about to ask that, Rose."

"Then, why didn't the author do the interview herself? Why the subterfuge...?"

Clifton pleadingly scanned the surrounding sea of faces now all tightly focused on him. No one would help him out, and now they all were intrigued. "Well, it's about anonymity. The writer needs anonymity to be able to write without intrusion, especially given the type of material she writes. On the other hand, however, every writer needs whatever publicity they can get."

"I wouldn't have thought Claudia Sanders needed much publicity," Rose replied thoughtfully. "I mean, she is a best-selling author and her work is good – very engaging."

"Thanks for that. Yes, her work sells well but every bit of promotion helps. Arrgh, what the hell; I hope I can rely on your discretion. As I said, anonymity is important ... and perhaps doubly so in this situation." Jeremy raised his eyebrows questioningly at his son. He sensed where this was heading. Clifton shrugged at his father and continued. "It might come as a bit of a surprise but Claudia Sanders is here with you now."

Several people looked around. Vera let out a howl. Grace clapped her hands to her mouth, and both women leant forward excitedly.

"Ahem, ladies and gentlemen, I am Claudia Sanders. Perhaps now you will understand why the author's identity needs to remain confidential."

Uproar erupted. Some were clapping. Congratulation came from all quarters. People reached across to shake Clifton's hand. Jeremy sat there smirking like the proud father he was.

At the beginning of that week, Edith advised Mariah that she would be unable to attend the wedding. She was going south for a few days and wouldn't be back in time. On Tuesday, Edith also shared news of her impending southern trip with the Busy Fingers crew, but without providing any details or explanation. As they drove into work on Thursday morning, Jane commented, "I think Edith must have left already, there were no lights on in her unit last night."

"I do hope everything is okay. It's not like Edith to go off like that. I don't think she's ever been away from the retirement complex since she moved in," Grace said.

"Yeah, it is a bit unusual and, when you couple that with the way her attitude is lately, you can't help feeling concerned," Vera added.

On the preceding Wednesday morning, Anthony also apologised to Mariah for not attending the wedding, but didn't offer any reason. It wasn't until the Friday night get-together that Gordon Bailey heard about it while in casual conversation with Mariah. Anthony hadn't mentioned to anyone that he wouldn't be going to the wedding, and Gordon wondered whether maybe he felt uncomfortable about going on his own now that Edith was going to be away.

After they arrive back at the retirement complex that evening, Gordon called at Anthony's unit. He knocked loudly on the door before realising no lights were on inside. Half expecting Anthony to come out and abuse him for waking him up, Gordon wasn't sure what to do next but decided to knock again anyway. Still no response, so Gordon gave up and went back to his own unit. He commented on it to the others as they drove into work the next morning.

"Ah hah, I knew it. There's definitely something going on with that pair, but I'm not sure I like what it might be," Grace said.

"I suppose we have to wait and see," Vera suggested, "But I have to admit to feeling increasingly concerned about what it might be."

While there continued to be speculation about Edith and Anthony's absences, the fact that they were away had little impact on the running of Busy Fingers. Neither of them had been involved in the day-to-day running of the store for some time. The impending wedding overshadowed everything else and the first week of the pair's absence came and went without any real impact.

The day of the wedding rolled around, hot and sultry as typical for so late in November. With none of their number directly involved in preparations for the wedding, the day passed much as any other day for the Busy Fingers crew. That was until about 5.30pm. Although normal closing time was six o'clock, there seemed to be a unanimous unspoken decision to close early that day. Anyone who could leave headed for home to change into outfits more appropriate for the occasion. Marilyn worked on the flowers until after six o'clock before delivering them soon after. The invitation was from 6.30pm, for drinks, and canapes supplied by Samira from Caffeine Heaven, until the ceremony at 7.00pm.

Gwenda, the marriage celebrant arrived a few minutes before the appointed time, and the ceremony got underway right on time. By then, a light cool breeze replaced the heat of the day. It wafted the loose floral chiffon coat that topped Mariah's mid-calf length peacock blue satin frock. Bella scrambled around taking photos and shooting video footage, and the assembled guests toasted the bride and groom with French champagne. Only a brief and basic ceremony, it still was enough for Rose and Lois to require tissues.

With the formal part of the evening over, everyone moved downstairs to The Quarterdeck for the reception. Mariah only vaguely noticed the tables looked lovely and that Elene had engaged an elderly couple to provide live music. Cecile's stunning wedding cake sat on a small side table beside a sinister-looking long bladed knife adorned with and enormous loopy bow.

The food was divine, speeches few and short, and Gordon ensured the evening flowed as it should. Soon after ten o'clock, it was all over and everyone was out in the carpark waving the couple off.

It was a somewhat deplete group that gathered in the rooftop garden on the Friday night following the wedding. The newly-weds and Edith and Anthony were missing, as well as Patsy Evans, who was an honorary member and who had told someone she wouldn't be there as she was exhausted after a busy day in Bedazzled. Clifton stayed only briefly, but shared with the group that the newly-weds were staying at a resort on one of the islands off Arkana Beach. He expected them home some time on Sunday. After a subdued couple of drinks, everyone headed home much earlier than usual.

November was slipping away, and heralding in the 'silly season' of Christmas and New Year as it did so. Everyone prepared for the promotions and events scheduled for December, as well as coping with the increased business in the lead up to Christmas. Although Mariah was back at Bedazzled, Patsy continued to help there and at Embellish where Moira looked exhausted.

As they prepared to open the Busy Fingers store on the last Monday in November, Rose asked the question that lurked in all their minds. "Has anyone heard from Edith or Anthony? Edith has been gone almost a week now. I know she didn't say how long she would be away, but it does seem strange without her." There was a collective shaking of heads.

"Let's work on the assumption that no news is good news, Rose," Grace said soothingly.

"It is concerning though…" Lois conceded. "…The pair of them going off like that, and especially with Anthony not saying a word to any of us about it. Do you suppose they are off somewhere together?"

"I suspect they are together. My concern is that something terrible happened in Edith's life and, when Anthony found out about it, he went to support her or help her through it in some way," Vera said.

There's nothing new in any of this, Gordon thought. They are the thoughts we all had over the past week… and we are no closer to finding answers.

"Well, that's end of November," Gloria announced as she joined the other Busy Fingers staff in the staffroom at closing time, "Wednesday 30 November already. Bring on December. I'm looking forward to having a couple of days off over Christmas."

The sound of the back door opening interrupted speculation about how busy they might be in the run up to Christmas. 'Statues' might be the best description of what the newcomers found on entering the staffroom. Nobody moved. Everybody was dumbstruck for a few moments as they all stared at Edith and Anthony. Rose felt her mouth gaping. She put her hand across it. Then the ruckus broke out. Everyone spoke at once. There was laughter and tears at the sight of a beaming Edith and Anthony fiddling with his navy blue bow tie. They stood in the doorway lapping up the group's reaction. Rose rushed forward to hug Edith.

After releasing Edith, Rose stepped back and eyed her up and down. "You look marvellous, positively glowing. The break did wonders for you."

"Yes, it was wonderful," Edith replied from under lowered lashes.

"If I didn't know better, I'd say Edith looks positively coy," Vera whispered to Grace.

"Hmmm … yes, if she were your daughter, you would be concerned about what she had been up to if she came home looking like that. Am I mistaken… is that the hint of a blush I see? …And, if Anthony is not careful, that smile of his will split his face in two."

Gordon poked his head between the two women, interrupting any further speculation. "Now ladies, don't spoil the moment. My sixth sense tells me we are witnessing the aftermath of the seniors' version of a dirty weekend." It was all Grace and Vera could to restrict themselves to silent giggles when more inclined to roar laughing.

A knock on the door brought the gathering to attention. Gordon opened the door to Samira Buttuta. On her way out to her car, she saw Anthony and Edith arrive and she wanted to welcome them home.

After allowing a few more moments of chatter, Anthony cleared his throat to announce, "It's getting late and everyone should be heading home. We do have news to share…" He gave Edith a conspiratorial look before continuing, "But I don't know when we will be able to get together to tell you."

"That's not a problem," Samira assured him. "Everyone is invited to dinner at my house … 7.30pm for eight o'clock okay? You may share your news with us then, Anthony, because I don't think we are able to wait longer than that."

A cheer went up and some clapped. Dinner at Samira's was something special at any time, but tonight it held the promise of an extra bonus. An immediate exodus followed Samira's invitation. The aroma of a mouth-watering tagine wafting through the cottage welcomed the group. Once everyone found a seat and had nibbles and drinks, Samira took charge. "Dinner will be about another 20 minutes at least. So, Anthony – or is it Anthony and Edith – you have the floor. You must share your news now, or the suspense will stop us from enjoying dinner."

There appeared to be some nonverbal negotiation between Anthony and Edith before Anthony cleared his throat and stood up. "Ahem, where to start…"

"At the beginning might be good," Gordon suggested.

"Oh, for goodness sake, Anthony, stop messing about. I'll tell them," Edith said.

"I know we have been difficult, but it has been a worrying few months. I haven't been well. The doctors didn't seem able to diagnose the problem – not accurately anyway. They would diagnose it as something and order a barrage of tests to confirm their diagnosis. When the tests came back negative, they would decide it was something else and order more – different – tests. That went on for months, with each new diagnosis – or guess – more frightening than the last … and its tests more expensive than the previous ones."

"You poor thing; you must have been nearly out of your mind," Rose said.

"Yes, it was that way. That's why it was so good when you suggested we work on the review instead of coming into the shop. It was easier to cope with everything at home. In the end, I couldn't take anymore and insisted on a referral to a southern specialist. It looked like it would be months before I could get an appointment, but then the specialist received all my information from the local doctors. I think it must have panicked the specialist a bit, and the next thing I knew, I was on a plane to Brisbane."

"So, that's why you left at such short notice. It must have been a relief though to know something was happening," Lois suggested.

"It was, and everything happened quickly after I got there. I flew down on the Tuesday night, saw the specialist on Wednesday morning and had some fancy scan that afternoon. I saw the specialist again on Thursday morning and was told I had been scheduled for surgery on Friday morning."

"That sent me into a tailspin," Anthony interrupted. "I took the first seat I could get, and flew down to be with her."

"It was all good news," Edith said in response to the anxious looks on the faces of the listeners. "There was some sort of fatty tumour – huge apparently –pressing on organs and blocking off vital processes. It was benign. I was only in hospital for three days after the surgery and then had to stay in Brisbane until I went back for a check later."

"I can see why you both look so relieved now," Vera said. "That's all great news."

"There is more good news," Anthony added smugly. "You won't be aware, of course, but I have been very fond of Edith for quite a long time." His audience dissolved into laughter and Anthony looked confused but continued. "Anyway, as I was saying, I was fond of Edith and had asked her to marry me more than a couple of times. She always turned me down. So, while we were both so euphoric after her good news in Brisbane, I proposed again. This time she accepted."

There was a gasp of surprise from a couple of the women, and then everyone was congratulating the couple, shaking hands and hugging them. When things quietened down again, Samira announced dinner was ready and they took their seats at the table. As soon as Samira took her seat, Gordon proposed a toast to the couple and the new future they were planning. Although it wasn't a late night, it was memorable. The news of more impending nuptials spread rapidly through Harbour Plaza's community.

Throughout the week after the Sinclaire wedding, that household spent every spare moment moving Mariah's belongings to Jeremy's house. With the last of her stuff jammed in the only bit of spare cupboard space, the scheduled cleaning of her unit by contractors came up in conversation over dinner.

"How long do you have before you have to hand in the keys?" Clifton asked. "Do you know if they have anyone lined up to rent the unit?"

Mariah, confused, took a moment to answer. "Oh, I see what you are asking. No, I don't have to hand in the keys. I don't rent the place. I own it. After I returned from the States and decided to stay in Oyster Point, I enquired about buying the place. The elderly owner didn't take much persuading. I will have to give some thought to what to do with it now I'm not living there."

"Would you be interested in renting it out?" Clifton asked.

Jeremy's brow furrowed as he tried to work out Clifton's interest in Mariah's unit. Mariah agreed that renting it – at least in the first instance – probably was the right move. Unable to curb his curiosity any longer, Jeremy asked the question. "Why the sudden interest in the unit, Son? Do you know someone who might be interested in renting it?"

"Uhmm, yes, me actually..."

"We've been through this before, Clifton. I thought you understood that nothing changed because Mariah and I married. Why do you want to move out?"

"This is your home, Clifton," Mariah assured him. "I would be deeply troubled if you moved out because I moved in here."

"No, it's not about your living here … you're a better cook than he is anyway. It's about something else, something personal … something personal to me."

"Surely it's not so 'personal' you can't share it with us. It will be a concern for us if we don't know what prompted you to move out."

"Okay, okay; I suppose I see your point. I want to move in with someone, someone … I'm in love with."

"That's wonderful news. Are we going to meet her? Invite her to dinner one night," Mariah said.

"Ahh, yes … here comes the difficult bit," Clifton responded with a wry grimace. "It isn't a 'she'. Kyle is a member of the male gender. …And, yes, before you ask, I have known for some time that I am gay, but I have never been attracted to anyone quite like this before."

Silence reigned for a couple of heartbeats after *that* revelation before Jeremy responded. "We still would like you to invite Kyle to dinner. He will be most welcome here, and he needs to meet us to know what he is letting himself in for."

"There is no question about you and Kyle renting my unit," Mariah assured him. "The place is yours to move into – rent free. I'll be happy to have someone I know looking after the place."

Later, when they were in bed, Mariah quietly asked, "How are you coping with Clifton's news… are you okay?"

Jeremy laughed. "I am absolutely fine with it. I'm surprised I hadn't worked it out before. There never have been any girlfriends – not the romantic kind anyway. I have seen him with a young man a bit lately … I think it might be Kyle … but I thought it was just two mates having a drink together or whatever. It never crossed my mind it was anything else. He has been happy lately. Maybe Kyle is good for him. We will just have to hold ourselves ready to pick up the pieces if it all falls apart."

"So many things have happened in this last month. It's almost exhausting to think on it all, and now we are in the run up to Christmas. Maybe after that, we can take a couple of days to settle down and become normal," Mariah whispered sleepily.

One Year On

Then December rolled around again. It is hard to believe 12 months have elapsed since the cyclone devastated Oyster Point. It took the last of my line, and removed my legacy, Green's General Store, from the map. There was no shortage of interesting moments leading up to the end of the year.

December brought with it a new focus for the business operators in Harbour Plaza. Discussion of pre-Christmas trading initiatives dominated Friday night gatherings in the rooftop garden. In addition to celebrating the anniversary of the cyclone that almost wiped out Oyster Point, there was unanimous support for creating a festive environment in the complex in the lead up to the holidays. There were sales and loyalty initiatives in place in individual stores, but the challenge was to organise various activities in the main areas of the Plaza in a bid to encourage repeat visits by families. Many of the suggestions put forward were for children.

Marilyn, the florist, although only recently moved into the Plaza, threw herself into the Friday night sessions. Her attendance at an extra mid-week meeting called to finalise Christmas Eve celebrations caused comment. "Marilyn seemed more subdued than normal tonight," Vera commented to Grace as they left the meeting. "She is usually so enthusiastic and full of ideas, but she hardly said anything tonight."

"I spoke to her when she was closing up this evening. Her eyes were very red."

"Hayfever…?"

"Could be I suppose – after all, she works with flowers all day – but I think it was something else. Maybe we need to keep our eyes open."

Rose caught up with the other two Busy Fingers women on the stairs. "Isn't he a lovely young man, that friend of Clifton's? I've seen them together a bit lately. They seem such good friends. It's good to see him getting out and about a bit; away from all those books." Vera and Grace exchanged a look, but shared unspoken agreement that it was simpler to leave Rose in blissful ignorance of the real situation. They repeated Rose's comments to Gordon as they drove back to the retirement complex.

"Harbour Plaza seems a dangerous place to be; not safe to work there at all," Gordon observed.

"What on earth makes you think that?" Vera demanded.

"Well, look at all the previously happy singles now married or paired off since the advent of Harbour Plaza. No, like I said, it's not a safe place for a single bloke like me to be."

When the laughter subsided, Grace asked tentatively, "Speaking of pairing off, has anyone else noticed that Samira and Jack Walker seem to spend a lot of time together?"

"Samira and Jack…? W-e-l-l, now you mention it, he was her 'and partner' at Mariah and Jeremy's wedding," Vera said.

"And she brought him to last week's Friday night get together," Grace added.

"That was because they were going on to something else afterwards. If you remember, they left early to go to something," Gordon reminded them.

"Hmm … maybe so, but I smell another pairing developing," Grace responded.

"Have you noticed Anthony's bow ties lately?" Vera asked.

"What about them?" Grace asked.

"Much more subdued these days. I sense Edith fair hand behind it."

"I wonder if we will start noticing a make-over of Jack Walker any time soon," Grace added with a giggle.

Conversation in the car then left Jack and Samira alone and turned to what special deals Busy Fingers might run to entice Christmas shoppers into the store. They swapped ideas for a couple of minutes before Gordon reminded them of something else. "All this fuss and bother about building up pre-Christmas sales might all be to no avail. Remember, Anthony and Edith called a Busy Fingers meeting for Sunday afternoon to discuss their review of the store's performance this year."

"Should we be worried?" Grace asked. "It seems to me we have done very well judging by the healthy dispersal of funds we receive. …And business seems to continue to grow."

"How would you feel if the review recommends chucking it all in and closing Busy Fingers?" Gordon asked.

"Do you know something we don't?" Vera demanded. "I would vote against it. To me, it seems to be doing very well and, more importantly, I think having something to do is good for everyone."

"I agree," Grace said. "I think the store gave all of us a new lease on life; gave us something to do and improved our outlooks." The discussion lapsed at that point as they had arrived home.

At the appointed hour, the retirees gathered under the pergola waiting for the 'show' to start. However, the main act, Edith and Anthony, were late, and Gordon hadn't arrived either. "Do you think the news is so bad that Edith and Anthony have bolted rather than face us?" Jane asked. It raised a nervous giggle from the assembly.

"Sshh, here they come," Grace whispered.

"Oh God, we are in for death by figures. Look at the pile of paper Anthony is carrying," Jane said.

"All we have to do now is to wait for Gordon. Maybe he is doing something about afternoon tea. I'll see if I can hustle him along," Grace offered.

"Don't worry, here he comes," Lois said.

Gordon marched up and plonked a laden tray on the table. While pouring the coffee, he commented, "Sorry to hold up proceedings, the scones took me longer than anticipated."

As everyone fussed over piling scones and jam and cream onto plates, Anthony cleared his throat. "Ahem, if starvation is now under control, may we begin…?"

"Please do," Gordon replied. "But please, may we have the executive summary rather than the whole chapter and verse of your report?" Anthony shot him a look and snorted in disgust.

Begin they did. The entire presentation took surprisingly few minutes… and it was all good news. "So, despite regular distributions, there is a quite healthy balance – a lot of money – in our account. We recommend a further hefty distribution to shareholders. The only thing to consider is the timing of the payment… now, or at the end of the year."

"It's almost the end of the year already. Why don't we leave it until after the Christmas trading is over?" Jane asked, and received unanimous agreement.

Rose had been quiet. She hesitantly voiced what was on her mind. "Well yes, I agree we leave the payment until after Christmas… uhmm … what I don't … what I'm not sure about is what all of this means."

"All of what? What is there that's so difficult to understand?" Edith demanded.

Ah-hah, the real Edith is returning, Grace thought and grinned to herself.

"Oh, the presentation was very good, Edith dear, but I just don't understand what it means. Are we going to continue with the Busy Fingers store, or not?"

When the laughter finally subsided, Anthony responded to the query. "Yes, Rose. The bottom line says we have done very well indeed, and indications are that we should continue with the store if we are all up to it. As this is a formal business meeting and is being minuted, I need a show of hands in response to my motion that we continue to operate Busy Fingers in the coming year."

"I second Anthony's motion," Edith quickly added. All hands went up in support … even Rose's after she had a quick look around to see what everyone else was doing.

A short lull followed. The news was something of an anticlimax and left a brief vacuum in its wake. Gordon rushed in to rescue the situation. "Right; now that's done, does anyone want more coffee?"

Early on Monday morning, Vera sidled up to Grace. "How about you and I take an early morning tea break?" Grace gave her a knowing look and nodded. The only time they did this was when one of them had something to share, but not with the rest of the group. About half an hour later, they headed to the staffroom together.

As they filled their coffee mugs, Grace couldn't hold back any longer. "Okay, come on. What's this all about?"

"Not what, who."

"Oh, even better … so, come on, who…?"

"Marilyn; remember we commented on how she wasn't herself?" Grace nodded and gave Vera a 'give me' gesture. "I watched a late night news program last night. It featured all the recent top news stories. They included something about that TV star who was rumoured to be taking a break at Arkana Beach. You know the one, long blonde hair and body of a barbie doll."

"She has developed a following for her role in that long-running soapie, and now she has launched a singing career. I thought that story about her being at Arkana was rubbish. Nobody saw her there."

"It seems that, by some coincidence, a reporter here in Oyster Point to cover something else supposedly saw the star in one of our parks with a bloke."

"I'm surprised there wasn't more fuss made about it. If it was a romantic getaway, I understand why she would want to avoid the media. That's all very interesting, but what has it got to do with Marilyn?"

"The reporter's 'scoop', accompanied by a film clip, aired earlier in the week. We must have missed it. The woman in the film wasn't the TV star, but was an exceptionally good look alike -- who was having a passionate lunch-break with her romantic interest."

"And the Marilyn connection is…?

"The bloke up close and personal with the blonde in the video was Marilyn's husband. The woman they mistook for the star -- the one he was kissing -- is his secretary."

"You are sure that's who it was? …And Marilyn saw the news that night?"

Vera gave an exaggerated nod in confirmation. "When he saw he was being filmed, he gave chase. They kept filming, capturing clear images of him as they scampered for their car. It was to be their big scoop. They had caught the big star and her mystery man up close and friendly while hiding out in a tiny seaside town. They buried it when they realised their mistake."

"It's no wonder Marilyn hasn't been herself. Should we do the tea and sympathy thing, or pretend we don't know anything about it?"

"Perhaps you and I should try just being friendly; supportive of the new person in the Plaza and see where it leads."

They had opportunity to follow through on their way out that afternoon. Grace and Vera stayed behind to close up and, as they were leaving, noticed Marilyn still in her shop. They stopped in for a chat. "Ladies, your timing is perfect. I was just debating whether to have an iced tea before going home or not. I'd enjoy some company."

"I wouldn't mind an iced tea," Grace said.

"Good; come through to the back." After a few minutes of chatter and a few sips of tea, Marilyn had the other two women squirming. "I suppose you both watch the news," Marilyn said.

"Uhmm, I saw a late program last night, but Grace hasn't seen what I think you are referring to," Vera said.

"I'm not as naïve as he thinks I am. I knew my husband was up to something funny. I don't know why I thought that. It was just a feeling. A few things weren't adding up. I wanted a new shop. He kept telling me we couldn't afford it. That he might be allocated a house out at the mine site, so moving into a new shop would be a waste of time and money."

"I didn't think they were building houses at the mine; only a workers' camp," Grace said.

"Yeah, I checked. There will be no houses. It was just part of his deception. That made me suspicious. I checked our bank accounts. He had been moving cash from my business account into our joint account, and then moving it on to his account. A couple of months ago, he paid a considerable amount to a real estate agent."

"I don't think I like where this is going," Vera said. "What did you do?"

"What you would do, I imagine. I found out details of the property he purchased and checked it out. It's a unit in that new block fronting the beach. Of course, I challenged him about it... after I transferred my money back into my account and blocked his authority to operate on it. He assured me it was an investment property that would appreciate considerably as the town grows."

"You bought that story...?" Grace asked.

"Don't be silly; of course not. I spent a lot of time watching the place from that coffee shop on the beach, and chatted up a gossipy woman who lives in another of those units. The blonde secretary spends quite a bit of time in the unit, but she and 'her husband'-- to quote the other resident – both work away and don't get to spend much time there. A couple of days after I discovered that, he rang to say he wouldn't be home for a couple of weeks as they were working on some big project with a tight deadline."

"He really did have you picked as a babe in the woods," Vera commented.

"I knew this shop was vacant, so I leased it and moved in before he came home again. On the first weekend he was supposed to be working on that project, my early morning walk went past the unit block. His vehicle parked outside was all the evidence I required."

"You are remarkably calm about all this," Grace said.

"I am now. I wasn't then, but I was ready for him when he finally came home again. I had all his stuff packed in removalist's cartons and in the garage. There wasn't much to pack. Much already had disappeared. He gradually had moved his belongings to the unit. Anyway, he is now gone. I am living in the residence attached to my old shop until the lease runs out in a couple of months' time."

"So, now you are house hunting," Vera thought aloud. "I wonder if there might be some possibility at the retirement complex." She raised her eyebrows in question at Grace, whose only reply was a shrug.

On their way home, Grace asked Vera what she meant by that comment about the retirement complex. "It depends on when Edith and Anthony tie the knot and what they plan to do with their extra unit. It could be that they will be looking to get rid of one of the units. It might suit Marilyn."

"Let me know if you work out how to ask the happy couple when their wedding is. There's no point in saying anything to Marilyn until we know something," Grace cautioned.

By the second week of December, summer was doing its best – or worst – to make life miserable. The humidity almost flattened anyone silly enough to venture outdoors. Most conversations seemed to include some comment about the weather.

"I hadn't seen Moira for a while until I saw her walk past yesterday," Jane said as they took a coffee break. "By the look of her, she must be nearly due. I don't know how she keeps working full-time. Even the best of us finds this weather debilitating. I don't suppose we know any more about what's going on there?" This last comment directed at Vera.

"Not really. Mariah is bringing in Patsy Evans almost on a full-time basis to help until Christmas is over. The intent was for Patsy to divide her time between Mariah's two stores, but Moira is so worn out that Patsy is spending almost all her time at Embellish."

"What's Moira going to do when the baby arrives?" Lois asked

"When Mariah challenged her, she admitted she was pregnant…"

"Well, she would have to, wouldn't she? She can't blame her current shape on poor diet," Jane said.

"No, but she hasn't told anyone else. She will take only a month off after she has the baby, and they agreed she would bring the baby into work with her. Mariah plans to have Patsy manage Embellish while Moira is away so I don't have to leave Busy Fingers in the lurch again."

"That's good news. I was a bit concerned your services would be required again," Lois admitted.

"I might still have to do a few hours here and there occasionally, but I won't be missing for large slabs of time."

Conversation lapsed and they were finishing their coffees when Rose rushed out of the stockroom. "It's happening again. I can't believe it. It's going to happen again." Rose's face had lost its colour. It was obvious to everyone in the staffroom she was in shock.

"Calm down, Rose, calm down. Sit down. Here's a glass of water. Now – *calmly* –what's happening again to upset you," Vera said as she shepherded Rose to a chair and plonked a glass of water on the table in front of her.

"It was on the radio. I just heard it on the radio… the weather forecast. We're going to have another cyclone."

Everyone stiffened for a few heartbeats. Vera recovered first and pursued more details. "Okay Rose, tell us what you heard, from the beginning and slowly so we can take it in."

"There's a low pressure system out there in the Coral Sea just like the last time. They say it will develop into a cyclone over the next day or so. I'm not sure I can go through another one, not so soon after the last one."

The other women exchanged worried looks. While they all felt a little as Rose did, they were not about to admit it. Cool-headed Vera continued to hose down the situation. "So, it is not a cyclone yet, and we don't know when or if it will be, or how big it will be. Am I right, Rose?"

"Yes … no … they *do* expect it to develop into a cyclone."

"But we don't know what category it will be … and there is an awful lot of Queensland coastline to choose from. There is nothing to say it will come across the coast at Oyster Point again. The odds are that it won't."

Nevertheless, everyone switched on their favourite news channel as soon as they arrived home. Rose's information was correct. They expected the current low-pressure system to develop into a cyclone some time the following day. A sombre mood prevailed when they gathered in the store before opening next morning. Gordon was the only one with anything practical to say. "Apart from worrying about our own units, we now have to think about what's here in the store. I'll go to the hardware store to purchase some of those plastic bins with tight fitting lids. If we do look like copping another cyclone, we can put the cash register, the computer and other stuff into the bins and store the bins in the storeroom. It's the safest room we have, probably safer than taking the bins home to our units."

As predicted, a late afternoon weather forecast confirmed a category one cyclone was likely to deepen to a category two by the morning. Slow-moving with no clear future direction yet, but everybody knew they were in for a couple of tense days as they waited and watched.

By the second day, the cyclone had reached category three and picked up speed. It was moving in a south-south-easterly direction. Its predicted path had it crossing the coast somewhere close to Oyster Point. That night and the next day were anxious times for the community. Apart from the 'old hands' who lived through the cyclone twelve months ago, a large proportion of the community now consisted of new residents, some of whom had never experienced anything like a cyclone before. Gordon brought a small battery-powered radio into the store. This one and the one in the storeroom tuned for the hourly cyclone reports by the Bureau of Meteorology. By the end of the third day, the cyclone was a category four. It now measured many kilometres across.

Before they left, all of the store's electrical equipment went into the plastic bins and was stowed in the storeroom. The Plaza closed early. Everyone wanted to get home to tape windows and generally batten down for the expected onslaught. Nobody went to bed early. The women sat knitting or reading. Gordon worked on an article he intended to write a month ago. Edith moved into Anthony's unit for the night.

The residents of the block of units at the retirement complex heaved sighs of relief when the 4.00am cyclone bulletin announced Cyclone Irma was now likely to cross the coast a few hundred kilometres to the north of Oyster Point. The Busy Fingers crew were not the only red-eyed people opening their Harbour Plaza stores later that morning. Buoyed up by the news they were safe from the cyclone, the release of tension put everyone in party mood. Plaza manager, Elaine Bennett, visited all the stores during the day inviting everyone to a get-together in the rooftop garden after closing.

Elaine supplied a few drinks and everyone who was able attended to celebrate. They toasted good luck, fate, God and anything else anyone thought of, but nobody stayed late. An early night and a sound sleep were on everyone's agenda that night.

With the cyclone threat over, the Oyster Point community got on with its preparations for the festive season, including completing its Christmas shopping. Harbour Plaza pulsed with activity from the moment it opened each day. Store operators went home each evening exhausted, but business was booming, and the mood in the community was upbeat.

At their Friday night get together, they decided to remain open until 10.00pm on the Thursday of Christmas Eve. The Plaza would close for Christmas and Boxing Days before opening again on the Sunday for the Plaza-wide post-Christmas sales. That left only one other issue requiring a final decision: whether to close the whole of the Plaza for the Saturday and Sunday immediately after New Year's Day. There was strong support for the move by those present.

"I do hope everyone supports the initiative," Grace said on the way home that Friday night. "I'm really looking forward to having three days off. The two days off over Christmas are only a tease. It's not long enough for us to relax properly."

It wasn't until a couple of days later that the retirees discovered the days off after New Year would not be entirely without obligations. At morning tea on the Tuesday before Christmas, Edith looked sheepish as she called the Busy Fingers staff to attention. "If you would give me a moment please," she began, "I have an envelope for each of you…"

"Not Christmas cards I hope," Lois said. "I haven't got cards for any of you lot."

Edith moved around the table handing out the envelopes. "No, Lois, they are not Christmas cards. They are your wedding invitations. Anthony and I decided that, as we don't have family to plan around, we might as well get married straight after New Year. Things should be quiet at the store in January after Christmas and the post-Christmas sales. It will be a good time for us to get away for a while."

Her news met with cheers and claps. "Oh, I almost forgot," she added, "No presents please. We already have two units full of belongings to sort out. It will only be a small casual affair, so don't dash out to buy a new outfit for the occasion."

After a few moments of chatter about the wedding, most left the staffroom to relieve Gloria and Grace in the front of the store. When the latter two women entered the staffroom, only Vera and Edith remained sipping their coffees. Edith handed them their invitations and Vera filled them in on the wedding plans. Gloria opted for an orange juice instead of a coffee, drank it quickly and left the staffroom. With only Grace and Edith left, Vera saw her chance to ask the question gnawing at her for a couple of weeks.

"Edith, what are your plans for after the wedding … I mean, what will be your living arrangements? Will you move into Anthony's unit, or will he move in yours?"

"We have decided to live in Anthony's unit. It has a nicer outlook than mine. I haven't decided whether to try selling my unit, or to lease it out. It probably will take me a while to move my stuff into Anthony's place. That is, after I've thrown out everything I absolutely don't need. I've been looking in cupboards. I've hoarded an amazing amount of rubbish, but so has he."

Vera shot Grace quick glance, took a deep breath and put forward her suggestion. "There is someone we all know who is house hunting at the moment. She might be interested in your unit, whatever you choose to do with it."

"I wasn't aware. I don't want to bring in someone who doesn't fit well with the rest of us. Who do we know that might be interested?" Edith asked.

"Marilyn…"

"Marilyn…? The florist that recently moved into the Plaza?" Vera and Grace nodded in unison. "Oh yes, she would fit in well. I'll talk to Anthony about it first."

Pleased with themselves, Grace and Vera went back to work, leaving Edith alone pondering what to do about her unit.

Christmas Eve in the plaza saw the community turn out in force for last minute shopping and to enjoy the various initiatives happening throughout the place. Many turned up in costume as was suggested in all the promotional material. The place was flooded with elves and Santa Clauses, mistletoe abounded, children had their faces painted and, for the cost of a gold coin, had a lucky dip in the wishing well to come up with a small gift. Live music filled the place through the day and into the evening. Storekeepers decorated their shops with cubic metres of mock snow, herds of reindeers, and a forest of holly.

"Doesn't the place look marvellous?" Rose said wistfully as she gazed down the length of the Plaza. "It's so good to see everybody so happy and everything looking so festive."

"Hmmf, it's a pity it doesn't look a little more Australian. When was the last time you saw snow or reindeers in Oyster Point?" Edith replied.

"…And I suppose you would like to see everyone turn up in shorts and thongs instead of those traditional costumes," Lois added as she walked past.

"Well, I don't think it matters," Rose retorted. "It's great to see the community happy and enjoying themselves."

When the Plaza closed shortly after ten o'clock, there was exhaustion and relief. The night went well, sales were good, and everyone was heading home to recover and prepare for Christmas day. However, there wouldn't be much rest. Although Saturday was Boxing Day, most storekeepers would be back at work repricing stock and setting up displays for the Plaza's post-Christmas sales.

At the retirement complex, Christmas passed uneventfully. The Busy Fingers crew, Gloria and Cecile and their husband, gathered at Samira's cottage for Christmas lunch. Jack Walker and Samira's daughter and son-in-law, Amina and Jacque, joined them. To accommodate that many people, Samira and Jack set up a makeshift banquet hall in her garage.

Everyone brought something to contribute to the lunch and the fellowship continued until after two o'clock. There were groans all round when someone mentioned having to go into work the next day to prepare for the sale on Sunday. Next morning saw a leisurely start, as they agreed not to go into the store until ten o'clock.

As they surveyed their morning's work, Jane said, "I expected it to take us longer than it did, but everything is done. We are ready for tomorrow's sale."

"I just went to my car for something," Jane said as she joined the others. "It's a miserable looking day outside. I think we are in for a storm. I'll be surprised if it doesn't rain before morning." Nobody paid much attention. It was summer, and rain was a part of summer in the tropics.

The weather deteriorated as the day wore on. By nightfall, the wind had strengthened and the afternoon showers turned into heavy rain. Conditions continued to worsen through the evening. The wind, now at gale force, howled through the retirement complex and the tropical downpour bucketed down. Most of the Busy Fingers mob stayed up until the early hours of the morning. Not much before midnight, Rose rang Grace. "Did the Bureau get it wrong? Is this that cyclone that hung around last week?"

"No, Rose, it's not a cyclone, just a tropical storm. Go to bed. It probably will blow over by morning." Graced hoped she sounded more relaxed than she felt. She heard a tree come down not far from her window, but couldn't see anything. The heavy rain whipped along by the wind created a 'white out', obscuring everything more than a metre away.

Grace was right. By morning, though still strong, the wind had weakened and the rain had backed off to a drizzle. What a dreary miserable day, grace told the empty unit as she surveyed the downed tree. Broken branches and leaves littered the retirement complex site. Bright blooms from the Bougainvillea hedge along part of the fence now carpeted one side of the grounds. You would have to be desperate for a bargain to go out in this weather, she thought as she made breakfast. Perhaps today's sale will disappoint.

With the Plaza due to open at 10.00am, at about 9.30am, the retirees sorted themselves into two cars and headed for work. The storm's damage was evident everywhere, but none more so than at Harbour Plaza's end of town. A couple of trees were down along The Esplanade, while others suffered varying degrees of damage. Palm fronds littered the area. The wind, still strong enough to cloak the bay in white caps, whipped spray and foam up over The Esplanade.

Of more significance was the army of high-visibility shirts swarming across the road in front of the hotel. The road, closed to traffic, allowed no one beyond that point. Powerlines brought down by the storm draped over trees, buildings and the road. A worker advised that everywhere from the hotel through to the marina was without power. Emergency power backup systems in the precinct kept fridges and freezers going.

The Busy Fingers crew held a hasty meeting on the roadway. "I don't think there are difficult decisions pending," Gordon announced. "We can't go in to the Plaza and nor can anyone else. There will be no post-Christmas sale today. Let's all go home again." They piled back into the vehicles and followed Gordon's suggestion.

Life seemed restored to normal by the time they arrived at the Plaza on Monday morning. However, a gaggle of workers seemed busy with something on the Plaza's roof. One of the big skylights leaked during the storm, filling the main aisle through the Plaza with rainwater. It remained contained in the aisle and didn't enter any stores. …But it brought accumulated dust from the roof along with it. Water plus dust equals mud, and the storm deposited a fine layer of it over the aisle's ceramic tiles. Cleaners worked most of the night to ready the place to open that morning.

Centre manager, Elaine Bennett, after conferring with her counterpart at the supermarket complex, visited each of the stores in the Plaza. Her message at each place was the same. When she arrived at Busy Fingers, she found the staff standing around wondering what to do next. Was there to be a sale or not? Elaine put their minds at rest.

"The proposal is to hold the sale on New Year's Eve. The Council has a program of activities planned for along The Esplanade to usher in the New Year. We will take advantage of that by staying open until about 11.00pm and organising various activities in the Plaza. Do you support this decision?" No one objected and a couple even called it a good move.

Later that day, Elaine again did the rounds of the Plaza's stores, this time handing out invitations. "What's this?" Gordon asked as she handed him his.

"It's a year since the cyclone. We're going to be open until 11.00pm. Let's gather in the rooftop garden for our own party to welcome in 2016."

There was little to do in preparation for the sale, everything already done the previous week. The week slipped by uneventfully. The only thing of note was Edith asking Grace to be a witness at her forthcoming marriage. Anthony asked Gordon While a little taken aback by the request, Grace was happy to oblige. She also felt compelled to do something else.

At her first opportunity, Grace went to Marilyn. "We have a wedding at the retirement complex straight after New Year."

"Yes; Edith and Anthony's wedding."

"Oh, you know about it. Good."

"Edith invited me to the wedding." Marilyn caught the surprised look that crossed Grace's face. "I bought her unit last week. I suppose I'm an *associate* member of the group until I join you at the end of January. That will give Edith time to move out and me time to move in before the lease on my present place runs out."

"Oh, I see. Welcome aboard and all that. Now, Edith insists there will be no fuss or fripperies involved with this wedding but, as her witness, I think she should at least have a magnificent corsage."

"Ah, that explains it. I was … well, I felt a bit put out that she invited me to the wedding, but didn't ask me to do the flowers. You are right. She shall have a corsage. Do we know what she is wearing?" Grace shook her head and shrugged. "That's okay. I'll do something neutral that will go with anything."

As Marilyn watched Grace leave, the florist gave a determined nod of her head and murmured, "…And the men shall have buttonholes and there will be flowers on the luncheon table."

Thursday, New Year's Eve arrived and the Plaza became a hive of activity. There was almost as much going on inside and there was in the surrounding area. The official sale didn't start until 6.00pm, by which time stores had tables and racks of products for sale out front of their shops. Local musicians entertained, there were activities to keep children occupied, and Sam Pelham, the wheelchair athlete, ran a couple of fitness sessions. Outside, the local Council's program of activities progressively moved along The Esplanade.

By 10.30pm, crowds in the Plaza began thinning out, and by eleven o'clock, the aisles were deserted. At that time, the outdoor entertainment reached an area just past the supermarket as it wended its way along The Esplanade towards the parkland adjacent to the marina. The fireworks, and whatever else Council had planned for midnight, would happen in the park. The Plaza closed at 11.00pm as planned, and its tenants wearily made their way to the rooftop garden. Some wondered if they could stay awake until midnight.

Elaine had hot and cold food, plenty to drink and champagne to toast the start of the New Year. After a few minutes in that environment, everyone seemed to come to life again and it developed into a lively party. After a while, Grace decided she needed to sit down. She made her way through the crowd towards the chairs now pushed to one side out of the way.

As she wrestled one chair from amongst its siblings, Grace noticed Moira standing alone against the back wall. Suddenly, Moira doubled over clutching her stomach. Grace abandoned the chair and rushed to Moira. "What's happening, Moira, are you ill?"

"It must be something I ate. A touch of food poisoning I think. I've been feeling a bit off all day. Then, this afternoon, these griping pains started. They are getting worse. I think I should go home and go to bed."

"You don't think it might be your baby? When is it due?"

"It's not due for another couple of weeks. You don't think this food poisoning might affect my baby do you?" Moira was barely able to finish the question before another wave of pain came. She gasped and clenched her teeth to stop herself crying out. Grace helped her slide down the wall until she was sitting on the floor with her back against the wall.

"Moira, listen to me. I don't think this is food poisoning. I think your baby is coming." As Grace spoke, further pains hit and Moira toppled sideways to lie curled up in agony on the floor. "Ah, there you are. Now your waters have broken. Your baby is definitely coming. Let me take a look."

Although not trained in such matters, it only required one quick glance for Grace to know her diagnosis was correct. Clifton Sinclaire, standing by himself at the time, noticed something happening at the back of the area and wandered over to investigate. He arrived in time to see Grace confirm the baby's imminent arrival. "The baby is coming. Clifton, we need an ambulance now," Grace shouted at him above the noise of the party.

Ashen faced and rooted to the spot after what he had just seen, it took Clifton a moment to get his feet moving. "I'll get Kyle," he said as he turned to rush away.

"No, we need an ambulance."

"Kyle's a paramedic. He'll know what to do." He rushed over to where Kyle was in deep discussion with Connor about the latest football scores. "Kyle; Kyle, I need you."

"It's nice to be needed," Kyle quipped and winked at Connor. "Oh, it's serious…! What happened, Clif?" One look at Clifton's face was enough to confirm this was no time for levity.

"It's Moira. She needs your help." Clifton grabbed Kyle's arm and raced him to where Moira was writhing on the floor. Connor followed on their heels. Kyle took charge after a quick assessment of the situation.

"Okay everyone," he shouted, although the noise had dropped as people realised something was happening. "We need a bit of privacy here. Could you all find somewhere else to continue the party?"

"This way," Elaine Bennett called out. "Grab something and bring it with you to the function room. We will continue in there." Everyone grabbed something off the tables and followed her in as she unlocked the function room.

Kyle looked up at Clifton who had stayed behind. His ashen face now took on a delicate shade of green. "You go too, Clif, and ring 000 for an ambulance please". Clifton wrestled his phone out of his pocket as he trotted towards the function room. Kyle turned his attention to Connor. "Are you okay with this?"

"I haven't delivered a lot of babies in my time, but blood and gore were a regular feature of my previous life."

Kyle glanced towards Clifton, halted at the function room door. Then Clifton turned and hurried back. "The ambulance will be delayed. They are all attending a serious accident up the highway." He found it a more subdued party when he finally joined the others.

"Has she ever said who the father is?" Lois whispered. "He should be here – or be told what's happening."

"No, she hasn't named the father and I don't think she intends to," Jane answered firmly.

Vera leant in to whisper to Grace. "This could go on for hours. It's her first and they are usually the longest labours."

"This one has gone on for some hours already and, from what I saw, I think there is only one question: will the baby be born this year or next year? It's almost midnight."

The sound of fireworks intruded on the hushed function room. All eyes swung towards watches or the clock high on the end wall. Then, cheering, the popping of champagne corks and salutes to 2016 mingled with the sounds of fireworks. The New Year had arrived.

A few minutes later, the cry of a new baby briefly plunged the function room into silence. More popping of corks, cheering and, in some cases, joyful tears welcomed Moira's baby. The guessing game about the baby's gender that raged for weeks before its birth broke out anew. The appearance of Connor holding a tiny bundle wrapped in his shirt brought renewed cheers ... and tears. "The newest member of the Harbour Plaza family has arrived safe and well. His mum doesn't have a name for the little chap yet."

Women rushed to coo over the baby who remained firmly in Connor's arms. An ambulance finally arrived. Kyle retrieved the little boy to send him to hospital with his mother. After seeing the ambulance off, he came back to the function room to face a barrage of questions about the birth and Moira's condition. Holding his hand up to silence the crowd, Kyle delivered his brief report. "The delivery was straightforward; no complications. Moira is well. She and her son will probably will spend a day or two in hospital. Connor's gone to find a clean shirt."

People started to drift off home. By one o'clock, the last of the partygoers sorted themselves into vehicles in the carpark. As they drove away from Harbour Plaza, Rose sighed heavily. "The New Year is already more than an hour old. It is so different from last year. Is that a good sign or not? ...And the safe arrival of a new baby surely must be a good omen."

"I didn't think last year was at all bad," Grace said. "The previous one ended disastrously with that cyclone and the havoc it wreaked, but last year was good. We all developed a new interest in life, became part of a wider diverse 'family' and did well financially. If this year turns out nearly as good, I will be perfectly happy."

"So much happened last year," Vera mused. "Already this year promises to be just as exciting ... a new baby, a wedding tomorrow and another new neighbour moving in at the end of this month. It's exciting to ponder what else might happen during the year."

It's Time

Ah, yes, what might this new year bring? There remains much scope for both happiness and heartbreak. However, I have every confidence in this family of Harbour Plaza tenants. If only my own line had proved as resilient and entrepreneurial.

I sought to ensure the success of that which replaced what the cyclone destroyed. There is nothing more to do here. It was such an interesting year -- so engaging, so satisfying. On many occasions, I intervened, but with no more than a gentle nudge in the right direction.

My work here is done. There is nothing to keep me here in Oyster Point now. The last of my line, Ted Green, is gone and left no heirs. My legacy, Green's General Store, is gone, as is the old shopping arcade I invested in so long ago when it too was only a dream. I intended to watch over the Plaza for its first year, but it has been so enthralling, and so satisfying to assist on occasions, I find it hard to contemplate leaving.

However, there remains unfinished business and dreams yet unfulfilled here in Harbour Plaza. Always there is potential for disaster. People have such difficulty seeing things clearly for themselves. So often, they need help to know what they really want or to see the opportunities. It would be remiss of me to abandon my role when more work remains. The universe would think me shirking my responsibilities. No, it would never do to sully my reputation after more than a century of good works.

Yes, it seems I must remain in Harbour Plaza for some time yet. Oh, not for long, just long enough to settle everything and render the place able to continue when I finally depart.

The End

About the Author

KAYLA DANOLI now lives in a small coastal town on the Queensland coast and works part-time on a charter vessel. In her spare time, she writes. Her previous published work is the *Harbour Plaza* series released in 2015 as monthly eBook episodes. *Revenge is not enough* was her first full-length novel. This book is an updated and extended compilation of the *Harbour Plaza* story.

Discover more about Kayla and her work by visiting

www.kayladanoli.com

or contact her at

contact@kayladanoli.com

www.ingramcontent.com/pod-product-compliance
Lightning Source LLC
Chambersburg PA
CBHW070011120726
47909CB00003B/889